OLD BONES

OLD BONES

A Bill Slider Mystery

Cynthia Harrod-Eagles

This first world edition published 2016
in Great Britain and 2017 in the USA by
SEVERN HOUSE PUBLISHERS LTD of
19 Cedar Road, Sutton, Surrey, England, SM2 5DA.
Trade paperback edition first published
in Great Britain and the USA 2017 by
SEVERN HOUSE PUBLISHERS LTD

British Library Cataloguing in Publication Data
A CIP catalogue record for this title is available from the British Library.

ISBN-13: 978-0-7278-8665-1 (cased)
ISBN-13: 978-1-84751-768-5 (trade paper)
ISBN-13: 978-1-78010-835-3 (e-book)

All Severn House titles are printed on acid-free paper.

Severn House Publishers support the Forest Stewardship Council™ [FSC™],
the leading international forest certification organisation.
All our titles that are printed on FSC certified paper carry the FSC logo.

MIX
Paper from
responsible sources
FSC
www.fsc.org   FSC® C013056

Typeset by Palimpsest Book Production Ltd.,
Falkirk, Stirlingshire, Scotland.
Printed and bound in Great Britain by
TJ International, Padstow, Cornwall.

To Tony, without whom very little would ever get done.
With thanks and love.

ONE

Party Politics

There comes a point in the life of a balloon when it has lost so much air that its taut, festive body becomes sagging, wrinkled and – well, frankly, sad. DCI Ron Carver's retirement party had reached that stage.

Slider cast an experienced look round the upstairs room of the White Horse and saw that the inevitable end was not far away. The young marrieds were eyeing their watches and wondering how soon they could leave. The young unmarrieds were eyeing each other and wondering how soon they could leave. The divorced and miserable were trying with increasing desperation to neck the equivalent of the gross national product of Belgium. A few career bunnies were holding the centre of the room and talking hard about Home Office initiatives and crime statistics. And a few old lags, Carver's bosom buddies, were making a lot of noise in the corner where Carver himself was getting determinedly bladdered.

Carver was a miserable bastard, who had raised resentment to an art form, and his leaving do was appropriately cheerless. The Osman Room – named with no apparent irony after some dreary character in a popular soap – had clearly been decorated by someone with terminal depression. There was a table with food – mini pork pies, scotch eggs, and the sort of sausage rolls that bend. There was drink – party kegs of beer, and a few grudging bottles of Australian *shar*donay for 'the wimmin': female police officers, and a boot-faced civilian clerk who had already done eight years hard as DS Benny Cook's mistress, with no hope of parole.

There was even a cake, a vast flat rectangle covered in rubbery fondant icing, decorated with Carver's name and two dates, as though it were his tombstone. Inside, Slider knew from sad experience, the cake would be a desiccated industrial 'sponge', sandwiched with a red substance in which even the most detailed DNA test would fail to find anything related to the raspberry.

It wasn't just that Carver was retiring. Because of the cuts every borough was having to make, his departure was being made the excuse to disband his firm. It was the end of an era, as someone was bound to say – as Borough Commander 'Dave' Carpenter did actually say in a short, all-purpose speech delivered when he 'popped in'. No one had expected him to find the time in his busy schedule. Slider couldn't decide whether it was a tribute to Carver's long service, or relief that he was going.

Carver belonged to the old-fashioned, Gene Hunt school of policing. Whatever it took to get chummy sent down, do it – just try not to leave marks. He'd had many brushes with the internal complaints system, but thanks to his golf and Masonic connections he'd always been snatched from the brink by some patron among the brass. But the times they were a-changing. When Slider and Carver had joined the Job, everyone, from the commissioner downwards, began the same way, out of Hendon and onto the beat to learn policing from the bottom up. It created a brotherhood. Now the brass parachuted in from the universities with degrees in sociology, and spreadsheets instead of blood in their veins. One could not imagine the likes of Commander Carpenter pulling Carver's chestnuts out of the fire. Carver had known when Carpenter's predecessor, Commander Wetherspoon (one of his greatest fans) got kicked upstairs that his time was running out.

'You should grab the chance and go as well,' he had told Slider at the beginning of the party, when he was still comparatively sober (his breath smelt of whisky, but he'd started early with a bottle in his room). 'Don't be a mug. Get out while you've still got some life in you.'

'And what are you going to do, Ron?' Slider had asked.

'Me? I'm retiring, full stop. More time for golf and the missus,' he'd declared smugly.

Most of Slider's firm had left the party now, and there was a definite feeling of winding down. He'd only stayed this long to see his own people safely off, and because Joanna was working, so home was not the irresistible attraction it might otherwise have been. But enough was enough. He drained the last of his eer and looked round for somewhere to deposit the plastic cup, and suddenly Carver was by his side.

'You going?' he demanded. Either he was swaying slightly or a tube train was passing under the building.

'Just off, Ron. Lovely do. I wish you all the very best,' Slider said.

Carver had reached the sad and frank stage of inebriation. 'It's a rotten party,' he said, slurring slightly. 'End of a rotten career.'

'Oh, don't say that.'

'What've they done to the Job, eh? Answer me that. Real coppers shat upon from a great height. Load o' bloody ponces in the top jobs, never walked a beat in their lives. And now there's not even going to *be* any beat.'

It was the latest pronouncement from on high: coppers were better employed in front of computers. Walking the beat never solved a crime. There would be no more of it. No more local bobby. No more *evenin' all*. No more size twelves pounding the pavement.

'It's the end of an era,' Slider said, with more sincerity than Carpenter had managed.

'You and me, we're old school. We know what's what. These bloody ponces, like Carp-Carpenter . . .' He stared at Slider, and veered off on a new tack. 'You should have got out while you had the chance. They'll be after your head now. You must have been bloody daft to go after Millichip. He won't forget it.'

'It wasn't just him. There are others.'

'He's the one that matters. Get him, you've got the lot. They gotta protect him. What were you thinking? He was gonna hold his hands up just like that? Operation Neptune, my arse! My dimpled bloody arse! He's not going down, chum, you are. He's an assistant commissioner. You must have been off your chump, accusing him. And you got no evidence, that's what gets me,' he went on peevishly. 'Nothing. One witness – a crackhead tart, say anything for a price. What made you think the CPS would wear it? You're fricking bonkers! But she won't testify – you mark my words. The fix has gone in.'

Slider felt a slight chill down the back. Carver had contacts. 'What have you heard?' he asked.

Carver didn't answer. His mind had wandered off, and he was surveying Slider with an expression usually reserved for things found on the bottom of a shoe. 'I never liked you, Slider,' he pronounced.

'And I never liked you, too, Ron,' Slider answered warmly. It didn't matter what he said now – Carver wasn't listening.

'You know what your trouble is? You never had any loyalty. It's us and them. Coppers and slags. That's it, in the Job. We stand together. But no, you thought you were better than the rest of us. Had all these fancy ideas about integ—' He belched. '—rity. Where's the bloody integrity letting some slag get off on a technicality? Rule number one,' he said, poking a forefinger into Slider's chest. 'You never. Shop. One. Of. Your. Own.'

The finger hurt. Slider gently redirected it. 'I'll try to remember that.'

'Going after Millichip,' Carver said with a disgusted shake of the head. 'He may be brass, but he's one of us, when kick comes to shove. But that's you all over. No bloody loyalty.' He swayed. Another abrupt change of tack. 'How's the wife? She not here tonight?'

'She's working,' Slider said. 'She's doing a West End show.'

Carver goggled at him in astonishment, trying to focus eyes and thought. '*Irene*'s in a *musical*?'

'Joanna,' Slider said patiently. 'I split up with Irene years ago.'

'I liked Irene,' said Carver. 'Nice girl. Smart dresser. Not like my old cow. You know what I hate most in the world? In the whole bloody world?'

Slider couldn't guess.

'Trousers on wimmin'. What's erotic about that? Whatever happened to skirts and stockings, eh?'

'Beats me,' Slider said.

'Wimmin everywhere. Menstruating. Having babies. Meno-pausing. Can't get a lick of work out of 'em. And they're all wearing bloody *trousers*! No more legs. No more stockings. What's the point of it all?' Actual tears came to Carver's eyes, and eased out onto his cheeks. 'Elastic-waisted trousers. That's what mine wears. Looks like a bloody whale. Arse the size of a football pitch. And I'm retiring. You know what that means?'

His voice went right off the pathos scale. *'More time for golf and the missus.'*

A hullabaloo behind Carver resolved itself into half a dozen voices shouting, 'The cake! Cut the cake! Time to cut the cake, Ron!'

'Fuck the cake,' Carver said quietly and with great sincerity. He looked into Slider's eyes. 'Real coppers, we were,' he said. There was an instant of connection between them, and a sense washed through Slider of all that was lost when the modern world forgot where it came from; a sense of time running out for all of them. Then Carver wiped the tears off his cheeks with a forefinger, turned and walked away, his normal cocky, slightly rolling walk, to join his cronies.

Slider was left with a bolus of sympathy he didn't know what to do with. It was most unwelcome.

Monday morning began with bones. McLaren took the phone call, breaking off from hand-to-mouth combat with a bacon baguette.

'You're disgusting,' Swilley said as he sprayed crusty flakes in the attempt to say 'CID room'. 'What would your girlfriend think if she could see you now?'

McLaren put down the baton carefully, balancing it across the top of his coffee mug, said, 'Yeah, I'll hold,' into the receiver, and had the leisure to answer Swilley. 'Nat wun't care,' he told her. 'She likes a bloke with an appetite. She's only little, but she can put it away herself all right.'

'Ah,' Atherton murmured on his way out. 'A gastro-gnome.'

But McLaren was now listening to the call. He didn't generally catch Atherton's witticisms anyway. He thought wit was a description of the weather in New Zealand.

A garden contractor starting to dig out foundations for a shed had unearthed a large bone and called the police. Uniform decided it ought to be investigated and Mackay from Slider's team went out. When he reported back that he thought the bone was human, Slider sent McLaren to assist while the SOC diggers were sent for, carefully to uncover whatever else might be there.

Mid-morning, Swilley appeared at Slider's door. 'The bones, boss,' she said. 'Mackay says they're definitely human.'

Slider looked up. 'How definitely?'

'The whole skeleton's there. Doc Cameron's on his way. The builder had the sense to stop when he uncovered the first one, so there's not too much damage. Uniform's got the owners corralled in the house – yuppie couple. The husband's kicking up blazes, apparently – wants to be let go to work.'

'All right, send someone down to keep him happy.'

'I'll go, boss.'

Slider eyed her. Tall, athletic, blonde and attractive. 'No, you might inflame the wife,' he said. 'Send Gascoyne – he's got an emollient personality.'

'If you say so,' said Swilley, though Slider didn't know whether she was doubtful about the man or the vocabulary.

He returned to the sea of paperwork that these days covered his desk. It never grew any less, because every time he left the room for a moment, elves would come and deposit some more. There had always been annoying paperwork, but of recent years, what with political correctness, pressure groups and the increasing litigiousness of the British Public, it had seemed to become not an adjunct, but the whole purpose of The Job. Sometimes he made an attempt at sorting the stuff into piles, but searching for something specific just spread them out again. It was an intractable mass. There were layers at the bottom that were turning into peat.

On a trip to the loo, to get away from it for a minute or two, he bumped into Detective Superintendent Porson, his boss, coming out, shaking his big chalky hands to dry them. 'Out of paper towels again,' he said irritably, glaring at Slider as though it were his fault. 'I hate them bloody blower things.' Slider whimsically pulled out his handkerchief, but Porson, with a stern look, advanced one hip and said, 'Get mine out of my jacket pocket.' And while he wiped his hands dry, still staring at Slider, he said, 'Got anything on?'

Slider repressed the facetious answer that sat up like a dog smelling sausage, and said, 'Human remains unearthed this morning in a garden in Laburnum Avenue.'

'Laburnum?'

'On the Trees Estate.' It was the officially unofficial name for a small development off the Uxbridge Road.

'Right. Laburnum. What sort of remains?'

'A whole human skeleton, apparently.'

Porson looked pleased, for some reason. 'Old bones. Lovely. Something for you to get your teeth into.'

'Sir?' Slider said with an effort. *Down, Fido!*

'Keep you busy,' Porson explained. 'Usefully employed and out of everyone's hair. You can't upset anybody looking into old bones.'

'You mean—?'

Porson took on a worrying hint of kindness. 'You know you aren't Mr Popular in some circles. Now *this* won't put anyone's toes out of joint. Sort it out, it's good publicity for The Job, bit of bon for you.'

'You want me to prioritize it?' Slider queried innocently.

'Get stuck in!' Porson invited, with a nod of his massive head, and strode on.

'Roger that sir,' Slider murmured. Direct order from the boss. Bye bye paperwork, hello fieldcraft. He returned via the CID room, where his minions were toiling over their various routines. 'I'll give it half an hour more for Doc Cameron to do his stuff, then I'll go over to Laburnum myself,' he announced. Eyes were raised in hope. DS Atherton, his friend and usual bagman, wasn't there – out on some business with the sergeant's envied freedom. He thought of the indignant yuppie couple and Fido grinned and wagged again. 'Hart, you can come with me.' Hart was black and sassy with a gorblimey London accent. Emollient she was not.

'Right, boss,' Hart said with a happy grin. 'Old bones. Lovely!'

Odd that Porson had used the same words, he thought.

When Slider's firm had uncovered an underage sex ring implicating many high-ups, including an MP, Gideon Marler, and their very own Assistant Commissioner, Derek Millichip, he hadn't expected to be Mr Popular. He half expected it to be buried. But the story had broken in the newspapers, so there was no covering it up. The media were all over it, as they always were in cases of celebrity sex. Glee, *schadenfreude* and prurience made a heady mix – one sniff, and newshounds bayed at the stars and lost all sense of proportion.

So a special investigation team had been set up by the Sexual Offences unit, and – the high point for Slider's optimism – they had issued the code name Neptune. A code name conferred legitimacy on an investigation. Operation Neptune had entered the media's vocabulary, and after the first excitement, there had been a steady updating of interest, with a piece every week or ten days to keep the show going.

But lately things had gone quiet and there had been no mention of Neptune in the papers for weeks. This was not altogether unusual when a complicated investigation was going on, but Slider couldn't help feeling uneasy. None of his firm had been included in the Neptune Team, which had disturbed him from the beginning. It looked as though they didn't trust him or his people. All their papers and notes had been taken away, and they had been told to keep their heads down and mind their own knitting.

The only aspect of Neptune that continued to exercise the great and good, as far as Slider was concerned, was the question of who had leaked the story to the newspapers. Officially, a witness had gone voluntarily to the press, and there was nothing anyone could do about that. But internally, the brass was convinced that someone had taken the press to the witness, and they wanted to know who. They wanted to discipline someone. They wanted revenge. The freelance journalist who started it all had decided, unusually, to remain anonymous and, in the face of police pressure, the fourth estate had closed ranks and kept it that way. Officially, nobody knew who it was. Unofficially, the grapevine said it was a female journalist newly returned from the States.

Slider was the obvious suspect for the leak, having been told over and over to back off, and having refused to. He had been in trouble before and was not liked at headquarters. Furthermore, Atherton's current lady friend, Emily, was a journalist and, coincidentally, had recently returned from the States. It looked like a dead cert: Slider, or Atherton with Slider's connivance, had brought Emily and Shannon Bailey together. Every member of Slider's firm had been separately questioned, and Slider and Atherton had been called in and grilled several times.

Slider had simply said it wasn't him and he didn't know who it was, or even if there had been a leak at all, which was the truth. What Atherton said he would never enquire. He had always been very down on leaks, and he did not want to suspect anyone in his own firm, particularly Atherton.

He didn't like to think that Atherton would deliberately leak the story, but he could see a scenario where, for instance, he hinted to Shannon that she go to the press, and dropped Emily's card somewhere Shannon would find it. Would that be enough for Atherton to face the IPCC and say, 'I didn't leak the story,' without blushing?

But here was another point: there was little doubt that without the pressure from the press, the case would probably not even have got as far as being assigned a code name. Was it unfair of him to believe that Atherton was capable of breaking the rules in a good cause and lying about it afterwards with a clear conscience? Was that even an accusation? Perhaps there was another, equal standard of morality that said achieving the right outcome was more important than following the rules.

He had always been something of an absolutist about the law. It was his way of dealing with an impossible world: the morass of human fallibility; the confusion of emotion and self-justification he met every day; the cruelty, stupidity and selfishness of wrong-doers. Something had to be clear-cut. You obeyed the law, whether you agreed with it or not, because anything else was chaos.

At the other end of the spectrum lay Carver and his boys. No doubt they had started off doing what they did for the very best of motives; but he was aware out of the corner of his mind that they had slipped from that purity. All power eventually corrupts. There had been shady doings that were not for the benefit of the community. There had been sexual favours and kickbacks. There had been revenge, prejudice, self-advancement – and just plain carelessness.

The question before Slider now was, did there exist a middle way that was morally superior to either end? As Carver had said, where was the morality in letting a slag get off on a technicality? Slider had always resisted that lure, because it led to a slippery slope. If the law does not decide, who does? Whose opinion, whose judgement, is better than whose? And yet, and yet . . . Those girls. Their casual abuse. Tyler and Kaylee, dead and tossed aside like screwed-up sandwich wrappers. It hurt him to let them down; and it hurt him more to think that perhaps he could not do his job within the constraints laid upon him by the law, by his superiors, by himself. If you could only beat corruption with corruption, the game was over.

He shook that thought away. No self-dramatising. Pragmatism was the way to go. Take it day by day, step by step. You did your best, and that was all you could do. And since he had difficulty with lying in response to a direct question, it was perhaps to the good that Atherton had done what he had done – if he had indeed done it; and better still for him, Slider, simply not to know about it, so as to be able to keep saying so with conviction.

Meanwhile, he could not help noticing the looks of dislike he got from senior brass when he happened to bump into them at Hammersmith, or the attitude of the inquisitors when he was called up yet again for questioning. Perhaps Porson was right, and these old bones might be a step on the way to rehabilitation. Of course, when Porson had told him to prioritize it, he had probably not meant Slider should go in person and do the footwork. But Slider was willing to interpret it any way that put a respectable distance between him and the festering midden of paperwork waiting for him on his desk.

Now *that* was pragmatism.

TWO
Posh and Vexed

The Trees Estate, so called because the streets had the names of flowering trees, was built by a speculator in the 1890s. Some had terraced houses, but Laburnum had small neat semis in red brick with white trim, designed for aspiring clerks and shop assistants. With the recent London property boom, they were now highly desirable properties, with the single drawback that they had been built, of course, without garages. That didn't prevent the current owners from buying cars. The kerb on both sides was parked, reducing the roadway to one car's width, and many of the houses had had their front gardens converted to hard standing.

Number fifteen was towards the middle of the street, and the SOC sprinter and Dr Cameron's Jaguar were parked on its apron. Presumably they had removed the owner's cars and the contractor's van to make room. Uniform had got the blue-and-white tape going, had temporarily closed the road to traffic and were keeping interested residents at a respectful distance.

Slider was aware of an unusual sensation as he hunted for a parking space, and paused mentally to examine it. Ah yes, that was it: time. With a skeleton, the murder had to have happened long ago. There was no desperate race to collect clues while they were still warm and interview witnesses before they dispersed, colluded or forgot. No pressing need to canvass the neighbours, leaflet at the nearest tube station, examine CCTV tapes. The old saying, you have forty-eight hours to solve a murder, didn't apply. You could go at it in a leisurely manner. It was a refreshing change.

He and Hart stepped out into the hazy autumn sunshine. The sky was milky blue, the sweet, warm smell of pavements was in the air, and though there was a marked absence of laburnums, those front gardens that hadn't been sacrificed to the great god

Car were still bright with summer bedders in jolly primary colours. 'It's a pity we didn't bring a picnic,' Slider said.

'Boss?' Hart gave him a worried look.

'I said, it's a lovely day.'

'Yeah,' said Hart, her expression clearing. 'I'd prefer a fresh corpse, but bones is all right. Better'n the Clapp family and their thievin' bloody kids.'

'Still having trouble with them?' It was a problem family on an estate she'd been dealing with.

'Sometimes think I should just move in with 'em,' she said.

Number 15, like its neighbours, was a halls-adjoining semi, built on the enduring plan of the London Dog-leg, with the stairs straight ahead and the passage dodging round them, past two reception rooms, to the kitchen at the back. D'Arblay, the uniform holding the door, told them that the owners, the Freelings, were in the front room with Gascoyne, and the contractor, whose name was Hobbs, was in the back room with McLaren.

'I'll have a look at the garden first,' Slider said.

The house was obviously a work in progress, because the two rooms he glimpsed as he passed seemed to be freshly decorated in modern style, but the kitchen had tired melamine units, and beige wall tiles decorated with a motif of tomatoes and corncobs. The worktops, however, were littered with top-of-the-range gadgets that had yuppie written all over them. His eye was caught by a gleaming multi-function coffee machine so complex it looked as if it could have launched space probes. It reminded him he hadn't had his mid-morning tea. If the householders were friendly and open-hearted, maybe they could be induced to brew up.

But first, the garden. It was a decent size for inner London, about eighteen feet wide by twenty-five long. There was six-foot high wooden fencing round the three sides, looking new and orangey, not yet faded by the weather to decent unobtrusive brown. Down the right side of the house was a passage leading to a high gate, the normal arrangement, and the only access into the garden other than through the house. The growing part of the garden was typical of the efforts of people who don't like gardening, consisting of a rectangle of lawn, an unkempt flower bed down the left-hand side, and a concrete path down the right side, scored in a clumsy attempt to make it look like crazy paving.

Beyond the side fences, all that could be seen were the taller plants in the neighbour's gardens. Over the back fence waved the top of a leylandii hedge, and behind it a glimpse of the upper parts of the house in the next street, Colville Avenue. It was an altogether more substantial building, evidently three-storeyed by the size of the dormer window in the roof. Laburnum was the last street in this particular development: beyond it the houses were from an earlier Victorian period.

The path on the right had evidently led to the old garden shed, which was now a heap of fractured wood in the middle of the lawn. Beside the heap was a wheelbarrow standing on a plastic tarp, together with some tools, a bag of sand and a bag of cement. Where the shed had stood, the forensic tent had been erected. Inside, the shed's footprint was a patch of bare earth about four feet wide and six feet long, and beyond that, between it and the back fence, was the grave. Freddie Cameron, the forensic pathologist, was kneeling beside it under the arc lamps, while a forensic digger leaned on his spade observing, in case he was needed.

'So he didn't find the body under the shed?' said Slider to Mackay, as they stood in the tent's entrance.

'No, guv. He took the old one down first, but the new one's going to be bigger, going right up to the fence, so he cleared that space and—'

'Cleared the space? What was there?'

'Plastic water butt. Empty. Then he starts digging out the foundations, and up comes this femur. He's a bit upset, the builder,' Mackay added, free of charge. 'The owners are more mad than anything.'

'I'll have a look at the grave first, before I talk to them,' said Slider.

'The Freelings have only been here ten months,' Mackay mentioned.

'Could hardly be their corpse, then,' said Hart chirpily. 'No wonder they're mad. I bet *that* weren't included in the fixtures an' fittings.'

Freddie Cameron, as always, was dapper as an otter, despite being clad in protective overalls. He gave Slider a minatory look as he approached, but Slider could not fathom what it was about.

It was quickly replaced by his usual urbanity. 'Nice change of pace from the usual frenetic investigation,' he said. 'Dem bones aren't in any hurry.'

'I was just thinking that,' said Slider.

He looked down over Freddie's shoulder. The skeleton looked up at him blankly, naked of flesh and infinitely pathetic. There was something intrinsically disturbing about this huddle of bones, all that was left of a human life once nature had had its way. It made you suddenly, uncomfortably aware of your own bones, safely tucked away out of sight, as they were meant to be, but waiting in the wings, as it were, for their ultimate emergence. There was nothing cheerful about a skeleton. It was the grin that put young people wrong. With no breath of mortality chill on their neck, they could think it was a jolly thing to get dressed up as. That grin was one of God's awful jokes. Slider had long suspected the Almighty had a somewhat warped sense of humour.

It was lying on its back, parallel with the back fence, and apart from some derangement of the right leg, presumably from the contractor's initial contact, it looked to have been laid out tidily, as though for a lesson in anatomy.

'What can you tell me?' Slider asked.

'Definitely female,' Freddie said. 'From the dentition, I'd say young – thirteen, fourteen, that sort of age.'

'Oh,' said Slider. That was not something he'd wanted to hear.

'Probably been here twenty years at least. The bones are bare and disarticulated, no shreds of periosteum or cartilage, but they still feel relatively solid. This is a nice, dry corner, thanks to the old British Leyland there sucking up the moisture.' He nodded upwards at the fronds of the hedge waving over the top of the fence. 'So the rate of deterioration won't be as fast as it would have been in wet, acid ground.'

'Understood.'

'So, taking one thing with another, I'd plump for twenty years, give or take.'

'Give or take what?' Hart enquired over Slider's shoulder.

Freddie gave her an old-fashioned look, the sort that showed itself to best advantage over a pair of half-moon glasses. 'It's not an exact science. Twenty years is an opinion based on experience. Could be twenty-five. Could be fifteen. What am I sure of? That it's not as much as fifty, not as little as five.'

'That's me told,' said Hart meekly. 'Sorry, Doc.'

'An historic case, then,' Slider said. 'Any obvious injuries?'

'No visible fractures. No trauma. Everything seems intact and undisturbed, bar the builder's work. Interestingly, there are no remains of any clothes.'

'Would there be?' Hart queried.

'Cloth, especially man-made fibre, deteriorates more slowly than human tissue,' Freddie told her. 'And it doesn't get eaten by ants and beetles and so on. It's not unusual to find scraps of clothing even after fifty years. Leather, as in shoes and belts, lasts even longer. Metal zips and buckles, longer still. Jewellery, more or less for ever. But there's nothing at all here. I'd say the body went into the grave naked.'

'Oh,' said Slider again. His mouth turned down at the implication, but he said neutrally, 'It's quite a shallow grave, isn't it?'

'Amazing how often they are,' said Freddie. 'Idiot mentality – out of sight is out of mind. Like sweeping the dust under the carpet. If you can't see it, it doesn't exist.'

'You'd think they'd worry about someone digging it up by mistake,' said Hart.

'I'm slightly surprised that it wasn't disturbed at any point,' said Freddie. 'Urban foxes weren't as prevalent twenty years ago as they are now, but they were around, and there are still dogs and cats and rats that can dig. But apparently there was a rainwater butt standing on top of it. Perhaps that protected it.'

'Perhaps it was meant to,' Slider said.

'Well, I'll get the remains back to the lab and do some more investigation, work out the height, make a record of the teeth, see if there's anything more I can tell you. Worth taking a DNA sample?'

'There'll have to be an official identification at some point,' Slider said. 'If we can find anything to match it against.'

'Right. I'll get one off, then.'

'Garden contractor' was too grand a description for Jim Hobbs: it appeared he was a one-man band, and only did small jobs, clearing overgrown gardens, putting up fences and building walls, laying patios and so on. He was a big man in his late fifties, weathered face, grizzled hair, and enormous hands, thick-fingered, scarred of knuckle, wooden from long and cruel exposure to cold and wet. He lived in Acton, where he had once had a larger enterprise employing several men and undertaking full garden makeovers.

'But you can't get the help nowadays,' he said. 'Kids don't want to do physical work. Sooner muck about with computers. Every time I get myself a boy, he only lasts a couple of weeks. I can do without that aggro. So I reckon I'm better off on my own.' He offered the first, tentative smile, as if he wasn't sure it was all right to smile at a policeman, or in the presence of death. His eyes were pale blue and direct. 'It's my semi-retirement, if you like.'

'More time for golf and the missus,' Slider murmured.

'S'right,' Hobbs said. 'D'you play golf?'

Slider avoided that one. 'How do you know the Freelings? Have you worked for them before?'

'No. I've never worked in this street before, though I did do a job in Magnolia last year – that's two streets over. But I've started putting an ad in the local freebie paper, and Mrs Freeling give me a ring from that.'

'When was that?'

'Be – what? – two weeks ago. Two weeks last Saturday. Wife took the call. Mrs Freeling said would I take down an old shed and put up a new one, and Judy – the wife – put her in the diary. Never met her till today. I got here just before seven – I like to start early when the light's good. And before the traffic starts. They were having their breakfast. They let me in down the side gate, I took down the shed – well, it was falling apart, prac'ly came down on its own. They said they didn't want the water butt or the slabs—'

'Slabs?'

'Butt was standing on two old concrete slabs – to level it, I s'pose. It must've been connected to the guttering round the shed at some point, but there was no pipe going into it when I got here, and it was empty.'

'Right. Go on.'

'Well, I put 'em on my van. I can always find a use for 'em.

Then I started digging and up come the bone.' A look of distress crossed his broad features. 'Straight away I thought it looked like a human bone. Too big for a dog to've buried it. What a life!'

Slider concurred. Hobbs seemed a straightforward bloke whose involvement was purely coincidental. He had already given his contact details to McLaren, who had been in the middle of taking his statement. Slider told him to finish it and let Mr Hobbs go. The gardener looked hugely relieved, but with a hint of disappointment. Slider supposed it made a nice change of speed to be at the centre of a drama – even one twenty years out of date.

The Freelings – Toby and Nicola – were smart young people in their early thirties which, if Freddie was right about the length of time the body had been underground, ruled them out from the start. Toby Freeling apparently hadn't thought that far, because he was seething with the self-righteous indignation of someone who thinks they are about to be blamed for something they didn't do.

'Look here,' he attacked Slider as soon as he appeared, 'it's completely outrageous to keep me here like this. This whole thing has got nothing to do with me. I've got important meetings I'm missing.' His smart phone, clutched in his hand, rang, and he gave it the distracted look of the owner at one of those small, yappy dogs that are constantly demanding attention.

Slider studied him while he answered it. He was slim and of middle height, in a sharp suit, with an expensive textured haircut, and enough designer stubble to have housed a clan of very picky field mice. His face missed being handsome by only a few degrees. Probably if he had smiled it would have made it. His wife was smaller, pretty, very dark of hair and eyes, and in a flowered print dress; she appeared to be slightly pregnant.

'If I lose business because of this I shall sue!' he resumed when he'd finished the call.

'Keep your hair on, sir,' Hart answered him. 'It's a serious thing, turning up human remains in your garden. We gotta do everything by the book.'

He gave her a furious look and was about to retort but the phone rang again and distracted him.

Slider turned his attention to the wife. She was placatory where her husband was angry, and answered Slider's questions the more eagerly for his rudeness, which had her flicking anxious glances at him as he snapped into the phone. She confirmed what Hobbs had said, that she had rung him in consequence of his entry in the small ads. She was a nervous and discursive witness, and Slider eased her along patiently, gathering that she had wanted to use a different firm but that her husband had vetoed it on grounds of cost and found the Hobbs advertisement himself.

He'd obviously been half-listening because, ending the call at that moment, he chimed in with confirmation.

'It's only a small job. No point in using a big VAT-registered contractor for something like that and getting screwed, cost-wise. Nicky wanted to go with the firm the garden centre recommended. I said no bloody way! They'll have fixed it so they get a kickback – and who do you think ends up paying for that?' He glared at his wife. 'The poor bloody customer!'

'I just thought—' she began weakly.

'You never do think, that's your trouble. Look here,' he addressed Slider. The phone gave a text message warble, he glanced at it and cancelled it. 'Look here,' he began again, giving Slider a firm, straight look as though trying to close a negotiation, 'that body can't be anything to do with us. We've only lived here eight months.' *Ah*, thought Slider. *He's got there at last.*

'Nine,' said Mrs Freeling, anxious to be exact. 'Nearly ten.'

Freeling ignored her. 'It's a skeleton, isn't it? So it must have been there longer than that. I mean, it takes – what? – years to, er, skeletonize. You can't pin it on us.'

'I'm not pinning anything on anyone, sir,' Slider said. 'I'm just making preliminary enquiries.'

'Well, can't you damn well make them and get out of our hair so we can get on with our lives? My wife's pregnant, you know.'

It was a fine non-sequitur. 'That's exactly what I'm hoping to do, sir,' Slider said, at his most emollient.

Hart caught his eye questioningly, and he knew what was on her mind. Where there was one body there might be others. The shadow of Fred West hung around in the back of the mind when female remains were discovered. Thank God these houses had no cellars. But the whole garden and ground floor would have to be scanned, and if anything showed up, excavated – which would necessitate the Freelings moving out.

Freeling's phone had rung again, and he had answered it, a modern rudeness Slider did not like, so he was saving, in order to relish it more, the news he was going to enjoy delivering – that they were a long way from being out of the Freelings' hair.

The Freelings had bought the house from the Barnards, an older couple – Freeling estimated in their late fifties. Slider had got him to turn his phone off at last, but he kept casting it fretful glances. 'We only met them once, when we first came to look at the house, but they just seemed like ordinary, respectable people.'

'How long had they owned the house?'

'I don't know. I never asked. But a long time, I think – the kitchen was very tired. Well, all the decorations were tired. As you can see.' He waved an arm towards the hall, to indicate the rest of the house. 'We've only just started putting it right. Have you *seen* the kitchen?'

It was a rhetorical question, but his wife opened her mouth to answer, and shut it again quickly when he glared at her.

'Do you know where the Barnards went?'

'No. Why should I?' He was growing indignant again.

'I think,' Mrs Freeling said hesitantly, 'the agent said some-where in Ealing. He thought they wanted somewhere with a garage. The parking here,' she said apologetically to Slider, 'is very difficult. We had to put our cars out this morning so the builder could come in.'

'He doesn't want to know about parking,' Freeling snapped at her. 'We don't know where the Barnards went, all right?'

It didn't matter. They could find out from the estate agent or the land registry, or if necessary the Electoral Roll.

'And have you done anything in the garden?' he asked. 'Have you worked out there, planted anything, dug anything up?'

'Nothing, except replacing the fence. It's just as you see it now, except for the shed, which only came down this morning. We haven't had time to do anything yet. We're not really keen on gardens, anyway.'

'But you prioritized the fence?'

'Security. It was in a terrible state, sagging all over the place. Anyone could have just pushed their way through it.'

'And the shed?'

'That was practically falling down. But I wanted a bigger one, anyway. I paint,' he added, with a hint of self-importance. 'Watercolours. I find it relaxes me after a hard day at work. I need a bit of quiet time to myself to wind down after dealing with clients all day, so we're putting up a studio for me.'

Mrs Freeling gave an eager, affirming little nod. Slider thought she'd probably be glad to have him go down the garden instead of hanging round the house bullying her. He wondered idly if the new shed would have a door that locked. From the outside.

'The water butt that stood beyond the shed – was that yours?'

'No, that was there when we moved in. I didn't want it – we don't intend to have any plants to water. We'll probably be getting rid of the grass – replace it with a polypropylene-polyethylene mix artificial turf. It's more practical and more hygienic. We've got a kiddie on the way – the garden's going to be his play space and we want it to be safe. It'll be—'

He stopped himself with a sudden thought. His wife made a small noise of distress and they exchanged a look which Slider could interpret easily enough: our precious child, to have to play in a garden where a corpse was buried?

He wouldn't give odds on their selling the house and moving somewhere else before the baby was born. In this age where everyone died in hospital, people were squeamish about dead bodies.

At that moment, another uniform, PC Lawrence, poked her head round the door. 'Doc Cameron's just going, boss. He'd like a word.'

Slider excused himself, leaving Hart and Gascoyne to start the statements.

Freddie was still outside, his back to the tent, staring absently around him at the garden. In the bright summer sunshine, he looked tired, as though under some strain.

'There was nothing underneath the skeleton when we moved it,' he said. 'I don't think it can have been disturbed at all from the time it was first planted. I'll get it back to the lab and do some more examinations, but I doubt there's much more I can tell you. Length of time it's been there is always going to be an estimate within wide parameters. My personal judgement.'

'I understand,' said Slider.

'Speaking of personal judgements . . .' He looked around, checking there was no one near enough to overhear.

'What's the joke, Freddie?' Slider prompted.

'Concerning Operation Neptune,' Freddie said. 'Have you heard anything recently? Do you know how it's going?'

'No. It's all gone quiet,' Slider said.

'Suspiciously so?'

'Why do you ask?'

Freddie looked uncomfortable. 'I've heard via the grapevine that they've called in another forensic pathologist to have a look at Kaylee Adams.'

'What for?'

'Who knows? But would it be paranoia to assume it's to second-guess me? I can't see why they would need a second opinion if they were happy with mine.'

It made ominous sense to Slider. 'That's bad,' he said. There was good reason to be paranoid when you knew everyone was out to get you.

'There's worse,' Freddie said. 'The FP they've called in is Sir Maurice York.'

'The Home Office pet?' said Slider. He was the establishment's go-to forensic expert, whose fame had spilled out of technical circles and onto the street, thanks to two popular books and a television series. It didn't hurt that he had a chiselled face and a mane of swept-back silver hair, and a voice so mellifluous you could have spread it on buttered crumpets for Sunday tea.

'The very same,' said Cameron. 'The Home Office has used him before to debunk evidence they wanted debunking. Hence the knighthood.'

'But surely he wouldn't falsify his report?' said Slider. 'Aren't there rules about that sort of thing? Couldn't he be thrown out of the Captain Marvel Club?'

'It's not a matter of falsifying,' said Freddie. 'There's always an element of opinion in these cases. I told you at the time it was my opinion Kaylee Adams had fallen. That was how I read the post-mortem signs. But another pathologist could read them differently – and given York's history, I'm afraid he's going to come up with an extremely persuasive narrative that explains exactly how those injuries are consistent with a hit-and-run incident. Otherwise,' he went on as Slider began to speak, 'why are they calling him in? Not just to confirm my findings, given what he charges per hour, and our current budget restraints.'

Slider met Freddie's eyes. It was what he had been afraid of from the beginning – but it hadn't happened at the beginning. 'But who's trying to quash it?' Freddie shrugged. It did no good to say it out loud. People at the top had been fingered. If there *was* something going on, that was the obvious place to look. 'And why now?' Slider went on fretfully. 'Why not before?'

Freddie had evidently given the matter some thought. 'Letting some of the steam out, would be my guess. If they'd had a fight about it at the start it would have got the newspapers even more worked up. It would have looked like a cover-up. Now the story's gone cold and nobody's interested . . .'

'*Why* aren't they interested, that's the question,' Slider said. 'Why have the broadsheets dropped it?'

Freddie shrugged. 'Not my province. Maybe they know more than we do. And I could be wrong about the reason for York being called in. There could be a perfectly innocent explanation.'

Yes, there was an explanation, Slider thought, but not an innocent one. The fix had done it, just as Carver said. Whatever his source of information, whether it was a Masonic thing or a nineteenth-hole thing, or just the product of an overactive imagination, he seemed to have been right on the money.

'Damn them,' he said quietly, but with feeling.

'Don't get involved,' Freddie said. 'That's my advice.'

'I'm too far down the food chain to get involved,' said Slider. 'They won't ask *my* opinion.'

'Well, don't go to the press,' said Freddie, with the hint of an 'again' at the end of the sentence.

Slider looked at him. 'It wasn't me. I told you that.'

'Of course you did, old boy. I believe you. I just mean, let it go. I'm more impugned than you, if it comes to that.'

'But it makes me mad.'

'You're jumping the gun. Maybe I've read it all wrong. Maybe they're preparing the case and they think York will look better in court than me. I just thought you should be warned, that's all. And now I'm off. Love to Joanna.'

'Yes – love to Martha,' Slider responded absently. He stood where Freddie left him, brooding, watching without seeing as the SOC team started their visual search, marking time, waiting for the GPR – Ground Penetrating Radar – equipment to show up.

Then Hart came out. 'Done 'em. Rude git, that Freeling, him and his bloody mobile! I give him the full street, accent and attitude, just to wind him up. It was fun.' She gave him a curious look. 'What now, boss?'

Slider came to. 'Back home,' he said. 'Nothing more for us here until we know the extent of it.'

'How many bodies, you mean?' Hart queried, with relish.

'Don't be ghoulish.'

'Can I help it if I enjoy my job?' she said.

THREE

The Anguish of the Marrow

I t was past lunchtime when they got back to the factory and Slider's inner man was raising Cain. He went up to the canteen for some cruel and unusual nourishment – in this case macaroni cheese, which the canteen manager, in a fit of transatlantic entrepreneurialism, had advertised as 'mac 'n' cheese'. It didn't help. It was so stiff you could have used it to mortar over cracks. Slider forced down enough to stun the inner man into silence, and headed back to his office, feeling as if he had a bowling ball in his stomach.

Hart met him at the foot of the stairs to say that two DCs from Carver's firm were waiting to report to him. 'They reckon they're joining us.'

'That's right,' said Slider. He had been promised new bodies for some time, and Mackay was leaving at the end of the week on secondment to one of the specialist units, a temporary re-assignment that usually turned out to be permanent.

'Why only two?' Hart complained. 'I thought we were getting the whole firm. I said to meself, where're they all gonna sit?'

'We were never getting everyone,' Slider said. 'Hewson, Botham and Cook are retiring as well.'

Those were Carver's closest henchmen, who couldn't be expected to live without him. Benny Cook was going the traditional route, into security – he had a job in a shiny new office block in Hammersmith Broadway. He was a man who would feel diminished without some kind of uniform. Botham was going into his brother's painting and decorating firm, and Hewson was opening a dry-cleaning business. He had savings to invest, apparently.

'Twenty-five percent discount for all coppers,' he'd said at the leaving do. 'Just show your warrant card. Bloodstains a speciality,' he'd added with a ghastly wink.

Cook and Botham had looked as though they couldn't see why that was a joke.

'And some of them are going to other stations,' Slider concluded.

'Well, I s'pose two's better than nothing,' Hart said sniffily.

'It would be,' said Slider, 'except that they'll be bringing Mr Carver's workload over with them.'

The two were standing by Slider's desk looking a little awkward. It was never much fun, he thought, being a new boy. Lessop was wiry and swarthy-dark, and cultivated a Captain Jack Sparrow look, with the whole facial hair thing, the big moustache and the beard ending in two short plaits. Regs had forbidden him the dreads and the beads, but the resemblance was still striking. Carver had loathed him, but had tolerated him on his firm because it was useful to have someone who could penetrate those areas of society that didn't respond so well to the cheap Burton suit, lace-ups and Hendon-approved haircut.

LaSalle was tall and gangling and rather retiring, and reminded Slider a little – painfully – of the late lamented Hollis, except that where Hollis had had feeble, failing hair, LaSalle's was red and tough. It sprouted out of his scalp and upper lip with so much vigour he looked as though he had a head full of coir under high pressure. Inconspicuous he could never be. Perhaps that was why he was so self-effacing, in a vain attempt to compensate.

They had worked together a lot on Carver's firm, the two outcasts. Their nicknames, Hart had told Slider on the way in, were Funky and Rang.

'Funky 'cos of the funky beard. And Rang's short for Rangatang. 'Cos he's got red hair and long arms.'

'He's tall,' Slider objected. 'He's bound to have long arms.'

'Yeah, but they're weird long,' Hart said. 'Like, he's always got to get his jackets made special.'

'I don't know why the fuss about orang-utans, anyway,' Slider complained. 'They're only auburn gorillas.'

The two newcomers looked at Slider with doubtful but hopeful eyes, like rescue dogs wondering whether their new home was going to be better or worse than life in the pound. Carver had not been an easy boss for those he did not favour.

Slider was not going to make any great speeches. He liked to see how people performed and judge them on that. He shook their hands and said, 'Good to have you aboard. You've brought some case files with you, I understand?'

'Yes, sir. Just ongoing stuff – nothing urgent,' said LaSalle.

'We heard you got some human remains this morning,' Lessop added hopefully. He had a faint Hertfordshire accent, oddly disarming in a pirate.

'Skeletal. Laburnum Avenue,' said Slider.

'My aunt used to live round there,' LaSalle offered. 'She was in Cherry Avenue. I used to visit her.'

'I expect you'll be useful, then,' Slider said. 'At ease, everyone'll get a chance to get out and about on this one. For now, find yourselves a desk and settle in. I'm sure you'll fit in just fine.'

'Thank you, sir,' they said formally, and shuffled off.

This concludes our little initiation ceremony, Slider thought. I hope you enjoyed it as much as I did. Happily he sat down and removed the entire centre section of his nascent compost heap to clear a space for Laburnum Avenue. Who had buried that body so long ago, and why? And why had it taken so long for it to re-emerge?

A new case, he thought with relish, without the fresh pain usually involved. Where there was death, there was always pain, but the old pain of old bones would be easier to cope with.

All he wanted now was a nice cup of tea, and he wouldn't have a care in the world.

The SOC team was still painstakingly scanning and searching the property – Bob Bailey, the head honcho, indicated to Slider that Mr Freeling had strutted some attitude at him and got right up his nose, so he wasn't going to hurry – and the Freelings had packed night bags and gone to stay with friends in Chiswick. Bailey was obviously hoping to find further remains, but Slider forgave him for that. His was essentially an archaeological discipline, and no archaeologist wants a dig that doesn't turn up anything.

'But there are things we can be getting on with,' Slider said to the assembled troops.

Atherton was still absent, but he had Lessop and LaSalle to make up the numbers; and Mr Porson had wandered in, being

as unobtrusive as was possible for someone who looked as though
he belonged up to his neck on Easter Island.

'Hart, you can make a start on tracing the people who owned
the house before the Freelings . . .'

'The Barnards,' she supplied.

'Right. They're the obvious suspects. Find out where they
are now. And how long they owned the house. If it was less
than twenty years you might have to go back to the people
before them. Maybe several owners before.'

'Whoever it was, they didn't half take a chance,' said Hart,
'leaving the body behind for someone else to find.'

'Connolly, you can go through missing persons. McLaren,
Mackay, have a look at any murder cases with similarities – same
area, same age of victim, same disposal method.'

'Right, guv.'

'We mustn't rule out the possibility that it was someone
from outside who used the garden to dispose of the body. It's
unlikely—'

'But fantastic if it worked,' Mackay put in. 'Pick someone
who doesn't do gardening, never goes out there – why would it
ever be discovered?'

Slider nodded. 'And I suppose on the same basis we must look
at the local sex offenders and child molesters. Any ideas, anyone?'

'Roger Radcliffe,' Mackay offered. 'The Hammersmith
Strangler.'

Porson spoke up. 'He's in Wakefield. Leastways, he was. Could
be out on parole by now, I suppose. Or dead.'

'Better check on that,' Slider said to Mackay. 'Who else?'

'Dismal Desmond?' Lessop suggested. 'He's more Acton, but
it's not out of his range.'

'But he's only in his thirties,' Swilley objected. 'Makes him
a bit young for a murder twenty years ago.'

'I was forgetting,' said Lessop. 'We need to look for someone
who was active then, not who's active now.'

'There was that priest,' LaSalle said. 'He come from round
there. That was back in the nineties, wasn't it?'

'Oh yeah,' said Lessop 'What was his name?'

LaSalle scowled with effort. 'Father something,' he came up
with.

'Brilliant,' Swilley muttered. 'Another McLaren in our midst.'

LaSalle gave her a wounded look but carried on. 'He was from that church, Our Lady of Sorrows – that's only half a mile from the house. I remember there was a fuss about him when I used to visit my auntie.'

'But he only did boys, didn't he?' said Mackay.

'You never know,' said LaSalle. 'He was only *caught* for boys.'

'All right,' said Slider. 'You and Lessop can look into the sex offenders. You'll have to go back into history. Newspaper archives might be a shortcut for you.' They nodded thanks for the suggestion. 'Swilley, you and Gascoyne can make a start on the neighbours.'

'Now, boss?'

Out of the corner of his eye, Slider saw Porson stir.

'No overtime,' the Old Man barked.

'Not until and unless it becomes necessary.' Slider softened the blow. 'Tomorrow will do. Find out if any of them were around at the time. And who was in the two adjacent houses – track them down if possible. Once it gets into the papers you might have people coming forward.'

'Yeah, right,' said Hart with broad irony. 'If I read a house I'd once owned had a body in the garden, I'd come running to get meself stuck on a spike and grilled.'

'Even if you were innocent?' Swilley asked.

'Specially if I was innocent,' Hart asserted.

'I hear I missed all the excitement,' Atherton said the next day, idling in casually like a cat that's been gone for two days and wonders if anyone's noticed.

'Where were you yesterday?' Slider asked.

'That pirate DVD ring. I had some leads to follow up. Looks as if it might get interesting – could be other goods involved as well. Not as interesting as a corpus, though.'

Hart came to the door at that moment. 'Guv, I've got something from Kintie's on the Barnards.'

'Did you say Kintie's?' Atherton said with an air of pricking up his ears.

Hart looked withering. 'I say a lot of things. Why pick on that?'

She knew, of course, as did Slider – Atherton had been doinking a solicitor from the firm of Kintie and Abram of Acton High Street. At least, he had before Emily came back. Slider assumed the affair was over, and hoped it was even more than he assumed. It was time that Atherton, the serial romancer, settled down. He was tall, handsome, elegant, and irresistible to females. Pure catnip. He could commit sexual harassment by sitting quietly in another room. Really, the world needed him to be taken out of circulation.

'Go on,' he said to Hart. 'What have you got?'

'Well, guv, the estate agent that sold the house to the Freelings told me the Barnards' had used Kintie's for the sale. So I got onto Kintie's, and they give me an address for 'em in Ealing. Bad news is, it was only a temporary address – apparently they were getting ready to emigrate to Australia, so the guy said, the guy at Kintie's. They got family there, in Adelaide – a son and daughter-in-law.'

'Blast,' said Slider. It would complicate matters horribly if they had to conduct an investigation on the other side of the globe, even with an Anglophone police force.

'But maybe they've not gone yet,' Hart said. 'Kintie's haven't had anything to do with 'em since, so they don't know. I've tried ringing the number they give, but there's no answer.'

'Better get over there and see what you can find out. Do you know how long they were in Laburnum Avenue?'

'Yes, guv. The Land Registry's got them there twenty-two years. So that puts them smack in the target zone. Before them was a Mr and Mrs Knight. They had it from 1974 to 1992, and before that the council owned it for six years and it was rented out.'

'We'd better hope it happened under either the Barnards or the Knights, then,' said Atherton. 'If you've got to start tracing council tenants of forty years ago, you're in real sticky.'

The SOC head man, Bob Bailey, rang through to say that the GPR had not discovered any more remains under the garden or the ground floor of the house.

'Searched the rest of the house too,' he said in leisurely tones, 'just to be sure. No stone unturned, sort o' style. Took my time over it. Couldn't have that lovely young couple coming back home to a house we hadn't checked out thoroughly, now could we?'

'He's been on the phone this morning to Mr Porson,' Slider told him, to cheer him up. 'Threatening to write a formal letter of complaint to the borough commander. He wants to sue the Metropolitan Police for inconvenience, casting aspersions on his character, and probably distraint of trade.'

'Couldn't happen to a nicer bloke,' said Bailey. 'However, our meticulous and very lengthy searches have not revealed any further bodies lurking in cupboards, alcoves or attics. Sadly.'

'Did you check for false walls? Boarded-up chimneys?'

'We certainly did.'

'The secret passage behind the panel in the library?'

'Come again?' Bailey was more literal than literary.

'I noticed a drain inspection cover in the front garden.'

'And there was one down the side entrance as well. It's all clean. Not so much as a dead mouse. So just the one body, looks like. Sorry about that.'

Slider wasn't sorry. He didn't want another multiple victim case, especially if they were young girls. He said, 'Good to know you've been thorough.'

In the Christie case, a human femur had been used to prop up the garden fence and the police had missed it. This was not the time for any of them to look foolish.

Freddie Cameron rang to say that closer examination had not found any evidence of trauma on the bones. 'No healed fractures, either. It looks as though she didn't break anything during her short lifetime.'

That was a relief in one way – made it less likely she had been abused – but healed fractures were a tool in identification, so it was disappointing in another.

'Now, there does seem to be a very fine fracture to the hyoid,' he went on.

Slider's ears pricked. 'Strangulation?' he said.

'In an adult, a fractured hyoid does strongly indicate throttling,' Freddie agreed, 'but it's not necessarily the case in children and adolescents, before ossification is complete. And remember, unlike other bones, the hyoid is only distantly articulated to other bones by muscles or ligaments.'

'Which means?' Slider prompted.

Cameron dumbed it down for him. 'It's a sort of floating bone, held in place by muscles. And when the processes of corruption destroy the muscles, there's nothing to keep it from dropping and possibly sustaining a hairline fracture from the process.'

'But it *might* be an indication of strangulation?'

'It might,' Freddie agreed. 'And there's nothing else to suggest any method of killing. But without the soft tissues, there's not much to go on. I've sent off samples of the grave soil, but after this long it's unlikely there could be any traces of, for instance, poison.'

'Right.'

'I've also taken a record of the teeth, for identification purposes,' Freddie went on. 'And I've sent off a sample for DNA profiling.'

'Fine,' said Slider. 'Anything else to tell me?'

'I'd put her height at about five feet one or two. No sign of congenital disease. Age, I'd stand by thirteen or fourteen.'

'And you'd still say the bones are twenty years old, more or less.'

'Sorry I can't be more exact, but that's how it is. Are you getting anything from your end?'

'It's early days yet.'

'Well, let me know if there's anything else I can do,' said Freddie, with a hint of dissatisfaction in his voice.

Worst case scenario, they would have to call in a facial reconstructionist to make a 3-D model from the skull of what the person would have looked like, and circulate it, hoping someone would recognize it. But it was a time-consuming and, above all, expensive process, which would not bring Slider and his firm any love or praise from upstairs. But they were a long way from those dire straits yet. The overwhelming likelihood was that the body had been buried there by an occupant of the house, probably these Barnards.

Identification was the one consideration that made it better that it was a child rather than an adult, for children were always missed and searched for. Adults disappeared all the time, and often nobody even noticed.

Hart came back from Ealing disappointed. 'The Barnards – they've moved on, guv,' she reported to Slider. 'The neighbours on one side said they'd heard they'd gone to Scotland. The ones on the other side said they thought it was Norfolk.'

'Well, not much difference there,' Slider remarked.

'One said Shetland and the other said Sheringham,' Hart translated. 'Neither of 'em had an address, though. And cos it was a rented, the estate agents'll be no help. The good news is, neither of the neighbours mentioned Australia, so maybe the bloke at Kintie's got that wrong.'

'He's more likely to be right than the neighbours,' said Slider. 'And I'm sure there are places in Australia beginning with "Sh".'

'Yeah, but one of the neighbours did give me the Barnards' car index, so there's a chance we might be able to trace 'em through that, if they are still in the UK – and only if they're pukka. If the body *was* theirs, they'll probably switch it again, but it might be worth a try.'

'All right – give that to Fathom. He's always happiest with cars. You can try the Post Office – see if they put in a request to have their mail forwarded. If not, you're back on electoral rolls.'

'Yeah, guv,' Hart said, without enthusiasm. She preferred a more hands-on sort of policing. She adhered to the maxim that what you were doing wasn't good police work unless someone somewhere wished you weren't doing it.

Connolly called him as he was returning to his room from a routine meeting, and he tacked over to her desk. 'I've hit a brick wall, boss.'

She turned her green eyes up to him. She was wearing navy mascara and eyeliner, he noticed, which made them look even greener.

'I've been through the Mispers and filtered out the unresolved ones, but they're all too recent. I checked anyway to see if there was any connection between them and Laburnum Avenue, in case it was part of a series, but I've come up with nothing.

The trouble with this case is it's too long ago to be in the computer system. Did they even *have* computers in 1990?' she added fretfully.

'The world was not then as it is today,' he told her.

'I know,' she said, outraged. 'I mean, no email, no mobile phones? Love a' God, how'd people live like that?'

'I can't believe we survived,' he agreed. 'But somehow we did. We had these things called pens and paper.'

'Woegeous,' she said – portmanteau of woeful and outrageous.

'As a system it had its advantage,' Slider defended. 'The thing with ink is that it's very difficult to alter without it showing. A computer whizz can alter an electronic record so that only an even better whizz can tell.'

'But I don't know where to even begin looking for a pen and paper yoke,' said Connolly. 'Assuming that's what there was back then.'

'You'll have to go and search the paper archive,' Slider told her. 'It's in the basement at Hammersmith. Every station used to keep their own, but it was all amalgamated years ago in the interests of efficiency, or thoroughness, or maybe just to have a handy source of paper for lighting the boiler. I don't know. Connie Bindman is the archivist. She's an institution – knows everybody and everything. She'll be able to help you.'

'A basement in Hammersmith,' Connolly grumbled, getting to her feet. 'It sounds dusty. And me with me hair washed this morning.'

'I thought you washed it every morning,' said Slider.

Connolly stopped, startled, and looked at him with a hint of wariness. 'How'd you know that?'

'I notice everything,' he said. 'That's why I get the big money.' And he went away, hearing Connolly's uncertain laugh behind him. He smiled inwardly. He liked to keep his staff guessing.

FOUR

De Profundis

I f Connolly had thought about it logically, she would have
guessed the archivist would be old. You'd hardly call a young
person an institution.

Slider could have told her that Connie Bindman, nee Fuchs,
had started with the police as a civilian clerk, and had gradually
burrowed her way into the system like a benign parasite until
she was indispensible. The ragging she had had to put up with
from the beginning over her name had made her strong, and an
insatiable curiosity and a photographic memory had made her
wise beyond her years.

When she did think about it, the word 'archivist' suggested
to Connolly someone who'd been around a good while. Even so,
she wouldn't have been prepared for the woman who met her at
the foot of the stone steps to examine the pass she had hung
round her neck on a lanyard. Connie Bindman, to Connolly's
young prejudices, looked about a hundred, and was vast, like a
shipping hazard. Her bulk seemed all sideways, and as she was
not tall, she gave the impression of having melted slightly and
be pooling inside her clothes.

She wore a strange grey smock of some tough material like
canvas over an enormous grey skirt which came almost down
to her ankles, below which could be seen a pair of fleece-lined
Ugg boots. She wore fingerless mittens on her hands. She
had two pairs of glasses on chains round her neck, which
she used alternately, one for mid distance and one for reading;
and there was a pencil and a Bic pen thrust through her wiry
grey hair – probably on the principle that it was as good a place
as any to keep them.

Yet the fingers of the hands were pointed and delicate, and
in the lardy face were traces of a past beauty, and a pair of very
intelligent dark eyes. She greeted Connolly with a smile of

lopsided charm and said, 'I was expecting you. You're Bill
Slider's girl, aren't you? How is he, the dear man?'
    'He's grand, thank you,' Connolly said dutifully.
    'Grand, yes – there is something grand about him. He thinks
on a bigger scale than most of us, bless him. But he's got over
losing poor Colin Hollis, has he? He must have taken that
badly.' Connolly looked blank, and she added, 'Responsibility.
You wouldn't feel it at your age, darling, but the weight of it
gets heavier the longer you live. And poor Bill is one of those
people who starts off with a guilt complex. Carries it round,
like a hump.'
    'You'd know him pretty well, then,' Connolly said, finding
the trend of talk embarrassing. This was her boss they were
discussing, after all.
    'Oh, I've met him here and there. Meetings. Conferences.
Someone's leaving bash.'
    'So you get out now and then?'
    'Yes, they take off the manacles once in a while. But I'm not
as isolated as you might think, sweetie. I get to hear everything
about everybody down here. And I'm interested in people. Well,
when it comes down to it, what else is there?'
    She gave a little laugh. Her voice was clear and beautifully
modulated, and though Connolly had read about a 'musical
laugh', it was the first time she'd heard anything that fitted the
description. She waited to see what else would be said, shifting
a little on her feet, partly in embarrassment and partly because
it was cold down here, below ground and on a stone floor.
    She didn't like basements anyway – didn't like any room
without windows – and this was the worst sort, with walls of
glazed brick, like her old school, and exposed pipes, and
cobwebs, and echoey, untraceable noises: watery gurglings, the
fitful buzzing of a faulty fluorescent tube, and occasional faint
thumps, as it might be of a member of the undead, heavily
bandaged, bumping into things as he came slowly towards
them, arms outstretched . . . She tried not to look over her
shoulder, but couldn't help it, and Connie Bindman's smile
widened. 'There's nobody down here but us,' she said.
'Buildings make funny noises. You'll soon get used to it. It
used to give me the awful whim-whams at first, but interest in

the work takes your mind off it. Now then, you want a missing person, I believe?'

Not the best choice of words, Connolly thought. Want one? Not down here, not in any state they were likely to be in. 'Human remains were found,' she said. 'In Laburnum Avenue.'

Connie Bindman put her head on one side. 'That name rings a faint bell. That's on the Trees Estate, isn't it? Now, I wonder why I recognize Laburnum?'

'Female remains. Doc Cameron says they'd been in the grave twenty years, more or less.'

'I know what that means. Anything from fifteen to twenty-five – and that's just for starters.' She sighed. 'It's an awkward time slot. Carbon dating's no good for anything less than a hundred years, so it's down to guesswork. And if it were seventy or eighty years, there'd be no investigation because the murderer would also be dead. With twenty years you've got the worst of both worlds. Well, darling—' she gathered herself together – 'here's the gig. We have them cross-referenced by name and date, but since you don't have a name, we'll have to trawl through in date order, which will take us some time.'

As well as exposed pipes, cable ducts and cobwebs, the walls were lined with metal shelving crammed with boxes, metal cupboards full of box folders, rows and rows of filing cabinets, and tall wooden chests of card drawers. It was to the latter Connie Bindman led her. The drawers were of varnished oak, with brass slots on the front for labels, unexpectedly grand and serious to someone from the age of throwaway plastic.

'It's quite simple,' said Connie Bindman. 'The card will give you the date the file was opened, which will be the date the person was reported missing, plus a few basic facts – name, age, address and next of kin – and a file reference. The files are in the boxes on the shelves over there, in numerical order. If you find anything of interest, let me know and we'll haul out the file. Assuming it's still in existence.'

'Why wouldn't it be?' Connolly asked.

'Oh, there have been accidents over the years. There was the flood of 1998 – we lost quite a lot of files then. An electrical fire in 1987, but luckily that didn't do much damage. There are advantages in being right next door to the fire station. We had mice in the 1970s – but they mostly ate the 1950s. And then there's been human carelessness. People borrowing files and not returning them, or returning them minus some of their material.'

'Really?'

'We don't have that sort of thing happening any more.' She gave Connolly a meaningful look. Connolly thought she meant that things going missing had not been altogether accidental. Gene Hunt syndrome again. 'We're *much* more careful. Everything has to be signed for and checked.'

'I'll be careful,' Connolly promised.

'Twenty years, you say?' Connie Bindman went on. 'All right, why don't you start here, in January 1995 and work forward five years, and I'll start in December 1994 and work backward five years. That will cover the most likely ten years between us. We won't get more than that done today.' She led Connolly to a stack of drawers and said, 'Don't rush, or you might turn two cards at once and miss something. Slow and steady wins this race, my pet.'

Connolly opened the drawer and stared in disfavour at the cards stacked along a metal rod which passed through a hole cut at the bottom of each. The cards had been white, but were browning slightly with age, their edges rubbed soft with handling. Some were unevenly typed, and some were written in a beautiful, neat hand in what was obviously fountain-pen ink, because it had faded in some places and changed colour in others.

Janey Mac, she thought, would you look at the cut of it! This was what came of people not getting on and building computers when they should've. Hadn't she read somewhere that Leonardo da Vinci had invented them in 15-something? Or the ancient Egyptians or somebody? And here they were in the twentieth century writing stuff on cards! With pens! There was no way simply to enter 'Laburnum' in a search engine and scan the results. You had to read each card, flicking it forward to expose the next, one card after another, on and on for ever.

Her fingers got cold. They got dirty. Her feet went dead. Some cards were packed closer together and tried to stick to each other. And the monotony worked on the brain so that after a bit you caught yourself reading without taking anything in. Had she missed something? Only way was to go back and repeat. Sweet Baby Jesus and the orphans! She'd be here for ever. She'd never get out. She imagined archaeologists digging through into the basement in several thousand years time and finding her fossilised remains, and wondering what she could have been doing here. Some kind of religious ritual, they'd think. They always thought that, didn't they? Sacrificial virgins buried with the Sacred Tin Boxes to ensure a good harvest . . .

Ah, maggots! She'd done it again, stopped taking anything in. Have to go back and re-read. Jaysus, lemme out of here . . .

And then, after all that, it was Connie Bindman who found it.

'Laburnum Avenue. Was it number fifteen?' she asked, with a lift of excitement in her voice. Well, stuck down here, it was as close to a thrill as you'd probably get.

'That's right,' Connolly said, keeping a finger in her place and hoping she wouldn't need it.

'A little girl went missing in August 1990. I thought the address rang a bell.' She read off the reference number, and shuffled in her fleecy boots over to the shelves; took down a metal deed box, carried it to a table and opened it. Connolly half expected a flock of bats to fly out. Instead Connie Bindman drew out a beige folder, double checked the reference number, and opened it. 'The case is still live,' she said. 'Which means she's never been found.'

Connolly met her eyes across the chilly basement, her mind working. 'It must be the same one. It can't be coincidence, can it?'

At that moment a telephone rang, loudly and nearby, startling Connolly so much she bit her tongue.

Connie Bindman answered it, and said, 'They're asking for you upstairs. Front shop. You'd better go. I'll send this over in the bag.'

'I can take it,' Connolly said.

'Bless you, not that I don't trust you, but who knows where you'll be going next? Bus, train, pub, home for the night. That's how things get lost. I'll send it over in the bag, then we'll be safe. You won't look at it before tomorrow morning anyway, will you?'

'Probably not.'

'All right then. Off you go. My regards to Bill Slider when you see him.'

*   *   *

Upstairs, in the front shop, it took a while to find out who had asked for her. Everybody seemed to be busy, nobody was willing to break off and help her. Obviously the activity was meaningful, she knew that; but beyond the security doors, the public who wanted to talk to a policeman sat around on benches waiting with the air of dead people in the ante-room of the afterlife: how long it would take to be processed, and where they would be bound afterwards, equally out of their ken.

Eventually, by the exercise of much patience and persistence, she got herself directed to a tall, curly-haired and moley wooden-top, who was engaged with a tablet and looked up at her with such reluctance she could almost hear the ripping sound as his eyes pulled away from the screen.

'You're DC Connelly?' he asked, frowning, as if it was hard to believe.

She flourished the visitor's pass. 'Yes. Rita Connelly. Shepherd's Bush. What's it about?'

'Come this way.' He led her through the pass door to an interview room, where he invited her to look through the glass.

At the table, looking both bored and defiant, was the skinny figure of Julienne Adams, dressed in pink leggings and sweat-shirt, alternately chewing her fingernails and making faces at the camera in the corner of the ceiling.

'Are you a relative or something like that?'

'Nothing like that,' said Connelly, puzzled. 'She was part of a case we had recently. What's she done?'

'Shoplifting. TK Maxx are getting really tough on theft these days. It's an epidemic.'

'What's it got to do with me?'

'She wouldn't give a name or address and she had no ID on her so they called us in. And then all she would say was we had to get in touch with you and you'd sort it out.'

'Oh, she said that, did she?'

He shrugged. 'Usually they start crying after a bit and blurt it all out, but not a tear, that one, and she wouldn't budge on the name or anything. She's a tough kid.'

'Her sister was killed and then her mum died and she was put into care,' said Connelly. 'That'd make you tough.'

'Well, do you want to talk to her?'

'I suppose I'll have to. What did she take?'

'Lipstick. Retail value £14.99. The store doesn't want to prosecute for that amount, but they want her frightened enough so
she doesn't escalate.'

'I think I can manage that,' Connolly said grimly.

Julienne Adams, age eleven going on forty, looked up with a
defensive scowl as Connolly came in, then her face lit and she
jumped up and ran at her, arms out.

Connolly fended her off, held her at arm's length by her
skinny wrists. 'None o' that,' she said sternly. 'What have you
been up to?'

At the rejection of her embrace, Julienne's face collapsed,
and she burst into tears. She wrenched herself free, ran back
to her seat, dropped her head on her folded arms on the tabletop,
and sobbed as though life were over. Connolly stood where
she was, arms folded, watching impassively for a break in the
storm.

Eventually the rhythm altered and she sensed a readiness for
dialogue, so she said, 'Knock off the waterworks. I want to talk
to you.' Julienne said something splurgey and tear-choked that
she couldn't catch. 'Would you stop the cryin', for Pete's sake?
I'm tryna help you!'

The child raised a wet face, mouth bowed like a Greek mask.
'You don't care! Nobody cares! I wish I was dead!'

At this hopeful sign, Connolly pulled out the chair catty-corner
to her, and dragged over the universal box of tissues. 'If I didn't
care, would I be here? Here, dry your face and wipe your nose.
You look like an explosion in a snot factory.'

Julienne sat up and obeyed, blew her nose, and muttered again,
'Wish I was dead.'

'You'll be a lot worse than dead if you don't stop this carry-
on. What the hell were you thinking? Robbing stuff from a store!'

'I didn't do nothing,' Julienne protested.

'Don't lie to me,' said Connolly. 'Exhibit one. A lipstick.
Colour Miss Fizzy. Price £14.99. You robbed it right off the
counter and the store detective nabbed you at the door.'

'I hadn't got £14.99,' Julienne said sulkily. 'I'd only got three
pounds.'

'You little eejit! If you can't afford something, you don't have it. That's it. End of. There's no just takin' stuff because you fancy it.'

'Why not?'

Connolly wasn't having a philosophical debate on capitalism with an eleven year old. 'Because it's the law,' she said shortly. Julienne took another tissue and wiped her nose again, avoiding Connolly's eye. 'So what's going on with you?' she asked in a kinder voice.

Julienne chewed her lip. She had a pale pointed face decorated with pink lips and, now, pink-rimmed eyes; thin, very fair hair caught back with a pink plastic slide. Her skinny little bod, still innocent of curves, seemed all joints, like a foal's. Connolly waited with the sort of silence that most people feel compelled eventually to fill – something DCI Slider had taught her – and eventually Julienne said, in an impassioned burst, 'I *hate* that place! I'm not going back there! They're mean to me.'

'Who's mean to you?'

'Everybody.'

'Why aren't you at school?'

'I hate that school. I don't know anybody. I hate the other kids. And the lessons are, like, really hard. It's really bo-o-ring. I hate the teachers.'

'That's a lot of hates. Anything you like?'

'No. I hate everything. I wanna go home.'

'Well, you can't, can you?'

Now Julienne looked at her, and her lip trembled. With an effort she said, 'No. Cos my mum's dead.'

There was a long moment of silence. Connolly looked at her steadily, noting her determination not to cry again. It was an heroic effort for so small a child. Fair play to her! she thought in tribute. At last she said kindly, 'Yeah. It's tough. You had a tough break, Jule.'

The child looked down at her hands, and heaved a long sigh, which was the fight and tension going out of her. 'What's gonna happen to me?' she asked.

'Well, I'm going to try and get you out of this. But you're never to do this again, you understand me? No more robbing. No more getting into trouble.'

She looked up. 'I like your trousers. I like your top. I wish I had nice things like you.'

'Then you've got to work hard at school, get good exams, and get a job. Then you can buy nice things for yourself.' The programme didn't seem to appeal to Julienne. 'D'you think it's easy?' Connolly asked harshly. 'D'you think I got given this stuff? Life is hard, kid. You either give up, or fight. I thought you were a fighter.'

Julienne tried to look tough, but her lip was quivering again. She met Connolly's eyes pathetically. 'Will you come visit me?' she asked in a mouse's voice.

An unwelcome surge of pity plus the vision of a waterfall of complications swept over Connolly and almost washed her away. *Damn, I don't want to get involved. I'm not responsible for her. I'm not a social worker. It'd do more harm than good if she got attached to me. It's not my job.*

Plus any number of other excellent reasons, excuses and caveats. But the kid was looking at her. There was a connection. Connolly didn't want it, she most passionately didn't want it, but it was there, like a sticky little paw creeping into hers. She had called for her when she was in trouble. *Out of the depths I have cried to Thee O Lord! Lord, hear my voice. Let Thine ears be attentive to the voice of my supplication.* They got you with poetry when you were a kid – what were the psalms but poetry? You could shed the homilies and the tellings off like a duck sheds water, but the poetry dug right in like a parasite and wouldn't be dislodged. She didn't suppose Julienne had ever had poetry. Her mother had been a drug-addict, part-time prostitute with no more sense than to name her daughter after a method of chopping vegetables. *Damn, I don't want to get involved!*

'Yeah, I'll come and visit you,' she said, and saw the light, which seemed as much relief as pleasure, in the eyes. 'But you've got to shape up. No more of this carry-on. All right?' Julienne nodded. 'And first off, the lipstick goes back, and you've to write a letter to the store, apologizing, and promising never to do it again.'

'All right,' said Julienne, a lot too easily for Connolly's liking. 'Will you help me write it?'

'You'll write it yourself. And you'll mean every word,' Connolly said fiercely.

'All right,' she said again, and grinned. 'Keep yer hair on.'

Connolly went out to talk to the constable on the case, came back in with a pad and pen, and sat across from Julienne as she began laboriously to write her confession, wrist crooked awkwardly, elbow stuck up, head on one side, tongue between teeth.

'How d'you spell "sorry"?' she asked after a minute.

'S–o–r–r–y,' Connolly supplied, and watched as the child wrote, in her crabbed and untaught hand: I am sory.

She just hoped she was.

FIVE

How Beautiful are the Feet

'Is that all there is?' Atherton asked disparagingly, fingering the file.

'It's a bit meagre,' Slider agreed.

'Thin as an adulterer's excuse,' said Atherton.

'You should know,' Swilley mentioned.

'Don't be illogical. You can't commit adultery if you're not married.'

'*You*'d be pushed to commit adolescentry,' said Swilley with unusual sharpness. 'Time you grew up.'

'Children,' Slider chided them. 'Shall we concentrate?'

The file was grubby, the cardboard softened with age, the pages inside faded. And above all, there was not nearly enough material there. It had all the appearance of something put aside and forgotten for many years, something that had never expected to be resurrected. You could almost imagine someone taking out a sheet at random to use as scrap paper, to jot something down on. This was what lay at the far end of those huddled bones in their shallow grave.

'To summarize,' Slider went on, 'Amanda Jane Knight, age fourteen, went missing twenty-five years ago. Only daughter of Ronald and Margaret Knight of 15 Laburnum Avenue.'

'They were the ones before the Barnards,' said Hart.

'I've not found 'em yet,' said Fathom.

'Maybe you won't have to,' said Hart. 'Kid goes missing, bones turn up. Can't be a coincidence.'

Slider resumed. 'Ronald Thomas Knight was a self-employed plumber, age fifty-four.'

'So he was forty when Amanda was born,' said Atherton. 'That's a late start. Unless there were others before her?'

'Only child,' said Slider. 'Mother, Margaret Emerald Knight, née Pirie, age forty-seven.'

'Thirty-three when she had the kid,' said Atherton. 'Elderly parents.'

'Mother worked nine to six Monday to Friday in the Jiffy Launderama on Uxbridge Road, doing service washes and taking in and handing out dry cleaning.'

'They sound like respectable people,' Lessop offered. 'We're not talking about a rackety young couple on drugs likely to kill their own sprog for a thrill.'

'Probably *was* the dad, though,' McLaren said, peeling the silver paper from a slightly melted Kit Kat. 'Always is, innit.'

'Boss,' said Hart, 'when you say "went missing" . . .?'

'She disappeared one Saturday afternoon from her own back garden,' said Slider. 'No one saw her leave, and she was never verifiably seen again.'

'Yeah, but she didn't leave, did she? She was there all the time.' Hart looked round the others. 'That's where she was found.'

Slider frowned. 'I know it's tempting to think that, but there is a difficulty. You'd have to be suggesting that someone came into the garden, killed her, dug the grave and buried her, all in broad daylight, and without anyone noticing anything.'

'The Trees Estate counts as the suburbs,' Atherton said, 'and people in the suburbs never notice anything, even when it's right under their noses. They don't even know their neighbours' names.'

'It's *technically* possible,' Slider said, 'but nobody would do it that way.' He let them think about that. 'Even if the killing was spur-of-the-moment, or accidental, the killer wouldn't set about digging a grave right there and then. He'd conceal the body somewhere and do the digging later.'

'In the shed,' McLaren said indistinctly.

'Can't hear you through your breakfast,' Swilley said.

'S'not my breakfast. S'my lunch,' McLaren corrected.

'That's what I like about you, Maurice,' Swilley said sweetly. 'Always ready to go the extra meal.'

'The problem with the shed is that the police were bound to have searched it,' said Slider. 'It seems more likely that she left the garden for some reason and was snatched, or waylaid, killed, and hidden somewhere for a time.'

'Her dad could have picked her up outside in his van. Kept

her there. If he was a plumber, he must've had a van,' LaSalle said eagerly.

'He did. But let's not get ahead of ourselves.'

'But if it was done outside the garden, whoever did it musta brought the body back,' Hart complained. 'That dun't make sense. Even if it was the dad. He'd've buried her somewhere out in the woods or something, wouldn't he?'

'Well,' said Slider reluctantly, 'if it *was* the father, he might have felt more secure about doing the digging on his own land. He'd know the ground, what the soil was like, where to find a spade, whether he could be overlooked. He'd know who, if anyone, was likely to disturb him. It would depend how intelligent he was.'

'And how cool,' said Swilley. 'Your average murderer's like a headless chicken. Rational thought doesn't come into it.'

'Unless he'd done it before,' said Lessop.

Slider nodded. 'Yes, there is that possibility. The more victims a killer has, the more cold-blooded he gets about it. We'll have to look him up, see if he had any criminal record.'

'Wasn't that done at the time?' Atherton asked.

'There's nothing in the file about it. We can't assume,' said Slider. 'The other possibility for a person who would bring the body back to the garden, would be a relative or close family friend, someone who knew the layout.'

'That'd be a bastard trick,' said Hart. 'Landing the parents with the corpse of their own kid.'

'But guv, the police at the time would see the freshly-dug earth,' said Mackay. 'I know there was a water butt on top, but they'd still have noticed, surely?'

'Again, it doesn't say here,' said Slider, 'but assuming that there wasn't any freshly-dug earth, that means—'

'The body was brought back after the police had done the garden,' said LaSalle. 'A relative or close family friend who was keeping up with things'd know when that was.'

'Were there any relatives?' Swilley asked.

Slider turned a page. 'Knight was an only child. Mrs Knight had a sister, Patricia Pearl Pirie, aged forty-two – five years younger. Married to Brian Bexley, an estate agent.'

'Ah, the sinister uncle,' said Atherton. 'When it's not the

father or stepfather, it's always the uncle. Was Uncle Brian interviewed?'

'Doesn't say. There's just their names, and the address – 27 Lupus Street, Acton Vale.'

'Just a 207 bus ride away,' said Atherton. 'So here's a thought – Amanda's bored on her own in the garden on Saturday afternoon, decides to go and visit aunty. Aunty's out, Uncle gets too friendly—'

'There's no point—'

'Or she gets picked up at the bus stop by a stranger and done away with,' LaSalle joined in eagerly.

'—in speculating like this,' Slider managed to finish. 'There are a thousand possible scenarios. We've got to trace these people—' he tapped the meagre file – 'and start afresh.'

'You're right. I was just doodling,' Atherton apologized.

'We need to find the Knights, the Bexleys, and the neighbours at the time.'

'Land registry. Electoral roll,' said Swilley. 'Census returns.'

'It wouldn't hurt to keep trying to find the Barnards as well,' Slider said to Fathom. 'It's a long time to have a garden and not find the body in it.'

'Right, guv.'

Slider felt the hair rise on the back of his neck, and turned to find Porson standing in the doorway between his room and the CID room. He wondered how long he'd been there. The old boy could move like a cat when he wanted to.

'Horse's mouth,' Porson said.

'Sir?'

'There's not enough in that file. I had a look when it came over. You don't know who was interviewed and who wasn't. You'll have to go back to the horse's mouth. Who was the SIO?'

'The Senior Investigating Officer was Detective Inspector Trevor Kellington,' Slider read. 'His supervisor was Detective Superintendant Edgar Vickery.' He looked up. 'I don't know either of them.'

'Before your time. Before mine, too,' said Porson. 'I've heard of Kellington – he was at Fulham a year or two when I was at Chelsea. Great big bloke. Had a good reputation. Vickery I don't know. He'd be older. Could be dead by now. See if you can get a line on Kellington. I fancy Mitchell Baxter over at Hammersmith might remember him. He might know where he is now. Find Kellington and pick his brains.'

'He might not remember,' Lessop was unwise enough to remark.

Porson's eyebrows snapped together like two stags locking horns. 'He'll remember,' he barked. 'Little girl goes missing on your watch, never seen again. That's a nightmare seraglio. You never forget a case like that. Those are the ones you like awake at night sweating for.'

'Boss, can I have a word?' Connolly said as everyone dispersed.

Slider invited her into his office, and she told him about Julienne Adams. She watched the frown develop between his brows as she spoke, and hastened to add, 'I talked to the police officer on the case. The store detective had left it up to him and he was fine with the approach, and he got in touch with the social worker, and she came over to escort Julienne back to the home. I did everything by the book.'

'But you didn't. She's a minor. You shouldn't have interviewed her alone.'

'She wouldn't give her name or age or anything until I got there, so technically they didn't know she was a minor.'

'Technically!'

'And I wasn't really interviewing her. She called me in as a friend.'

Slider sighed. 'I know you meant well, but you can't be too careful in these cases. If a complaint were lodged against you, it could be very serious for you.'

Connolly let a corner of her anger show. 'The kid's got no one! She turned to me for help, and I'm supposed to tell her to get lost?'

'I don't—'

'That's how these kids get into this mess, because everyone's too scared to use their common sense.'

'Don't rant at me, constable,' Slider said mildly. 'I'm not responsible for the system.'

She breathed out hard through her nose, remembering that he had done his own share of regs-breaking in good causes. 'Sorry, sir. I know you're on my side.'

'I'm just warning you to cover yourself. If anything like this happens again, get the social worker in first.'

Connolly gave a wry smile. 'She hates the social worker. She likes me. I think I can be a good influence on her.'

Slider said nothing, and she felt compelled to add, into his receptive silence, 'I told her I'd visit her sometimes.' She hadn't meant to tell him that. Oh, so that's how it works, she thought.

Slider gave her a level look. 'What you do in your own time is your own affair,' he said. 'But I would advise you not to get involved.'

'I don't want to,' Connolly admitted. 'But I've seen it back home, good kids going bad for want of anyone paying them just a bit of attention.'

'Back home – in Dublin, you mean?' Slider asked lightly. Connolly was famously tight-lipped about her personal life and her past, and seemed to be on the brink of revealing something.

But she only grinned and said, 'I didn't mean *me*, boss. Jaysus, I was so good, it'd sicken you.'

DI Trevor Kellington had long since retired. Mitchell Baxter at Hammersmith, who had indeed worked under Kellington at Fulham, remembered him.

'Hard to forget him. He was a hell of a big bloke, six-four or five,' he told Slider. 'Not heavy, I don't mean, but powerful, massive hands he could crack nuts with. Great big head and a great beak of a nose. When he stood up with his head thrown back, he was so imposing, he could scare the shit out of a slag just by beetling his brows.'

'But what was he like as a policeman?' Slider asked.

'Oh, he was all right,' Baxter said with a slight diminution of enthusiasm. 'He was straight, you know. Hard-working, careful. But a bit lacking in imagination. A by-the-book man. Not a whole barrel of laughs, if you get my drift.'

'Any idea where he is now?' Slider asked.

'None, sorry. But he'll be on a pension, if he's still alive. The pension admin will have an address.'

Of Edgar Vickery he had no memory or knowledge. 'Before my time.'

'One's enough to be going on with,' Slider said to Atherton in the car.

'Kellington was the SIO, so he'll have the more hands-on knowledge anyway,' Atherton agreed.

Kellington was widowed, and was living in a house near Tring with his daughter, son-in-law and youngest grandson. It was a small, modern house in pinkish brick the colour of salmon pâté, on a raw-looking new estate. The daughter met them at the door, a patient, faded woman, so bland in every aspect it was hard to remember, the instant you turned away, what she looked like. She had evidently given her whole life to being a wife and mother and, latterly, carer of the elderly, so that over the years their demands had worn her smooth, as water rubs away at a pebble.

Behind her in the cramped hallway lurked the grandson, a lanky youth in tracksuit bottoms, T-shirt and bare feet, who gave them an aimless grin when they caught his eye and then hastily slunk away. Slider wanted to ask him why he wasn't at work on a weekday, but sadly felt he knew the answer.

'Dad's through here,' the daughter said. 'You won't upset him, will you? Only, if he gets in a state, he can't breathe. It's his emphysema.'

'We won't upset him,' Slider said soothingly. 'We're just here to pick his brains, about the people in an old case.'

She nodded, not entirely appeased. 'He'll remember. He's got a wonderful memory for his old cases. Always did have a wonderful memory for names and faces.'

'Yes, we heard that,' Atherton said mendaciously. He smiled, and she looked faintly startled. Atherton's smile could have that effect on females.

She seemed to grope for an appropriate response to it, looked at him and away, and finally said, in softened tones, 'Can I get you a cup of tea?'

'That'd be nice, thanks. If it's no trouble,' Atherton said.

She beamed. 'It's no trouble. I'll be making it for him anyway. Come this way, won't you?'

'I hope I'm getting tea as well,' Slider whispered into Atherton's ear as they followed her. 'What do you do to women?'

'It's a gift,' Atherton murmured back.

'Give it back,' Slider suggested.

'Visitors, Dad,' the daughter announced, and stood aside to usher them into the narrow through-room. Kellington was in an armchair at the far end, by the French windows that looked out on a small, careful garden whose most lively feature was a bird table enjoying brisk traffic. The former giant was now gaunt, with sunken cheeks and blue lips, and he breathed like a broken-winded horse. He didn't smoke any more, but his right hand twitched and jumped constantly as if blindly seeking that sustaining tube, as a piglet noses for the teat. He was wearing an old-mannish grey cardigan over an open-necked white shirt, and grey flannels, and his feet looked both enormous and pathetic in crimson velvet carpet slippers where there should have been shiny black boots, capable of kicking down doors. How were the mighty fallen! At the sight of him so reduced, Slider found a limerick running unbidden round his brain.

> There once was a copper called Kellington,
> Who looked like the old Duke of Wellington.
> He pounded the street
> With his size nineteen feet
> And wore himself down to a skellington.

Without turning his head, Kellington said, 'Goldfinch. Two of 'em. They always come in pairs. It's called a charm. Charm of goldfinches.'

They moved into his line of sight.

'Like birds?' he said. 'I could watch 'em all day.' He gave a wheezy, mirthless laugh. 'Not much else to do. Pull up a chair and sit down. You'll be Bill Slider. Mitch Baxter rung me and said you were coming.' He passed rheumy – but nevertheless still copper's – eyes over them, pausing a little over Atherton as if unsure where to put him in the filing system. Atherton *was* an anomaly – too smart, in both senses. 'What's your name, son?' he asked. The 'son' was meant as an insult, to see how he would react.

Atherton bore it nobly. After all, he reasoned, Kellington would soon be dead. 'Detective Sergeant Atherton,' he replied. 'Jim.'

'Come in through the university programme, did you, *Jim?*'
A casual tone, a disingenuous question.

'Hendon,' Atherton said, returning the look steadily. 'The old
way.'

Kellington relaxed, all except his right hand, which jumped
towards his pocket and away. This would have been the moment
to hand round fags, cementing the trust. Instead, he reached
with his left hand into his cardigan pocket and brought out a
handkerchief, carefully to wipe his eyes. 'All right,' he said,
just as if they had all lit up. 'What's it about?'

'Amanda Knight,' Slider said. 'Laburnum Avenue.'

They could see the names filtering, the machinery whirring,
the index cards coming up. 'What's your interest?' Kellington
asked warily.

'If you don't mind, I'd sooner not say until afterwards.
I'd like your recollections of the case without . . . let's say,
contamination. The case just as it presented itself to you.'

Kellington regarded him sharply for a moment, and then said,
'All right. I suppose you've got your reasons.' He settled himself
more deeply into his chair, folding his hands across his stomach
and interlinking the fingers, and stared into the garden with a
little frown of concentration. 'Amanda Jane Knight, age fourteen.
Disappeared from her back garden one Saturday afternoon in
August. Middle of the school holidays – would be about the
eighteenth, nineteenth?'

'Eighteenth,' Atherton supplied. The frown deepened slightly
and Slider gave him a quelling look.

'She was playing in the garden on her own. Her dad was out
at work – he was a plumber. Self-employed. Saturday's a busy
day for him. Mum was home. She worked Monday to Friday.
Laundromat. She was in the sitting room working on the sewing
machine. She made a lot of their clothes. She goes into the
kitchen about three o'clock to put the kettle on, looks out
the window and Amanda's not there. There's the rug she'd been
sitting on, but no sign of the kid.'

'She couldn't see her from where she was working?'

'Nah, the sitting room's at the front.'

'So she hadn't seen her since . . .?'

'They had lunch around half-twelve, Mum started sewing about one. So she'd had a long start.'

'And it got longer,' Slider said. 'It seems the alarm wasn't raised until after eleven that night.'

Kellington frowned and sniffed. 'Dad come home about half-five for his tea, by which time Mum's anxious. It's not like Amanda to wander off without saying. Dad tells Mum to wait. He's more angry than frightened – says, I'll give that young lady what for when she turns up, worrying her mother like that. He's got another job to go to, so he goes out again. Comes home around half-ten. Amanda's still not tipped up, so after a bit of argy-bargy, they call the police.'

'But no one came out?' Slider said neutrally.

Kellington was unembarrassed. 'There wasn't the same atmosphere then about missing teenagers. You know what they're like – go out with a friend, stay overnight, never think of ringing their parents. Turn up the next day full of attitude. Call handler told 'em to ring round friends and relations, report again in the morning if she wasn't back. Which they did.'

'And you attended?' Slider asked. 'On the Sunday?'

'Duty sergeant went round first, and once he'd had a talk with them, he decided it was serious and rung me. Monday, the machine goes into gear.' Kellington shrugged. 'The usual routine. But there was never any trace of her.'

'No sightings at all?' Atherton put in.

Kellington looked at him. 'O' course there was sightings, everywhere from Land's End to John O' Groats,' he said sourly. 'Once it goes public, everyone's a clever clogs. But they was all rubbish. No one saw her leave the house, or walk down the street.'

His daughter came in with tea on a tray, and there was a little bustle as it was distributed, questions were posed about sugar and milk, biscuits were offered, little tables placed. Then she went away to a sofa and took up some knitting, effacing herself and apparently uninterested in their conversation – though the room was too small for her not to have heard it.

Kellington sipped his tea, watching the blue tits flicking from the creeper over the house wall to the feeder and back. Slider guessed he needed courting.

'Please go on. You said no one saw her in the street?'

'Not Laburnum or any other street nearby. We assumed she'd gone out the garden of her own accord. Gone to visit a friend or buy a comic or something. But she'd not been in any of the local shops. We canvassed the neighbours. Knocked on doors for streets around. The lib'ry, swimming pool, rec centre.' He took out his handkerchief. 'Never got a tickle. A whole lot o' bloody nothing.' He wiped his eyes again. The slow trickle of infirmity made it look as though he was weeping for the lost child. Slider hoped somebody had. 'O' course, there was no CCTV in those days. No mobile phones, either,' he added. 'And she didn't have any friends.'

'No friends?' Slider queried.

'Not that she visited, or visited her. Apparently she was a loner. Anyway, you know how it is with these cases. You don't find 'em in the first forty-eight hours, you're not going to. Either they've run away to London to go on the streets – though she didn't seem like the type, but you can't always tell – or they've been snatched. And if they've been snatched, you're not going to find 'em anyway. Not alive.'

'Did you suspect anyone at any time?' Slider asked.

'We thought she'd run away,' said Kellington, 'but naturally we had a look at the father, just in case. He's out and about in his van, unaccountable. We looked into the jobs he was supposed to be at that day, and they looked pukka, but o' course the timings weren't exact, there was a lot of leeway. And there was a gap, when he was supposedly having his lunch in the van. The wife made him sandwiches and a flask, and he sat in his van with the *Daily Mail* from about quarter past one to about two. But there's nobody to confirm it or otherwise. He could've come back. Trying to get confirmed sightings of a white van in a London street is like . . .' He failed with a simile.

'Quite,' said Slider helpfully.

'But we couldn't get anything out of him, or on him. No blood in his van. No blood on his clothes. We kept an eye on him, in case he had done away with her, and led us back to where he'd stashed her, but nothing. Not a dicky.' He shrugged. 'Nothing anywhere. So we let it go. You got to give it up some time or other. There's always too much else to do.'

'So you thought he was the most likely suspect?' Slider asked.

'No, like I said, we had no reason to suspect she was dead. No evidence of any foul play. We did look at local nutters and sex offenders as a matter of course, but there was nothing to link any of 'em to the girl or the place or the time. So, with no evidence and no leads . . .' He shrugged again. 'Course, with the benefit of hindsight, it's most likely she *was* dead, and if she was, it was most likely the father, but at the time . . .'

Behind him, Slider heard the knitting needles pause, and the daughter shift in her seat. It always was the nearest and dearest wot dunnit, and not for the first time he wondered what the nearest and dearest of policemen thought about that. Fortunately, most civilians never had cause to doubt their kin, but a copper's family had their noses rubbed in it week after week.

Kellington drained his tea mug, put it down, and fixed Slider with as firm a look as he could manage with eyes like a week-old cod. 'So what's all this about? You going to tell me? Don't tell me someone's confessed.' It was not unusual for a murderer late in life to decide to unburden himself, to lead the police to the bodies. It was always portrayed in the press as 'making their peace', but Slider believed it had more to do with the last desperate bid of a failed man for fame and attention.

'We've found a body,' Slider said.

Kellington was suddenly alert, seemed on the instant taller, his face younger by the tightening of the muscles and narrowing of the eyes. 'Where?' he barked.

Slider hesitated, because he quite liked the old boy and didn't want to show him up; and in that moment he saw that some of Kellington's tautness was apprehension. He didn't want to know.

'Buried in the garden,' said Slider.

Kellington stared, as though trying to comprehend the incomprehensible. 'The garden? What garden?'

'Number fifteen. The Knights' garden.'

'No.' Kellington began shaking his head slowly in denial. 'No.'

'I'm afraid so,' said Slider.

Kellington continued to shake his head, but in anger now. 'God damn it,' he said – growled, rather. 'God damn it!' His voice grew louder with each repetition. 'God damn it! God damn him! He did it! He had to go and do it! Oh, God damn him!'

He began to cough, and his daughter got up hastily from her sofa and said, 'Dad?' with a little, doubtful, birdlike cry. 'Dad? You all right?'

Kellington coughed, his face darkening, and flapped her away with one enormous, skeletal hand, the other fumbling for a handkerchief.

She looked at them reproachfully. Atherton glanced at his boss in query, but Slider waited impassively. The coughing went on and on, and to Slider, each explosion sounded like another furious *God damn it*! from the angry old man.

SIX
Gripes and Wrath

It seemed very peaceful in the room when the coughing was over. Kellington seemed to have passed almost into a pensive mood. The daughter (she didn't seem, in her self-effacingness, to need a name) had ceased fussing and returned to her seat and her knitting. Outside the day was declining, and there was a hint of fog in the air. The little birds were coming and going with an air of urgency, getting one last meal in before dark.

Slider didn't advance the questioning. He was interested to hear what Kellington would say unprompted. Atherton was waiting for his lead, sitting back, seemingly relaxed in his chair, one elegant leg crossed, his long hands quiet in his lap. Slider knew that when he looked the most indifferent, he was listening the hardest.

'Well,' Kellington said at last. 'Well. So he did it after all. I knew it. I said all along . . .' He stopped himself, and looked at them with a sort of wariness, as if he suspected them of trying to trick him. 'Ronnie Knight. Musta been him. Who else would have buried her in the garden?' Then he frowned. He was a policeman. He would see the snag just as Slider saw it. 'Wait a minute!'

'You'd have noticed if there was any freshly-turned earth,' said Slider.

'There wasn't,' said Kellington 'No signs of digging. We searched the house. That's SOP. Searched the shed and the garden. Of course we did. Besides . . .'

'It wasn't likely the perpetrator would do the digging in broad daylight,' Atherton supplied.

Kellington nodded agreement without looking at him. His eyes were fixed on a very distant scene. 'No, he must have stashed her somewhere else. Buried her there later.'

'With only skeletal remains, there's no way to tell if the body was moved at any time before burial,' Slider said.

'I suppose it was a calculated risk, burying the body where he could keep guard over it, see that nobody found it?' said Atherton, with a faint question mark.

Kellington shook his head. 'By that point he wouldn't have cared. Just get rid of her – that's all he'd care about by then.' He said it bitterly, almost as if he had a personal resentment.

'What was the latest time you would have noticed any disturbance in the garden?' Atherton asked.

Kellington came back slowly from his thoughts, and had to have the question repeated. 'Monday,' he said. 'It would have been the Monday. Yes. She went missing on Saturday, Monday we searched the house and garden. Not that we expected to find anything. We thought she'd walked out. Of course we did.'

'Anyone would have,' Slider said.

Kellington fixed him with a resentful eye as if he'd disagreed. 'There was no reason to think otherwise. We searched the house and garden the Monday. That was just routine. After that, we were in and out the house, talking to the parents, but I don't recollect we ever looked at the garden again. There was no reason to.'

Kellington pouched his lower lip and slowly scratched his sparse hair, thinking hard. He looked tired.

'If it was the father—' Slider began.

'O' course it was,' Kellington interrupted sharply. 'Who else would it be?'

'If it *was* him,' Slider resumed evenly, 'it's likely that he had her in his van for some of the time.'

'Obviously he must've used it to transport the body,' Kellington said impatiently. 'But there was none of this DNA business back then. We looked for bloodstains, signs of a scuffle, but what else would we do? Even if we'd found one of her hairs in there, there was no reason it shouldn't be there.'

'Quite,' said Slider. 'I'm sure you did everything by the book.'

'Damn right we did!'

'I wonder, though, why there's so little in the file.'

He seemed startled. 'What? What file?'

'The Misper file. There ought to be far more detail on how you conducted the search, dozens more interviews. Even if the actions proved unproductive, one would expect them to be logged in the file.'

'One would. One would.' Slider thought he was mocking him, but he seemed almost dazed. He was thinking. 'Everything ought to be there. The whole paperchase. Everything – but it was so long ago. Twenty – twenty-five years. My God. Files – they get set aside. Forgotten. Things get lost. And,' he seemed to rally, 'once they go into storage, who knows what happens to 'em? You don't ask, do you?'

'Have you any idea what became of them – the Knights?' Slider asked.

'We kept an eye on 'em for a while, like I said, in case he led us to the body. They were still in the same house a year later, I know that. After that, I dunno. You move on, don't you? You know you're not going to find her.' He fixed Slider suddenly with a terrible eye. 'So you've not traced him yet?'

'We're working on it.'

'He'll be – what? – knocking on eighty now. You'd better get a move on. You don't want him to die before you find him. Twenty-five years! It'll be a wonder if any of 'em's still alive.'

'Speaking of which, have you any idea where we could find your old boss, Mr Vickery?'

Kellington took in a breath to answer, and seemed to suck it the wrong way, because he burst again into a fusillade of racking, painful coughs. Through them he seemed to be trying to answer in the negative, shaking his head. His daughter appeared again at his side with a glass of water, and he took it and drank and the bout subsided, leaving him flushed and breathless.

The daughter gave Slider a reproachful look, and he obeyed it and stood up. 'I think we'd better be going,' he said. 'Thanks for all your help. If you think of anything else that might help us . . .'

Kellington made a flapping motion with one hand to stay him, while the other fumbled the handkerchief to his face. Slider waited, feeling Atherton stirring uneasily at his side – fearing some inappropriate confession of failure from the old man, probably. A lead missed, a stone unturned.

But when Kellington emerged from his mopping and blowing, what he said was, 'Let me know what happens. All right? It was my case. I'd like to see it closed.'

'I'll let you know if we make any progress.'

Something about that, or the way he said it, seemed to sting the old man. Kellington struggled to his feet, in itself a disturbing phenomenon to witness. Upright, even with the shrinkage of old age, he towered over Slider, and even topped Atherton by a couple of inches. He must have been daunting in his prime. 'You lot have it easy these days,' he wheezed angrily. 'Mobile phones. Satellites. Cameras everywhere. Surveillance bloody society. We had to do it the hard way. Hands and knees. Every bloody inch. I'm telling you, there was no trace of her. Not – a – dicky.'

'Nobody's blaming you,' Slider said.

'Bloody right they're not!' It was almost a bellow – a bull with laryngitis. 'Like to see any of you do as well without your fancy IT and all your gadgets!'

Slider thought of the dusty, etiolated file with its meagre, nibbled pages. Twenty-five years ago was a foreign country, all right.

Outside, Atherton said, 'So all we have to do is find Ronnie Knight, and we're home and dry.'

Slider knew he was half joking, but felt constrained to say, 'We'd still have to prove it, and if they couldn't do it back then when the trail was fresh . . .'

'I don't suppose they tried very hard,' Atherton said. 'I got the impression they assumed from the start she'd wandered off and would never be seen again.'

'They had no reason to think it was Knight, after all,' Slider said fairly. 'They didn't have the body.'

'Once we nab him, he'll confess,' Atherton said with confidence. 'After all this time, it'll be a relief to him. Make his peace, as they say in the tabloids.'

They got into the car, and Slider drove off.

'Still, I wonder why he did bring the body back,' Atherton mused.

'As you said, a calculated risk. Someone might stumble on it if it was stashed somewhere else. In his garden he could keep an eye on it.'

'I suppose so,' Atherton said, dissatisfied. 'But how did he creep back in, heaving the body, do all the digging, and his wife not notice anything? Unless she was in on it?'

'Seems unlikely.'

'I didn't mean in on the murder. But she might have been the sort of wife that felt she had to support her husband, no matter what.' Slider threw him a sceptical look, and he said, 'Joanna wouldn't shop you if you'd murdered somebody, would she?'

'I'd shop myself.'

'Or she might have been terrified of him.'

'That seems more likely.'

'I suppose loyalty would depend to an extent on why he did it.'

Uxbridge Road traffic was light in this direction, and Slider sped past the westbound build-up with the sense of smugness one always feels about other people in traffic jams. The street lights were on, and made haloes in the fog; the traffic lights looked pretty through it, like Christmas decorations.

'Kellington didn't suggest a motive,' he said, 'so I suppose they never discovered one.'

'Mr Kellington doesn't strike me as the sort of person who'd care about airy-fairy, arty-farty, psychological bollocks like motives. Find a man with a bit of lead pipe standing over another man with his head stoved in, and who cares about motive?'

'Juries do, nine times out of ten,' said Slider mildly.

Porson was in his office – you could always tell from a distance because the door was open – so Slider went in to bring him up to date.

'What did you make of Kellington?' Porson asked when he had finished.

Slider considered. 'I thought he was a bit defensive.'

'Not surprising.' Porson nodded. 'Must have felt a twat hearing the body turned up right there in the garden. Bound to feel people'll think he didn't do his job properly.' Slider hesitated, and Porson barked, 'What? Spit it out, laddie. Don't mince about the bush!'

'I do wonder whether they *didn't* take it seriously enough at the time. Whether there was more they could have done but didn't. And then she didn't turn up and it was too late.'

Porson didn't pooh-pooh it. 'We've all made mistakes. Let something slide that turned out to be important.'

'I was wondering, you see, about the file having so little in it. Whether someone slimmed it down a bit afterwards. Without the paperwork, it would be harder to show that things weren't done that should have been.'

Porson shook his head, and did a turn or two along the strip of carpet between his desk and the window. It was down to the backing in places. 'Don't go there,' he ordered. 'Not our provenance. Things get lost. Accidents happen. Lot of water under the carpet since then. You just concentrate on getting *your* job done.'

'Yes, sir,' Slider said.

'Get out there, start knocking on doorsteps. They've got a long start on you.' Yes, Slider thought. Twenty-five years. But the good thing was, people who had something to hide back then probably wouldn't worry about it now, so would be more likely to tell you the truth. One of the most frustrating things was that people lied to you to protect a secret you had no interest in. It happened all the time. Mind you, people lied to the police automatically, for no reason at all, just out of habit.

Porson had followed a different thread. 'Good thing is,' he said, 'no one can blame you if you *don't* crack it, not after all this time.' He sounded positively pleased about that.

'I'll blame myself,' Slider replied.

'Help yourself,' Porson said generously. 'Long as the commander's happy.'

Joanna came home, bringing in a swirl of outside air, moisture jewels in her hair. 'It's getting really foggy,' she said.

'I know,' said Slider. 'I'm glad you're back.'

She knew he worried about her whenever she was out in her car. It had annoyed her at first, thinking he didn't trust her driving. Now she realized it was everybody else's he didn't trust. So she didn't pick up on it. 'It was rather lovely along the Embankment, with those globe lights like strings of furry pearls,' she said.

'G and T?' he offered.

'Lovely,' she said.

He mixed it while she took off her coat and dumped her bag and violin case, and met her with it on the sofa. 'Good show?'

'Lots of entries,' she said. 'You've got to keep your wits about you. But it went OK.' She took a deep draught and sighed with satisfaction. 'There are only two rules to depping in a show,' she told him, leaning back on the sofa. 'Don't change the markings on the part. And don't be better than the person you're depping for.'

'I may be in something like that position,' Slider said.

'What, these bones of yours?'

He told her about Kellington, and the emaciated file.

'But he's retired. He's out of it. It won't matter if you're better than him. And you're bound to be.'

'Spoken like a loyal wife.'

Her mind jumped to Porson's comfort. 'At least they can't complain if you *don't* do any better – not after all this time.' She read his expression and said, 'I know, *you*'ll care.'

'It's my job. You wouldn't want to give a bad performance, however unimportant the concert.'

'True. But that's not why.'

He got up and fetched a copy of the photograph from the Knight file that he had brought home with him, and gave it to her. 'That's why.'

It had been a school photograph, so the girl was in uniform. She had straight mouse-fair hair cut in a bob just below jaw length and a short, square fringe – it was before the current fad for long, straggling locks. She had a narrow face, a straight nose, a dusting of freckles. She was narrowing her eyes, so it was hard to tell what colour they were, but the file had said blue; the smile was faint and perfunctory. She was smiling because she had been told to, not because she felt any hilarity. There was really nothing distinctive about her: she was just ordinary, and the ordinariness made it all the harder, somehow. A great beauty or a great talent would be remembered. Amanda Knight had left nothing behind to mark her short tenure. Nothing but some bones.

Joanna studied the photograph. She said, 'She looks like the kind of girl that keeps her bedroom tidy and does her homework without being nagged.' She handed it back to him. 'Yes, I see why,' she said.

'I shouldn't have shown you. It's upset you.'

'I can stand a little upset. You're my husband and my lover

and the father of my child, and you have to share things with me.'

He remembered an earlier conversation. 'If I committed a murder, would you stand by me?'

'You wouldn't commit a murder.'

'That's not an answer.'

'It's all the answer you'll get. Come on, don't be morbid.'

'I'm not being. It looks as though it must have been the father that did it.'

Her mouth turned down. 'I've never understood how anyone could kill their own child. I know it happens all the time, but how could they? Top me up?'

She drained her glass, and he got up, feeling guilty, and refilled them both. He shouldn't have brought the subject up. He searched for a new topic. With his back to her, he said, 'I was thinking, it's been a while since we had Jim and Emily over for supper. Do you think they're on a firm enough footing now to risk it?'

He turned back with the glasses and saw her expression of amusement. 'Nice save,' she said.

He pretended innocence. 'What? I mean it.'

'If it had come up in your mind spontaneously you'd have said Atherton. You never call him Jim.' She took her glass from him and clinked it with his. 'Thank you for caring about my state of mind.'

He gave her a crooked smile. 'Didn't want you having nightmares.'

'And yes, I think their relationship can probably stand exposure to the white heat of our domestic bliss. I've got Friday off, and Sunday, if you want to check diaries.'

'I'll talk to him tomorrow,' Slider said; and she began to talk about her day and the show. Later, in bed, he realized she had done it for his sake, to keep his mind off. She didn't want him having nightmares either.

SEVEN
Skin and Blister

Twenty-five years is a long time in a London street, especially in an upwardly-mobile area like Shepherd's Bush. Few people stay that long. And in London people generally only know their immediate neighbours, if that. Even the people straight opposite across the street are likely to be strangers, perhaps known by sight but rarely by name. As for anyone further away – forget it.

So it was not surprising that only two people in Laburnum Avenue had been there at the time Amanda Knight went missing, and neither of them had known the Knights personally, or knew anything other than what had been in the public domain. Swilley had a long and frustrating day and came up dry.

Gascoyne had done better in getting a handle on the Bexleys, Amanda's aunt and uncle. They were no longer at the address in Acton Vale, but a neighbour remembered them and said with some authority that they had moved to Ealing. With the search area thus narrowed, he was able to find a Patricia Bexley on the electoral register, at an address in Haven Lane. A telephone enquiry established that she was, indeed, *the* Pat Bexley, née Pirie, and that she was willing, even eager, to be visited.

'Get the story first,' Slider warned, 'before you tell her anything. And find out where the Knights have gone.'

Haven Lane was a narrow road of roomy Victorian houses, popular for its proximity to Ealing Broadway station. Unusually, it had two living pubs, the Haven and the Wheatsheaf, and adjacent to the latter was a short terrace of original two-up-two-down workmen's cottages, gentrified now into bijou residences, ideal for singles or childless couples.

The shiny red front door was opened to Gascoyne by a smart woman in jeans and a jaunty haircut. He knew from the records that she was now sixty-seven, but she was evidently making an effort, and with a disciplined figure, expensive highlights and artfully-applied make-up, she was managing to look ten years less. Her movements were spry, her smile fizzy; having shed ten years, she seemed to be trying, by applying the modern nostrum that fifty is the new forty, to lose ten more.

The house, though small, was bright, modern and well-lit inside. Wood strip flooring, pale walls and minimalist furnishings maximized the impression of space; and there was an agreeable smell of good coffee.

'Come on through,' she invited cheerily. 'Gascoyne, you said your name was? Any relation? I suppose everyone asks you that. Names! Honestly, what our parents make us suffer! Like me: I started off Patricia Pearl Pirie – three pees. Imagine what the other kids made of that at school! Patricia Pearl and Margaret Emerald – what was my mother thinking?'

'Rather pretty,' Gascoyne managed to get in before she was off again.

'Pearls and emeralds were her favourite stones – or is a pearl a stone? Whatever. I suppose it could be worse. Could have been amethyst! Think of that! Amethyst Pirie, my God! I've always insisted on just Pat ever since I left home, but Mum always called me Patricia right to the end, or "my little pearl", when I visited her. Ended up in a home – I felt bad about that, but what can you do? But at least she kept her marbles. Bodes well for me. What do I call you?' She gave a little laugh. 'It seems a bit old-fashioned to be calling you "constable". Or "detective", or whatever. Like something on TV. I've got some coffee on. How do you take it?'

Gascoyne felt that only the last question needed answering. The two tiny downstairs rooms had been knocked together to make one long narrow one, and the scullery at the rear had been demolished and a glass-roofed kitchen built across the back. Here the smell of coffee was joined by the smell of oil paint.

'You don't mind if I carry on working while we talk, do you?' she asked, plonking down a mug of coffee and indicating a chair at the table for Gascoyne. The table had been pushed back against the wall to make space in the middle of the tiled floor for an easel, on which stood an unfinished painting. Propped up next to the canvas was a photograph of an Alsatian dog, which she was evidently copying.

'It's a commission,' she explained. 'It's what I do. "Your pet in oils". Ghastly, isn't it?'

'I don't know anything about art,' Gascoyne said cautiously.

Mrs Bexley wasn't fey about it, he gave her that. She just laughed and said, 'You don't need to be polite. It's not art. It's only one step up from painting by numbers. I taught myself for a hobby, when I retired. A friend asked me if I'd do her dog, and it came out not bad, though I says it as shouldn't. She showed it around, and someone else asked, and so it went on. Now I advertise in the newsagents, and the local freebie mag, and I'm doing a couple a month.'

'Do you make a living at it?' Gascoyne asked.

'Oh, God, no. Just pocket money, but it keeps me in gin, as they say.' Another gay laugh. 'Have you got a pet you want immortalized? Take my card. I'll give you a professional discount.'

'I don't have a pet.'

'Funny enough, neither have I, not now, though we always had dogs. I miss them, really. More than I miss Brian, and that's a fact.'

'Your husband's not here?' Gascoyne asked delicately.

'Never was. We got divorced fifteen years ago. He got himself a twinkie, the idiot – one of the girls at his office, half his age and about a quarter his size, because it has to be said, he liked his grub, did Brian. Well, I was fed up with him by then, so I didn't mind. Good luck to him. We sold the big house – we had one of those double-fronters in Madeley Road – and split the money, and I bought my little nest here free and clear. He had to take on a big mortgage to satisfy Lolita's ambitions. And of course the effort killed him. Working every hour God sends and running around after her the rest of the time, bloody fool. Big heart attack, boom! Bye-bye Brian.'

'I'm sorry,' said Gascoyne.

'Oh, don't be,' she said easily. 'After a certain age, a man is just a drag on you, you know? I mean, you have to cook for them and clean up after them, and all they do is slump in front of the telly, and fart, and snore – no offence. I'm sure you're not like that. But he was like a smelly old dog I kept tripping over.

Now I can eat what I like, when I like, go where I like. I had a
fortnight in Japan last month. Brian would never have gone to
Japan. Raw fish? He'd have thought they were trying to poison
him. Do you like sushi?'

She had picked up the palette and was working her brush into
a patch of green paint, staring critically at the painting. Gascoyne
wondered how you got green into a brown and black dog, and
said, 'What about your sister? Are you close to her?'

'Maggie?' She gave him a sidelong look. 'I guessed it wasn't
me you wanted to talk about. Are you opening up that old case
again? I'd have thought you'd all got plenty to do without that.'

'There were just the two of you, weren't there?' It was a tip
he had got from Slider. Don't answer a question you don't want
to – ask another question of your own. And Mrs Bexley seemed
happy to talk about herself. Gascoyne guessed that despite her
robust ideas about being divorced, she missed having someone
around, a captive audience.

'That's right. We got along all right, but I was the bright one,
I got ahead and made something of myself, and Maggie – well,
she never had a decent job. She was a school dinner lady at one
time. My sister! Then she worked at a launderette. You see what
I mean? Whereas I got myself qualifications, I always worked
in an office. I was always a step above Maggie. And it didn't
help when she married Ronnie. Oh, he was a decent enough
bloke, but not very bright. I suppose by the time he came along
she thought it was him or nothing. She was over thirty when
they got married, you know? I mean, I always had loads of
boyfriends. Tons. I could have my pick. But Maggie – well, I
don't know that anyone else ever asked her.'

'You didn't like Ronnie?'

'Oh, don't get me wrong. He was all right. But he was . . .
old-fashioned working class, if you know what I mean. Whereas
Brian and I . . . Well, we had a different lifestyle. Ronnie'd come
home for his evening meal about half past five and call it his
"tea". I don't think he ever drank wine in his life. And they never
entertained. Unless Brian and I went over for Sunday lunch, I
don't think they ever had anyone in the house.'

'Didn't he have any relatives – Ronnie?'

'No. Only child. Or, wait, I think he had a brother that died when he was a kid. No, he didn't have any relatives, or friends. It was just the three of them. Amanda never had friends in, either. It was just the way their minds were set. Our parents, mine and Maggie's, were just the same. I don't remember anyone but relatives ever setting foot over the threshold.' She dumped the green brush in a jam jar of turps and took a clean one, working brown and white together on the palette.

'Tell me about Amanda,' Gascoyne invited, seeing they had reached her naturally.

'Oh, that poor kid,' said Mrs Bexley, frowning at her painting. 'I don't suppose we'll ever find out what happened to her. Unless you've got something new to tell me?'

'What was she like?' Gascoyne asked.

'She was a good kid. Good at school. I always thought she was more like me than Maggie – wanted to get ahead, make something of herself. She wasn't lively like me. Very quiet. Sort of *intense*. Always thinking. But she was very fond of me. I think she was more fond of me than her mother, in some respects. Used to love coming to visit us – mind you, that was partly because of the dogs. We always had dogs. We couldn't have kids, you see. Amanda loved dogs. Mad about animals. She wanted to be a vet when she left school, you know? I told her she had to work hard at her lessons if she was serious about it, especially maths and science. Otherwise—' she glanced at him – 'I could see her turning into one of those drudges, cleaning out kennels and so on. You know? End up like her mum. Instead of being a proper vet and making a lot of money and having a nice house and everything.'

'And did she work hard at school?'

'Oh, I think so. Well—' a smile – 'she didn't have much else going on. She didn't have a big circle of pals like I did at her age. I was very popular at school. Amanda didn't seem to have any friends. Well, not friends that she visited. And of course, like I said, she wasn't encouraged to have anyone in.' The smile switched off. 'That last day, she was playing all alone in the garden. In the middle of the summer holidays. Can you imagine that? I'd have been off out somewhere with my gang from dawn to dusk. But that was the sort of girl I was.'

'When had you last seen her?' Gascoyne asked.

'The Sunday before. They all came over to our house for lunch.' She made a face. 'I made a point of it, at least once a month. Otherwise Ron would never have stirred out of that house at all. Liked eating at his own table, that's what he always said. But I wanted Maggie to have a break now and then. And Amanda – at least she ought to know what a napkin was, if she was going to get on. Ron called them "serviettes".'

'Do you remember anything about that visit?'

'I remember everything about that visit. Had to go over it often enough at the time.' She stared moodily at the photograph. 'Is it my imagination or are this dog's ears different sizes?'

'What did you talk about?'

'Just what people always talk about. Except that the topic of holidays came up. I mentioned Brian and I were going to Marrakesh. In September, though, when the prices came down. Of course, Maggie and Ron had to go during the school holidays because of Amanda, and they could never afford to go anywhere interesting. Not that Ron would have wanted to – a fortnight in a caravan in Weymouth, that was nirvana to him. Anyway, I remember he got a bit grumpy when the topic came up, said he didn't think they'd be able to have a holiday at all that year because he was too busy. I saw Maggie look at him, but she would never say anything in front of anyone else, not even her own sister.'

'She was loyal to him?'

'Well, yes, but it was more like keeping up a good front. She'd never admit everything in the garden wasn't rosy. And then Amanda piped up and said she was glad they weren't going away, she'd sooner stay at home. And I saw Ron give her a surprised sort of look. I suppose he thought she was sticking up for him.'

'You don't think she was?'

'Backing up her mum, more likely.'

'Didn't she get on with her dad?'

'Not a lot. I don't suppose she saw much in common with him.'

'Did they have rows? Did he tell her off?'

She seemed to sense a trap, and paused, brush in hand, looking at the painting to sort out her answer. 'He was a bit of a Victorian father, in a way,' she said carefully. 'Old-fashioned, you know? Wouldn't let her wear modern clothes, or make-up. All the other girls wore mini skirts, but Amanda's had to be right down to the knee.'

'And she complained about that to you?'

'Oh, not really complained, as such, but she must have minded it, mustn't she? She was always interested in my make-up, when she came to visit. I offered to do her face once, and she blushed like fire and said, "Oh no, Dad would kill me".'

'Did he hit her?'

'Ronnie? No,' she said at once. Then: 'Well, not that I ever heard. I mean, he wasn't abusive. He didn't knock them about.'

'But you think he might have hit them now and then?'

'Oh no, I'm sure he didn't,' she said. 'Maggie would have said something. No, I'm sure he never hit them. But he did have a bit of a temper on him. He'd get red in the face and you could see he was wanting to blow. I went over one day when they weren't expecting me – oh, years before, that was – and I could hear him before I got to the front door, shouting at Maggie about something. It stopped when I rang the bell like it was cut off with a knife, and Maggie came to the door looking embarrassed and pretended like nothing had happened.'

'Did Amanda have a boyfriend?' Gascoyne asked.

Mrs Bexley laughed. 'No! She didn't know boys existed. She was very young for her age in that way, though intelligence-wise she was streets ahead. No, like I said, she was mad about animals. A lot of girls go through that stage, before they get into boys. With me, it was when I was about ten, but Amanda, like I said, she was young for her age. I don't suppose it would have been long, though. She'd have discovered boys soon enough. If she'd had the chance,' she added despondently. Her brush paused. It seemed a genuine emotion: to Gascoyne it was the first time she had not been playing to the gallery, watching her own performance.

'That day, the day she disappeared, did Maggie telephone you?'

'Yes, she did. Around six'ish. I couldn't say the time exactly. She asked me if Amanda had come to visit me. Well, I said no.

I was surprised, because that wasn't something Amanda would do, just come on the off-chance. Not that I'd have minded – she was always welcome – but they didn't do things like that. Not without an invitation. They weren't dropping-in sort of people. So then I asked, why? And she said Amanda had gone. She was trying to sound calm, but I could hear underneath she was in a panic. I said, Gone where? And she said, Just gone – she'd been in the garden, and now she was nowhere to be found. So of course, I told her not to worry – God help me! Well, you do, don't you?'

She seemed to need it, so Gascoyne gave her a nod.

'I said she'd probably gone down to the library or something, and she'd turn up any minute. And Maggie said, Yes, that was probably what it was, and rang off.'

'And what did you *think* had happened?'

'Well, I didn't know. Amanda wasn't the sort of kid to wander off without saying. That wasn't how she was brought up. I suppose in the back of my mind, maybe I thought she'd finally reached the age where she broke out – you know, defied them, rebelled against the rules. But Maggie had never said anything about her starting to give trouble, and usually there are signs, aren't there, a build-up? But I never, never thought anything had happened to her. You don't, do you? It happens to other people, not you.'

'How did they take it, Maggie and Ronnie?'

'Well, they were devastated, of course they were.' She looked at him as if it was a stupid question. 'Maggie didn't know what to do with herself. Ronnie went through all the stages, anger at first that she'd gone off without a word, then fear something had happened to her, then absolute despair. I never saw a man so crushed. I mean, I never really *liked* Ronnie, if you want to know the truth – he just wasn't my sort of person – but I had to feel for him, the way he went to pieces. And, of course, poor Maggie, it just got worse and worse for her, when the police started making out that Ron must have had something to do with it.' She met his eyes, straight and level. 'I mean, what kind of a thing was that to suggest to her?'

'You never thought that yourself?'

She hesitated. 'No, I didn't. Not at the time. He was too

upset about it. But afterwards I thought – well, it could have been. No more than that. Just could have been. If, say, he'd found her walking along the road, and lost his temper because she shouldn't have been out without telling anyone, and maybe hurt her without meaning to. I don't believe he'd ever *mean* to do it, but say he killed her by accident, well, he'd have had to try and cover it up, wouldn't he? Take the body somewhere in his van and get rid of it.'

'At what point did you start thinking that? That it could have been him?'

Unexpectedly, she blushed. She averted her eyes from him, put down the brush and palette and turned away. 'Like some more coffee?' she asked, in a voice that was probably meant to sound casual but came out gruff and brusque.

'No thanks,' said Gascoyne, watching her. She went over to the kitchen counter where the coffee machine was keeping it hot, but did not touch it. She had her back to him, and he guessed she was trying to rearrange her face. He didn't want to give her too much time, so he said again, 'At what point did you—?'

And she turned abruptly to face him, her cheeks still pink, her eyes bright. 'If you want to know, it wasn't all sweetness and light between me and Brian and Maggie and Ron. I mean, we felt sorry for them, terribly sorry, of course we did, and we tried to do everything we could to help them get through it. But what can you do, in the end? Something like that – it's unimaginable. You just don't know what to say or do. And there was no end to it. If she'd been found . . . If a body had been found, well, at least you've got closure. I mean, I don't suppose you ever really get over something like that, but you have to move on. But they just didn't know. The agony just went on and on. And I suppose you have to lash out at the people nearest you, don't you? Because that's all there is.'

'And they lashed out at you?'

'Things got strained,' she admitted, looking down at her hands, which she had locked together. 'Things were said. Maybe – maybe I let Maggie see that I had *entertained* the idea that Ronnie might have had something to do with it. I mean, I never said it, I wouldn't say it outright.' She looked at him quickly. He saw she was ashamed. 'And then *she* said, What about Brian?'

He waited, but she didn't seem to be able to go on. 'She suggested Brian was involved in Amanda's disappearance?'

She nodded. 'She said a lot of things. She said Brian was in and out of empty houses all day with his job being an estate agent, so he had opportunity. She said I never knew where he was from one minute to the next. She said he had a bad reputation where women were concerned. She said I ought to get control over my own husband before I started throwing mud at someone else's.' She swallowed. 'She said he'd always been a bit *too* fond of Amanda, and she'd been thinking for some time they ought to stop visiting us before things got out of hand.'

Ouch! thought Gascoyne. He could see the whole scenario being played out in his mind's eye – the two women throwing ever more vicious barbs at each other, a lifetime, perhaps, of jealousy and resentment coming to a festering head, fed by the poison of fear for the missing girl. He would like to bet that at some point Maggie had said, 'You don't know what it's like – you don't have a child', thereby striking Pat the one blow that could never be forgiven.

He said, gently, 'I have to ask you – did you ever have any suspicions that way yourself?'

She gave a short, mirthless laugh. 'No. Not for a second. Brain loved his twinkies, it's true, but Amanda wasn't to his taste. He liked 'em older, and he liked 'em obvious. All eyes and mouth. Fully developed – udders like a dairy cow. He was definitely a boob man – the stinker!' she added with parenthetic disdain. 'He'd always had women on the side – I always knew that. But what can you do? At least it meant he didn't bother me too much with all that malarky. I could do without it, if you want to know the truth. He was seeing some girl anyway, at the time Amanda went missing. I could tell – he wasn't exactly subtle about it. So he didn't have a vacancy, if you like.'

'All the same—' he began, even more gently.

'No, listen,' she interrupted him. 'The police back then looked into him. I suppose they have to look at everyone. But he was covered. He was at the golf club all morning, had lunch with half a dozen of his pals.'

That didn't cover the important part of the day. 'And afterwards?' Gascoyne asked.

'I told them he was at home with me all afternoon.' Her expression was stony now. Gascoyne felt a quickening of interest.

'Was he?'

She seemed to hesitate, as if wanting to say something but having some block on it. 'We had a terrific row afterwards – probably the worst we ever had. It was so stupid. He *wanted* to tell them where he was. He said she'd give him a complete alibi. But I didn't want to admit it. To anyone. It was one thing knowing where he was, what he was doing. But to say it out loud, to strangers, washing our dirty linen . . . It was humiliating. I couldn't do it. So when they asked me, I said he was with me, at home, all afternoon. I got my word in first. So when they asked him, he had to go along with it. But he was furious. He wanted to show off his manhood, all blokes together – stupid, macho shit that he was! Wanted the police to think he was a great guy. Ho ho, nudge nudge. I wasn't having that. He was doing Karen Beales from the office, at her place, but I told the police he was home with me. I said we were doing a jigsaw puzzle together,' she added with vicious satisfaction. 'One thousand pieces. A Cottage Garden. That hit him where it hurt!'

'That must be nearly unique,' Gascoyne reported to Slider afterwards. 'Giving a man a false alibi he didn't want, while knowing he had a genuine one.'

'*She* may have known it,' Slider sighed, 'but we don't. We'll have to check his alibi. It gives us one more person to find. Damn.'

'She's given me this Karen Beales's address at that time. I'll make a start on her, guv. But . . .'

Slider saw from his expression that he had seen the snag. Even if Karen could be found, and even if she confirmed Brian was with her, there was no way to be sure she wasn't just saying it. And if she didn't confirm it, they might suspect him, but what good would that do, when he was dead already?

'I suppose there's not a lot of point,' he said, 'but you have to go through the motions.'

'You know what they say,' Slider told him kindly. 'If you can't take a joke, you shouldn't be in the Job.'

'Yes, guv,' Gascoyne said with a reluctant grin.

The best solution, Slider thought, would be if she told them Brian had confessed the whole thing to her one night under the influence of passion, with full details of how he had gone about burying the body. But who was ever that lucky?

'How did Mrs Bexley take the news about the body being found?'

'Just what you'd expect,' said Gascoyne. 'Surprise. Disbelief. Sadness. She said she supposed that meant it must have been Ronnie, but I don't think she'd *really* thought he did it, not in her heart of hearts.'

Heart of hearts. Gascoyne was a sweet, old-fashioned boy, Slider thought. 'And did she give you a line on where the Knights are now?'

'I'm afraid not,' Gascoyne said, obviously reluctant to disappoint him. 'The sisters had a falling out after the big row, when Maggie said Brian might have done it. They patched it up, but things were never the same again. She said the Knights moved away about eighteen months later – to try and make a fresh start, was the way she put it. I suppose Ronnie could never have a normal life once it was known the police had suspected him. They moved to Reading first, and Ron got work with a construction company, but after a couple of years things broke down again and they moved on to Swindon. Pat and Maggie sent Christmas cards to each other for a few years, but one year no card arrived from Maggie, and the next year the one Pat sent was returned undelivered. So she doesn't know where she is now.'

'Oh joy,' said Slider.

'At least it narrows down the field of search a bit,' Gascoyne tried to comfort him. 'It could have been anywhere, from John o' Groats to Johannesburg.'

'It still could,' Slider pointed out.

EIGHT
Making the Red One Green

A therton had been called away again, for another grilling at headquarters. Slider found it comforting in an obscure way, a sign of life in Neptune, which otherwise, from his position, looked as lively as a botoxed brow.

The parallel investigation by the Fraud Squad into the finances of the North Kensington Regeneration Trust – he had suggested the line of inquiry, along Al Capone lines, as another way of getting to some of the perpetrators, since many of them were involved in both – had also gone quiet, though that was not surprising, since fraud investigations were highly technical and generally took years. You couldn't expect the tightly knitted financial arrangements of terminally rich men to be unpicked in a brace of sheiks.

Repetition had lulled any concerns he had about Atherton's standing up to the inquisitors, so he was startled when his bagman returned, came into his room and shut the door behind him. Closed doors were not a big part of his firm's routine.

'What?' Slider said. 'Has something happened? Was it bad?'

'No,' said Atherton. 'It was worryingly *not* bad.' He took his usual position, sitting on the windowsill, the day outside another sweet, fog-and-fruitfulness backdrop to his lean good looks. 'It started off the usual way. They shoved me in an empty room, and left me there for three quarters of an hour to contemplate my sins. I spent the time working out how much my enforced idleness was costing the taxpayer. Do you want to know what the answer was?'

'No. Get on with it. Who interviewed you?'

'Medlicott from the IPCC.'

'Oh, bloody Nora!' said Slider. He was the top inquisitor. 'It must have been serious.'

'You'd think so. It had me sweating when I saw him come in.

But here's the thing – he didn't seem to know what to say. He seemed almost embarrassed.'

'*Medlicott?*' Slider exclaimed in disbelief. Medlicott embarrassed was like Ivan the Terrible watching *The Sound of Music*. And reaching for the Kleenex.

'I know. He kept fiddling with his papers and clearing his throat. Then he said, "It was you, wasn't it? You leaked the story." And I said no, it wasn't me, and that was it. Dismissed.'

'Seriously? That's not a grilling.'

'Hardly a light toasting. I thought, well, maybe it's his time of the month or something, but . . .'

'It's worrying,' Slider agreed.

'We know they must really, *really* want to know who leaked – if anyone did – so if they're walking away from that aspect of it, maybe they're losing interest in the case. And here's the thing—'

'I thought we'd already had the thing.'

'No, this is the real thing – when I came out of the room, I headed for the lift, but something made me look back, and I saw someone coming out of the observation room. He went the other way so I only caught a glimpse of his face, but I'll swear it was Assistant Commissioner Millichip.'

'*Millichip* was observing your interview?'

Atherton nodded. 'So what's going on, guv?'

'I don't know,' Slider said, thinking. Millichip back in the driving seat? The newspapers dropping the story? Freddie Cameron's revelation that they had appointed a new forensic expert?

'Ron Carver tried to warn me in his cups,' he said. 'At his leaving party.'

'Had a load on, did he? Isn't he known as a bit of a fantasist?'

'You weren't there,' Slider said. 'It was one of those booze-induced moments of embarrassing frankness. And whatever we think of him, he knows people.' He lapsed into thought again.

Atherton was watching him like a cat waiting to be fed. Come on: tin, can opener, bowl. How hard is it to put them together?

Slider stood up. 'I think I'll go and have a word with Mr Porson,' he said.

*   *   *

Porson was standing by his window, reading something, his bushy eyebrows pulled down to the bridge of his nose like two Arctic fox stoles. He didn't look up as Slider tapped politely on his open door, but he said, 'I thought you'd be in.' He turned a page. 'You've read this, then?'

'Sir?'

Now Porson looked, examining his face. 'You're on the circulation list. Must still be on its way. They're filing Neptune.'

'They're dropping it?' Slider had been half expecting it, but the actual words came as a shock, like the bang when the watched rocket goes off.

'I said filing,' Porson said, in a reasonable tone, which was a warning. 'As in, anything new comes up and we open it again.'

'So the fix *has* gone in,' Slider said bitterly.

'What's that? What fix?' Porson scowled at him. 'Don't start getting off on one of your high hats. They haven't got enough to go on, that's all. Lack of evidence. I told you from the beginning it was thin.'

'Anyone'd be thin if you starved them,' said Slider.

'Now look here – you want to keep your feet firmly on terra cotta. Start seeing conspiracies everywhere and they'll be carting you off to the giggle farm.'

That was all very well, but Porson wasn't meeting Slider's eyes. 'Sir,' said Slider. Now Porson looked at him, and there was a guilty hesitance in there somewhere which Slider hastened to exploit. 'Please tell me what's been going on. I know you know.' Porson's eyes shifted to the document he was still holding, and Slider added, 'And I don't mean the official version. The truth.'

Porson sighed heavily. 'Your witness withdrew her statement. Said she'd made it all up.'

'But—'

Porson allowed himself a touch of irritation. 'It's all here. Black and white. Shannon Bailey was never a creditive witness, and now she's voluntarily withdrawn her statement. No other witnesses have come forward. The whole thing's a storm in a mare's nest. Nothing anyone can do. DPP's comment's very fair. Doesn't blame you, says appearances were all your way, but on examination there's nothing to go on. Case filed.' He put the report down on his desk with a terminal thump.

Slider stared. 'They put pressure on her. Frightened her. Or maybe paid her off.'

Porson's eyebrows lifted, revealing frosty blue pools. 'Will you get a grip on yourself! Why have you always got to be right and everybody else wrong? You've had enough experience of so-called witnesses who make it all up to get attention. Fantasy land.'

Yes, he had – enough experience to know the difference. Shannon hadn't wanted to tell, and it had taken patience to win her trust and get it out of her. He had spoken to her, watched her face. He knew how scared she had been.

Well, in fairness, he had to admit she might have been scared enough to withdraw her statement without any further pressure being put on her. But if anyone had actually wanted the case to go ahead, they would have dealt with her fear. *He* would have dealt with it if he was handling her. That's what they did. But they hadn't done it. They'd sided with the AC against the teenage sex toy. Carver would have thought that was exactly the right thing to do. Us and Them. Shannon wasn't exactly a Them, but the AC was definitely an Us.

'And Kaylee Adams?' he said, but he knew the answer to that already.

'Hit and run. It was only Doc Cameron's opinion she fell. They've got another forensic pathologist to look at it—'

'I know.'

'You do?'

'And I bet he'll explain exactly how those injuries could come about in an RTA.'

'Well, there you are.' Porson started walking his beat again. Displacement activity – like a caged tiger. 'Does it ever occur to you that Cameron could be wrong? I mean, he's not God. And neither are you, by the way.'

Slider said, 'What about the sex parties at Holland Lodge? Drugs and underage girls?'

Porson paced. 'Where's your evidence? Anyone can have parties. No law against that. No proof there were drugs or minors there.'

No, there wouldn't be, Slider thought, if none of the girls wanted to talk, and why would they unless persuaded? The people attending the parties wouldn't incriminate themselves. 'And Peloponnos? His list of names?'

'List of names – what does that mean? Could have been anything. Anyway, he was a bit of a nutter, wasn't he? Unstable. Topped himself.'

'Sir.' Slider gave him a reproachful look, and Porson made an irritable turn.

'He wasn't some knight in shining arbour, you know. Financial improprieties. You were right about that. That trust of his was as crooked as a pig's hind leg. The Fraud Squad hasn't got to the bottom of it yet, but I've heard they're saying old Ploppyloss was cyphering off money right and left. Secret bank accounts.'

Slider was silent. So they were going to blame everything on Peloponnos. Well, it made sense. He was dead, and his only family, his aged mother, had gone back to Greece. If there were ever any need to publish anything, who could object to Peloponnos taking the fall?

'Look,' said Porson, 'this is good for you. You brought forward your suspicions, which was right and courageous, they were looked into. This report's quite complimentary about you. They'll be even pleaseder if the Fraud Squad gets some of the money back, thanks to you. So you can go on your merry way with a clear conscience.'

'And the establishment doesn't get rocked to its foundations,' Slider said.

Porson scowled. 'Is that what you wanted? To overthrow the establishment?'

'No, of course not.'

'It's hard enough to do our job as it is, without more scandals eating away at public confidence. We've got the press on our backs, politicians taking pot shots at us, and if our own start trying to bring us down as well—'

'That wasn't what I wanted, sir,' Slider said unhappily.

'Just as well. People who pull down ceilings get buried under the rubble. And who'd have been the better for it? It's always the little people who get hammered in a revolution.'

Slider looked up, surprised at this piece of insight. The Old Man could be quite sharp.

Porson said, more kindly, 'All you've got to do now is keep your head down and do your job and everything will be fine. Things could have got very nasty, very nasty indeed. I don't think you ever fully realized what sort of hornet's nest you were poking. You've had a let-off. Look at it that way. A case like this, rumbling on for years, everyone pissed off at you – if there *had* been anything in it, I mean. You'd have had a miserable life.'

Slider thought about it. It was Kaylee that smarted most. What's dead can't come to life, I think. But nobody cared about the likes of Kaylee Adams. 'Sir,' he said, 'if you knew all this, why didn't you tell me?'

'I *didn't* know it, not till I got this report. Anyway,' he added, giving himself away, 'you were in purdah, as long as you were under investigation by the IPCC.'

'Were?'

'They cleared you. I heard this morning. That'll be on its way to you as well. You're all clear. Another win.' He looked at Slider's long face and added, ironically, 'Hooray.'

'Thank you, sir.'

'This is all good,' Porson said, trying to jolly him. 'Just keep your nose clean and you'll be fine. What have you got on? Oh yes, the Trees Estate. The bones. How's that coming along?'

'Slowly.'

'Good. Fine. Just the ticket. Get stuck into that.'

'Absolutely sir. I'll do that,' said Slider.

Porson's eyes narrowed. He suspected satire. 'Slow and steady wins fair maiden. The less your face is seen around the place the better, for a while.'

Slider understood the interview was at an end, and turned to leave. But when he reached the door, Porson said, 'That leak?'

Slider turned, expressing a wary blank.

'It was Atherton, wasn't it?' Porson asked with deceptive indifference.

Slider said, 'He says it wasn't. And I believe him.'

He left. No good deed goes unpunished, so it was said. And everything left a trace of DNA.

It took him the length of his walk back from Porson's office to his own to make up his mind. He called Hart in.

'What are you working on?' he snapped.

She grew alert at his tone. 'Trying to find the Knights. Searching electoral registers.'

'Hand that over to someone else – LaSalle will do. I want you to find Shannon Bailey. You're the one who had the contact there, you've got the street cred.'

'Shannon? What's happened to her?'

'I don't know. Maybe nothing. But she's withdrawn her evidence.'

'Bastard!' Hart said – meaning the situation, not the girl. 'Someone's got at her.'

'I need to know that she's all right.'

'And if we can turn her back,' Hart added with relish.

'Just find her,' Slider said warningly. 'Then ring me. Ring *me*, do you understand? Don't talk about this to anyone else.'

'Gotcha,' Hart said smartly, and went. Thank God for an intelligent copper, Slider thought.

Atherton sloped in. 'Well?' he asked.

'Shut the door,' said Slider. The report hadn't reached his in-tray yet. When it did he'd have to tell the rest of the firm. For now, he just wanted a sounding board against whom to try out the ramifications.

'It's not good news, is it?' Atherton said whimsically.

'When is it ever?' said Slider.

The report had Shannon staying with her sister Dakota. Hart tried there first, calculating that Dakota would have got up by now, but would not yet be working, but there was no reply when she rang the doorbell. A policeman develops an instinct for when a place is empty and when there is someone inside ignoring the bell. She went back to her car and sat watching, and was rewarded half an hour later when Dakota appeared, turning into the street from the far end, a tall, slim figure in a very smart jade wool coat and long boots, with a Morrison's carrier bag in either hand. She crossed the road right under Hart's nose without seeing her, heading for the front door, and Hart let her get her key in the door before nipping across nimbly and saying, 'Hello, Dakota. Can I have a word?'

The girl started violently. 'Bloody hell fire, you frit me!' And then, seeing who it was, her expression soured. 'Oh fuck, it's you again. What do *you* want?'

'Language, love,' Hart said mildly. 'I just want a word. Can I come in? You don't wanna discuss your biz in the street, do you?'

Dakota looked up and down the road, and then shrugged. 'Oh, all right,' she said. 'But you can't stay long. I got to get ready.'

Inside the flat it smelled clean and warm and was very quiet. The passage from the front door led past the two bedrooms, one either side, and Hart noted that the door to Shannon's was closed. Dakota strode into the living area at the end, shrugged her coat onto a stool at the kitchen counter, and went straight to the coffee machine, which was on. 'Want some?'

The coffee had been made long enough ago to lose any aroma. 'No thanks,' said Hart.

Dakota poured a mug and carried it over to the French windows which gave onto a tiny balcony. She opened them and stuck a cigarette into her mouth. 'You don't mind if I smoke, do you?' she asked indifferently.

'S'your lungs, babe,' said Hart. She could see Dakota was arranging her defences, but that was all right, because it suggested she had something to defend. 'So where's Shannon, then?' she asked when the woman had taken her first drag.

'She's not here,' Dakota exhaled.

'I didn't ask where she wasn't.'

'I mean, she's moved out.'

'Where to?'

Dakota's eyes shifted. 'Look, what d'you want with her? I thought this was all over.'

'What was all over?'

'All the questioning. She told you lot what she knew, and you blew her off. Now you're back again. Can't you leave her alone?'

'I just want to make sure she's all right,' Hart said genially.

'She will be if you lot just sod off.'

'Where is she, babe?'

'I told you, she moved out.'

'Why don't I believe you?'

Dakota rolled her eyes in an exasperation that appeared genuine. 'Look, she *was* stopping with me, but there was police in and out all hours, hanging around outside, sniffing about, asking questions. It was affecting my business. I mean, people don't want the filth looking over their shoulders when they're on the job, do they? Shan's a good kid, she didn't want to ruin my life. So she went.'

'Where did she go?' Dakota didn't answer, and Hart shifted a little closer and added a little menace. 'Look, babe, you ain't exactly on strong ground here. *I* don't mind what you do for a living, but there's others might. So I won't ask again – where did Shannon go?'

'She went up Auntie Hallie's,' she said sulkily.

'Where's that?'

'She's got a West Indian restaurant down Notting Hill. She said Shan could waitress. She's gonna work there till she decides what to do.'

'What's the name of the restaurant?'

'I'm not telling you,' Dakota said, with a renewed rush of defiance. 'You leave her alone. Haven't you done enough?'

'I told you, I just want to make sure she's all right.'

'She won't be if you go barging in asking questions, showing her up. She's trying to make a fresh start, all right?'

Hart changed tack. 'Can I have a look in her room?'

'There's nothing to see.'

'Then you won't mind me looking, will you?' Hart said.

Dakota hastily stubbed out her cigarette and followed her, but Hart had enough of a start to get the door open before Dakota could stop her. The room contained a single bed, wardrobe and chest of drawers which before had been crammed and crowded with Shannons's effects. Now the cosmetics and other clutter was gone from the top of the chest, and the drawers and the wardrobe contained a few less favoured items of clothing and a lot of empty space. She *had* gone then, at least to the extent of taking her immediate requirements with her.

'I know that restaurant,' Hart said casually, pretending to examine the clothes in the wardrobe. 'I've et there a coupla times. It's not bad, the Jerk Shack.'

'The Pepper Pot,' Dakota corrected without thinking.

Hart was ready with another question to distract her. 'Did Shannon say anything about Jessica Bale? Her friend?'

'Like what?'

'Whether she was still seeing her. They were close, weren't they? She was stopping with her before.'

'I dunno. She's not mentioned her in a while. Look, what are you after? Your lot questioned Jess as well as Shannon. You ought to know how she is. Why're you asking me?'

'Oh, this isn't official,' Hart said with a grin. 'This is just me askin', cos I'm a nice person.'

Interestingly, a look of alarm crossed Dakota's face, slightly beating a blush of annoyance to it. 'I think you better go,' she said, trying for dignity. It wasn't far to the front door. 'And don't come back!' she added as Hart opened it.

Hart turned, out in the corridor. 'You might not know it, babe, but I'm on your side. Remember that, if you find you need help.'

'Yeah, real Samaritan,' Dakota sneered, and closed the door.

Dumb Dora, Hart thought affectionately as she trod down the stairs. She didn't even realize she'd told her where Shannon was.

NINE

Downtown Addy

Just before dawn a thick white fog came down, silencing the world, blocking out all sight. Slider stared out of the window at the faintly luminous whiteness. It was like being inside a ping-pong ball.

Joanna was still asleep. As he walked along the passage he could hear George chatting quietly in his cot. In the mornings he liked to wile away the time until his day started up by telling himself stories, acting them out with his toys. Slider moved quietly until he could see into the room, and watched for a moment as the cars and plastic marines bounced and jerked to the murmuring narrative. Then George sensed him, turned, and his face lit in a ravishing smile. Slider was one of the two people in the world he was happiest to see just then, and he knew how to show it.

To provoke such utter bliss in another human being was beautiful and terrible. A pang of absolute love gripped Slider, making it for a moment hard to breathe. This intensity of feeling and minuteness of observation belonged to second families, were what made it worth while starting all over again in middle age. It was not that he had loved his other children less, but that life the first time around had not granted the space for such contemplation. Hours had been longer, money shorter, difficulties more pressing because he'd had less wisdom and experience to cope with them. Life had been one damn thing after another. Looking back, it felt as though he and Irene and the kids had been like four peas in a maraca, bouncing around in their preoccupations and only touching to collide.

And of course he had not had the same sort of relationship with Irene: they had not been two halves of one whole, but ill-matched horses pulling a cart, out of step with each other. Irene had never understood the Job. To her, it was simply the way he made money for them to spend in their *real* life. It was where he went for annoyingly long hours, and from which he notably failed to mine sufficient money or status to compensate her for his absence. It wasn't her fault. Few people who had not done it could understand, which was why the Job was littered with broken marriages.

But Joanna was a musician, and she did understand, because it was the same for her. A musician always had to turn up. There was no calling in sick. You went even if you felt like death. There was no being late. There were no duvet days. There was no saying *the hell with it* and turning back because the traffic was impossible. There were no excuses. And there was no giving less than a hundred percent to the performance when you did arrive. You had to be there, and you had to be perfect.

And it wasn't just because you would lose the work if you failed. There was an imperative beyond that: the work itself. Music called you like the grim god in a pagan world, demanding service, utter dedication, the whole self. And, of course, you wouldn't have it any other way. That's what the outsider couldn't grasp – why you would do that to yourself, serve such a rigid tyrant, when you might lollygag about at some other employment and probably earn twice as much. They didn't understand. Musicians and policemen did.

George was watching him, curiously, and when he said quietly, 'Want to come downstairs, boy?' he held out his arms and made that impatient snatching motion with his hands, so Slider went and reached into the cot, lifted out the divine weight and lodged it on his hip, smelling the warm, new-bread scent of his sleep on his skin. He kissed the perfect curve of hot, silken cheek, and thought that some years hence such kisses would be rebuffed as the self-consciousness of boyhood kicked in. He couldn't kiss Matthew any more – would probably never kiss him again in the whole of his life. Kate allowed kisses, but they were counters in her own private power game, not tokens of affection. But for now, any touch of his was welcome to George. Love bloomed between them, uncomplicated and perfect. He had a few years of it yet; and this time around, he knew it and would cherish them.

But in the kitchen, as he made tea and boiled George's egg, and his child chattered to him, he listened and responded with his whole heart but only half his mind. The fog outside was thinning and the world was claiming him. He was remembering the scene at work when the Neptune report had finally arrived, and he had summoned his firm to give them the bad news. They had listened in stony silence, and he realized that it had already reached them, in that mysterious way that 'grapevine' worked.

'I know you feel let down,' he had concluded. 'You feel your work has not been rewarded, you made all that effort for nothing. But sometimes that's the way it goes. Not all cases come to court – you don't need me to tell you that. Sometimes it just isn't possible to assemble the evidence that will carry the thing home. As long as you know in yourself that you have done everything you could have done, there's nothing to regret. Put it aside, and move on. We're here to do a job, not win awards.' He observed their expressions and added the old saw. 'If you wanted to be popular, you should have joined the fire brigade.'

They gave him reluctant laughter for that, and seeing he had finished, got up and began gathering themselves to go home, looking more relaxed.

He had told Joanna about it in the evening as she prepared supper, and she had looked at him over her shoulder from in front of the gas stove and said, 'Nice speech, but was that really what you thought? That it was just one of those things?'

'I've read the report. It's very carefully phrased, very balanced. It makes sense. Not to believe it – to believe there's some sort of conspiracy going on – would make me a paranoid nutter, wouldn't it? A swivel-eyed loony.'

She looked at him carefully, and went back to stirring the ragu. She said, 'Was every lead followed up the way you would have done it? Were there things not done that you would have done? I know it was taken away from you before you'd properly finished.'

He hesitated. 'I'm starting to wonder, you see, if I *wanted* to see more than was there. If it all unravels when you pull one thread, maybe it was bad knitting to begin with. If it weren't for Kaylee . . . But as Porson kindly pointed out to me, Freddie Cameron isn't God. His opinion could be wrong. It's far more *likely* that she was knocked down by a hit-and-run driver. The simplest explanation is generally the right one.'

Joanna turned the gas off from under the spaghetti, carried the pot to the sink and tipped it into the colander. 'But you don't think she was, do you?' she said from within the cloud of steam. 'Knocked down?'

'It doesn't make *sense*,' he said fretfully.

She ladled the sauce over the pasta. 'Can't you just forget it?' she asked. 'Take your own advice, set it to one side and move on? Maybe you were wrong: it's possible.'

He thought about it as he followed her to the table. 'When you play,' he said, 'you *know* when it's right, don't you?' He saw her raised eyebrow and said, 'I don't just mean you're playing the right notes. I mean, when it's *right*.'

She nodded. 'I know what you mean. Like when you're playing darts and you need a double top to go out – you know as it leaves your hand, before it reaches the board, that you've done it.'

'I've developed an instinct over twenty years of being a detective. And if I lose that, I lose everything.'

She heard the frustration in his voice, and the fear underneath it, because a musician lives with that fear all the time: *can I still do it? Am I finished?*

'Well,' she said lightly, 'if you were right all along, something else is bound to come up, sooner or later. After all, look at this Laburnum Avenue thing. Everybody must have believed that poor child would never be heard of again. But here you are, twenty-five years later, hot on the scent.'

He smiled at her painfully. 'I can't wait twenty-five years! I shall be too old to care.'

'Good God, I hope not!' she said sharply, as she served him. 'George won't even have finished his education.'

'In twenty-five years?' Slider protested.

'Oh, he's going to be a doctor, didn't you know? Look at his hands.'

'I thought they were the hands of a concert pianist.'

'He can do both, can't he?'

'Of course he can. Silly me.'

One of the few statements included in the Knight file was from a schoolmate, Adrienne Tusk, and she turned out to be quite easy to find. Her parents still lived at the same address in Adelaide Grove, and were able to give Swilley her new address.

'We saw that about the skeleton on the local news, on the telly,' Mrs Tusk said in a suitably hushed voice. 'And that was Amanda, was it? What a terrible thing.'

'Terrible,' her husband echoed. They were meek and decent people in their sixties, on their best behaviour in the presence of the police; retired now, growing closer and more alike now that there was just the two of them. They sat side by side in their meek and decent sitting room, the same height, the same build, the same short grey hair – almost, with the androgyny of age, the same face.

'That poor girl,' said Mrs Tusk. 'I remember at the time, when she went missing, we were so sorry for her parents – weren't we, Geoff?'

'So sorry!' he agreed.

'And now it turns out that she was there all the time. Buried in the garden.'

'Shocking,' said Mr Tusk.

'Really shocking,' Mrs Tusk echoed.

'Do you remember Amanda?' Swilley asked, since she was there.

They looked at each other, as if swapping thoughts. 'Not really,' said Mrs Tusk. 'I suppose we saw her a couple of times, but she didn't sort of stand out, if you know what I mean.'

'She was ordinary,' said Mr Tusk.

'Ordinary,' Mrs Tusk confirmed. 'A quiet little girl, I'd say. Of course, they said at the time our Addy was her best friend, but I don't know really that they were close. Addy had lots of friends – she was a very popular girl – and I suppose Amanda must have been one of them. I remember she came to Addy's birthday party that year – that was in May, the May before it happened. So they must have been friends then. But she wasn't in and out of the house all the time, like the other girls.'

'Girls in and out, all the time. Our Addy had lots of friends. Very popular girl.'

'But I don't recollect that she was ever invited to Amanda's house – do you, Geoff?'

'No, I don't recall that she was. Mind you,' he added, striking out an independent line for once, 'I'd be at work then. I wouldn't get back until gone half-past six. It'd be Lin – the wife – who'd know more about it.'

'That's right.' She lifted a daring look to tall Swilley's face. 'I s'pose she was – *murdered* – poor thing?' The word was mouthed, soundlessly, as though that would make it less real. 'Do you know who did it?'

Mr Tusk was more robust. 'I s'pose it'd be the father, wouldn't it, with the body being in their garden?'

Swilley didn't indulge them. 'Did you know them – the Knights?'

'No,' Mr Tusk said with regret, as though knowing a murderer would have added to the richness of his life. 'I don't know that we ever met them.'

'Oh, we did, Geoff – once, at school, at the concert, you remember? Our Addy pointed them out. They were standing with Amanda, over in a corner, not talking to anybody.'

'Oh, yes. That's right.'

'But we never heard anything bad about them,' said Mrs Tusk quickly. 'The police asked us that at the time, and we told them.'

'We never really *knew* them,' said Mr Tusk. And he exchanged another look with his wife, as if the not-knowing of them was a significant factor – because a murderer would be bound to keep himself to himself, wouldn't he?

Adrienne Tusk was now Adrienne Hopper, living in St Albans, and working for a computer training company there. Her husband had his own specialist commercial and domestic cleaning firm, and she had two children at school, a boy and a girl, aged eleven and twelve. All these facts were matters of intense pride to the Tusk parents, as Swilley gathered from the array of framed photographs on the sideboard behind them, which included one of the whole family standing in front of the Hoppers' house – new and, she was assured, *detached*. 'Her Tony's doing *ever* so well for himself,' Mrs Tusk had cooed.

Swilley caught up with Adrienne Hopper at work, so she never got to marvel at the discrete nature of her abode. She was a neat, brisk woman with tidy hair and a black cloth skirt and jacket over a white shirt that had 'work suit' stamped all over it. When

Swilley introduced herself, she surveyed her with intelligent eyes and said, 'Is this about Amanda? I did wonder if you'd be wanting to talk to me. Let's see – the small conference room'll be empty. Come this way. Would you like some coffee?'

'Unusual name, Adrienne,' Swilley said to warm her up, when they had settled at the conference table with mugs of coffee in front of them.

'I was named after Adrienne Corri,' she said. Swilley looked the question, and she smiled. 'No, I didn't know, either. She was an actress my dad had the hots for – used to be in all those schlocky horror films. I always quite liked it as a name. Better than being another Sarah or Lisa. There were two Sarahs and two Lisas in my class.'

'But only one Adrienne,' Swilley said. 'And only one Amanda?'

The smile became a frown. 'Oh dear, poor Amanda. You know, the press at the time said I was Amanda's best friend, but I'm not sure that was really true. Or, at least, it probably *was* true, but only because she didn't have any other friends.'

'Why was that, do you think?'

'Oh, she was very quiet. And – maybe a little weird.'

'Weird how?'

She thought about it. 'Maybe that's not fair. She probably wasn't weird, exactly, just different from the rest of us. We were all miniskirts and eyeliner and Afro hair. She looked like something out of the fifties – skirts down to her knees, lace-up shoes with socks, page-boy haircut. But I suppose that was her mum and dad's fault. And we were all Stones and Rod Stewart, and she had this thing for David Essex.'

'I get the picture. So how did you become friends with her?'

'We sat next to each other in class for a while and . . . well, I suppose I felt a bit sorry for her. Some of the other girls used to tease her, and she was never really in with any of the groups. Not that she seemed to mind – she was a bit of a loner, really – but of course afterwards you do wonder whether she was a loner by choice, or because it was forced on her, don't you?'

'Afterwards?'

'After she disappeared. I mean, of course, at the time we all thought she'd run away.'

'Did that surprise you?'

She thought about it. 'No, not really. I always knew there was something underneath that mousey front – I mean, she wasn't stupid, by any means. She was always near the top of the class, and she gave the impression of thinking a lot. We'd all be messing around and making a noise, and she'd be just standing there watching us, and you always got the feeling her brain was running at higher level and she was thinking we were pretty silly really. The idea that she'd got sick of her life and gone off to find a better one sort of appealed to me. I liked to imagine her living in a commune somewhere, you know? Smoking dope and having free love and laughing at the rest of us nine-to-five clones.' She gave a nervous laugh. 'Of course, we had no idea then she'd been murdered.'

'Even when she didn't come back?'

She shook her head. 'No, I must say I never thought that. I suppose you don't when you're a teenager. You assume you're all going to live for ever. I'm disappointed really,' she said with an apologetic smile. 'I thought she was the one that got away. I don't like to think of her being . . .' She stopped and bit her lip, staring into the past thoughtfully.

'So how close were you?'

'Well, she sort of hung around with me and my group the last year. I saw quite a lot of her at school. I suppose – yeah, we were friends.'

'After school?'

'No, not really. We lived in opposite directions, and she'd go off home and I'd go off home and that'd be that.' She shrugged. 'I don't know what she did in her spare time. Homework, prob-ably.' She gave a nervous smile at her own joke.

'What about boys?' Swilley asked.

'What about them?'

'I assume you all had boyfriends by then – age fourteen. Just the age to be boy mad. Were you sexually active?'

She blushed and looked annoyed. 'What a question to ask! No, I wasn't, as it happened, but some in our class were. I had a boyfriend, sort of. Someone I was keen on, but it wasn't serious, and we never really did anything.'

'Did Amanda have a boyfriend?'

She expected a quick negative, but to her surprise Adrienne

thought about it. 'I wouldn't have said she was the sort to,' she said slowly. 'You know, with the old-fashioned clothes and no make-up and so on. And she was mad about David Essex – I mean, really dopey. Had a big picture of him on the inside of her locker, and she carried one around with her, a little thing this size she'd cut out of a magazine and kept in her purse. She used to talk about him as if he was a real person – I mean, as if she knew him. She was always going on about what he liked and didn't like. "I wouldn't do that," she'd say. "David wouldn't approve." And she'd say stuff like, "David doesn't drink coffee, he only likes tea." It was a bit weird.'

'So you think that took the place of a real boyfriend in her life?' Swilley asked.

'Well, yes,' she said, 'that's what I would have thought, if I'd thought about it at all. I mean, I was fourteen, you don't analyse. But looking back, she'd changed the last few months, and I wonder whether that wasn't part of it – that she'd got a boyfriend. A real one.'

'Did she say anything about a boyfriend?'

'No. But if she did have one, I reckon she'd have to keep him secret – I mean, I can't see her parents approving.' She paused a moment in thought. 'But she did talk about a new girlfriend. Somebody called Melissa.'

'You didn't know this Melissa?'

'No, she wasn't at our school. We went to Poplar Road. According to Amanda, Melissa went to St Margaret's, where the posh girls went. She was very proud of that fact, was Amanda. Melissa lived in a big house, Melissa went to St Margaret's, Melissa had everything, she was the bees knees. A couple of times I wanted to say to her, if she's so marvellous, why's she interested in you? But I didn't.'

'You were jealous?'

'Good God, no!' But she blushed a little as she said it. Then she said, 'Well, maybe I was, looking back. I mean, I'd always been the only one standing up for Amanda. I felt sorry for her and took the trouble to be friends with her, and then suddenly—'

'Instead of being grateful she went off with someone else?'

'It sounds silly when you say it now.'

'No, it's very understandable,' said Swilley.

Adrienne shrugged it off. 'Anyway, I got fed up with hearing about wonderful Melissa. And then Amanda stopped talking about her.'

'When was that?'

'That summer. The summer term. I suppose, the last few weeks before we broke up. She didn't talk about anything, really – went all silent and distant. She changed, you know? She even looked older. Thinner in the face and more – more like a teenager and less like a kid. I think she had a secret.'

'But you have no idea what it was?'

'Not really. She never said anything to me. But – well, looking back, it's the sort of change you might see if a girl like that suddenly gets mixed up with a boy. A real one, not David Essex.'

It was also, Swilley thought, the sort of change you might see if a girl suddenly found out about sex from the wrong end of the spectrum. Becoming silent and withdrawn is often a first sign that abuse is going on. And abuse could so easily lead to murder.

'This Melissa – do you know her other name?'

'No.'

'Or where she lived?'

'No. Just that it was a big house.' She looked at Swilley unhappily. 'If she existed at all,' she said.

'Did you think she was made up, then?'

'Not at the time, no. But now – well, you've found her bones, haven't you? Which means she must have been murdered. So maybe something was going on at home – you know what I mean. And she made up a new best friend to sort of comfort herself. I mean, I'm not a psychiatrist, but . . .'

'Quite,' said Swilley. 'Did you talk about this to anyone else at the time? To the police who interviewed you back then?'

'No, of course not. I was just a kid. And they were grown ups. You don't tell stuff to grown ups. And in any case, this is really stuff I've thought about since.' She read Swilley's face. 'I know, hindsight and all that sort of thing. Maybe I'm making too much of it. But she really did change that summer.'

TEN

Occam's Razor

LaSalle had been searching public records in Swindon for Ronald Thomas Knight. There were about 200 Ronald Knights nationwide, but the 'Thomas' narrowed the field considerably, and none of them was working or voting in Swindon. However, given that the age of the subject would now be close to eighty, he had one last place to look.

'Found him, sir,' he said, tapping respectfully at Slider's open door.

Slider examined the expression being presented to him. 'You don't look happy about it.'

'Dead,' LaSalle admitted glumly.

'Damn!' said Slider.

He didn't say, 'Are you sure?' – he was *that* good a boss – but LaSalle told him anyway.

'Found him in the register of deaths, seven years ago, checked the address against the 2001 census and it had him and a Margaret Emerald Knight living there. Well, you don't get many of *them* to the pound, so it's got to be the right one?'

'It sounds like it.'

'It's a bummer he's copped it,' LaSalle grumbled. 'Cardiomyopathy – that's heart failure, isn't it?' Slider assented. 'The wife's not still at that address, and I couldn't find her in Swindon, but then I thought, maybe when her old man popped his clogs, she'd want to go back somewhere they were happy together.'

'We've searched in Shepherd's Bush.'

'No, not there. I meant *relatively* happy,' LaSalle said. 'It must've been a relief to get away at first, and Ronnie got a job, and they must've thought they were making a new start – I meant Reading. So I had a look.'

'And?' Slider prompted patiently. LaSalle evidently liked a story and an audience.

'Found her!' he said triumphantly. 'In a rented house in Tilehurst. She's on the 2011 census, and the current electoral register, living alone. D'you want me to go out and interview her?'

He looked so hopeful Slider was almost sorry to have to crush his dreams. But Mr Porson had told him to prioritize, hadn't he? And if Ronald Knight was dead, this was now the last link, and the last hope of finding out what had really happened. 'No,' he said, 'I'll go myself.'

The house was one of a terrace in a new development, and represented the meanest of ambitions on the part of the builders. Slider had looked up the layout online before they left, part of his preparation, gauging the subject's prosperity. The basic house was an oblong shoebox thirteen feet wide, with a living room at the front, which had an open-plan staircase in it, and a kitchen at the back, just big enough to turn round in. Upstairs there were two bedrooms, thirteen by nine, with a windowless bathroom between them, and at the back the garden, inevitably thirteen feet wide, was twelve feet long, just about big enough to house a rotary washing line.

Slider stared at the terrace with disfavour as they stepped out of the car. The façade was flat, the roof line was unsullied by chimneys, and had each house not been blessed with a tiny porch tacked on the front, there'd have been nothing to break the outline at all.

Atherton read his expression and said, 'It's no different from a Victorian two-up two-down – probably bigger, in fact.'

'But a Victorian two-up two-down would have window detail and a bit of fancy brickwork to lift the spirits,' he said.

'Not everyone cares about architecture.'

'Not everyone knows they do, but it affects them all the same. And the ceilings would have been higher and it would have had a fireplace with handy alcoves for shelving, and picture rails, and cornicing, and pretty architraves round the doors.'

Atherton made a dismissive 'pfft' noise. 'You can't eat architrave.'

'That doesn't even make sense.'

'You know what I mean. It's clean and new and full of straight lines, which is what people want. Cornice just harbours the dust, and who wants a fireplace when you've got central heating? I wonder if she's in.'

'She's seventy-two, of course she's in. Where else would she be?' But he felt an unusual thrill of nervousness as they walked up the path of the unfenced front garden (seven feet by – yes, you've guessed it – thirteen). The enormity of Margaret Knight's experiences, plus the question about how much she knew at the time or had learned later, made it a delicate, even a nerve-racking interview to contemplate.

The television was on, spewing out its daytime Prozac, and there was an elderly armchair with a dent in the seat facing it, while next to it the top table of a nest bore an empty mug, the TV remote and a glasses case. Slider concluded she had been sitting watching – or at least staring in the direction of – the screen when they rang the doorbell.

She seemed almost dazed when she opened the door, and stared at them, not so much questioningly as apathetically, the archetypal victim waiting to be told what to do by the friendly conman or crim.

Slider spoke to her gently, trying to ease her into an under-standing of who he was, placing his warrant card into her hand and giving her plenty of time to look at it. He expected some reaction of shock, or fear, or even horror, but she only looked up and said helplessly, 'I've not got my glasses on. I can't read it.' Then, catching up with his words, she said, 'Shepherd's Bush? You said you were from Shepherd's Bush?'

'That's right. Detective Chief Inspector Slider. And this is Detective Sergeant Atherton.' He gave their names again, care-fully. 'May we come in and talk to you?'

'You're police?' She got there at last.

'Yes, that's right. May we come in?'

And so she let them in. She moved back towards the chair as if there were rails along the carpet, and having reached it, waved her hand vaguely at the sofa. 'D'you want to sit down?' she said.

'Thank you – and could we have the television turned off?'

'I forgot it was on. I wasn't really watching,' she said. She picked up the remote, and with one click produced a blessed silence.

She was small, thin, old, with a lined face, glasses, and grey hair in what Connolly called a 'mammy hairdo' – cut short and permed. In a supermarket with a shopping trolley she would have been indistinguishable from any other lone female pensioner. She had not let herself go completely, Slider concluded, for the perm looked relatively recent; and she was decently dressed in a grey wool skirt and a blue jumper, with a grey cardigan open over the top, and nylon tights on her legs, and bedroom slippers on her feet that were not old and broken down. But she was not wearing make-up, or any jewellery apart from a plain broad wedding ring. She had dressed for decency, but not to be seen.

The furniture in the room was old, brought with her, presumably, from previous homes, and there were no pictures on the walls, and no ornaments apart from a struggling maidenhair fern in a fancy cachepot, and some framed photographs on the sideboard under the window. One of them, he could see, was a wedding photograph – presumably of Margaret and Ronald; one, he thought, was of Amanda in school uniform; and a third, a family group of some sort, seemed much older and browner, so perhaps it was something from her childhood.

It was not a great deal to show for seventy-two years of life, and for a moment the thought of what she had lost appalled him. It was not something you could ever get over, was it? And if she didn't know, if she had never known, if she had not been involved, how much worse was what they had come here to do?

'Mrs Knight,' he began.

She forestalled him. 'It's about Amanda, isn't it?' She had turned her head towards him and the light from the window reflecting in her glasses stopped him reading anything from her expression. 'After all these years,' she said. 'I thought you'd finished with all that. Why have you come bothering me now? Ronnie's dead and gone, don't you know that? Driven to his grave, by the worry of it. The shame. All that stuff in the papers – he never got over it. People thinking he'd done away with his own daughter. Hounded, that's what he was. How could you even *think* such a thing? I pity your poor wives and families, if you've got minds like that.'

The unexpected fluency, coming out of the previous silence, surprised Slider. While he was digesting the content, Atherton picked up the cue and said, 'Mrs Knight, there's been a development. Haven't you seen anything about it on the news?'

'I don't watch the news. It's all rubbish. Nasty rubbish, too, all death and bombs and such like. As if we didn't have enough trouble in our lives without that.' She caught up with the word and stopped herself abruptly. 'Development? What development?' She looked from Atherton to Slider. He had moved slightly so that he no longer caught the reflection from the window, and he saw instead a slow and agonising hope that must have burned like gall all the way up from her heart to her throat. Her thick, misshapen hands gripped the chair arms. 'You've found her?' she whispered. 'You've found our Amanda?'

There was no way round it. You had to tell them. 'I'm afraid it isn't good news,' Slider said. 'I'm sorry to have to tell you that human remains have been found—'

'Remains?' She jumped on the word, and then repeated it, her face screwed up with pain. '*Remains?*'

'A skeleton has been found. I'm afraid that's all that would be left, after twenty-five years.'

'She's dead?' Mrs Knight looked from one face to the other, but she was not seeing them. 'Amanda's dead?'

'I'm very sorry,' Slider said.

She didn't cry. She was absorbed with thought, and he wished he could interpret it. When she spoke, it was unemphatically, more to herself than to them. 'I suppose I knew it, really, after all this time. I mean, we'd have heard something. But I never believed it, not inside. You don't, do you? You can't. I kept hoping one day she'd come back. You see things on telly, where people have been found years later. Daddy used to say, "Face it, Mags, she's gone," but you can't, not a mother, not after you've carried them for nine months and given birth to them and . . .' She fumbled a handkerchief out of her cardigan pocket, but it was to wipe her mouth, not her eyes. 'The last time I saw her,' she said in a stronger voice – and Slider guessed it was something she had said many times – 'was having a cheese sandwich and a cup of tea at the kitchen table. We had our bit of lunch together, just as normal as could be, and then she went out in the garden and I went to my sewing machine, and I never saw her again. But I always thought she'd come back in the end.' She looked at Slider and said, almost indignantly, 'She was only fourteen! Who did this? Who did it?'

'That's what we have to find out,' Slider said gently. 'You see, up until now Amanda was officially a missing person. Now I'm afraid we have to investigate a murder.'

Her expression sharpened. 'Why d'you say that? Maybe it wasn't murder. Maybe it was an accident. Maybe she fell down a quarry or fell in a river and it was just an accident. I don't want . . .' She swallowed. 'I can't think of her being killed deliberately. I can't.'

'I know it's hard for you, but—' Slider began.

'No!'

'The body had been buried, you see. That was a deliberate act by someone. Someone buried the body to conceal it, which I'm afraid suggests it was no accident.'

'Buried? Where?' Mrs Knight asked sharply.

Was her keenness anything more than a desire to know the worst? Slider wondered. 'In the garden of number fifteen, Laburnum Avenue,' he said.

Her lips moved soundlessly, rehearsing what he had said. Then she said, 'In *our* garden? Oh my God. Oh my good God. In our *garden*?'

Well, he thought, glancing at Atherton, she hadn't known the body was there, that at least was clear. However much she had known – or suspected – about the rest, she hadn't known that.

'What did . . .? How did she . . .? But she *left* the garden. She was sitting out there, and then when I looked out, she wasn't there, so she must have left the garden. So . . . someone brought her back?'

'It looks that way,' Slider said, giving her time to come to terms with it.

'Someone brought the – brought her back and *buried* her there?' She shook her head in bewilderment. 'But I don't see how they could. I mean, without us knowing? Digging and such-like? I mean, we'd have heard something. We'd have seen. We'd . . .' Her eyes widened, her lips tightened, and a look of old, old anger came over her face. 'You're thinking *he* did it, aren't you? Ronnie. You're back on that old story.'

Atherton took over. 'As you say, it would have been hard for anyone else to do it without you knowing. But your husband could come and go at times when he knew you wouldn't be at home. Or he might creep out at night when you were asleep.'

She was red with anger now. 'He wouldn't do that! You can't come here saying these things to me! It's disgusting, when he's not here to defend himself. I won't listen to any more of it. You get out! You hear me? Get out this minute or I'll . . .' She tripped herself, obviously having been about to say, 'or I'll call the police'.

Into the silence, Slider said, 'I'm very sorry to have to put you through this, but we have to talk to you. You must see that. It's our job to find out what happened to your daughter, and you're the person now who was closest to her.'

'You think he did it,' she accused, but quietly.

'I don't think that. I don't *know*. And I have to try and find out.'

'He wouldn't, you see,' she said. 'You didn't know him. He was so proud of her. He would never lay a finger on her, I promise you that.'

'Wasn't he sometimes prone to losing his temper?' Atherton asked.

Slider flicked a glance at him. He didn't want her provoked, he wanted her talking. But she seemed now to want to explain things, rather than protest about them. 'He did have a bit of a temper on him,' she agreed, 'but it wasn't violent. He would never hit anyone. Pat – my sister Pat?'

'Yes, we've spoken to her,' said Slider.

Her mouth soured. 'Oh, have you. Well, no doubt she gave you a few of her ideas to be going on with. She made a big thing afterwards that he had a temper, but it was only shouting with him. You see, he wasn't all that good with words, and he'd get in a muddle sometimes and blow up, but it was all over in a moment. Pat, she was always hinting that him blowing up meant he'd hit us, but he never lifted a hand to either of us, nor would he. He was a kind soul, always ready to do anyone a good turn – as *she* ought to know. Did all their plumbing for them for nothing, when she had that second bathroom put in. It was that good-for-nothing husband of *hers* she ought to have been looking at. Running around with other women! I say if a man breaks one law, he's more likely to break another. My Ronnie never did a dishonest thing in his life. Paid his taxes, worked hard – he never even took a cash job, like most of 'em do. Honest as the day is long, Ronnie. But her Brian – well!'

'What did he do that was against the law?' Atherton asked.

'He committed adultery,' she said hotly. 'That's against God's law, isn't it?' And seeing Atherton was not impressed, she went on: 'And he was a great one for things that fell off the back of a lorry, things he got from a man down the pub. That's how he got a microwave before everybody else had one. And a video player. Loved his toys, Brian did. And how come he always had hundred-packs of cigarettes around the house? And a sideboard full of bottles of gin and whisky and you name it?'

'You think they were stolen?'

She sniffed. 'All I know is, they were supposed to be some great bargain. He got Pat this fancy watch. I said to her, *I* wouldn't be comfortable wearing something that I didn't know where it came from, but she wasn't so particular as me. And Brian, he wasn't particular at all.'

Slider noted that while she resented unproved allegations against her husband, she didn't mind doing the same for Pat's. The sisters were more alike, perhaps, than either of them thought.

'But Brian had an alibi for the whole day, didn't he?' Atherton asked innocently.

'Pat said he was home with her all afternoon,' she said.

'You didn't believe her?'

'It wouldn't be like him, on a Saturday. More likely he was off with one of his floozies, and she didn't want to admit it.'

She was sharp, Slider thought. She saw through that one. But she didn't follow through to realize it was still an alibi. 'I believe you suggested at one time that he might have been interested in Amanda in an inappropriate way,' said Slider. 'Did you ever see him do or say anything to her that you didn't like?'

She looked slightly shamefaced. 'I said that really to rile Pat, because she'd been saying things about Ronnie. I mean, he was a devil for the women, but Amanda, she was only fourteen, he didn't look at her that way. He used to give her sweets, and tease her, you know, like the way uncles do, but I never thought . . .' She pondered. 'No, I never saw anything like that. She used to like going over there, but that was for the dogs, really. She was mad about dogs. She was always asking why we couldn't have one, but Daddy always told her we couldn't afford one. Truth was, he didn't like dogs. He'd been bitten more than once, when he was doing work at people's houses. He was afraid of them, if you want the truth, but of course he wouldn't say that. A man has his pride. It was one of the things him and Amanda used to row about, her wanting a dog and him saying no.'

'They used to row about it?' Atherton asked, trying not to sound too interested.

But she wasn't spooked, well into her memories now. She probably hadn't had many people to talk to in the last twenty-five years. 'Well, they were a lot alike, Daddy and Amanda. Quiet, not big talkers, but there was a lot going on inside. And stubborn, once they'd set their minds on something. But she'd got the schooling that he hadn't, she was really bright. Not that he was stupid, not by a long chalk, but he'd not had much education. Growing up during the war, there was a lot of disruption with the bombs and everything. And he couldn't wait to leave at fifteen and start his apprenticeship. He got his City and Guilds, he was a good plumber, he made a good living, but he always regretted he hadn't had the book education. He had all these thoughts he couldn't find the words for, and Amanda, she could talk rings round him. It used to make him mad. And he'd end up shouting and banging out of the room. It was just frustration,' she added pleadingly. 'He'd never hurt a fly, really.'

'That last weekend,' Slider asked, 'had they had one of their rows recently?'

'Oh, I can't remember that long ago. They were all right at breakfast, I know that. He went off to work just like usual. I don't remember any atmosphere.'

'Was it normal for him to work on Saturdays?' Atherton asked.

'Course it was. Saturdays were the busiest, truth be told, because people were home from work and wanted things done while they were in. They'd have had him out Sundays as well, but I put my foot down. Not on Sunday. There's got to be one day of rest.'

'Were you churchgoers?'

'No, not really. Pat and me were brought up to it, but Ron

– well, his mum and his brother Ted were killed in the Blitz, and after that his father got very anti-God, and wouldn't go near a church, so Ronnie grew up without the habit. We were married in church, and Amanda was christened, but aside from that we never went, only Christmas Day when we were over Pat and Brian's, and then it was just Pat and me and Amanda. Ron and Brian would go down the golf club for drinks.'

'So that Saturday he was working all day?' Atherton asked mildly.

'That's right,' she said, with a look of annoyance, 'and the police checked every job he'd done, and he was accounted for every minute of the day. So you don't need to start with the insinuations.'

'Except for his lunch break,' Atherton said, so bland now he'd make magnolia look fluorescent. 'There was a gap of fifty minutes, I believe.'

'Well, a person's got to have his lunch, hasn't he? Cheese sandwiches I put up for him, same as Amanda and me had, cheese was his favourite, only he had Branston with his, Amanda couldn't abide pickle, and a piece of fruit cake, and his flask of tea. He sat in his van in a lay-by outside Chiswick House, because his last job had been Chiswick Mall and he'd got to go up Turnham Green next, this old lady with her leaky pipe, she ought to have had the whole house replumbed but she was too tight with her money, though living in this big house she must have had plenty. Ron was over there every couple of months, you never knew such a patient man as him, especially with old people. I told him it wasn't worth his while but he said he couldn't let her down. So what with the traffic, he must only have been sitting there twenty minutes, hardly enough to choke his lunch down and give himself indigestion.' Her indignation was growing. 'And then the police made all this fuss about how he'd got no witnesses – as if a person has to have a witness to eat his lunch! And how the old lady couldn't remember if he'd been there or not because she was going a bit dotty. So he showed them the work he'd done, and *then* they said it could have been done any time in the last few days. Why would he want to make up a story like that?' she demanded angrily. 'If he said he'd been at Mrs Whittaker's, that's where he was. And then they made out there was something funny about him going to another job after his tea, but he'd *promised* the Morrises he'd come and he wasn't one to break his promises. Their boiler was out of order, which is a hardship when you've got three kids and a baby. And then they tried to make something of it because he said he got there at quarter to seven and they said it was more like half past – well, with three kids running wild who *ought* to have been in bed that time of night, it's a wonder if they knew which way was up, never mind the exact second someone arrives, who was actually doing them a favour, not that you expect any gratitude from people like that, they can afford to have a detached house and four children but they argue about the plumber's bill when it's after six o'clock on a Saturday, which ought by rights to be *double* time, never mind time and a half.'

At which point she had to stop for breath.

ELEVEN

Reason as a Way of Life

'You didn't call the police straight away,' Slider said. 'Why was that?'

'Well . . .' She looked puzzled. 'I mean, you don't, do you? You don't want to be calling them for nothing, making a nuisance of yourself. We thought she'd gone off somewhere, and you don't want to be setting the police on your own daughter, as if she's a criminal, even if she shouldn't have done it. It wasn't like she was a toddler or anything. We thought she'd come back.'

The last sentence was unbearably pathetic.

'Your husband told you not to call, when he came home for his evening meal?'

'We didn't think it was needed, not then.'

'And then he went off to work again?'

'He'd promised the Morrises.'

'He didn't think of searching for her?'

'But where would he look?' she said. 'We didn't know where she'd gone. But when he got back from the Morrises, and she was still not back, he said, Go on then, better call the police. Not that it did any good,' she added bitterly. 'They just said leave it till tomorrow. And when they did come, they didn't do anything. Had a look round the house, as if we were hiding her somewhere, and that was it. That one in charge, that tall one, he just said she'd be bound to turn up again and not to worry. Didn't seem like he cared one way or the other.'

'Detective Inspector Kellington?' Slider asked casually.

'That was him. Acted like he had his mind on other things half the time. And that other one, who came later, Vickers his name was—'

'Vickery?'

'That was him. He was this other one's boss, and if you ask me, he was telling him not to bother with us. Very contemptuous he was, the way he looked at us, as if we was beneath his notice. Kept saying to me, "Now, now, Mrs Knight, you mustn't be imagining things." Kept saying teenage girls went off all the time and came back all right. He didn't know Amanda. He reckoned she'd gone off with some boyfriend, like some bad girl.'

'Did he say that?'

'No, but I could tell that's what he thought. He didn't know her. She would never have done anything like that. Kept talking behind his hand to that Kellington and looking at us like dirt. Of course, when days went by and she didn't turn up, then they had to start searching for her.' She looked bleak. 'But I suppose it was too late then. As it turns out.'

Slider tried a different angle. 'It was the summer holidays. What had she been doing with herself, with no school?'

Mrs Knight thought about it, but with a puzzled crease to her brow. 'Well, I don't know, really. What do girls do? Just hung around the house, I suppose. Listening to her pop music. She liked to read a lot,' she added on an inspiration. 'She might have gone down the library.'

'You worked during the daytime, I believe,' Slider said.

'That's right. At the Jiffy, down Uxbridge Road – the launderette.' She seemed puzzled by this new direction.

'So Amanda would have been at home alone during that time? Every day, during working hours?'

'Well, yes,' she said warily.

'So, in fact, you wouldn't know what she was doing at all during those summer holidays. Or where she was at any time?'

'I suppose not,' she said, offended. 'But she could look after herself. She was a very sensible girl.'

'Did you notice any difference in her that summer?' The question seemed to need clarifying, and he added, 'She was fourteen. She was growing up. Things can seem difficult to girls at that age, coping with the changes in their lives. Had she seemed different to you lately?'

'What, you mean, like, moody?' Mrs Knight asked, seeming eager to understand, to help. 'I suppose all teenagers are, aren't they?'

'More withdrawn? Quiet? Keeping her thoughts to herself?'

'She was always a quiet one,' Mrs Knight said. She frowned in thought. 'I suppose she was a bit more . . . mopey.'

'Depressed?'

'No, not that – sort of in a dream. In her own world. Some evenings she'd be up in her bedroom, instead of watching telly with her dad and me. Like, you'd say, What are you doing up there? And she'd say, Oh nothing. But as long as she wasn't getting into trouble . . .' Her shrug said: what can you do?

Slider saw it: the parents, not very well educated, not having the sort of intimate, involved, all-talking relationship parents were supposed to have with their children these days; tired from work, happy just to sit quietly and have a daughter who did the same. It wasn't that they didn't understand her, but that they didn't see there was anything to understand. Never trouble trouble till trouble troubles you.

While he was thinking, she remembered something. 'She had this diary. We bought it for her for her last birthday. She was always writing in that.'

Slider felt Atherton glance at him. *A diary! Now you're talking.*

'Did you ever read any of it?' Atherton asked casually.

'It had a lock on it,' she said simply. 'That's what she asked for, a diary that locked.'

'What happened to it afterwards?'

Her brow furrowed. 'Well, I don't know. I haven't thought about it since then. I suppose it was in her room with her things. I didn't look – there was so much else to think about.'

'What happened to her things?' Slider asked, showing nothing in his voice, no exasperation, no hope.

'We packed them all up in a box when we moved to Reading, in case she came back and wanted them. We took them with us.' She wiped her mouth again, slowly, a gesture of pain. 'When we went to Swindon, Ron said there's no point keeping her clothes, they won't fit her any more. So we got rid of them. But her books and bits and pieces we kept.'

'Do you still have them?'

She nodded slowly, trying to think along with him. 'You think she might have written something in her diary? I never even thought of that. But what . . .? I mean, she couldn't have known what was going to happen.'

'There might possibly be some clue as to where she went that day,' Slider said. 'Maybe it was somewhere she'd been going regularly. Or some new person she'd met. Would you mind if we had a look?'

She was gone a long time. Slider got up and went to look at the photographs. The brown one was obviously of the sisters Maggie and Pat, aged about five and ten, in very 1950s garb: cotton frock, Fair Isle cardigan, sandals and socks and hairslides. They were holding hands, standing with their parents behind them, with a seafront in the background – Brighton perhaps. The parents were smiling dutifully for the camera (one of those street photographers, probably – otherwise, who was holding the camera?) Little Pat was grinning gappily, Margaret self-conscious, with her head slightly lowered and her upper lip tucked in. A holiday snap, a memento of a happy day: how families should be. How Margaret must have expected her life would be. You didn't think your only child would disappear, and turn up dead twenty-five years later.

She came in with a large cardboard box, big enough to have to hold with two hands, but obviously not very heavy. It was very dusty, sealed with sellotape that was browning and lifting with age, and it had 'Amanda' printed in uneven capitals on the side. She put it down on the small dining table, and stepped back from it, as if leaving it to them. 'I've not opened it since we left Shepherd's Bush,' she said. 'I've never looked in it.' She gave them an apologetic glance, upward from a lowered face, and Slider saw the resemblance to the child in the photograph. 'Couldn't face it, somehow.'

The sellotape came off willingly, long tired of its task. Slider took out the objects reverently, laying them on the table, while she watched, chewing her lip, but otherwise controlled. There were books; a swimming certificate; a little box of childish jewellery – beads and bangles, hairslides, a ring evidently gleaned from a Christmas cracker. There was a scrapbook, mostly of pop stars, but including other pictures cut out of magazines that had appealed to her for some reason – cute animals, pretty scenes. There was a brown leather purse containing £3.47 in coins, some hairgrips, a white button that might have come off a school blouse, and a small, square, rather creased picture of David Essex. There was a collection of china and plastic animals, mostly dogs and horses. There was a tiny transistor radio. There were some seashells. There was a Royal Wedding Commemorative Coin in a blue velvet box. There was a single short white sock that had got tangled up with a hairbrush.

There was no diary. Slider packed the things away again.

'I suppose it got lost,' Mrs Knight said. 'The diary. Or thrown away. I don't remember much from the time straight after. It's all a bit of a blur. People coming and going. The things in the paper. Waiting for her to come home.'

'Quite understandable,' Slider said. He pressed the sellotape back into place, hoping it would hold for a bit. He could see she was tiring, and said, 'Just one last question, and we'll leave you in peace.' She looked up from her contemplation of the box, and seemed, absurdly, almost disappointed. Well, they were company; and she probably hadn't talked about Amanda to anyone for years. 'Amanda had a new friend, Melissa. Do you know her other name? Or where she lived?'

She shook her head slowly. 'I don't know any Melissa. Mind you, I didn't really know much about her friends at school. She used to talk about Adrienne sometimes. And I think there may have been a Lisa?' She looked hopeful.

'This wasn't a girl from her school, apparently.'

'Oh. Well, I'm afraid I don't know. I don't think she ever mentioned her. Is it important?'

'I don't know. It may be. If you do happen to remember anything, please give me a ring.'

'All right,' she said, accepting his card. And she looked up at him sternly. 'And you find out who did that to her. Because it wasn't Ron.' There was no answer to that. There was one more thing to do, and Slider was working up to it when she inadvertently gave him an opening. 'I suppose I can't see her?' she said wistfully, and then answered herself. 'I suppose there's nothing to see. What happens now to her – to the . . .?'

'As soon as all the tests have been done, I'll let you know, and you can arrange for a funeral. But before a death certificate can be issued, there is just the question of formal identification. Obviously that can't be done visually, so I would like to take a DNA sample from you for verification.'

'How do you do that?' She looked nervous.

'It's very simple, just a swab from the inside of your mouth. It doesn't hurt. I have the kit here.'

When it was done, she followed them to the door to show them out, seeming reluctant to let them go. It was hardly surprising, Slider thought: their visit had raised as many questions as it had answered. Almost he didn't like leaving her there, old and alone in the doorway of her meagre box, with nothing left to her but her wondering. 'Thank you for coming,' she said, as if remembering her manners. And then, suddenly: 'In the garden?'

Slider turned back. He didn't know what she wanted from him. 'At the bottom,' he said at last.

'Oh my Lord,' she said quietly, and they left her.

The Pepper Pot, in Portobello Road, was jumping, even though it was earlier in the evening than you would expect people to be out eating. The place had been decorated to look like a beach shack. The ceiling was covered in rattan, the walls in carefully rusted corrugated iron sheets, on which colourful graffiti were painted at artistic angles. Behind the bar was a promise of sixty-seven different rums, and posters for Afro music concerts. The tables were bare scrubbed pine, with wooden benches for seats, the floor was bare boards, and the piped music was skull-splitting. A six-foot carved wooden giraffe stood beside the door with an 'open' sign hanging round its neck, and Hart wondered mildly how many giraffes you saw ambling along the Caribbean beaches.

Most of the tables were occupied with trendy-looking young blacks, drinking coffees and cokes, with a few whites sprinkled among them, all talking at the top of their voices in the effort to be heard above the music. There were one or two older men, more working-class in appearance, who were eating with silent dedication, and the smell of jerk seasoning and fried chicken was in the air, plus a whiff that might have been barbecue smoke and Hart hoped was not ganja.

She scanned the room casually, but didn't see Shannon anywhere. The waitresses were wearing black miniskirts and multi-coloured shirts in the sort of patterns you get if you rub your eyes too hard. (Hawaiian shirts, her mind told her, but that was a confusion too far.) They were scurrying about serving, and it was a while before one came to her with a wide grin and said, 'Help you? Table for one?' She glanced back over her shoulder and said, 'You might have to share.'

'No, it's all right, babe,' Hart said. 'I'm looking for Shannon. She on tonight?' The girl looked puzzled. 'Shannon Bailey. She works here.'

'I don't think so,' the girl said. 'I don't know the name.'

'Is the owner here? Can I have a word?'

'The owner?'

'Hallie, isn't that her name?'

'Oh, Mrs Labadee. She's the manager. She's in the back.' The girl looked suddenly doubtful, examining Hart's appearance for clues. 'Is it important?'

'Yeah, mate, dead important.' She didn't wait for an invitation. 'Through here, is it?'

At the end of the bar was a doorway covered in a multi-coloured bead curtain, and Hart sidestepped the waitress and pushed through into a sort of hallway with boxes stacked along one side and a staff lavatory on the other. Ahead, through another doorway, she saw more stacked boxes and three steel beer barrels. A woman was stooped over changing the feeds from one to another. She straightened abruptly as Hart approached.

'Who are you? What do you want?'

'Mrs Labadee?'

The woman was short and wide, light brown, with a handsome face and quick, dark eyes. 'That's me. And you would be . . .?'

'I'm looking for your niece. I was told she was working here.'

'My niece?'

'Shannon Bailey.'

'Your information's out of date, honey. She's not here any more. And she's not my niece.'

'Oh. She calls you Auntie Hallie,' Hart said.

'Lot o' people call me auntie. It's a Jamaican thing.'

'But you know her – you offered her a job.'

'I knew Shannon's ma way back, that's all. Are you police?'

Hart knew better than to deny it to that sharp face. 'Yeah, but this is not official. I was just worried about her, that's all. Checking up, to see if she's all right.'

'That's nice of you,' said Mrs Labadee with what Hart took

to be irony. 'Well, I don't know where she is. I only took her on as a favour to her mum. She worked here for a couple of weeks, slept in the flat upstairs, but her heart wasn't in it. She moved on. I wasn't sorry – she was a lousy waitress. And . . .' She paused, scanning Hart's face keenly. Hart returned the look steadily. 'Are you sure this isn't official?'

'Swear on my mother's grave,' Hart answered.

Mrs Labadee monitored her a moment longer, then gave a minute nod. 'Well, I wasn't sure about her. She was nervous and secretive, like she had something to hide. I'm afraid she was up to something. She said she was going to come into some money. Where's a girl like that, her age, going to get money? Then one day she said she was off.'

'Did she say where?'

'No. She just packed her bag and left.'

'Did she say *anything* to give me a clue?' Hart pleaded.

The woman shrugged. 'I'm sorry, I can't help you any more than that. Now I must get on. It's getting busy out there.'

'If she comes back . . .'

'I'll tell her you're looking for her,' said Mrs Labadee firmly, to eliminate the other possibility – that she should call Hart herself.

That was one smart cookie, Hart thought, and took her leave, out through the throbbing restaurant into the teeming streets. This was the perfect area for a young black girl to hide herself. Without some lead, it was going to be a needle in a haystack search.

For the supper date that evening, Atherton and Emily arrived separately, and Emily was late, having been caught in traffic coming from the West End.

'I was interviewing that new child star in *Matilda*,' she explained. 'They seem to change every couple of months but this one's got an interesting background – overcoming hardship on the way to stardom, blah blah blah. So *The Sunday Times* wants to run a feature.' She shed her coat and handed it to Joanna. 'You're not in *Matilda*, are you?'

'No violins in it,' Joanna said. 'No strings at all, apart from one cello.'

'Oh. I knew you were doing a West End show, so I assumed it was a musical.'

'There's nothing *but* musicals in the theatres these days,' Atherton complained.

'And lots of long-running ones,' Joanna said cheerfully, heading for the drawing room. 'The longer they run, the more they want deps. It's all good.'

'It's all brain rot,' said Atherton. 'Are you not getting any orchestral dates?'

'Not many. I'm afraid I've slipped down the fixers' lists, having had all that time off, first with George and then the miscarriage. Gin and ton?'

'Thanks.'

'I'm getting a few dates with the Whitaker circus, that's all.'
'What's that?'

'Hugh Wharton Whitaker. He's a conductor-impresario who does these Sunday concerts in Aylesbury. Scratch orchestra. It pays peanuts, but it's all work. We call him Huge Warty Whitaker.' She shrugged. 'It's not much of a revenge, but you take what you can get.'

'Why do you need revenge?' Atherton asked.

'Because he's a megalomaniac, and royal pain in the bassoon. And he treats the orchestra as his own private seraglio. There's always some poor little second flute dashing out of his dressing room in tears.'

'And otherwise it's the West End? What piece of musical pap are you depping in at the moment?'

'*Whistle Down the Wind*,' Joanna said. 'You can have a lot of fun during dialogue breaks altering the title to Dribble Down the Window. It can be done with satisfyingly few pencil strokes. Mind you, deps aren't supposed to graffiti the parts, but the regular player is an old mate of mine. He often leaves me scabrous notes in the margin. And one of the keyboard deps does obscene caricatures and passes them round. Which is great as long as you don't get surprised into a snigger. The MD's a frightful misogynist, so we girlies have to mind our Ps and Qs.'

'MD?' Emily queried.

'Musical director. It's what you call the conductor in a show.'

'This is great,' Emily said. 'Background stuff. I'm taking it all in.'

'Well, they're nearly all potty,' Joanna said. 'Conductors in general, but MDs even more so. But don't say I said so or I'll never dep again.'

'I should think you'd be happy not to, when it's wall-to-wall Lloyd Webber,' said Atherton.

'You're prejudiced,' said Joanna. 'It's all right. It's all work.'

'But you must want to play proper music.'

'There speaks a music-lover, not a musician.'

He bristled a bit at that. He thought of himself as intensely musical. 'I don't see the difference.'

'The difference between admiring a horse for its beauty, and riding it.'

'I like that,' said Emily. 'Can I quote that?'

'Feel free.' Joanna turned back to Atherton. 'You know what a musician *really* wants?'

'Fame and glory? A solo career?'

'Nah. Just to play – doesn't matter what. All we want is to play the dots all day, and then have someone say, "Here's some money, can you come back tomorrow?"'

Emily laughed, but Atherton said, 'I don't believe that. You wouldn't do it if you didn't love music.'

'Yes, love *playing* it, not listening to it.'

'Well, listening to it as well,' Slider said, in the interests of accuracy. She smiled at him, and went on: 'I'll tell you a story. I was doing a concert at the Festival Hall once, years ago, and as I walked over Hungerford Bridge I could hear a busker playing the trumpet. I thought, "I know that sound," and sure enough, it was a bloke I knew. I used to bump into him doing sessions, or with the orchestra when we did the big brass numbers, Bruckner and Berlioz and so on.'

'Poor bloke,' said Atherton.

'That's what I thought. He'd got old, his lip had gone, he couldn't play professionally any more. I asked him delicately if he was short of money, but he said no, he was fine. He just went down there to play. He'd sooner belt out "Stormy Weather" under the bridge than not play at all. If he took a few quid beer money in the process, all to the good. But it was the dots he missed. Just the dots.'

Slider saw Atherton was going to argue, and stepped in. 'Did you really recognize the sound? I mean, you knew it was that particular person?'

'Of course,' she said in surprise. 'Every trumpet player sounds different. The same as you'd recognize someone's voice if you heard it.' She got up. 'I have to go and do things in the kitchen. Eating in ten minutes.'

She'd made goulash, with rice, and Atherton had brought two bottles of a peppery Lirac, which went nicely. While they ate, Slider and Atherton caught the women up on the case.

'It has to be Ronnie,' Atherton said when they were up to date. 'The father.'

'I wish I didn't agree with you,' Emily said, 'but on what you've told us, it looks most likely.'

Atherton nodded. 'Those missing times in his day. Suppose he didn't stop and eat lunch. He was only a mile and a half, two miles, from home. He knew Amanda was there—'

'He knew his wife was there as well,' said Slider.

'True, but we know Amanda must have left the garden. He could have come across her in the street. Or he may have known where she was going.'

'The lunch break doesn't give him much time,' Emily objected.

'But didn't you say there was some doubt as to whether he did the job in Turnham Green?' Joanna queried. 'The old lady who was a bit confused?'

'He probably knew exactly how confused she was,' Atherton said. 'After all, he'd been doing jobs for her for years. He may have counted on that. But anyway, how much time did he need?'

'To kill her and stash her somewhere? Quite a bit, I'd have thought,' said Emily.

'He may not have stashed her anywhere. She may have been in the van all the time. In fact, I think it's most likely she was. You run far more risk of being discovered if you're moving a body about from place to place.'

'That's all very well,' said Joanna, 'but you haven't given any reason.'

'Reason as logic? Or reason as motive? Or reason as a way of life?' Atherton said.

'I think that's pretty impressive for someone who's drunk as much as you have,' Emily said with a grin. Joanna gave them an 'uh?' look, and she said, 'He was quoting. From *Tinker Tailor*. I was finishing the quote.'

'Oh,' said Joanna. 'Well, how about reason as motive, to start with?'

'The obvious one,' Atherton said. 'He was working every day in the vicinity, his wife was out at work all day, Amanda was home from school for the summer. He could have popped home any time he liked without anyone knowing.'

'You mean, he was abusing her?' Emily said.

'That's a big conclusion to jump to,' Joanna objected. 'Why has it always got to be that?' She sounded angry.

'Not a conclusion, just a suggestion,' Atherton defended himself.

Slider, who'd been letting them run to see where they ended up, said, 'There are some elements that fit the hypothesis. Her school friend said she changed that year, her mother said she'd become more withdrawn and moody. She'd started keeping a diary, asked for one with a lock on it—'

'Every teenager with a diary wants one that locks,' Joanna objected. 'I know I would.'

'It's just something to take note of,' Slider said. 'And the diary went missing after her death. It's possible there was something in it that someone wanted kept out of circulation. And who had a better chance to remove it than the father?'

'The mother?' Emily hazarded.

'Well, yes,' Slider conceded. 'In every case, you have to allow that we only have her word. There are no witnesses, and he's not here to speak for himself.'

'Doesn't that rather make the whole thing fruitless?' Emily asked. 'If he did it, how will you ever prove it? And since he's dead, he can't be punished for it anyway, so what's the point?'

Joanna was ready with the answer. 'He wants to know,' she said. 'He always wants to know.'

'You may have to settle for presumption this time round, my dear old guv,' Atherton said. 'I doubt we'll ever get to the truth.'

'Probably not,' Slider said, 'but there are a few more steps to take before we stop. Oh, and one other thing to take into account

– when she left the garden that day, she didn't take her purse with her. She wasn't going out to buy anything.'

'Interesting point,' said Emily.

'So I'd just like to know where she *was* going,' Slider concluded.

'And you'd be satisfied with that?'

'I doubt it,' he said. 'I'm never satisfied.'

TWELVE
Death and Glory

Julienne was easy to please. She bounced, Tiggerishly, down the path to meet Connolly, and had to be bounced back inside so that she could be signed out. But the formalities over, she hopped excitedly alongside Connolly with her usual litany of: 'I like your coat. I like your boots. I like your hair. I wanna do mine like yours. Is that your nachral colour? Where are we going? Is that your motor? Cool! What is it?'

'It's a Skoda.'

'Oh. Aren't they, like, pants?'

'Not any more. They're the same as Volkswagens now.'

'Cool! Can we go for a drive? Like, bomb down a motorway or something?'

'Of course not. I'm a gard. We can't do things like that.'

'You're a what?'

'A gard. It's what we call the police in Dublin. Short for *Garda Siochana*. Keepers of the peace.'

'What language is that, then?'

'Irish – what d'you think?'

'I never knew you had a language. Say some more in it.'

'Can't. You hungry? I thought we'd get some lunch. D'you like pizza?'

'Duh! Everybody likes pizza.'

Julienne was impressed that they went to a Pizza Express, which she said was 'well posh, posher than Pizza Hut', was delighted to be told to choose whatever she liked, and was thrilled with her Classic 11 inch La Reine and chocolate milkshake.

If only dates were this easy, Connolly thought. The skinny little creature opposite chattered like a happy budgie and was in a mood to be pleased with everything.

'So what's happening with, like, Kaylee and that?' she asked at length, a slice of pizza in her hand and a smear of tomato on her lips. 'You know. The bloke that done it. When's he gonna be, like, up in court, and that?'

Connolly had hoped that question wouldn't be asked, but she supposed it was inevitable. 'There won't be a court case,' she said. 'It's been shelved.'

'What does that mean?'

'Dropped,' she explained, and watched the frown of disapproval arrive on the pale, pointed little face.

'But they can't!' she wailed.

'They can. They have. There's no evidence, you see. We only had one witness, and she's changed her mind. Withdrawn her testimony.'

'What, Shannon? She's, like, saying he never done it?' Julienne asked from the depth of her confusion.

'I don't know exactly what she said, but basically she's saying she doesn't know anything and can't give evidence in court.'

'Why would she do that?'

'I don't know,' Connolly said. 'I expect she's not sure any more. It's a big thing to accuse somebody of something like that if you're not sure.'

Julienne thought about that. 'I bet she is, but she's just scared. You're gonna, like, make her change her mind, aren't you? Make her do it? She's gotter!'

'She's done a legger. We don't know where she is.'

'Have you looked?' Julienne asked suspiciously.

'Everywhere we can think of. Apparently she said she wanted to make a fresh start, so she could be anywhere by now. And even if we could find her, we can't force her to change her mind.'

'But you could try.'

'If we knew where to look. But we don't. Have you finished that? D'you want any afters?'

Julienne hastily swallowed the last of the pizza unchewed and licked her fingers. 'Yeah!' she affirmed with enthusiasm, and forgot everything for the time it took her to comb the menu and choose a Chocolate Glory, ice cream with chocolate sauce and chunks of chocolate fudge cake. And a chocolate straw. Connolly, blenching quietly, had a coffee. Julienne didn't do much talking until she was at the bottom of the dish, but she had evidently been doing some thinking, because she said at last, in a voice clotted with synthetic glory, 'You know Shannon?'

'Ye-es,' Connolly said cautiously.

'Well, you said she, like, wanted a fresh start?'

'That's what I heard.'

'Well,' said Julienne, nibbling daintily on the chocolate straw, which she had saved until last, 'her and Kaylee used to talk about what they'd do.'

'Do?'

'Like, when they grew up. I heard 'em talk about it a *lot*. They wanted to be beauticians. There's this beautician school they looked up – had some funny name with tits in it – the something Academy. They was gonna do a course, and get jobs, and one day they was gonna open their own beauty place.'

'All that'd cost some money,' Connolly said.

'Yeah, well, they was gonna start with the course and get the diploma,' said Julienne. She finished her milkshake with a noise like a carthorse freeing its hooves from deep mud. 'They was saving up. Kaylee was, anyway, and I bet Shannon was. They were, like, getting money from these blokes, weren't they? So I bet that's what Shannon's done, 'f you say she wanted a fresh start – gone to beauty school. I bet she had some money saved up. She's smart, Shannon. I bet she got out all right,' she concluded, a touch wistfully. 'Not like Kaylee.'

Connolly saw damp eyes and a quivering lip looming on the horizon, and sought to distract her. 'D'you want to go and look round some shops?'

She brightened instantly. 'TK Maxx?'

'Are you kidding me? We can't go there.'

'But I told you I wouldn't nick stuff any more.'

'I believe you. But they'll be on the lookout for you. How about Primark?' *God, I know the way to a girl's heart!*

'Yeah, Primark! Cool!' said Julienne, appeased.

Half an hour wandering round fingering things, and the purchase of a cherry-flavoured lip salve and a pair of aubergine tights with the pocket money that was burning a hole in her purse, and Julienne was back on an even keel. It lasted until Connolly said it was time to take her back. Then her face registered instant woe. 'I don't wanna go back!'

'Well, you've got to. We all have to do things we don't like,' Connolly countered.

'I hate it there! I wanna go home.'

'But you can't, can you? Home's not there any more. Sorry, kid. Tough break.'

The child changed tack with a suddenness that suggested she'd been thinking about it for some time. 'Why can't I come home with you?'

'Me?'

'Yeah. People do. They, like, foster, don't they?'

'I'm not in the market for fostering. I doubt they'd think I was suitable anyway.'

'What? You're a copper. You're a guard,' she changed the word beguilingly, and smiled up like the world's cutest crocodile. 'They gotta like that.'

'I work long hours, unsocial hours,' Connolly began. 'I'd never be there.'

'I don't mind being on my own,' Julienne jumped in. 'My mum was always going out. I could get your tea ready for when you come home from work. I done it for my mum – not that she ate a lot anyway. I'm all right left alone. I can look after myself,' she added pleadingly.

'I know you can,' Connolly said kindly, 'but that's not the point, is it? The idea is that you should be looked after. That's what fostering's about – to give you people to take care of you, like parents would.'

'I could keep house for you,' Julienne said. 'I could do . . . dusting and stuff.'

It was too sad. 'Sorry, Jule,' Connolly said with all the firmness she could muster. 'You'll just have to get through this part as best you can. Keep your nose clean, work hard at school, then when you're older you can go where you like and make a proper life for yourself.'

Julienne's face was down and her lower lip out. She looked up at Connolly pathetically from under her eyebrows. 'But you'll still be my friend? You'll still come and visit me?'

'If you behave yourself,' Connolly said sternly. 'No shenanigans.'

'No what?' Julienne asked, bouncing back on the instant to her default setting of lively curiosity.

'Messing. Playing silly beggars.'

'She– what?'

'Shenanigans.'

Julienne repeated it to herself several times, grinning. 'You don't half talk funny! Is that Irish? Say some more.'

'Well,' Connolly obliged, 'our prime minister's called the *Taoiseach*.'

'The Teapot?'

'And the present one's name is Enda Kenny.'

'That's a girl's name! Your Teapot's called Edna!' Julienne crowed delightedly. 'Say some more!'

They were heading back for the car park and the journey into darkness, but Julienne hopped along beside her, chatting and giggling, clutching her bag of small treasures, and Connolly felt horribly like someone taking their unknowing pet to the vet to be put down. So when a small, sticky hand was slipped into hers, she let it stay there. She didn't have the heart to shake it off.

St Margaret's School did not keep its old records on the premises. 'We're a venerable foundation,' the current head told Swilley, 'and there just wouldn't be room. We keep ten years' worth to hand. Everything else is in the archive, which is looked after by one of our former headmistresses, Miss Wheatcroft. I can give you her address.'

'Thank you. And where is the archive itself?'

'Oh, in her house. Or rather, she has a barn next to her house which we've had specially remodelled – fireproofed and humidity controlled. But she's the present archivist, and she's also tremendously knowledgeable about the school, so if anyone can help you, she can.'

And so on Saturday morning Swilley found herself driving out into the countryside to a village on the border of Essex and Hertfordshire. Into the countryside *again*, she thought – she who hated winding lanes, hedges, cows and mud with a visceral passion. She liked pavements, shops, tube stations, red buses – she was a Town girl through and through, which made it all the stranger that she so often got sent to these one-horse, carrot kingdoms.

Even she, with her inbuilt prejudice, could see it was a pretty village, on a river, with a desperately cute little twelfth-century church, and more timber-framed houses than you could shake a stick at. The Dower House, where Miss Wheatcroft lived, at least had the decency to be on the main road, and was easily spotted, a square fifteenth-century house, painted white between its black beams, with the massive Tudor barn standing right next to it with – thank God – a wide gravelled parking area between the two. Whoever had converted the barn to a modern storage facility had done a good job: butter wouldn't have melted in its mouth. You couldn't see a thing, and even the building behind which housed the generator for the climate control had been designed to match and looked like the big barn's timber-clad offspring.

Miss Wheatcroft was expecting her, and came out to meet Swilley as soon as she got out of the car. It had been clear during the night, and evidently cold out here in the sticks, for there was still frost lingering along the shadowed edges out of the sunshine, and Swilley saw her breath rise as she spoke a greeting, to join the misty haziness that clung to the surrounding trees. She shivered involuntarily at the realization that it was all trees and fields for miles around.

Miss Wheatcroft misinterpreted the shudder and said, 'Come inside, come – it's lovely and warm in there, and I've got coffee on the brew. I don't notice the cold myself any more, but I expect it was much warmer in town when you left, wasn't it?'

She was hospitable and exuded a calmness and warmth that Swilley thought would be invaluable in a head teacher, as they were called now – though if anyone was ever a headmistress, it was this lady. She must have been in her eighties, but was brisk and healthy and bright-eyed and handsome, dressed in a smart tweed skirt and a lavender twinset, with a silk scarf round her neck twisted together with a string of pearls, pearl earrings in her ears, and her silvery hair prettily waved and styled. She could have opened the annual flower show there and then, without changing a thing.

Inside the house it was, as promised, warm. It was spacious and beautiful with antique furniture and pictures on the walls, if you cared for that sort of thing, but the kitchen was modern and well-equipped, and it was to the kitchen Swilley was led, to be greeted with slow stretching and peaceful smiles by two Siamese cats and two dogs – a black Lab and a terrier mix – who had been lying in baskets in front of the gleaming new Aga.

'You don't mind the chaps, do you?' Miss Wheatcroft asked. 'They're very well-behaved. I can't stand people's pets that jump on you without being invited. Just ignore them if you don't like them and they won't come any nearer.'

'I like animals,' Swilley said cautiously. She held out a hand and the dogs came to sniff, but the cats sat on their tails and squinted at her from a polite distance, then went back to their basket. The dogs went to the back door and Miss Wheatcroft let them out, then brought coffee to the table in bone china mugs, with a plate of shortbreads.

'How do you take your coffee?'

'Just as it comes,' said Swilley. 'Thanks.'

'Good girl,' said Miss Wheatcroft. 'I always think of Steinbeck: "If ya wanted a cup a cream an' sugar, why'd ya ask for coffee?"' She did a passable American accent. Swilley didn't know the quotation and smiled politely but blankly, and Miss Wheatcroft pulled herself together. 'Now then, you wanted to pick my brains, I understand, about some of my girls from back in 1990?'

'That's right. Or at least, one particular girl, who would have been about fourteen then.'

'Yes, quite. That could have been either the third year or the fourth year, so I looked up both. They have a yearbook, American-style nowadays – there's so much copying of the Americans these days, isn't there? – but we didn't have them then. But I've got out school magazines and various other bits of the records, so I hope we can find what you want. The class registers, to begin with. If you have a name, that's the place to begin.'

'All I know is that she was called Melissa – that is, if she existed at all. Our victim told people that she had a new friend called Melissa, who went to St Margaret's, but of course she may have been making it up.'

Miss Wheatcroft had lifted a number of files and documents onto the table, and was now examining an attendance register, running her finger down the names. 'Well, there was a Melissa in class F,' she said. She examined two more registers, and said, 'The only one in the year, fortunately – or unfortunately, as the event dictates. Here—' she showed Swilley – 'Melissa Vickery.

This is the record for the summer term, 1990. Quite a lot of absences, I note. Is she the one you're looking for?'

'I think she may be. What can you tell me about her?'

'Let me find her pupil record – that will probably trigger something. There'll be a photograph, and it's faces that bring back the memories for me, more than names. It's remarkable,' she added as she searched through files, 'how many children one can remember out of the thousands that pass through one's hands. Of course they're all unique, but children do like to disguise that uniqueness by behaving in accordance with pack dictates. Strange little creatures . . . Do you have children?'

'One,' said Swilley, shortly.

Miss Wheatcroft smiled. 'Sorry. Unprofessional of me to ask. I never had any myself. I never married. Dealing with a school of six hundred girls and thirty-odd teachers day after day, not to mention governors and civil servants, was quite enough emotional exercise for me. I couldn't have gone home to more demands. I always marvel at teachers who can. Here we are. Melissa Vickery.' She opened the file and took out the photograph on top. 'Oh yes! I remember her now. Quiet little thing. Poor attendance record. Not in the top rank academically, but I remember she had a sweet smile. And helpful – always the one to offer to carry books, that sort of thing.'

She passed the photograph to Swilley. The girl in school uniform gazed at the camera with a closed-mouthed smile, thin fair hair in a bob with a fringe and slightly anxious brown eyes. An ordinary face – a face there was nothing to say about.

'We kept a copy of each year's school photograph on file, but she left at the end of that term, so that's the last photograph we have of her,' said Miss Wheatcroft. 'It was rather sad. Her mother died the previous year. She lived with her father, and I remember there was an adjustment period when she was coming to school without breakfast and in dirty clothes, until he got into a new routine. After that, they seemed to be managing quite well together. Often girls in that position have to do a lot of growing-up very quickly, have to take over their mother's role in the house. They learn to cook and iron and control the household budget – it can be very good for them in the long run.'

'Do you have an address?' Swilley asked.

'Yes, of course.' She looked up. 'Though it's hardly likely she'll still be there, all this time later.'

'I know, but it's a place to start.'

'Quite. Here we are. Father's name David; mother Caroline, deceased. No other siblings. Address: 22 Colville Avenue – do you know where that is?'

'Yes,' said Swilley.

Miss Wheatcroft was still reading notes. 'Ah, I thought I remembered something like that – you certainly won't find her still at that address, because the reason she left school was that they moved away. It was quite sudden. He sent a letter halfway through the summer holidays, and she didn't come back to school that September.'

'Did he say where they were going?'

'You're still hoping to interview Melissa?' Miss Wheatcroft said curiously.

'If she was close to our victim, she may be able to tell us something about her circumstances in her last days. What was going on in her life.'

The level brown eyes said they understood what was being suggested here. 'Sometimes they confide in their friends about that sort of thing,' she said, 'but more often they don't. They get very secretive. Just so you don't get your hopes up too high. Here we are. He says in his letter they are moving to Gloucestershire, to Tetbury. He was going to enrol her in the Edward Tenney school there.' She looked up. 'We have to inform the Department of Education, to ensure that schooling continues. They will have checked that the girl did arrive there.'

'What did the father do – does it say?'

'Yes, where is it? He was a technical designer, self-employed. Whatever that means. I think they were pretty well off – the houses in Colville Avenue were large and expensive in my day.'

'Even more so now,' said Swilley.

'So I imagine,' said Miss Wheatcroft. 'I have a photocopier – I expect you'd like copies of some of this?'

'Yes please,' said Swilley.

She left twenty minutes later with a neat manila folder and triumph in her heart. Melissa Vickery! Surely, surely that couldn't be a coincidence? And if not – well, what ramifications were they looking at? She looked around at the village as she drove away with more kindly eyes, not even minding that there were miles of countryside between her and the factory. All those country lanes had led her to a pot of gold. The road to glory could take many different forms.

THIRTEEN
Rocking the Cash Bar

Joanna was working on Saturday, rehearsal in the morning and concert in the evening, but she would be home for a couple of hours in the afternoon. 'We can have a late lunch together and take George out to the park or something,' she said.

'Good,' said Slider. 'I'll look forward to that.' They didn't all that often have time together as a family. His father and Lydia were happy to have George in the morning and take him grocery shopping with them, so he didn't feel bad about going into the office for a couple of hours and bashing through some paperwork he had been neglecting for the Amanda Knight case.

So he was at his desk when a call was put through from Mrs Knight. She sounded quavery and infinitely old. He could imagine that she had lived the past twenty-five years in a sort of rigid state, braced against the loss of her daughter, with the unanswered question pervading her bones like cancer. Now the question was answered in the worst possible way, the bones had crumbled, and there was nothing left to keep her upright.

He pushed the pity away and tried for professional kindness. 'Is there something I can help you with?'

'Yes,' she said. 'I wondered – you said – I keep thinking about what you told me, but you – you didn't . . .'

'Yes?' he encouraged.

'You didn't say *how*. I mean, what happened to her. I suppose you think she was – killed deliberately . . .'

'That's not necessarily so,' he said. 'It could have been an accident, and the person panicked and tried to get rid of the body for fear of the consequences.'

'But *how*? I mean, how was she killed?'

'I'm afraid there's no way of knowing that,' he said. It was an awful question. 'There doesn't seem to be any traumatic damage to the bones. No skull fracture, for instance.' Which left all the other possibilities – poison, strangulation, smothering, drowning. The mind could run riot – a mother's mind perhaps particularly. There was nothing he could do about that.

'Why do you think it must have been my Ronnie that did it? It could have been anyone.'

'There's the problem of access to the garden, you see,' he said carefully.

'You don't even know it's Amanda. You don't even know it's her.' He didn't answer that, and she went on fiercely: 'Even if it is – you didn't know him, you didn't know my Ronnie. He would never have harmed her, not a hair on her head. I'm glad he's not here now to hear all this. It would have killed him.'

It was said without irony. There was nothing he could say except, 'I'm sorry.'

There was a pause, and then she said, 'When do I – get her back?'

'It shouldn't be long,' he said. 'A few more days. I'll let you know as soon as it's possible to release her.'

'And then what do I do?'

'I'll have someone talk you through it all, when the time comes. Try not to worry.'

'I got nothing else to do,' she said, and rang off.

He feared there was never going to be any closure in this case – not for her, but not for him either. They would assemble every bit of information they could, and it would still all add up to an implausibility wrapped in a mirage inside a figment.

Gascoyne had tracked down Karen Beales, the supposed mistress of Amanda's uncle Brian. Given that she had been, in the words of the wronged wife, a 'twinkie', he had assumed she had been a good deal younger than the old dog, and would therefore still be working. And once an estate agent, always an estate agent. That was the easy part. The hard part was that estate agencies had proliferated in London like black beetles in a basement.

But he found her at last employed by one of the newer entries to the field, Zingybrix, who went in for a bright, breezy advertising style and fluorescent orange-and-lime plastic fascias on their shops. Her name was now Karen Redondo, and she was working at the Acton branch.

The former good-time girl was now an overweight woman, and the once-pneumatic bust was now a solid shelf that blended into the general bulk without differentiation. She wore a lime green skirt suit over an orange blouse – presumably corporate wear – which didn't help; but she had done her best with full make-up, perky highlighted hair, funky earrings, and heels so high it made Gascoyne queasy just to look at them.

She greeted him with many teeth, perky and flirty, until she learned who he was and what he wanted. Then she seemed to abandon the whole act with something like relief and relax into worn middle age for a bit of a rest.

'I read in the paper about the skeleton being found. I must say I didn't put it together with that old business. So that poor little girl was dead after all? All this time . . . I have sometimes wondered what happened to her.'

She conducted him through the shop into the employees' lounge, which had a cheap sofa and chair and a coffee machine, but was made less than welcoming by the presence of two filing cabinets and a photocopier which presumably wouldn't fit into the shop, or into its image.

'Mind if I take me shoes off?' She heeled them off and sank with a huge sigh onto the sofa, whose cheap foam seat pads sank alarmingly under her onslaught. 'I tell you I'm getting too old for these buggers.' She bent and massaged her toes tenderly. 'So, you want to talk about Brian, do you? Blimey, that's a long time ago. Lot of water under *that* bridge. I was still on my first back then. Karen Beales, I was. Kevin Beales, my first. Karen and Kevin, what a lovely couple,' she added with heavy irony. 'We got married too young, that's what it was. Thought we were in love. *That* didn't last. Alec's my third – Alec Redondo. He's a bit younger than me,' she mentioned with a coy look at Gascoyne, who was younger than her and also good-looking, in a clean cut, eager-young-fellow way.

He was used to the reaction, and didn't take it personally. A policeman got a lot of offers, and they were all fatal to accept. In any case, he was working, quietly and privately, towards an accommodation with the daughter of an old friend and colleague of his policeman father, who would therefore understand the Job. When he got married, he intended it to stick.

He nodded a neutral reply, and she sighed again and let her face sag. 'Big mistake, marrying a younger bloke. I've not got the energy for it any more. Get to my age, you see sex more as a chance for a lie-down.'

'So, you and Brian Bexley,' Gascoyne prompted her gently.

'Oh, yeah. Course, you don't want to hear my sad story. His was sad enough. Married to a real ball-cutter. She despised him – there's a lot like that. They don't want a real man, they want a tailor's dummy – looks good, knows its place, never speaks. She was a go-getter. Ambitious. Always pushing him. He was out of his depth. Course, he'd've been out of his depth on a wet pavement. He came to me for a bit of a rest from it all.'

Gascoyne nodded encouragingly but offered no comment. Anything he said at a moment like that could lead to trouble.

'Funny thing, we'd been working at the same branch a while before it clicked. It was actually at a do at the golf club. Silver wedding bash, the club captain and his wife – pair of old farts! Mean, too. Not even a sit-down: catered buffet and a cash bar, then a disco and a charity raffle. Cheek of it! I'd gone with Kevin, Brian was there with Pat, they both had faces like boots. Pat never did like the golf club crowd, and Kev was in a mood about something, I can't remember what. So Brian asks me to dance, and – well, I'd had a few drinks. So had he. Long story short, we slipped outside and did it on one of the greens. We got a bit silly. Coming back, we stuffed my knickers into the captain's exhaust pipe.' She grinned.

'How did that work out?'

'Didn't hang around to find out. Anyway,' she went on, 'that was the start of it. I wasn't the first. I knew that. I didn't mind. I wasn't interested in marrying him. I was happy just having a bit of fun. He wasn't a bad bloke, really. Anyway, it was a change from Kevin, who, frankly, was an arsehole of the first water. Complete shit. And to be totally frank with you—' Was she ever anything else? he wondered – 'not all that well endowed in the bedroom department. I mean, I kid you not, it was like Braille down there. And no staying-power. Our first night together, I thought to meself, is that it? I've been vaccinated slower. But old Brian, well, he'd not got much imagination, real meat-and-potatoes man, but at least he had stamina. Anyway, that's all it was, with Brian and me, a bit of fun, no pack drill, nobody gets hurt.'

Gascoyne gave her a gentle push. 'Do you remember the time when the little girl went missing – his niece?'

'Oh my goodness, yes. You don't forget a thing like that. I mean, you're always upset when a kiddie goes missing, because so often they turn up dead a few days later, don't they? But when it's someone you know – I mean, when it happens to someone you know – it's even worse, isn't it?'

'There was some question, I believe,' Gascoyne said delicately, 'about an alibi?'

She gave him an open-eyed look. 'For Brian, you mean? Oh yes, there was a rare old fuss about *that*. I mean, it was a lot of nonsense, him even needing an alibi, because *he* never done anything to that poor kiddie, and anyone who knew him would've known that. But I suppose the police have to do things by the numbers, don't they? I mean, *they* didn't know him personally. Poor old Brian was really upset about it, though, just the thought that they could suspect him at all. It would have made him a kiddie-fiddler, and it made him sick just to think about that. Because he was as normal as white bread, poor old Brian, in that department, if you get my drift. He liked it a lot – and I mean *a lot* – but it was plain vanilla all the way with him.' She looked at Gascoyne with an anticipatory smile, as if waiting to see if she had made him blush.

Gascoyne made sturdy notes in his notebook. 'But did he, in fact, have an alibi?' he asked, without looking up, as though it was a matter of not very much importance.

'Oh yes. Well, he was with me all afternoon, the day she went missing, wasn't he?' she said matter-of-factly. 'I thought that was what you come here asking about.'

'You're quite sure about that?'

'Course I am. See, the thing was, he was worried about me having to give evidence in case anything happened, and it all coming out, me being married at the time. I told him, I don't care if Kevin does know, because *he's* not Snow White. He was doing it with this barmaid down the Sun in Barnes, which I knew all about, though he didn't know I knew, so if he'd wanted to make something out of me and Brian I had my defence all ready.

But when it came to the point, his wife told the police that he'd been home with her all day.' She gave a malicious smile. 'I reckon she was just yanking Brian's chain, because she made out they were doing a jigsaw together, like he was some poor old henpecked hubby – which he was, in a way, but he didn't like to think it. It put him in a right old froth. I reckon he was half hoping it'd all come out about him and me, so's he look like a real lad, you know what I mean? But once she'd said it he had to go along with it, didn't he? But he was with me all right, the whole afternoon, so there was no harm in it, from that point of view.'

She seemed both frank and honest on this point, and Gascoyne put a line under another possible theory with an inward sigh.

'Did he talk much about his niece?' he asked.

'Well, not before it happened,' she said. 'We had other things on our minds, if you get my drift. But afterwards, yes, he did talk about it a lot. In the office, generally, *and* when we were alone. He was very upset, you know,' she said, giving him a nod. 'Actually, he was sure at first she'd run away, but as time went on—'

'Run away?'

'Yeah. Well, her and her dad were always rowing. Brian thought she'd run away, like teenagers do – like a cry for help, if you know what I mean?'

'What did they row about?'

'Oh, I don't know. Everything. Brian said they were at it like knives all the time. He said she was very bright, and her dad was a bit stupid, and they couldn't see eye to eye on anything, but they were both stubborn as donkeys, so it was all shouting and banging around.' She heard herself and stopped, and looked at Gascoyne round-eyed again. 'Here, d'you think he done her in, her dad? Is that what this is all about? I thought you were after poor old Brian again, but all this, you were just trying to get to his opinion of her dad, weren't you?'

'You're very sharp,' Gascoyne said, to flatter her.

'Oh, I'm not just a pretty face,' she said.

'Did Brian suspect anything like that?'

'Well,' she said reluctantly, unwilling to pass up on a drama, 'he never said anything to me about it, no. He just said they rowed all the time. See, Amanda, she wanted to be a vet when she left school, and her dad wanted her to work in a bank or a building society or something like that. Nice steady job with good prospects. Didn't want her messing about with animals and earning peanuts. They had a big blow-up about it not long before she went missing, round Brian's house – they used to go there for Sunday lunch. Brian reckoned that argument'd been going on a long time, and he thought she'd finally run away from home to, like, draw attention to herself. Sort of blackmail – let me be a vet or I'll run away again. Of course, he thought she'd come back.'

'And when she didn't come back,' Gascoyne said, 'what did Brian think then?'

'Well, that some pervert'd done her,' Karen said, looking serious. 'He was very fond of her, and of course when the days went by and she wasn't found, he knew, same as we all did, that it was most likely she was dead. You know when you see it on the telly, if they've been gone a few days, that's it. It's a rotten thing to have happen.'

'So it never occurred to him that her father might have killed her?'

'Not that he ever said to me.' She thought for a moment. 'No, he never thought that, I'm sure. He'd have talked to me about it if he had. We talked a lot, between the time the kid went missing and we broke up. Tell the truth, talking was about *all* we did. And we didn't last a lot longer. He sort of went off sex, and I didn't feel the same about him. I mean, it was just supposed to be a bit of fun, but it's no fun with a missing kiddie always between you. And him talking about her being raped and murdered by some pervert. It was in the August, as I remember, that it all happened, and the end of September I got myself a transfer to another branch, because it's awkward working with a bloke when you're not sleeping with him any more. And all the talk about the kid give me the willies.'

'Well, thank you for your help,' Gascoyne said, closing his book and getting up.

She rose too, and looked up at him, considerably shorter without her five-inch heels. Under the make-up her face looked old and plain. 'So she was murdered after all?' she said glumly. 'Where was it she was found?'

'In the garden of the house where they lived.'

She nodded seriously. 'So it must have been her dad. I see now why you were asking. Well, all I can say is that Brian never suspected him. Poor old Brian. I wonder what he'd think if he was here now? It's probably a good thing he never knew, because he was really fond of that little girl. It'd have broke him up. He was a nice man, really,' she added with a sentimental smile. 'His wife never understood him.'

Atherton rang Slider on Sunday morning to tell him that they had got into the Sunday papers. '*The Times* and the *Telegraph*,' he said.

Slider rarely had time to read the papers, and depended on his friend to catch him up. 'Much in there?'

'No, it's just a short piece, tucked away on page five. Interview with the Freelings about how it feels to have a skeleton found in your garden. Interview with the gardener about how it feels to dig one up. Separate boxed shortie from an archaeologist about how to date old bones – bit out of left field, that one, because he's talking about carbon dating and dinosaurs. Nothing about the Knights.'

'That's good,' Slider said.

'It is?'

'Proves we're not leaking. Anything else?'

'There's a photograph of the house. Mentions the road but not the number.'

'Well, we'll see if that stirs anything up.'

It was a delightful rarity to have a Sunday at home when Joanna was not working, and he intended to enjoy it to the top of his bent. His other children, Matthew and Kate, were coming over. Their mother, Irene, delivered them at around two o'clock – Matthew had had rugby in the morning – and when she mentioned that her husband Ernie was away, at a high-flying bridge tournament in Gatehouse of Fleet, Joanna invited her to stay for lunch, and she accepted with apparent eagerness.

Slider tried not to feel dismayed. It was like Joanna's generosity to ask her, but she and Irene were always awkward with each other, and though there was no longer any animosity between him and Irene, she never seemed at ease in his presence, and particularly not in his house.

He gave her a sherry and she sat on the edge of the sofa and made brittle small talk. She was looking well, he thought. She had put on a little weight, which suited her – she had always tended towards the too-skinny. She was perfectly turned out, even for delivering children, in expensive-looking slacks and a nice wool jacket, silk scarf and some chunky costume jewellery; Ernie was both well-off and generous. Her make-up was perfect, her short dark hair shiny and trim as though it had been painted on. She looked what she was, a prosperous middle-class wife, and he found himself staring at her with amazement at the idea that he could ever have lived with her, slept in the same bed with her, talked to her across the breakfast table. She seemed so alien to him, even when she met his eyes and called him 'Bill', that it was, frankly, an embarrassment to remember that he had once known what she looked like naked. He felt hot and ashamed at the thought – as if he had been caught looking up the Queen's skirt.

It was a relief when Dad and Lydia arrived, coming in from the granny flat, for Dad had always had a soft spot for Irene – in a slightly sorry-for-her way, but nevertheless – and Lydia had terrific social skills. She could make anyone feel comfortable, and soon had Irene chatting easily about colour schemes and soft furnishings, from which Slider concluded she was about to begin on one of her restless redecoration jags.

So with George in his booster seat, they were eight around the dinner table, which was very pleasant. He carved the beef and dispatched plates and felt like a paterfamilias. This was what it was all about, wasn't it? The reason for living. Perversely, by the time the roast beef and Yorkshire course was getting down to the dirty plates, the same thought had shunted him off into a copper's siding, from which he observed the happy, animated faces chewing, talking and smiling like someone shut out from the feast.

Yes, it *was* what it was all about: keeping the city safe for ordinary happy families like this; and because on the whole they were successful, it meant that for the vast majority of people, the world of crime was a parallel universe which they had heard about but knew nothing of.

But it was where he lived for much of his life. It was the contaminated flood water through which he waded day after day, with the turds of pointless stupidity and greed bobbing against his legs, and the sewage smell of lies and cruelty clinging to his clothes and hair. He climbed out of it onto dry land when he came home, but he was always afraid he would bring some infection back with him.

He worried for his children. Knowing what he knew of the Dark Side, he wondered what sort of world would be there for them when they grew up. Little George, frowning in concentration over the mechanical challenge of marrying roast potato and fork, had no other concern at present but the mastery of his own body. Matthew, looking more like Dad every day, was pinkly scrubbed from his post-rugby shower, and had an interesting bruise and scratch on the side of his face. His eyes were on his empty plate, his mind, Slider was sure, far away. He was a dreamer, and had still to discover what direction his dreams ought to take him. And there was Kate, who was doing her hair differently – parted in the middle and long and straight, the current yard-of-tapwater style. She had already acquired the tic that went with it: every few seconds she would tilt her face upwards and shake it once each way, to get the hair out of her eyes – like a swimmer coming up out of the water. She was confident and knowing, with the automatic slight contempt for the hopeless, bumbling male half of creation that she had learned from her mother. But would that be enough to protect her?

She had caught him staring at her. He managed a feeble smile, but she twitched her hair again and said loudly, 'You can stop giving us the third degree with your old detective eyes, Dad. I'm not doing drugs and Matthew isn't watching porn – are you, Matt?'

Matthew turned crimson and threw his father a brief, horrified glance. It looked like guilt, but Slider recognized pure embarrassment when he saw it.

'I wasn't thinking that,' he said.

'I bet you *were*. You've been staring at me for hours.'

'Thinking how pretty you look with your new hairdo.'

Kate contorted her face wildly and said, 'Oh yuck, yeuch! Hairdo? What am I – forty with a perm? Get with the programme, Dad! Twenty-first century, hello?'

She meant it humorously, but Slider was suddenly cold to his core, and couldn't respond. He was looking at her, but he was seeing the huddle of lonely bones, yellowing and forgotten, all that remained of Amanda Knight. He had thought bones less unsettling than the flesh, but it wasn't so. He felt his own inside him, warmly fed with roast beef and family cheer, but grimly marking time all the same, waiting for their eventual, inevitable cue to appear at the end of everything. It was what they all came to, what was waiting for them all. *Golden lads and girls all must . . .*

He saw his father look at him, then was aware of an exchange of looks between Dad and Joanna. And then Joanna stood up and said, 'Can you help me clear the plates, darling? No, don't you move, Irene. We'll do it.'

And in the general movement and clatter of plates being put together and passed along, he was able to stand up, received his freight of gravy-stained china, was able to stir his frozen limbs into movement, stepped out of the cold pool of horror and walked the few yards along to the kitchen. He put the plates down carefully and turned as Joanna came in. She put down her stack too, and put herself into his arms. He wrapped his around her, rested his face on the top of her head, closed his eyes, felt her pressing hard against him all the way down, giving him her heat and life. Her bones pressed against his. No, he wouldn't think about bones any more. He could smell apple pie and custard in the air, and it was the smell of home, of childhood, of safety.

'But she wasn't safe, even there,' he said.

He hadn't meant to say it aloud. But Joanna's response was a grunt, and a harder squeeze. He drew a long breath, then gently released her. She looked up into his face. 'Better?' she asked.

He gave a shaky smile. 'How did you know?'

'Foolish question. Your face is not a kabuki mask, you know.'

'Sorry.'

'And anyway, I love you. Custard in the saucepan, jug over there – can you transfer the one to the other while I get the pie out?'

He knew what she was asking. 'I'm all right now. It's just –
she was the same sort of age as Kate.'

'I know,' said Joanna. 'I saw the photograph.'

'So you did,' he said, and went to the stove for the custard
pot. 'Thank God for you,' he added, now in a normal voice.

FOURTEEN
Ingots We Trust

In the absence of Hart, Connolly had gone down to Mike's snack van for the breakfast sandwiches. Slider opened his paper bag, took one horrified look, and bellowed. Connolly appeared in the doorway with an enquiring expression.

'Tomato sauce on a *bacon sandwich*? Were you raised by wolves?'

'Sorry, boss.'

'On a sausage sandwich, yes . . .'

'Sorry, boss. You must a' got McLaren's by mistake.' She glanced back over her shoulder. 'Ah, Jayz, he's already taken a bite. D'you want mine? I'll swap you. I haven't touched it.'

'What have you got?' he asked suspiciously.

'Fried egg.'

Slider was tempted, but a fried egg sandwich took careful management. Like mangoes, they were best eaten in the bath. 'I'll pass, thanks,' he said with a sigh. 'Here, McLaren might as well have this one as well.'

'Will I go back to Mike's for you?'

'No, it doesn't matter. There's not time before the meeting.'

'I'll get yiz a cup of tea,' she said contritely. 'And a biscuit.'

Gascoyne was the first to report. 'I don't know that it's helped much,' he said, having précised his meeting with Karen Beales Redondo. 'But it does look as if we can rule the uncle out.'

'It's given us a possible motive, anyway,' Slider said. 'A family row that got out of hand.' *Better than abuse*, he added inwardly.

'So, how does it work?' Connolly mused. 'He goes home. Finds Amanda, starts givin' out to her, loses his temper and lamps her. Where does all this happen? In the garden?'

'My view is that it must have been in the van,' Atherton said. 'Say he saw her walking along the road – it'd be natural to call to her to get in. If it was anywhere in the open air, it would surely have been seen.'

Connolly shrugged. 'In the van, if ya like. Makes it simpler. Now he's got to think what to do. Maybe he drives around in a panic. Realizes he needs an alibi. Remembers the owl lady, knows she's a bit confused. Reckons he can say he was at her house – she won't remember which day he did the repair. Comes back for his tea, tells his wife not to raise the Gards. Goes and does his other job with the body still in the back of the van. Couple of days later, he brings the body back and buries it.'

'No, he must've stashed it somewhere,' Lessop said. 'Once the police were called they'd've checked in the van first thing.'

'Maybe they didn't,' said LaSalle.

'Yes, but he'd have expected them to. So he couldn't have left her there.'

'People do stupid things all the time. And get away with it.'

'And the police at the time don't seem to have been very thorough,' Gascoyne said apologetically.

'Whatever,' Connolly resumed, 'it sounds reasonable, but how do we prove any of it?'

'Yeah,' said McLaren, moodily peeling the paper bag off a rather squashed sausage roll, his second course. Or rather, Slider thought resentfully, remembering where his sandwich had gone, his third. 'That's where it all falls down, innit?'

'I can't see it matters anyway,' said Fathom. 'They're all dead. S'not like we're gonna bring someone to justice.'

'Well, I've got something to throw in to the mix,' said Swilley. 'Might make it a bit more interesting for you, you poor delicate flowers.' She told them about her visit to Miss Wheatcroft.

Atherton sat up straighter. 'Vickery!' he exclaimed. 'That's got to mean something, hasn't it?'

'Yeah, but what?' Connolly said.

'It's not *that* uncommon a name,' Slider put in.

'It's a Shepherd's Bush name,' LaSalle offered. 'Quite a lot of Vickerys around when I was a kid.'

'*Was* Detective Superintendent Vickery a local man?' Swilley asked, but no one could answer.

'We need to find that out,' Slider said.

'It could be just a coincidence,' LaSalle said soberly. 'Colville

Avenue's the next street to Laburnum. No reason she couldn't have met the girl walking home from school one day and they became friends. The fact that the Det Sup on the case happens to have the same name—'

'Yeah, what *are* you suggesting?' Lessop said to Atherton derisively. 'That Det Sup Vickery was involved somehow? That *he* killed the girl?'

'I'm not suggesting anything,' Atherton said, with a Vulcan eyebrow. 'Keep your pants on. It's a coincidence, that's all, and it's my belief that a coincidence is God's way of telling you to pay attention.'

'I said it would make it more interesting,' Swilley muttered, with a glance at Slider. 'Sorry, boss.'

He shook his head slightly, cancelling the apology. 'Let's find out about Det Sup Vickery. LaSalle, you're the local boy, you're on it. Lessop, you can help. Where he lived, whether he had any family, what became of him after the Knight case. Did he have any connection to this David Vickery. It probably *is* just a coincidence, but we'd look like idiots if it wasn't and we didn't check. And of course we need to find Melissa Vickery. She might hold the key to the last days.'

'I'm on that,' Swilley said.

'But boss,' Connolly said restlessly, 'what *are* you accusing Det Sup Vickery of?'

'Nothing at all,' Slider said. 'I just want to know if there was any connection.'

But it had jumped into his mind – as he suspected it had into Atherton's – that the thinness of the Misper file might not have been accidental, or the attrition of ages, after all. He had an uncomfortable feeling that the sleeping god Complication had stirred, and opened one eye, and blearily but with incipient menace was looking – where else? – at him again.

'No, no, no,' said Porson. 'No, you don't.'

'Sir?'

'You can't make official enquiries about a detective superintendent. Dammit, man, that's the very sort of thing I'm trying to keep you away from.'

'But it was twenty-five years ago,' Slider objected.

'And what if he's still in? Or only just left? Or still has friends among the high and mighty?' Porson demanded. 'You've got to learn to self-preservate. That's why I thought these old bones'd be just what you needed. Keep your head down for a bit.'

'Just a simple computer search—'

'On our state of the ark computers? It's diamonds to doughnuts any enquiry like that'd be flagged up. You don't want people looking in your direction just now, you really don't.'

'I didn't think there were no-go areas when it came to serious crime,' Slider said sourly.

'Oh, don't pout at me. Why can't you come at it the other way? Look into this David Vickery – you'll soon find out if he was related. But even if he was, don't come to me with anything but a cast-iron case, not unsupported innuendoes. You're a good copper, Slider, but you're too quick to think the worst of the higher echelongs.'

'But if there *is* something there,' Slider insisted.

'*If* there is, and *if* you assemble some evidence that actually stands up, and doesn't disappear overnight like mother's gin . . .'

'Then you'll support me?'

'We'll see.' He raised an eyebrow at Slider's expression. 'I'm trying to protect you. You've put up a lot of backs lately, but bring in a really clever case that doesn't hurt anybody they care about – well, they'll be laughing on the other foot, then.'

'Yes, sir.'

'Meanwhile, call your dogs off this Det Sup Vickery, before they do any damage.'

'Yes, sir.'

Porson looked at him for a long minute. 'So what *are* you thinking now? If the father did it, what's Vickery got to do with it? Either Vickery?'

'I don't know,' Slider admitted. 'Maybe there was some connection between Knight and Vickery – our Vickery. The Mispers file was very thin. I want to know where the body was before it was buried. If it was in the van, why didn't the police at the time find it? If it was elsewhere, surely to God someone must have seen something – and maybe they did, but the evidence was suppressed.'

'There you go again.' Porson gave him an incredulous look. 'On the supposition express and heading for La-la Land.'

'I just have a feeling—'

'Oh, a *feeling*!'

'You used to trust my feelings,' Slider complained.

'Shouldn't've married me then, should you?' Porson said, and jabbed a forefinger towards the door. 'Out!'

After the morning meeting, Swilley and Connolly had gone to Tetbury on the trail of David and Melissa Vickery. Outside the magic heat-circle of London it was bitterly cold, and the trees were at last shedding their leaves, bare branches scratching at a pale sky. The hedges were thick with rime, and the newly-ploughed fields were brown waves with white crests.

'Bloody countryside again!' Swilley snarled over the steering wheel. 'I hate the bloody countryside.'

'Ah, it's grand to get out for a bit,' Connolly countered cheerfully. 'Don't you get sick of it all, sometimes?'

'Sick of what?'

'The big city. People everywhere.'

'I love London.'

'All the gougers and the gobshites. The crime. Now here—' she gestured out of the window – 'nothing but fields and trees and cows as far as the eye can see.'

'I hate cows. Going about with their tits hanging out. It's indecent!'

'Aren't you the Miserable Margaret? Look on the bright side – we can get lunch out. Find a nice pub. I'm so hungry I could eat a baby's bum through the bars of a cot.' Swilley grunted unreceptively. 'Anyway,' Connolly tried, 'I need to go.'

'You should have gone before we left.'

'That was two hours ago! Ah, c'mon, don't be narky. A bit of time out is no harm. I won't tell if you don't.'

Swilley gave her a glance, and gave in. 'Ten minutes, then. And no beer. We can't go breathing fumes over the general public.'

'You're no fun on a road trip, Thelma,' Connolly remarked.

Tetbury was a pretty town full of grey stone, mediaeval buildings, but it had the slightly worn air of a place that had hit hard times. The big old coaching inn, The Crown, was boarded up, and several shops were closed, but there were people about, and a teashop on a corner in the centre seemed to be doing brisk trade.

The Edward Tenney school was easy enough to find, standing at the end of the main street, where the town gave way to the country again. It occupied a large stone house with mullioned windows, evidently once some great merchant's pride; but behind it, the extensive grounds had been colonised by additional buildings from a variety of periods in a variety of styles, including Twentieth Century Insensitive.

Inside the main building, they waited in a grand hall to see the head teacher, and Connolly had her own moment of the horrors. 'You know how you hate the countryside?' she whispered to Swilley. 'Well, I hate schools!' There was that institutional smell, and the distant murmur of voices, the whisper of movement, the sense that behind closed doors there were desks, and books, and teachers, and the seething mass of emotions and unsatisfied desires that were teenaged girls, all trapped together and forced to disobey the centrifugal power that was urging them to get the hell out of there.

But their wait was not long, their request was well received; and being such a venerable institution, the school had comprehensive records, and looked after them. They were put in charge of Mrs Anderson, the librarian, who took them to the well-appointed library, produced old ledgers, and quickly found the evidence that Melissa Vickery had indeed joined the school that September, and had attended for another two years.

Attended not very well, however. 'A lot of absences,' Mrs Anderson noted. 'And she left school the moment she could, when she was sixteen. Of course, that wouldn't happen nowadays,' she added with disapproval. 'We are a private, fee-paying school, and there's tremendous competition for every place. Our girls work extremely hard to justify their parents' investment, and our belief in them. But things were rather different then, when we were under the local authority. Back then, intake was a simple matter of geography.'

Connolly, for some bizarre reason, felt driven to defend the absent. 'She'd just lost her mother,' she mentioned.

Mrs Anderson bent a stern look on her. 'We all have

difficulties to overcome. The mark of a Tenney girl is that she has the character to turn negative experiences into positive strengths.'

I bet that little gem's appeared in a lot of speeches, Connolly thought.

They got an address, and were directed to a plain, flat-faced stone cottage in a steep, cobbled lane called Chipping Steps. The house was cheerful with a newly painted green door and boxes of summer bedders hanging on in the tiny sliver of front yard behind the wall that divided it from the precipitous street. The door was opened by an alert-looking woman with unlikely red hair and two Manchester terriers.

'Sorry, they're a bit uppity. I was just about to take them out,' she shouted over their clamorous greeting. 'I'll just shut them in the kitchen.' Having muted the barking behind a stout oak door, she came back and said, 'The school rang to say you were coming. Come in. I'm not sure I can help you much, but come in out of the wind. It roars down the Steps, doesn't it? Straight from Siberia today.'

They stepped straight into the living room, which was low-ceilinged and crammed with oaky and chintzy furniture and cottagey ornaments, so that every movement had to be thought out beforehand. She guided them to a saggy-looking sofa, which sank under them and absorbed them like quicksand, so that Swilley, who was tall, was wondering from the start how she would ever get out again.

Mrs Bristowe was cheery, lipsticky, and salt-of-the-earth friendly. 'So, you want to ask me about the Vickerys? The people I bought the house from. We, I should say – my husband passed away two years ago.'

'I'm sorry,' Swilley said. 'How long ago was it you bought the house?'

'Twenty-three years last July. We've been very happy here. Our little nook, Henry used to call it. We had a big house before, but when the children went away, it seemed so empty. So Henry said, sell it, buy somewhere snug. It's a white elephant, he said. It cost the earth to heat. You wouldn't believe the draughts! It was listed, you see, so we couldn't put in double glazing. Never buy a listed place, my dear, it just isn't worth the hassle. Still, I wasn't keen to move at first – all my memories were there. But when I saw this place, it all just clicked. I could imagine how we'd snuggle right in, just the two of us – and we did. It's small, but I was sick to death of being cold.'

Swilley nodded as if she was interested in all this. 'So tell me about the Vickerys.'

'I'm not sure there's much to tell. We only met them a couple of times, when we came to look at the house. He was good-looking – trust me to notice that!' She gave a social laugh. 'Very dark, almost swarthy, with gorgeous black wavy hair and blue eyes. Irish looks, you know? A bit like that doctor on *Grey's Anatomy* – the one they called McDreamy?' Swilley nodded. 'She was more mousy. I don't really remember much about her. Except that she was more friendly than him. She seemed to want to chat, but he kept shutting her up. What else can I tell you? Hmm.' She thought a moment. 'Oh, he worked from home – I don't know if that helps? One of the bedrooms was his study. I think that's partly why they were moving. The bedrooms are pretty small here.' She thought again. 'He didn't strike me as a happy man. It didn't feel like a happy household. But we didn't mind – I knew we'd make it a real home. We're nesters, Henry and me. *Were*, I should say.'

'Do you know where they moved to?'

'Only that she said they were looking at farms in the area.' She thought. 'That was one of the times he shut her up. I don't think he wanted their private business talked about. You get people like that. Henry was a bit that way. "No need to tell everyone your shoe size, Bar," he used to say. He always had a neat way of making a point, like that. And he was a private sort of person, except with people he knew well. Me, I'd tell anyone anything. Not that there's anything interesting about me to tell!' She laughed again.

'How did she behave when he shut her up?' Connolly put in. 'Was she cowed? Afraid of him?'

Mrs Bristowe shook her head. 'You're talking about a very long time ago. I don't remember all the little details.' She thought again. 'I don't *think* she was afraid of him – or I *should* say, I think if she'd seemed really scared of him I'd remember that. But maybe I wouldn't. That's all I can say, really.'

'And they didn't leave a forwarding address?'

'No. As a matter of fact, I don't remember any post ever coming for them. But if there had, I'd've just given it back to the postman.'

'And you never saw them again?'

'Not that I remember. If they did move somewhere in the area, you'd expect to bump into them now and then, when they came in to shop. People hereabouts are very friendly. And nobody ever moves far away. Once a Tetburyite, always a Tetburyite! Of course, they may have been closer to Cirencester and shopped there. Ciren's only ten miles away, so say they were halfway between the two. That's if they *did* buy a farm in the area. I don't know why they'd've wanted a farm – I can't believe they were farmers. Perhaps they just wanted the space. They could always have let the grazing. That's what most people do.' She gave them a rueful smile. 'I'm sorry, I don't think I've been much help.'

'It was a long time ago,' Swilley said. 'Thank you for racking your memory for us.'

'I suppose you can't tell me what it's all about? They weren't Russian spies or something, were they?'

'They weren't Russian spies.' Swilley heaved herself up with immense effort, and tried not to punch her head right through the ceiling. Alice-like, she seemed to have grown bigger in the time they had been here. She handed over her card. 'If you do remember anything else about them, anything at all, please let us know.'

'I will. But I don't think I will, if you know what I mean. They were a funny couple, or I don't think I'd remember them at all. But I think I've told you all I know.'

Hart was as surprised as dismayed to discover how many beauty salons there were in the general Hammersmith area. It struck her as astonishing that so many women were willing to put on a nylon cape, lie down and have some teenage mouth-breather do things to their faces. How could they regard it as a treat? As something desirable to book in advance and look forward to? And how come they had the time and the money for it? Why weren't they at work? Or getting on with something productive,

or at least useful? She came from an old-fashioned West Indian
family where the mother was the lynchpin, and quite capable of
lynching any of her children who lazed around, leeched on others
or just generally wasted their substance when they could be
Getting On.

Besides, Hart had always hated anyone touching her head. It
was bad enough having to have your hair done, but the face was
the place more than anywhere else in your body that you lived.
To close your eyes and allow a stranger to put their hands all
over it, let alone come at it with sharp implements . . . And for
what? Eyebrow tinting – what was *that* all about? What did they
think God gave them eyebrow pencils for? Dermabrasion, peeling
– yeow! It made her think uncomfortably about Egyptian
mummies, embalming, and what they'd told her at school about
pulling the brains out through the nose with a hook, which, even
though it was done to dead people, had still caused her to scrunch
up in horror.

But it was evidently a lucrative field, because 'Beauty
Academies', as they laughably called the training schools, had
proliferated like spiders in a corner, and since they were all private
enterprises, they wouldn't have existed if there weren't sufficient
wannabe pluckers and buffers to take up the places. She made a
list of the most likely ones, and started to work through them,
but her enquiries were met with blanks, not to say frequently
incomprehension, as though the idea of taking the names of
trainees or keeping records was a ludicrous notion. Probably in
many cases it was. At the smarter, longer-established academies,
the administration was at a higher level, but so were their fees,
and Hart doubted Shannon Bailey could have afforded them – if,
indeed, Julienne's guess had any merit. Connolly seemed to think
it worth a try, and Hart had no other leads, so what the hay?

And then, thinking again about ancient Egyptians generally,
snake rods, golden masks and those tall hats, something clicked
in her mind. Connolly had told her Julienne had said the beauty
school Shannon and Kaylee talked about was 'something with
tits in it', which she had dismissed as meaningless. Now she had
a light bulb moment, and thought, *Nefertiti!*

There was on her list a Nefertiti Beauty Therapy Training
Academy. She parked the car and brought it up on her tablet.

Make £££s as a Beauty Therapist!!! it urged the reader.
Enter the exciting world of Beauty Therapy at one of our
Training Academies! Our world-beating 11-day course will
put you on the road to a satisfying and money-spinning
career!! When you have completed the course you will
receive a Beauty Academy Diploma which will open the
door to Beauty Salons and Spas all over the country! Or
treat paying customers in the comfort of their own homes!
Nefertiti is recognized UK-wide. Become a Nefertiti Beauty
Therapist and you can earn £££s!!!

From the number of exclamation marks, they were looking for
a more excitable and less thoughtful sort of candidate; and Hart,
who had read a large number of advertisements for academies
that day, noted that they did not mention NVQs or City and
Guilds qualifications. She concluded the Nefertiti Academy was
a gnat's short of totally pukka. It said they had training centres
in Birmingham, Manchester, Chelmsford and Basildon as well,
but she didn't know enough about those places to know if the
addresses were genuine. But judging by their Hammersmith
address, which was in one of the less gorgeous parts of Askew
Road, they weren't going to be palaces of learning.

She had a look on Google Street View and found the place in
the upstairs part of a neglected building whose street level was
a shabby-looking estate agents. That, she thought, was much
more Shannon's speed. It was certainly worth a try. She drove
down there, parked across the road, and settled down to watch
the door. By any reasonable calculation the day's course should
be ending soon, and if Shannon was there, it was better to try
and catch her coming out, than announce herself and risk her
having it away down some back exit.

Half an hour later, her vigil was rewarded. The door opened
and two Asian girls came out, arm-in-arm and heads together, and
walked off down the road. After a pause, two white girls and –
surprise, surprise – a tall youth came out, paused talking for a
moment, then split up, the youth and one of the girls one way,
the other girl walking to the nearby bus stop where she waited,
fidgeting from foot to foot in the cold wind. Another pause, and
another female figure came out, so bundled up in a quilted coat

and a woolly hat with lappets that Hart almost missed her. It was as she walked away, hands stuffed in her pockets, that she gave what seemed like a nervous look around, and Hart saw her face.

The girl turned down Becklow Road. Hart slipped into gear and followed her, and caught up just as Shannon was turning into the gate of a terraced house, two storeys and a basement, which was obviously divided into flats. *Gotcha!* Hart thought. She idled past, noting that Shannon was going down the basement steps, and then had to find a parking space. Fortunately some of the residents were still out at work so she was able to snag a residents'-only space and slap the ON POLICE BUSINESS notice in her windscreen.

Moments later she was facing a considerably startled Shannon, still in her coat but with the hat off, who opened the door, looked at Hart blankly for a moment, said, 'Oh fuck!' and tried to close it again.

Hart's booted foot was in the way. She smiled and said, 'Too late, babe. C'mon, don't get antsy, I'm not here officially. I just wanted to find out if you're all right. Can I come in?'

And Shannon, with an air of recognizing inevitability when it jumped up and peed on your leg, let her in.

FIFTEEN

More Sinned Against than Sinning

Some nifty footwork on the part of Lessop, comparing census returns and electoral rolls, established that the householder at number 24 Colville Avenue had been there for thirty-five years, and had therefore been next-door neighbour to the Vickerys.

They were a Mr and Mrs Clavering, Bernard and Georgette, in their late eighties. Lessop, who did the initial phone contact, said the woman had a dead posh accent, and combining that with the size of the house, Slider sent Atherton to interview them – *him wot could talk the lingo, orright?*

The houses in Colville Avenue were a mixed bunch, from 1850s cottages through late-Victorian detached to a rash of 1930s maisonettes, and a couple of oddities slapped up post war where a bomb had dropped. Numbers 22 and 24 were detached, solid two-storey, late-Victorian, yellow brick and Welsh slate, with what looked like original dormers in the roofs, making them probably six-bedroom properties. Atherton noted that they were still single-occupancy. In an earlier age they would have been divided up into flats or even bedsits, but the wheel had turned and Shepherd's Bush was attracting more wealthy people now, people who couldn't afford Notting Hill, but still wanted a big house with high ceilings and 'original feachers' as the estate agents called them – cornices, doors and fireplaces. He also noted, with a little more interest, that number 22 was directly behind 15 Laburnum Avenue: their gardens backed on to each other.

The old lady who opened the door certainly had a cut-glass accent. 'Oh yes,' she said, 'they rang to say you were coming.' Atherton observed her taking mental note of his suit, and then, tellingly, his shoes. Evidently he passed muster, for she smiled and said, 'Do come in.'

It was certainly a big house – the hall was the size of most people's principal reception room these days. It had stairs to one side, a door to the left and another straight ahead, with a passage off at right angles leading, one assumed, to the kitchen region. Mrs Clavering led him straight ahead into the living room, which had French windows looking onto a well-kept garden. 'Please sit down,' she said, gesturing towards a vast chesterfield, and taking a chair facing it, on which she perched very upright.

She was tiny, her face wrinkled like a store apple, and she had evidently had difficulty in applying her make-up, for the lipstick was askew, one eyebrow was darker than the other, and the blusher had not been blended in, giving her a clownlike look – except that her natural air of authority made it impossible to find it amusing. She was neatly dressed in skirt, silk blouse and knitted jacket, with pearls, and most notably was wearing polished shoes rather than slippers.

The house smelled cold and stale, and Atherton did not need a detective's eyes to see that dust was thick on every surface. The grate contained the cold ashes of a fire that had not been burning very recently, on top of which several used tissues and an apple core were awaiting the final translation; and in a dim corner a forgotten vase of flowers had shrivelled to brown mummification. But she had got herself up in full fig, and he would have been willing to bet she did so every day, as a matter of course. *One of the old school*, he thought. Slider would probably have called her 'old county'. The big, cold, dusty house reared round her, too much for her to cope with; but it was her home, and she would live there, whatever the struggle, and pride would keep her warm.

'Is your husband here, ma'am?' he asked, the 'ma'am' slipping out without his volition. 'I had rather hoped to speak to both of you.'

'My husband is in a home,' she said, without emotion. She would never ask for sympathy. 'Looking after him became too much for me. He has dementia, so I'm afraid he wouldn't be much help to your enquiries. He doesn't really remember anything very much now.'

'I'm so sorry—' Atherton began, but she waved it away with a small queenly gesture.

'I understand you want to know what I remember of the Vickerys.'

*   *   *

The Vickerys – David, Caroline and Melissa – had moved in only two years after the Claverings; but Mrs Clavering's father had owned the house before, and it was where she had been born, so she had known the road all her life.

'Next door was rather a mess,' she said. 'There was an old couple there, the Sweetings, when Bernard and I took over this house, and they'd rather let things go.' She said it with no self-consciousness, Atherton noted. She evidently did not think of herself as an old person, or of her house as less than pristine. 'They died within months of each other and the house went on the market.'

'And the Vickerys bought it,' he helped her along.

She gave him a cool look that said she didn't need helping, and continued, 'We liked the look of them when they came to see the house. They were in their late twenties, I suppose, a very nice-looking couple. David, in fact, was strikingly handsome, very dark, lean, charismatic. We were glad it was a young couple. We hoped they'd take care of the house. It's not good to have a neglected property next door.'

'And what about his wife – what was she like?' Atherton asked.

'Caroline was a sweet person. Fair, quiet, rather shy. Surprisingly so, since she'd been a nursery teacher before she married. But Melissa, their little girl, was about five or six then, so she couldn't have taught for long before she had her. She talked about going back to work now that Melissa was at school, but I gathered that there was no need for her to work – they were quite well-off. And I'm not sure she had the energy for it. She was always a bloodless creature, always seemed rather *ailing*, you know. Very pale, with that limp, fair hair. She always seemed to be getting colds and headaches.' Mrs Clavering had been staring at nothing as she remembered, but now she looked up, sharply. 'Of course, we learned later that she *was* ailing. She died dreadfully young. But one didn't know that at the time. I'm just giving you my impression of her.'

'Were you friends?' he asked.

She considered. 'A little more than neighbours, a little less than friends. We had them in for drinks, for dinner sometimes, we babysat for Melissa once or twice. But I wouldn't say we were very close. There was quite an age difference. Bernard and I were in our fifties, and we had our own circle. But we liked them – were fond of them, even – and we tried to be good neighbours.'

'What did David do for a living?'

'He was a design engineer, and apparently quite brilliant. An inventor. It was a little out of my league—' she moved a deprecating hand – 'but I understand some of his innovations were quite important. Some kind of new valve that revolutionized car engines, for instance. And something to do with the guidance system for those robots that land on the moon and Mars and so on. I can't remember much about them, but he earned a great deal of money from his patents and licences. A very great deal. He worked tremendously hard. He had a study at the top of the house, and we'd see the lights burning up there late into the night.'

'That must have been difficult for Caroline,' Atherton suggested.

'It must have been a lonely life for her,' Mrs Clavering agreed. She pondered a moment. 'I've always thought it important in a marriage that there's a certain equality, that each partner brings a strength to the table. I didn't see that with them. She was a sweet girl, but he was an extraordinary person. I had the impression that she worshipped him but didn't understand him. That's not healthy. And he could be quite brusque with her. She sometimes seemed quite cowed by him.'

'Do you think he was ever physically abusive?' Atherton asked.

She look affronted. 'Good heavens, no. Why do modern minds always jump to that? There are more ways of being cruel than with fists. But I don't think he was *consciously* cruel. He was on a different intellectual plane, that's all,' she concluded. 'He must have been hard to live with.'

'What about the little girl?'

Mrs Clavering gave a minute shrug. 'She was just a little girl. Nothing unusual about her. She had nice manners, was always tidy and well turned out. Rather shy. I can't say I noticed her very much. I had grandchildren of my own who were much more fascinating. As far as I could see she was never any trouble.'

'Did her father have a good relationship with her?'

'I really couldn't say. He never talked about her, but then, when we were in company with him, it was at grown-up parties, and children were not a topic. He might have been devoted, for all I knew. The difference in generations meant we didn't see that side of them.'

Atherton took her back to the last year of the Vickerys' residence there. Caroline's death was quite sudden. 'Pancreatic cancer. It takes them off horribly quickly. We hardly knew she was ill when she was gone.'

'How did David Vickery take it?'

A slight shrug. 'We offered all the help we could, but there wasn't much we could do. Of course, he worked from home, so that was one problem that didn't arise – childcare. I think they rather turned in on themselves, and we didn't see them . . . oh, for months.'

'It's Melissa I'm particularly interested in. Did she have a lot of friends?'

She gave him a patient look. 'She was just a child who lived next door. I had no reason to take notice of her.'

Atherton nodded, and sought for another approach. 'Do you remember the case of a little girl who went missing, who lived in the next road, Laburnum Avenue? It happened that summer, the last one the Vickerys lived next door.'

She frowned. 'I have a vague recollection of it. It wasn't the sort of news story I would pay much attention to. Why do you ask?'

'Because the girl who went missing, Amanda, referred to Melissa as her "best friend". She told the other girls at school that she was spending a lot of time with her.'

Mrs Clavering looked at him blankly, waiting to know what this had to do with her.

'We know that Melissa didn't visit Amanda's house, so the inference is that Amanda spent her time at Melissa's.'

The word 'inference' seemed to reassure her. 'I'm afraid I wouldn't . . .' she began, and then stopped. 'Wait, though. Now I think about it, I do remember a time when I was seeing *two* little girls playing in the garden next door. That would be not long before they went away, and it must have been in the summer, during the summer holidays, or they'd have been at school, wouldn't they?'

'What were they doing?'

'Just sitting on a rug, talking. Exchanging secrets,' she added with a deprecating smile, to show that she didn't fully approve of flights of fancy. 'Sitting with their heads together. The Vickerys' garden was dreadfully overgrown – they'd never been very interested in gardening, and since Caroline died, David hadn't bothered at all. It was upsetting to us, because we were keen gardeners, and weeds don't recognize fences. And I'd often look down from our bedroom window and deplore the state it was in. That's why I remember seeing them there together, day after day, on a rug, with the grass far too long around them. Like sisters.'

'You mean they looked alike?'

'From that distance – same size, same age, the same sort of mouse-fair hair, cut in the same bob. Of course, I've no idea who she was – whether she was this other child you're speaking of.'

'Did you ever see her close up?'

'Not that I'm aware.' She seemed a little impatient. 'I don't suppose I'd have recognized her if I passed her in the street. And it wasn't long after that that they left, and I haven't thought about them from that day to this.'

'You mean they moved house?'

'David took Melissa on holiday – it *was* August, you know. He came one morning to let us know. We used to keep an eye on their house when they went away and vice versa. We had each other's keys, in case of emergency.'

'Did he say where they were going?'

'I have an impression it was Devon or Dorset or something like that. For three weeks, to give Melissa a change of scene before she went back to school. But in fact they never came back. The next thing we knew, there was a "for sale" notice outside.'

'Had he mentioned to you that he was thinking of moving?'

'No, not at all. I suppose it was a sudden decision.'

'So you were surprised?'

'We were a little hurt that he didn't bother to say goodbye – not so much as a note through the post. But of course they were only neighbours, not really friends. Perhaps once he got away from it, he realized the house held only sad memories for him.' She shrugged. 'I don't know.'

'Did you ever see him again, or Melissa?'

'No. I don't know if he came back in the time before the house was sold, but if he did, I didn't see him.' She looked at him, waiting for enlightenment. 'Are you going to tell me what all this is about?'

'It's about the little girl who went missing, Amanda Knight. We'd like to talk to Melissa, but we don't know where she is. We hoped you might have some more information about the Vickerys that would help us find her.'

'I'm sorry. I don't know where they went,' Mrs Clavering said. 'I could have told you that from the beginning,' she added, a trifle impatiently.

'Anything you can tell us about them may be helpful.'

'I can't imagine how.'

Atherton ducked that one. 'Do you know if they had any relatives – the Vickerys? Brothers or sisters, uncles or aunts?' She shook her head. 'David, for instance – did he ever talk about a brother? Please think for a moment. It might be important.'

'You hope to trace Melissa that way?' She thought, evidently quite thoroughly. 'They had visitors,' she said musingly, 'just like any other couple, but whether they were friends or relatives I couldn't say. I'm trying to think – did Caroline ever mention . . .? I talked to her more than him.' She frowned with effort. 'Yes, we did once have a conversation about how brilliant David was – that was a frequent topic with her – and she said that he came from a high-flying family. She said, "They've both done terribly well for themselves, him and his brother." Something like that.'

'Did she mention the brother's name?'

'I don't remember. I don't think so. Perhaps if I'd been more interested I'd have asked, but her conversation was not very stimulating. She was such a pallid creature. One tended to smile and nod and think of other things.'

'She didn't mention what the brother did?'

'Not that I remember. You must understand, it was a long time ago, and I didn't pay that much attention.'

'Well, if you do remember anything else, however trivial it may seem to you, please let me know,' Atherton said, producing his card. 'It isn't always apparent at the time, but it could mean something in the whole pattern of things.'

'Like a piece of a jigsaw,' she said with a smile. 'You can't tell it's a nose until you put it into place.'

He smiled back. 'Exactly. So please, anything at all.'

She rose to see him out, and gave a gracious bow of the head. 'You may be sure I will.'

'What do you *want*?' Shannon demanded, with more irritation than fear, though there was certainly a wariness at the back of it.

Hart was taking care to keep between her and the door. Shannon was home, and didn't look like scarpering, but it didn't hurt to be vigilant. It was a tiny place, typical rental, a bed-sitting-room-kitchen with a door to one side presumably leading to the bathroom – or more likely shower-room. It had cheap beige carpet and was meagrely furnished from IKEA, but it was clean and warm, and Hart could guess how much it meant to Shannon as a place of her own.

'Like I said, I just wanted to find out if you're all right,' Hart said.

'Will be, if you'll just leave me alone,' Shannon said crossly. 'New start, remember? Make a fresh start, you said, forget about all that other stuff. Well, I'm trying to, all right?'

'I know. The Nefertiti Beauty School,' said Hart.

'Academy,' Shannon corrected.

'And this flat. Very nice. Who was it said that, about making a fresh start? It wasn't me.'

Shannon rolled her eyes. 'You *lot*,' she said, as though it was not worth correcting.

Hart smiled kindly. 'Ah, well, you see, there's lots and then there's lots. There's us, at Shepherd's Bush, who got you out of the hands of the bad men and did our best to get them put away. And then there's other lots, high-ups, who don't necessarily talk to us, or tell us what's going on.'

'I dunno what you're talking about.'

'*I* didn't tell you to make a fresh start. Not without clearing up old business first. But now I hear you've withdrawn your testimony. Is that right, babe? You not gonna help us take them bastards down?'

Shannon didn't answer at once. She studied Hart with some apprehension. 'Who sent you?' she asked at last.

'Nobody sent me. I sent meself.'

'Bollocks!'

'S'trufe. I told you, this is not official.'

'How did you find me?'

'Intuition. And a little help from your friends. Why? Are you in hiding?'

'No, but they said . . .' She stopped herself, warily.

'What? Said what?'

'Not to talk about it to anyone.'

'You can talk to me. I'm on *your* side.' She glanced around. 'Nice place you've got here. Small, but nice. I know what places cost, even gaffs this small. And that course you're doing – got to pay for that, haven't you?'

'Once I'm qualified, I'll make a really good living.'

'Yeah, maybe, but you got to pay first. Earn later. Where'd you get the dosh from, Shannon?'

'My sister,' she said, not quite quickly enough.

Hart shook her head. 'No, you didn't. Try again. Your auntie, maybe? Auntie Hallie?'

'Yeah, that's what I meant. Auntie give it me.'

'No, she didn't. She don't even know where you went. I talked to both of 'em. Don't lie to me, babe, cos I'm one step ahead of you all the way.'

'Oh, leave me alone!' Shannon cried, half angry, half alarmed. 'I'm doing all right now, and you're gonna spoil it all!'

'Just talk to me. Why did you withdraw your testimony?'

'I wasn't sure any more. I dunno what I saw.'

'You saw Kaylee being thrown off the roof,' Hart said brutally.

'I never!'

'You told me you did. And I believed you.'

Shannon looked down, twisting her hands together miserably. 'You don't know what it's like. They keep asking the same thing over and over. They keep talking at you and talking at you till you can't remember what you saw and what you didn't. They tell you that's not what you said last time, and you can't remember what you *did* say, and in the end you just – don't – know – any more.'

'But you do know, really,' Hart said gently.

'I don't!' Shannon looked up in desperation. 'Look, I'd been drinking. I'd been doing charlie. I'd had a couple of E's. I was out of my fucking head, if you want to know. I didn't know if it was Christmas or last week. I prob'ly couldn't've told you my own name. I was out of it. And Kaylee was never even there that night.'

'Is that what they told you?'

'They *proved* it. She was out some place in the country with a boyfriend. She got run over. She was never *there!*'

Hart felt a deep sadness come over her for this girl, caught in the middle of things. And for the first time, a tremor of doubt. 'When you told us about Kaylee being chucked over the roof, you were pretty sure about it,' she said quietly.

'I made it up,' Shannon said. She withstood Hart's steady gaze remarkably well.

'Where'd you get the money for all this?' Hart asked next.

The gaze wavered. 'They were really nice to me. Nobody's ever been nice to me like that before, not, like, you know, *proper* people. They said they didn't blame me. They could've sent me to prison for false witness or something, but they said it wasn't my fault, I'd got caught up in the drugs and everything, and they was gonna give me a second chance. To go away and make a fresh start. So I went to Auntie's, but I knew I didn't want to be a waitress. I knew what I wanted to do. And when the money come, I done it.'

'Become a beautician,' said Hart. 'It was you and Kaylee's dream.'

'Yeah.'

'But Kaylee's dead.'

'I know.' A tear squeezed out, and Shannon's lip trembled. 'I can't help her. But if you make trouble, they'll take the money back and I'll be fucked,' she said miserably. 'I don't wanna go back to the way I was. I wanna have a good life.'

'Babe,' said Hart with infinite gentleness, 'I don't wanna make trouble. I want you to have your fresh start. Good for you, girl! All I ever wanted was justice for Kaylee. I swear on my mother's grave you won't get in trouble, but just tell me the truth, so I know. Just so I know, all right? Did you see Kaylee thrown off the roof?'

'I don't *know!*' Shannon wailed. 'I was out of my head that night, I don't remember. It's all just a big blur.'

'Think about it, girl. Just think.'

'I can't think any more,' Shannon said wearily. 'I done thinking. I don't remember nothing about that night, and that's the truth.'

'D'you swear to me? Mother's grave?'

'I never saw nothing. Mother's grave. I made it up.'

SIXTEEN

How do you Solve a Problem Like Diarrhoea?

The merry-go-round of English weather delivered a mild wet day on Tuesday, with a sky like damp towels. Atherton had brought in a whole box of Krispy Kremes, to prime the morning motor. 'Including two plain ones for you, guv,' he told Slider as he came out to join the throng. Slider didn't like things on or in them. He thought pink icing and sprinkles was a terrible thing to do to a self-respecting doughnut, like putting clothes on a dog. A doughnut, he said, had a natural dignity which should never be violated.

Coffee and tea went round with the reports from the previous day.

'Don't you find that provocative?' Atherton prompted, when he'd finished with Mrs Clavering's evidence. 'Vickery selling the house so suddenly, like that?'

'What, are you thinking *he* had something to do with it, now?' Swilley objected. 'Why him? Why not the Pope or President Obama?'

'The Pope's name's not Vickery,' McLaren growled through custard filling, but Swilley silenced him with a look.

'It's not just the coincidence of the name,' Atherton said. 'Look, if he went away for three weeks, and school usually starts around the seventh of September, that brings it back to around the 18th of August, doesn't it? The date Amanda went missing.'

'That's the *latest* they could go. But Mrs Clavering didn't know the date. You don't know they didn't go earlier than that,' said Gascoyne, reasonably.

'And you don't know he was even meaning for her to *go* back to school the first day,' said McLaren, swallowing valiantly. 'Parents are always keeping kids off school for holidays.'

'We know she *did* go back to school,' Connolly said. 'Just not the same school.'

'Look,' said Swilley patiently, 'even if the date *is* significant, isn't it more likely Melissa was upset about her friend going missing, and he took her away to take her mind off it?'

There was a brief silence in acknowledgement of the argument.

Atherton rallied first. 'But then why did he suddenly sell the house?'

'Like Mrs Clavering said, probably it just had sad memories for them, which they realized once they got away,' said Swilley. 'I'd buy that.'

'It doesn't seem a bit sudden to you?'

'We don't know he hadn't been thinking about it for ages,' said Connolly. 'Only that he didn't discuss it with Mrs Clavering. And why should he? D'you tell your neighbours all your biz?'

'True,' said Atherton reluctantly. 'That's the trouble with this case, everything's so long ago, you can' be sure of anything. So where does that leave us?'

'We have to find Melissa,' said Connolly. 'She was there, she'll be the one that knows.'

'So we're no better off than we were yesterday.'

'We've got an area to look in,' said Connolly.

'What about this brother?' said LaSalle. 'Could that be our Mr Vickery?'

'Even if it is,' said Atherton, 'I don't see that it gets us any closer to Melissa. We don't know where he is, either. That's just displacing the search by one person.'

'For me,' said Swilley, 'it's the father that did it, no mystery about that.' There were murmurs of agreement. 'What we don't know is the why and the how.'

'I can't see how we're ever going to know,' said Gascoyne. 'He's dead, and he's not likely to have told anybody else. Finding Melissa might tell us more about Amanda's state of mind, but is that going to get us any closer to the why and how?'

Slider could see his troops were getting discouraged. He caught Hart's eye – she had been sitting quietly at the back. She had reported to him privately already, and he reckoned there was nothing like a toothache for taking your mind off a stomach ache. 'Hart,' he said, 'tell us about your day.'

She stood up, and related her interview with Shannon. It was received in silence.

Then: 'She's been nobbled,' said Fathom.

'Let's not say anything we wouldn't want to be heard outside this room,' Slider warned. 'Hart, what did you think about her?'

'I dunno,' she said. 'I started off thinking she'd been nobbled, what with the money and everything—'

'Bought off,' said Fathom.

'Shut up,' Swilley told him sharply.

'But the more I listened to her, the more I thought, she really doesn't know any more. And it's probably true what she said – she'd been on the vodka and snorting charlie, so she could easily've been imagining things. Or maybe not even that – just dreamed it up afterwards, then forgot she'd dreamed it. You know what they're like.'

They did. In a state of terminal confusion – and very, very suggestible. Slider felt a pang of doubt. Had they pushed her into remembering what they wanted her to remember?

'In any case,' Hart concluded, looking at Slider, 'she ain't a witness any more, that's for sure. *I* wouldn't find it easy to believe her now.'

'Well, that's the point, innit,' said McLaren, disgruntled. 'They've done her like a kipper. Done *us* an' all. They didn't like us putting the finger on Mr—'

'McLaren!' Slider said sharply, and his mouth snapped shut. 'Let's not give the conspiracy theories an outing. We did our job, to the best of our ability. Things didn't work out as we expected. We move on.'

'Yeah, but—'

'Maybe,' he went on firmly, 'we were wrong. Has that ever occurred to you?' They all looked at him. Porson's words rankled in the back of his mind. *You're too quick to think the worst of the higher echelongs.* Had he been trying to be too clever? Was vanity his sin? These were people's lives they played with every day. It could induce a god complex without one realizing. *I just have a feeling.* They developed a copper's instinct over the years, a little voice, and mostly it turned out to be right, but that didn't mean it *couldn't* be wrong. 'Maybe we were wrong,' he said again, looking around them, meeting gaze after gaze.

But we weren't wrong, said the expressions looking back at him. 'There's such a thing as being in the game too long,' he said. He hadn't known he was going to say it, but he went with it to see where it took him. 'You can start to jump at shadows. See things that aren't there. This Amanda Knight business might be just what we need. Something we can examine without pressure, without haste. No careers rest on it. But that can be a good thing. I want a result on this, and I know it's going to be difficult. But she deserves justice like anyone else. Just because she's been dead twenty-five years doesn't mean it matters any less. So let's do this. Be thorough, be forensic – be *right*.'

He didn't often make speeches, but hearing it come back to him he was rather impressed. So were they. Connolly applauded, and they all joined in for a beat or two.

Atherton lounged over to him as the group broke up. 'Where did that come from?' he asked ironically, but Slider could see he was impressed too.

'Deep inside,' he replied in like manner, thumping the manly chest. 'This is the start of a new era. We're going to kick bottom. We're going to take this case by the seat of its pants and look it in the face.'

'We're going to a contortionists' convention?'

'I'm in charge here,' Slider said grittily, 'and as soon as I know what the questions are, I'm going to want some answers.'

'That's fighting talk.'

'You'd better believe it.'

'Bravo. Show me a man who laughs at defeat, and I'll show you a chiropodist with a twisted sense of humour.'

Refreshed by this interlude, Slider gave him a stern look. 'What are you going to do now?'

'Look for Melissa Vickery,' Atherton said meekly. 'In a forensic and thorough manner. Are you going out?' he added as Slider headed for the door.

'I'm going to Cumae,' he said.

Gascoyne had a telephone call from Pat Bexley. 'You know, Amanda Knight's aunt? You came to visit me last week?'

'Yes, of course I remember. How can I help you?'

'Well, I wondered whether you'd managed to find Maggie, my sister Margaret. I mean, with all your resources—'

'Yes, we did trace her. My boss went to see her and had a talk with her.'

'Broke the news to her?'

'Yes, of course.' He couldn't discuss the interview with anyone else, and tried to distract her. 'What can I help you with today?'

'Well, I wondered if you could give me her address and phone number. Or phone number at any rate. I'd like to get in touch with her. It must be a terrible time for her right now. After all these years – and I know she must have suspected Amanda was dead, but that's not the same as knowing, is it? She must need someone to support her, and family's family when all's said and done.'

'I'm afraid I wouldn't be allowed to give you that information—' Gascoyne began, but she jumped back in.

'And there'll be a funeral won't there? I mean at some point. She'll need help with that. She shouldn't be alone at a time like this.'

'I can't give you her contact details,' Gascoyne said firmly, to stem the tide, 'but what I can do is give your contact details to her, and tell her that you want to be in touch with her. How would that be?'

'Oh! Right – well, that'd be better than nothing,' Mrs Bexley said, with hope in her voice.

'I'll just run it past my boss to make sure it doesn't breach any protocols,' said Gascoyne.

'Thank you. And do you know when the funeral will be?'

'I haven't any information about that at present. I don't think the body has been released yet.'

'Oh. Well, give Maggie my details and tell her to get in touch. Tell her I really want to hear from her.'

'I will.'

'And tell her, I know we parted brass rags, and there was bad blood between us, but that was a long time ago. It's all water under the bridge, and I've got no hard feelings. Forgive and forget, I say, especially when you're up against it. Blood is thicker than water, after all, and I want to be there for her in her hour of need. Family ought to stick together at times like this, and Amanda *was* my niece. And *she's* my sister, no matter what. Tell, her, will you?'

'I'll tell her,' Gascoyne said, writing it all down.

After he had rung off, Slider passed his desk on his way out and, looking over his shoulder, said, 'Practising for the Annual Cliché Competition?'

Gascoyne explained. 'Shall I pass it on to Mrs Knight?'

'Yes, all right. I expect she'll welcome the chance to bury the hatchet. What's this about the funeral?'

'I said I didn't think the body had been released yet.'

'We don't really need it for anything now. Look it up, will you?'

Gascoyne found the file on-line, and said, 'Oh, here it is, sir – we haven't had the DNA test back yet. The doc didn't fast-track it, so I expect it's caught up in the queue somewhere.'

'All right, well goose them up a bit, will you? We ought not to keep that poor woman waiting longer than we have to.'

'Will do, sir.'

Despite the rise in temperature outside, Connie Bindman's basement was horribly cold. She had added two woollen scarves to her usual polar gear, one round her neck and one tied over her head. 'I keep asking them to fix the heating,' she said to Slider, 'but it's always the same answer. "Budget," they say. "You'll have to wait your turn," they say. I tell them paper needs to be kept dry, but they don't care. I think they'd be happy if the archive would just go away, and me with it. I swear to you, I wouldn't be surprised if I tried to go home one evening, and found the door at the top of the stairs boarded up and the building scheduled for demolition.'

'If I ever hear it's going to be, I promise I'll come and check that you got out,' said Slider.

She beamed. 'You're a good man, Bill Slider. One of the gentry. What can I do for you, darling? I had one of your girls down here last week, looking for a misper. Are you still on that?'

He nodded. 'It's developed ramifications. One of which is that the missing girl was allegedly best friends with a girl called Melissa Vickery.'

'Oho!' said Connie. 'As in Detective Superintendent Edgar Vickery?'

'I don't know. That's why I came to pick your brains.'

She had an access of caution. 'What do you mean by "allegedly"?'

'Con, this case is twenty-five years old. Everything's alleged. People who were children then are middle-aged now, people who were young are old. And people who were grown-up are dead.'

Connie winced visibly. 'Don't be so dramatic, darling. Twenty-five years is nothing in the scheme of things.'

'In the scheme of *me* it's a lot of water under a lot of bridges. And I want a result on this very badly.'

She gave him a shrewd look. 'Don't tell me it's a rehabilitation thing? You shouldn't pay too much attention to those children upstairs. They throw their little toys out of the pram, but you and I, dear boy, we've seen it all before. We've survived it. In a few years there'll be different children with different toys. But the Job is always the Job.'

'I'm not sure it is any more,' he said dolefully. 'They keep changing things. In the end, there's nothing left that you recognize.'

'I can see you're in defeatist mood. That's not like you. Don't tell me they've finally knocked the cheek out of you? Not Bill Slider, the Met's answer to James Dean?'

He had to grin. 'You do me good, Con! Everyone should have a course of Connie Bindman prescribed every so often—'

'Like a purgative?' she interrupted wryly. 'Thank you so much, my cherub. But you really don't want to start venting bodily secretions down in this morgue, I can tell you. Have you any idea how many flights of stairs separate us from a WC at this moment? It's a good job I have iron control over everything, including my bladder. But all things have their season, so shall we get on with some work? What do you want to know?'

'Vickery. Kellington and Vickery,' he added, for good measure.

Connie produced two folding chairs – rejects from one of the conference room make-overs upstairs – and set them up, and they sat facing each other, close, knee to knee, in an unconscious bid to preserve body heat.

'Kellington was Vickery's boy,' she pronounced.

'You mean . . .?' Slider asked, with a raised eyebrow.

She looked annoyed. '*No*! Don't be obvious, Bill Slider. You're better than that.'

'I was surprised, that's all. I've met Kellington.'

'Appearance proves nothing,' she said briskly. 'But you're right. It wasn't that. Kellington worshipped him, that's all. He was a big, slow, dumb giant – as stupid as it's possible to be in the Met and still get on – so, not dangerously stupid, just . . .'

'Lacking in imagination?'

'Yes. Good.'

'That's what Mitchell Baxter said.'

'He's a good boy, Mitchell,' said Connie. The 'boy' was close to retirement, but Slider let it go. 'Yes, lacking imagination. Whereas Vickery was brilliant. Quick. Inventive. Bags of imagination. I used to think of them rather like those two chaps in *Of Mice And Men*, what where they called – George and Lennie?'

'Good lord!'

Her brows snapped down. 'Not literally, fool! Just the relationship. Kellington did Vickery's bidding, Vickery protected Kellington. Kellington thought Vickery was the cat's pyjamas, Vickery explained things that were above Kellington's brain-grade.'

'This is good. More!'

'Vickery was one of those wiry, restless, fizzing people, who tend to go off at the wrong time if they're not given enough to do. An unstable firework. Impulsive.'

'Crooked?'

'No, I wouldn't say that. Perhaps a bit too brilliant for his own good. It made him impatient with people who didn't see things the way he saw them.' She stopped, brooding over memories.

Slider thought about that, concluding that crooked was as crooked did. An impatient, brilliant person might cut corners to get the hard-of-thinking to the destination that he could make in a single bound. If the destination was a good one, he might justify corner-cutting very happily to himself. Hadn't they all done things like that from time to time? Hadn't *he* gone to interview Gideon Marler against direct orders from his borough commander?

'Where is he now?' Slider asked.

She came back. 'Who? Oh, Vickery? I can't tell you. He left the Job a long time ago.'

'Left, how?'

'Just resigned. Had enough, I suppose. Burned out, maybe – your brilliant ones often do. You should watch your pet Jim Atherton that way.'

'Atherton's all right,' Slider replied, meaning that he had had his breakdown, years back, after being knifed on the Job. Done it, come back, got the T-shirt.

But she gave a wry smile and said, 'Yes, I know – he's got you. Equally, though, you've got him. It doesn't do to get too reliant on one person.'

'We're not talking about me,' Slider said hastily. 'When did Vickery leave?'

'October 1990,' she said without hesitation.

'How the heck—?'

'I looked it up, simpleton! I knew you'd be back. That file didn't have nearly enough in it, so I knew you'd want to pick the Bindman brains. Vickery handed in his notice, and left at the end of October 1990. Kellington went on to retirement – but you said you'd seen him, so you'll know that?'

'Yes,' said Slider. 'Did Vickery have any family? Wife, children?'

'He was never married while he was in the Job. Afterwards, I couldn't tell you. He was a noted cocksman, in trouble for it from time to time, when he didn't keep it zipped when he ought to have. Witnesses confused. Evidence compromised and so on.'

Slider nodded understanding. 'As to children – I never heard he had any. Probably *he* didn't, either.'

It was a joke, and Slider smiled. 'What about other family?' he asked casually, his mind on tiptoe. 'Brothers? Sisters?'

But she wasn't fooled. She gave him a wise old grin and said, 'If the girl's name was Melissa Vickery, we're not looking for a sister, are we? Or the surname would be different. Did Edgar Vickery have a niece called Melissa? I couldn't tell you.'

Slider's disappointment was sharp.

But she continued. 'He did have a brother, however. Who could well have been married and have had children.'

'Name?'

'I don't know his name. But what I heard was that this brother was brilliant as well, and our Edgar was intensely proud of him. Some high-flier in the scientific community. A generation further on and he'd probably have been one of these IT wizards. The Vickerys had brains, that was Edgar's boast.' She looked at Slider thoughtfully. 'Kellington might know. He and Vickery worked together a lot. He probably talked about his brother to him. Almost certainly, I'd have thought.'

But if there was anything funny about the case, Kellington was probably involved, and he didn't want to go to him now, before he had his ducks in a row. Little niggles were working away in his mind, but he didn't really know what he suspected, or of whom. All he knew was that, like Atherton, he was made uneasy by coincidences.

'And,' Connie went on, still studying him, 'if there's something funny about Vickery in relation to his brother or this case, Kellington might not tell you. He might prefer to be a good dog. These rather stupid people can be loyal beyond all reason.'

'You could be right,' said Slider. He mused. 'Were they a local family?' he asked. 'One of my new boys, LaSalle, says Vickery is a local name.'

'Oh yes,' said Connie. 'Born and bred. Came from Godolphin or Coningham – one of those roads. LaSalle's local, too – I suppose you knew that. Not his name, of course. His grandmother married a French refugee during the war. Scandalous! She was a Pierce before that. *That*'s a Shepherd's Bush name, too.'

He had to laugh. 'You really do know everything, don't you?'

'Except how to get those bastards upstairs to fix the heating,' Connie said sourly.

SEVENTEEN
O Tempora O Maurice

Joanna was depping in the West End again, and Slider had a happy couple of hours being a father. Dad had already fed George by the time he got home, but he played with his son on the floor with his Lego junior construction kit, then gave him his bath, tucked him up in bed and read to him. His favourite bedtime book at the moment was *Goodnight Moon*, which was so soporific Slider had difficulty in staying awake long enough to see George off.

George would be three next month, Slider thought as he went downstairs to prepare his own supper, and was due for some more grown-up brain-fare. He didn't hold out much hope, however. Bedtime rituals were exactly that – change them at your peril. When he himself had been very small, he always had to stroke the dog goodnight before he went to bed, which had driven his mother crazy because it meant she had had to wash his hands again. The dog loved to roll in cowshit, and she was convinced he would suck his thumb during the night and give himself dysentery. Goodnight Dog. Hello A&E.

Over supper, the thoughts he had sent out for a walk while he enjoyed himself with George came back to plague him. He tried to ignore them, but they sent his appetite packing. The washing machine had come on on the timer, and made an unholy racket – Wagner's Rinse Cycle, as Joanna was wont to call it – so he gave up on food and went into the drawing room. He tried to read, but the words wouldn't grip, so he watched a bit of *Mad Men* on the boxed set Dad and Lydia had given him last Christmas. Thanks to the vagaries of work, he was still only halfway through it. It was quite good as a distraction because he could never remember who anyone was or how they related to anyone else, which had his forensic skills running around until they were tired.

And when Joanna came home, he had the gin already in the glass, waiting for the tonic, knowing that she would be both tired and 'up' and would need winding down before bed.

'How was it?' he asked, bringing her the glass on the sofa.

'Ah, lovely! Thanks. I've been thinking about this all the way home. The show? Oh, much the same. Flippin' chaos held in check by the brilliance of the musicians. The MD was off tonight, so we had the AMD, who's a keyboardist in real life, which is fine by us, but it put the lead soprano in a temper, because she's having it off with the MD and she's convinced he's seeing someone else whenever he's out of her sight. So she was obviously determined to make his life a misery by ignoring him – the AMD, I mean.'

'Why doesn't she just make the MD's life a misery?' Slider asked.

'Because she depends on him for work. She's not really that good, you see. But as long as he's bonking her, he has to come up with the jobs.'

Slider smiled. 'You're kidding me. It doesn't really work like that, does it?'

She raised her eyebrows. 'Have I taught you nothing? The MD is all powerful. He dispenses patronage. He can accept or reject a dep, for instance, on the basis of whether he likes them or not. Or whether they've sucked up to him enough on other occasions.'

'But this soprano – she must be able to sing the part?'

'Up to a point. What she has is decibels. She's got a voice like a power drill boring through sheet metal. She fills the theatre, all right. You can hear her in the back rows. Whether you'd *want* to hear her is another matter. But she's the darling of Classic FM, she's got recording contracts, and she can snub a poor humble AMD-keyboardist with impunity. Hey, have I told you the old joke? Why is being a lead soprano like staying in a cheap lodging house?'

'I don't know,' Slider said obediently.

'Because you can come in when you like and you don't have to worry about the key.'

'Ho-ho,' he said. She had finished her drink. 'Another?'

'No, thanks, I'd never sleep. How was work? You look frazzled.'

There was no fooling her. 'Hart found Shannon Bailey.'

'And?'

'She says she doesn't remember any more what she saw, if anything at all. She was on vodka and cocaine and everything's a blur.'

'I see. Well, that's possible, isn't it? Even likely.' She studied him. 'And she was all you had, wasn't she?'

'She was the only witness to Kaylee's death. Except that, without her testimony, there's no knowing if that's how Kaylee died. Or if she was even there. They've got a top forensic expert to say that her injuries were consistent with being hit by a car where she was found. So the whole roof thing is now officially just a junkie's drug-fuelled fantasy.'

'Officially? But you still think—'

'No. That's the problem. I now worry that I pushed her into it. Junkies are very suggestible. Young girls are suggestible. I got the answer I wanted.'

She looked troubled. 'What about the parties? The underage sex?'

'None of the other girls will testify. There may have been parties, they may have gone to them, but there's no evidence any of them had sex with anyone.'

'Oh, come on – why else would they be there?'

He shook his head at her. 'That's just innuendo. Give a dog a bad name and hang him. They could have been having Bible reading classes in there for all we know. A fine group of worthies trying to improve the lot of poor girls and set them on the strait and narrow. The Gladstones *de nos jours*.'

'Do you believe that?' Joanna asked, a touch raucously.

'Doesn't matter what I believe. In fact, I *shouldn't* believe. Facts, evidence, a proper case, that's what I have to have, or I'm not doing my job. I'm afraid,' he said slowly, coming to the hard part, squeezing it out, because she was his confessional and he needed her to understand, even when it hurt to tell her, 'that I *wasn't* doing my job. I was running a vendetta, because I was angry about Kaylee – her life, her death, and the fact that no one cared about either. I turned myself from a policeman into a vigilante.'

She nodded – acknowledgement rather than agreement. She

saw he was shaken – perhaps ashamed. This was a crisis in his life. She had been with him through aftermaths before, seen him depressed because, although he had caught the villain, it didn't make any difference to the victim. They were still dead. He didn't really have the robust temperament his job demanded, she thought. Pointless death troubled him too much. He should have been a farmer, and helped things grow. But he needed her now, and she had to come up with something, though she had no idea what. She opened her mouth and hoped something appropriate would pop out.

'I don't know if you did wrong or not,' she said. 'But if you did, the important thing is that you know it. That's how we grow – learning from our mistakes.' *Too much?* she wondered. He was looking at her, she thought, a trifle blankly. She couldn't tell if he was warmed by her words, or incredulous that she'd said them. 'Now you have to forgive yourself and move on,' she concluded. 'Otherwise, it's all a waste.' *Say something!* she urged him silently. *I don't know what I'm doing here!*

Finally, he nodded. 'You're right,' he said, and she almost sagged with relief. 'The Job is still the Job.'

She didn't know they were Connie Bindman's words. '*I* was going to say that,' she objected, to lighten the mood.

'I got it out of a cracker in the canteen,' he said.

'They have crackers in the canteen?'

'What else do you have your cheese on?'

Joking, she thought, put a layer of essential padding between the raw nerves and the world. He'd be all right now. 'Don't make me your straight man,' she said, standing up.

He stood too, and put his arms round her. 'Oh, you're anything but straight, I'm glad to say. Bed?'

'Are you all better now?' she asked suspiciously.

He pressed against her. 'Try me, and see.'

Hart was not there on Wednesday morning, but she rang in as soon as Slider was at his desk – how did she manage that? Some kind of second sight – and said, 'You don't need me for anything in particular, do you, boss?'

'I can manage. Why?'

'I rather not say.'

Slider frowned. 'Is this something to do with the matter we weren't going to talk about any more?'

'Maybe, maybe not. Depends how much you want to know.'

'I don't want to know,' Slider said. 'Also it's over. We gave it our best shot, and that's the end of it.'

'Well, maybe it is and—'

'Sergeant!' Slider said sharply. 'And remember, promotions are reversible.'

She weakened. 'I had an idea, that's all,' she said, without the sass. 'I'd like to follow it up.'

Slider sighed. 'You'd better tell me.'

'It's the other girls. I know they won't testify about the sex parties and the drugs and that, but if I could just get them to say that Kaylee was *there* that night, that throws this new forensic gig out the window, dunt it?'

'I'm afraid not. She could still have gone out to Harefield afterwards.'

'But if the big boys all say she *wasn't* there, and we can prove she was, they must be covering something up, mustn't they?'

'And who do you think would be believed, if it came to a straight contradiction. You've got nothing there, Hart. I'm sorry. Let it go.'

There was a silence. 'If you say so, boss.'

'I do.'

'Can I take a personal day, then? If you don't need me in.'

'What for?' Slider asked suspiciously.

'Oh, just girl things,' Hart said, chirpy again. 'You don't want me to spell 'em out, do you?'

'Certainly not. I'll mark you on holiday, then.'

'Ta, boss.'

'Just don't go poking sticks down holes,' Slider warned.

'Never!' said Hart, and rang off.

LaSalle came gangling in rather shyly, still uncertain as to how his new boss reacted to individual thought. Carver had liked things done his way. To him, initiative was the sound you made when you sneezed.

'I've been doing a bit of research, sir,' he said modestly. 'In the BD&M.'

Register of Births, Deaths and Marriages. Like many public records, it now had an online presence. Slider remembered long, peaceful hours at Katharine House when he was a detective constable, poring through the giant leather-bound ledgers in the hushed, library-smelling fastness. It was a wonderful way to keep out of your guv'nor's line of sight for a day. Alas, no more. Oh the times, oh the customs!

'Into?' he prompted.

'Vickery, sir. Knowing they were local made it easier. I got our Mr Vickery's date of birth from the records, then looked him up, got his parents, and went through with them to see if they had any other children. And there *was* a brother called David.' He lifted his eyes, hopeful for praise. *Good* orang-utan!

'Well done,' Slider said.

LaSalle relaxed and became expansive. 'Born 1952, sir, which made him 30 in 1982 when Mrs Clavering said the Vickerys moved into Colville Avenue – she said late twenties, so it's a fit all right. Our Mr Vickery, Edgar, was five years older, just right for idolising a brilliant younger brother. And . . .' He hesitated.

'Go on,' said Slider.

'Well, sir, maybe feeling he had to protect him. If he'd been set to look after his kid brother all the time when he was a boy, the habit might stick.'

'Hmm,' said Slider. 'Well, we won't speculate about that. The only connection we've got between David Vickery and this case is that his daughter was friends with the victim. Doesn't make him guilty of anything.'

'No, sir.'

'But it's good to have that point cleared up, anyway. Now we just have to find Melissa Vickery.'

'Yes, sir. She'd be 39 now. So she could be anywhere,' LaSalle said with a slight lowering of the tail. 'Or any*one* – if she married she won't even have the same name.'

'If it was easy being a detective, everyone would do it,' Slider comforted him, and he went away.

It was a day for wonders. Not long afterwards, McLaren came bursting in, for once with no food in his mouth or his hand, though the piece of paper he was holding did have a greasy thumb-mark on it, and he bore about him the faint aroma of gravy and onions. Ginster's individual steak pie, Slider concluded.

'I've got it, guv,' McLaren said.

'Well don't scratch, or it'll never get better,' said Slider.

McLaren was used to him after all these years. He ignored that bit. 'I had this idea, y'see, about how to find David Vickery. If he was an inventor, if he had patents, he'd have to register them at the Patents' Office, or he wouldn't get his royalties. And if he'd invented something really important, like Mrs Clavering said, for the space programme – or even for the motor industry – he'd have wanted the royalties all right. They'd be worth a fortune.'

'She said he was well-off,' said Slider. 'But that was a long time ago – no likelihood he'd be at the same address.'

'No, guv – you have to re-register a patent every year,' McLaren said proudly. 'Otherwise it lapses.'

Another good dog. 'I didn't know that. Well, go to it. Find him. Sic, boy!'

'Already done it,' McLaren said, beaming.

'Well?'

'Patents only last twenty years,' said McLaren.

This was like one of those 'I've got some good news and some bad news' routines. 'Don't toy with me, McLaren,' Slider warned.

'Yeah, but he didn't stop inventing right away,' McLaren went on hastily. 'He done other stuff after he left Shepherd's Bush. So there's patents still active.'

'So you've got an address for him?'

'Not for *him*. He's dead.'

Mentally, Slider reached for a rolled-up newspaper. 'Dead, is he?' he said patiently. Too patiently.

'Died four years ago, apparently.'

'Well, well. How unfortunate.'

McLaren spotted the signs in time, and hastened to make good. 'No, guv, the point is, patents are like property, you can leave the royalties to someone, like in a will. So if the person they're left to wants the dosh, they got to keep in touch. Vickery left 'em to his daughter. I got an address for Melissa.'

Good dog! 'Have a biscuit,' Slider said.

'Biscuit?' McLaren said suspiciously.

'Where is she?' Slider translated.

'In the same area. The old dame in Tetbury was right,' McLaren said. 'They moved to a farm between there and Cirencester. Oathill Farmhouse, Oathill Lane, Rodmarton, that's the address.'

'And she's still there?' Slider was taking nothing for granted by now.

'I rung up the local boys just to make sure,' McLaren said, with an eager nod. 'They say she's still there, lives there alone. The farmland's all rented out, it's just the farmhouse and a couple of outbuildings. Never been any trouble, so they don't know much about her. Bit eccentric, they say – but they'd say that about any woman living alone, my opinion.'

'You could be right,' said Slider. 'Or they could. Well, this is good news. At last we can talk to someone who was around at the time.'

'Yeah, but she was only a kid then. Who remembers stuff properly from when they were fourteen?' McLaren said.

'Thank you, I can do my own pessimistic adjustments,' said Slider.

EIGHTEEN
Armed and Dangerous

The house in Wornington Road with its scabby rendering and flaking paintwork was the sort to look all the better for the morning fog, wrapping it in a benign lack of definition. It was gloomy enough to need lights indoors, but there were none showing upstairs. There was a glow behind the drawn curtains of the basement, however, where the caretaker, Anita, lived. Hart descended and rang the doorbell.

As the door opened a cloud of cigarette smoke rushed out, like baby fog wanting to join its mamma, and there was the sound far back in the flat of the television blurting the witless shouts and laughter of some confessions show. Anita filled the space, a very large West Indian woman in a beige velour tracksuit, a mauve scarf tied over her rollers, a cigarette burning between her fingers. Her eyes narrowed when she saw who it was.

'You've got some nerve, comin' round here again! What you pushin' your ugly face in ma house again for?'

'Gimme a break, ma,' Hart said. 'I'm looking for Jessica.'

'I ain't your ma. You show me some respec', copper. I pay your wages.'

Hart sensed that this was not just jousting – that she was really annoyed. She spread her hands apologetically. 'I didn't mean no disrespect. I need to talk to Jessica. I fought I should clear it with you first, seeing as you look after her so good.' She thought the flattery might calm her, but Anita's face was as hard as her eyes.

'She ain't here.'

'Is she at work? At the restaurant?'

'No, she ain't. She lost that good job, an' it's all your fault – putting the filth on her. Coppers goin' round there all hours, pokin' about, askin' questions. Course they give her the shove!

They don't want no trouble. Nobody wants no trouble, and these girls, they get the fuzzy end o' the stick. She lost her job, and now she gone. I hope you satisfied!'

Hart didn't entirely believe her. 'Can I look in her room?'

Anita bristled. 'You can look all you want, you won't find nothing. She ain't here, an' I don't know where she gone. I wouldn't tell you if I did. We was gettin' on all right before *you* showed up.'

She tried to shut the door but Hart had her foot in the way. 'Look, love,' she said, 'I'm not the villain here. I want to help these girls, same as you do.'

'You got a funny way o' showing it, stickin' the filth onto 'em.'

'That's not how it was. They were being exploited by some very bad people, and we needed their help to stop them.'

'Well, stop 'em, then!' Anita snapped. 'Do your job, copper! Just keep your nose out of my life.'

The door was hurting Hart's foot now, but she wasn't going to give it up. 'Just tell me where Jess is, and I'll go. I just want to know she's OK.'

A voice from inside the flat said wearily, 'Oh, for God's sake!' And Jessica Bale appeared behind Anita. 'If I tell you I'm all right, will you leave us alone?'

She looked older than when Hart had seen her last, the rounded parts of her face mutated into adult planes, the shadows of late nights under her eyes. But she didn't have the spiky, unstable look of being on drugs, for which Hart was grateful.

'Oh, there you are, girl,' Hart said cheerfully. 'You livin' with Anita now?'

'She's just visiting, all right?' Anita snapped. 'She got her own place, nice flat, sharing with some other girls.'

'Give it up, 'Nita,' Jessica said. 'I'm in my old room. I'm clean. And I got a job in a food packing factory. I'm doing all right.'

'I'm glad to hear it,' Hart said. 'But why did you withdraw your testimony? I know why Shannon did, but we can't take the case forward without *somebody* helping us.'

Jessica sighed. 'It's all over, all that. Can't you just let it go? There's not going to *be* a case.'

'It doesn't have to be over. Listen—' Hart began.

But Jessica interrupted her. 'No. *You* listen. You've got your career and you want someone to be banged up for it, so's you can feel good about yourself. I get that. But I'm out now, and I ain't going back in for anybody.'

'Babe, you was all under age,' Hart urged. 'You was exploited. These people broke the law—'

'Oh, stuff the law. It's against the sodding law to have a fag in a pub.'

'You told me you left because you got scared, because you didn't want to end up like Tyler,' Hart reminded her.

'Yeah, well I didn't, did I? I got out, Anita got me straight, I got a job, I'm all right now. That stuff, that's like a nightmare, all I want to do is forget it, but you want to start stirring it all up again. Well, I ain't gonna do it. So just go away and leave me alone, willya. I ain't testifying about anything to anybody, and that's that.'

'So she never married,' Atherton said as they headed down the M4.

'Or married and kept her name. Or got divorced and changed back. Don't jump to conclusions,' Slider admonished.

'It's all the exercise I get,' said Atherton. 'I wonder why she didn't come forward. It was in the national papers.'

'Very small, inside page, only once,' said Slider. It hadn't struck the fourth estate as very gripping, the skeleton in the garden. Too many other juicy stories breaking at the same time. 'She could well have missed it. And not everybody reads newspapers. And even if she had seen it, she might not have thought there was any reason to come forward. She might not have anything to tell us.'

'You're determined to spoil my pleasure, aren't you?'

'I should have brought something for you to play with. You're hell on car journeys.'

'Let me drive, then.'

'Just sit still and look at the scenery.'

Rodmarton was just off the main road from Cirencester to Tetbury. They drove through the village – it had pleasant cottages around a small green, and a pretty stone church with a spire atop a square tower – and on northwards, past rather scrubby fields in which sheep busily cropped, building up body weight against the winter to come.

There was no sign for Oathill Farmhouse, and they missed the lane at the first pass. They had a brief argument with each other and with Sat Nav, who insisted she was right, returned and paused doubtfully at the entrance to a narrow, muddy lane, only one car wide and leading between high, overgrown hedges. 'This must be it,' Slider said.

'It doesn't look like a road, more like a farm track.'

'We *want* a farm track,' Slider pointed out.

'People ought to put up signs,' Atherton complained.

'Not if they don't want visitors,' said Slider.

'Oho. You think . . .?'

'I don't think anything.' He turned into the lane and bumped carefully through the ruts. 'We didn't have a sign at the end of our lane when I was a kid,' he said. He'd been born in a farm labourer's cottage. 'Everybody knew what was down there, so there was no need.'

'What if a stranger wanted to find you? There was no Sat Nav then.'

'Why on earth would a stranger have wanted to find us?' Slider countered with irrefutable logic. 'Get out and open the gate, will you?'

'What if there's a dog?' Atherton objected.

'There is a dog. Can't you hear it barking? Just do the gate. It'll be chained up.'

'You hope.'

'They always are.'

Slider observed from Atherton's struggle that the gate was old, heavy, and ill-balanced on its hinges. Beyond lay a large, muddy yard, decorated with puddles that looked to be of long standing. At the far side stood the farmhouse, Cotswold stone with a slate roof, flat-faced and plain, the sort of square with four windows and a door that a child might draw, and managing to be unusually, for a Cotswold farmhouse, unattractive.

To either side of the yard were outbuildings, on the right an open-fronted shelter in which stood a very muddy Landrover plus various pieces of rusty machinery, pallets and packing cases. On the left was a wooden barn with a tiled roof which seemed to be gently collapsing into its component parts. Parked by the house was an elderly Volvo estate car, even muddier; and the corners of the yard were colonized by an enormous roller, seized with rust, a Morris Minor lacking wheels or doors, several wheelbarrows, a decrepit bicycle, a pram circa 1958, and various nameless and abandoned implements, rolls of wire, buckets, and general junk. Long grass and weeds were growing between and rampantly through them. It was, Slider thought, a typical farmyard.

In one corner was a wooden kennel, at the entrance to which an Alsatian dog barked monotonously, jerking at his chain with every woof. The top of the kennel was covered with several layers of sacking, on top of which a large cat couched looking inscrutable, and rather spoiling the dog's reputation for ferocity. There were several other cats, slinking in the shadows or looking out from hidden places amongst the junk, and a number of chickens, some fancy bantams and a few ducks were foraging about, unconcerned about the cats or the visitors.

They got out of the car. Atherton took two steps, paused, lifted his foot to inspect the sole of his shoe. He gave Slider a grim Sundance Kid look, and said, 'Bolivia! Hah!'

'It's the countryside. You get mud in the countryside,' Slider said serenely. 'This could be the Atlantic City, New Jersey of all Gloucestershire for all you know.'

'Let's go. There's nobody home.'

'She's home,' Slider said, pointing to the faint smoke rising from one chimney.

'Why doesn't she come out, then?'

'Probably got her hands all floury making a fresh batch of scones for us. Are you going to sulk all day?'

They approached the door. The dog reached a crescendo of warning and then stopped abruptly, the rubber nubbin of its nose working frantically in what Slider assumed was astonishment. Probably never smelt Townies before.

There was no knocker on the door, or a doorbell – 'Not keen on visitors,' Atherton remarked – so Slider rapped good and hard with his knuckles on the wood. The dog watched them with interest. And just at the moment when Slider concluded there would be no answer and a new strategy would be needed, the door was opened roughly, and a woman stood there, frowning at them.

She was of middle height, and looked bulky in layers of multiple woollens topped off with a chocolate-brown cardigan with holes in the sleeves. Below were what looked like a man's brown cord trousers which were too big for her, tucked into green wellingtons, the whole ensemble bound in the middle with a webbing belt. Her hair was no-coloured and frowsy, the front parts held back with a child's plastic hair slide; her face was weathered, with deep creases from nose to mouth and a sullen underlip. And far from being innocently floury, her hands were ingrained with dirt like a gardener's, and her first and second fingers were heavily stained with nicotine.

Of more immediate and piercing interest was the fact that she was holding a twelve-gauge shotgun. It wasn't raised and aimed at them, but even from the casual position she had it in, she couldn't have missed them at that range.

Slider raised his hands very gently to chest level in a don't-shoot-till-we've-talked gesture. 'It's all right, we're police officers,' he said.

She hefted the gun suggestively. 'What do you want?' she demanded. Her voice was harsh and toneless, as if she hadn't used it much recently. 'I didn't call you.'

'We're not local police. We're from London,' Slider said. 'We'd just like to talk to you. You are Melissa Vickery, aren't you?'

He had not noticed her eyes before, but now as they widened slightly, he saw a flash of blue, as though light had shone through from two sudden rips in her skin. Then it was gone. Her eyelids were heavy and shielded her eyes very effectively from scrutiny, and her frown, which seemed habitual, all but concealed them.

'Who wants to know?' she growled.

Slider introduced them.

'Have you got some ID?'

Slider reached for his, and the gun shifted slightly in warning, so he drew out his warrant card slowly and held it out to her. She inspected it. 'What do two policemen from London want to come out all this way for?' she said, her voice grating with suspicion.

'We want to talk to you about Amanda Knight,' said Slider.

In the silence that followed, he could hear a crow yarking some distance away, and closer to hand the croodling of the hens in the weeds, and the jingle of the dog's chain as it shifted position. He was aware of the tension of Atherton beside him and the alertness of the woman in front of him.

'That's a name I haven't heard in a long time,' she said at last. Her suspicion seemed to have lowered a notch.

'May we come in and talk to you?' Slider asked politely.

She seemed to consider, looking round the yard behind them as if expecting to spot commandos wriggling through the undergrowth on their elbows. Then she said, 'All right,' and turned away, letting them in.

Slider gestured Atherton to go first – Atherton gave a grim quirk of the mouth to express dismay, disbelief, and comical alarm as he passed – then followed him and closed the door. It caught against the stone-flagged floor, until he tried lifting it a little – the hinges had dropped and the door had swollen. Inside it was dark, chilly, and smelled damp. He caught a glimpse of a dim brown parlour on the right – the best front room, he supposed – but she led them to the left and into a large farmhouse kitchen which, while not exactly straight from *House & Gardens*, was at least comparatively light and, thanks to the range, warm.

The floor was stone-flagged, and a large wooden table took up most of the centre of the room. There was a wooden bench under the window, and the range and its surrounding chimney dominated the opposite side. On the wall above the mantelpiece were two gun rests, one empty and the other holding a four-ten. There was an old-fashioned wooden dresser against the far wall. There was a rug on the floor in front of the range, on which two collies were lying tangled together, asleep, a cat was sitting on top of the cool plate, and two more cats perched on the windowsill.

So far, so Famous Five. Sold to a yuppie, it would have been made into a delightful room. As it was, it smelled of dogs and cigarettes, and it was comfortless and cluttered. There was a single very old and disgusting armchair beside the range, the seat worn into a basin by years of use, the wooden arms runnelled with cigarette burns. The dresser was buried under old correspondence, items of clothing, tools, balls of string, nameless bits of metal, tins and jars, a box of dog biscuits; all the things carelessly put down there and never cleared away. Likewise every other surface in the room; and on the kitchen table, in addition, was a large bucket crusted inside with what looked like chicken meal, a heap of muddy vegetables, and two dead and bloodied rabbits. Even the front bar of the range, which should have been decorated with a pretty dishtowel depicting common English wild flowers and perhaps a cheery red-and-white checked oven glove, bore instead a very dirty towel that might have been used to dry a dog and some rather grey underwear.

The woman stood by the table, watching them come in, her head slightly lowered, like a bull wondering whether or not to charge, her brows frowning, her lower lip stuck out. She examined them afresh, and then sighed slightly, straightened, and put the gun back in its rest. 'Sorry about that,' she said, with a jerk of her head towards it. 'When strange men come up the lane in these parts, you get nervous.' She gave a mirthless grin. 'No use calling the police. Time they get here, you're dead, and they've stripped the house bare. You learn to look after yourself when you live in the country.'

'I understand,' Slider said soothingly.

She gestured towards the bench under the window. 'Sit down if you want. Shove those things on the floor.' They did as they were told, and she came and perched on the edge of the table, thereby putting herself at an advantage, and between them and the guns. 'Why the sudden interest in Amanda?' she asked. 'That was a hell of a long time ago.'

The question sounded casual, but Slider sensed an alertness, perhaps a tension, in her as she asked it. Well, that was natural enough, he supposed. Anything unexpected tends to put you on your guard.

'You didn't read anything about it in the papers?' he countered, watching her face.

'Don't read papers,' she said gruffly.

'Well, then – I'm sorry to tell you that human remains were found.'

She frowned. 'What? You're saying you've found Amanda? What makes you think it's her?'

'They were found in the garden of the house where she lived. 15 Laburnum Avenue.'

She stared. She repeated the words, '15 Laburnum Avenue!' as though it were a thing of wonder. She seemed to remember something. 'I never went to her house. Never once.'

'It backed on to your own house in Colville Avenue.'

'People were never invited in. They never had people in. She couldn't have friends like a normal kid. If you don't invite them home, they don't invite you.'

'But she had you. You were her friend,' Slider said.

'Yes. She had me.' She sounded almost dazed. 'It was such a long time ago. I never thought I'd hear that name again. Amanda Knight!' She stood up abruptly, walked away to the dresser and, with her back to them, rummaged around until she found a pack of cigarettes and a box of matches, and lit one. She turned back with it in her mouth, her face screwed up against the rising smoke. She gestured with the packet. 'Want one?'

'No, thank you,' Slider answered.

She resumed her place, seeming more collected, almost brisk. 'So, what do you mean, remains were found? What remains?'

'A skeleton,' said Slider.

'You mean she was buried? In her garden? And nobody found her? All these years and nobody found her?' She gave a short bark of laughter. 'All those people scouring the park and dredging the canal and thinking she'd run off to live on the street, and all the time she was dead and buried in her own garden.' She examined their expressions. 'Oh, come on, you have to laugh.' She sucked on the cigarette, and shrugged. 'All right, you don't have to laugh, but you have to see the irony.' She sighed out the smoke. 'Poor old Amanda. No, I'm sorry for her, really. So she's dead, is she? How did she die?'

'We don't know that yet. That's why we've come to see you.'

'What d'you mean?' she said sharply.

'To try to find out what was going on in her life the last few weeks or months. It seems as though you were the person closest to her at the end.'

'I don't know about that,' she said vaguely. 'I don't see how I can help, really.'

'Well, if we could just ask you a few questions,' Slider said.

She shrugged. 'Go ahead. For what good it'll do. It was a long time ago. I don't remember much about those days.'

She looked at Slider for a question, then at Atherton. Atherton, seeing Slider had gone into a frown of thought, took up the cue.

'Let's start with how you met her,' he tried.

'Who? Amanda? I don't remember,' she said unhelpfully.

'You didn't go to the same school,' he said.

'No. I was at St Margaret's, where the posh kids went. Amanda had to go to Poplar Road. She was really bright. If anyone should have gone to St Margaret's it was her. She'd have got a good education there, she'd have got a chance to get on in life. It was wasted on me. I was dumb as a nail.'

'So how did you meet?' He tried slipping the question in isotonically.

'Walking home,' she said without thinking. She looked at him. 'Yes, walking home one day. I dropped something. My gloves. I dropped my gloves and she picked them up. Gave them to me. I said thanks. We got talking. She said where did I live. I told her. She said her parents were both out at work, so I asked if she'd like to come home with me for a bit. I think I said, *for tea*.' She pronounced it with an ironic emphasis, as though it was an extraordinary thing to have said.

'Did you have a lot of friends?' Atherton asked.

She seemed to think. 'No,' she said, quite abruptly, and lapsed into silence.

Atherton thought he'd better prod her, or they'd be there all night. 'Your mother had died the year before, hadn't she? Quite suddenly. You must have been still learning to live with it. You must have been lonely.'

She stared at him, her mouth turning down. She removed the cigarette deliberately, and said, 'Oh, very nice! Yes, tactful reminder. "By the way, your mother's dead, how does that feel?" And you do this for a living, do you?'

'It was a long time ago, as you've already noted,' he said, interested by her reaction.

'You never get over losing your mum. Take it from me. You're right, I was upset, I was bewildered, I was lonely. I was a mess. Amanda – she was different. She always knew what she wanted,

and she was determined to get it. Anyone who got in the way
– look out. She was tough. A tough kid.'

'And she befriended you. That must have been nice for you.'

'Nice?' her eyebrows went up. Then she took a last drag on
the cigarette, butted it, folded her arms over her chest, and said,
'Yes, it was nice. Nice for poor little me to have a friend. Amanda
was nice. I was nice. We were nice together.'

Atherton nodded receptively, thinking that Melissa Vickery
might just be a little bit bonkers. But living alone in a place like
this, where anyone knocking at your door unexpectedly needed
to be met with a twelve-bore, might well send a person spiralling
off to a distant planet. And from where she started – losing her
mother at age fourteen – it might not have been a very long
journey.

NINETEEN
Females of the Species

'That summer, you saw a lot of Amanda, didn't you?'

'Yes,' she said. 'We'd meet after school and she'd come home with me for a bit, until her mum and dad got home from work. She helped me with my homework sometimes. Or we'd talk. Or have tea. We were better off than her, we always had cake and stuff. They didn't have nice stuff at home. And I had sweets. She didn't get much pocket money.'

'And when the summer holidays came?' Atherton prompted.

'She came most days. Her parents were out at work, so she was on her own.'

'Your father worked from home, didn't he?'

She looked at him sharply. 'He didn't mind. He had his study up at the top of the house. But he liked Amanda, anyway. He was glad I had a friend.'

'Did you go out together, during the holidays?'

She shrugged. 'Sometimes. But mostly we just stayed in. Talking and so on.'

'What did you talk about?'

She looked irritated. 'How do I remember? All those years ago! What kids talk about.'

'So she spent most days with you, at your house. But her parents didn't seem to know about it. Her mother didn't seem to have heard of you.' The woman shrugged again. 'Why do you think Amanda didn't talk about you?'

'How should I know?' she said roughly. 'Maybe she just wanted to keep something for herself. I don't think she liked them very much. They didn't understand her. They were stupid and uneducated. Her dad was like some kind of dinosaur. They were always rowing, he was always trying to stop her doing things.'

'What things?'

She seemed to regret her sudden expansiveness, and answered that with a closed-mouthed shrug.

Atherton glanced at Slider but got no message from him, so he carried on. 'That last day, the day she disappeared—'

'I don't know anything about that,' she said indifferently.

'It was in the middle of the summer holidays, August the 18th. A Saturday. Did Amanda visit you that day?'

She was irritable again. 'I don't remember. It was a long time ago. I don't remember *dates*.'

'When did you find out that she had gone missing?'

'I don't remember.'

'All right, *how* did you find out? Did a neighbour mention it? Did someone ring up? A schoolfriend, perhaps? Did your father see it in the newspaper? *How*?' She just shook her head, and reached for another cigarette. 'When you did hear about it, why didn't you go round to her parents and offer your condolences?'

She looked incredulous. 'I was just a *kid*!'

'Well, then, your father. You said he liked Amanda, was glad you had a friend. Why didn't he?'

'*I* don't know. He didn't know them, why would he?'

'You went away on holiday about that time,' Atherton said, watching her light the fag.

'Did I?' she said through the smoke.

'Was that because you were upset about Amanda? Did your father take you away for that reason, to get you away from it all?'

She took the cigarette from her mouth and looked at him consideringly. 'Maybe. How would I know? Look, I was a kid, what do kids know about why their parents do anything? You just go along with it, don't you? You're asking the wrong person.'

'But we can't ask your father, can we?'

'No. because he's dead. Want to make a joke about that? I'm an orphan, isn't *that* hilarious?'

Atherton had decided it was best to ignore her changes of mood. 'How did he die?'

'He blew his head off with the shotgun,' she said brutally, looking to see if she had affected him. He returned the look steadily. 'He found he'd got cancer. He didn't want to go the way my mother went. He was suffering. So he took the shotgun and went behind the barn and blew himself away.'

'That must have been terrible for you,' Atherton said gently.

She blinked. She seemed about to say something and change her mind. Then she took another drag on the cigarette and said on the exhale in a quieter voice, 'It was a quick end. You do it for a dog – you don't let them suffer. It's better that way.'

'You must miss him dreadfully,' Atherton said. 'It's been just the two of you all these years.'

'Of course I miss him,' she said harshly, turning her head away. 'What do you think?' She removed a fleck of tobacco from her mouth with a forefinger and examined it. 'I loved him.'

'It was quite a sudden decision, when you moved from Shepherd's Bush out here,' Slider said. His voice, quiet, unemphatic, seemed to ease into the air between them like a gentle zephyr from an open window, nothing to be regarded.

'I suppose it was,' she said.

'Did your father tell you why you were going? You must have wondered.'

'He was sick of it all. Sick of that house. Sick of the place. You couldn't breathe, people all round you, everyone wanting to know your business. Out here you can be alone. People leave you alone. Sometimes you don't see another soul from one week's end to the next. It's quiet.'

'And you like the quiet?' Slider asked. By the hearth, the dogs sighed and changed position. Behind him, on the windowsill, he heard one of the cats purr in response to the movement.

'Of course,' she said. 'Who wouldn't?'

'That last summer,' he went on in the same inconsequential voice, 'what was on Amanda's mind? You talked together, for hours, almost every day. What was going on in her life?'

'Just the usual things. Nothing in particular,' Melissa Vickery said. 'Why? I don't remember. It's too long ago.'

'Was there someone new in her life?' Slider asked. 'A boyfriend?'

'She wasn't interested in *boys*,' she said scornfully.

'A man, then. Was something happening to her that she'd want to keep secret from her parents, from grown-ups in general?'

'When you're fourteen, you want to keep everything secret from your parents,' she said, with unusual perspicacity.

'Had her relationship with her father changed? Worsened, perhaps. You said they rowed a lot. Did he hit her? Was she afraid of him?'

'She wasn't afraid of *him*! She wasn't afraid of anyone. He didn't hit her. She thought he was a stupid little man. What's the point of all these questions, anyway? I don't know what happened to Amanda. I didn't see her that day. I can't help you. What does it matter, anyway? She's been dead twenty-five years, and nobody misses her.'

'She was your friend. I expect you miss her,' Slider said.

'Not after all this time.' She stood up. 'I want you to go now. I'm sick of you. I told you I couldn't help you, but you *would* come in. Now go away, and don't come back.'

They had stood too, but Slider did not yet move from the spot. He regarded her steadily, until she stopped fidgeting, stopped puffing at her cigarette, and looked back, frowning but attentive.

'I think there is more that you know, but you don't want to tell me. You think it doesn't matter after all these years, but Amanda's life was cut short, she was cheated of what was lawfully hers, and that matters to me. So I will keep asking questions until I find out what happened. And I will come back here if I need to. Do you understand?'

She sneered. 'Do you think I'm an idiot? Of course I understand. And you'd better understand that I defend my property against intruders if *I* need to.'

Slider nodded. 'Very well,' he said. He jerked his head to Atherton, to send him first, and followed him; and she followed them as far as the passage, where she stopped to watch them go out of the front door. As he turned to close it behind him, he said to her calmly, 'You know Amanda kept a diary?'

She looked blank, then there was a slow seeping of alarm into her face. 'You found her diary?' she said.

'You knew she was keeping one then, that last summer?'

'Yes. No. I suppose so.' She rallied. 'Most girls keep a diary, don't they?' Her eyes narrowed. 'You haven't got it, have you? Otherwise you wouldn't be asking me.'

'No, we haven't got it. I just wanted your confirmation that it existed. And what was in it.'

'I don't know what was in it. She never showed it to anyone. Probably a lot of childish nonsense anyway. If it existed at all. If you haven't got it, how do you even know there was one?'

'I spoke to her mother.'

For a long moment, it looked as though Melissa Vickery was going to say something, and then she shrugged. 'For what that's worth. Close the door behind you. And don't forget to shut the gate.'

They went. Slider felt better with the door closed behind them, and didn't really think she would come busting out and blast away at them with both barrels, but he'd feel even better when he was on the safe side of that gate. The morning mistiness had cleared away and the yard was peaceful in the sunshine. The chickens were taking dust baths, and the ducks had discovered the puddles, and the chained dog watched them with interest and perhaps wistfulness as they made their escape.

'Mad as a sack full of cats,' Atherton said. 'I didn't think we'd get out of there alive.'

'You do get upset about trifles,' said Slider.

'A gun is not a trifle.'

'It can be an assault trifle,' Slider offered.

'Ha! You joke now, but don't tell me you weren't nervous.'

Slider didn't answer. He was thinking. 'I'm not sure we learned anything essential from risking our lives like that in the line of duty,' Atherton said.

'I think we'll realize we learned a lot when we've had time to digest it,' Slider said.

'Speaking of digesting, do you realize we didn't get any lunch today?'

'It's too late for lunch now,' Slider said, glancing at his watch.

'But we could stop in Cirencester for a pint and a sandwich. Can't run the engine without petrol, you know.'

'Engine?' Slider said vaguely.

'The brain,' said Atherton. 'See, you'd have understood that straight away if you weren't hungry.'

Slider turned the car out onto the road and headed back towards Cirencester. 'Did she strike you as stupid as a nail?' he mused.

'Dumb as a nail, she said,' Atherton corrected. 'And no, she didn't. Mad as a parrot, but not stupid.'

It was past going-home time when they got back to the factory, but Swilley and Gascoyne were still there. 'What happened? Did you see her? What's she like?' Swilley asked.

Slider let Atherton tell, and he made the most of it, while Slider went back through his memories of what had been said, and almost as important, what had not.

'So you think she knows something?' Swilley asked, when Atherton came to a pause.

'I'm certain that she does,' Slider said, 'but I can't work out what.'

'What makes you suspect, sir?' Gascoyne asked respectfully.

Slider winkled it out. 'She couldn't say – or wouldn't say – how she found out that Amanda was missing,' he said. 'She kept saying it was a long time ago and she didn't remember any details, and that's fair enough, but *how* did she hear Amanda was missing? According to her there was no contact between the families, so Amanda's parents wouldn't have telephoned her father. In fact, she said that they didn't even know Amanda visited her, and we have Mrs Knight's word that she'd never heard of a Melissa.'

'So her father heard it from someone else,' Swilley hazarded. 'Friend, neighbour – or read it in the paper.'

'Maybe our Mr Vickery mentioned it,' said Gascoyne, 'seeing it was just the next street.'

'All quite possible,' said Slider, 'except that she didn't say her father told her. And when I suggested another schoolfriend might have rung her with the news, she just shook her head. She rejected all the possibilities. I know it was a long time ago, but I think she would have remembered who it was broke the news to her that her friend, the friend she'd been seeing nearly every day, had disappeared – unless she knew something about that disappearance.'

They thought about it. 'So – you think she was with Amanda when it happened? She saw it?' said Swilley. 'And was too frightened to say anything? Say the two of them had gone out somewhere, and Ronnie Knight found them and was angry for some reason – they'd gone somewhere he disapproved of, or something – and he got into a row with Amanda, killed her, probably by accident? No, but she wouldn't just keep it quiet, would she? That's mad.'

Gascoyne shook his head. 'Even if she was afraid back then, she wouldn't still be, not all this time later. There'd be no reason not to shop Amanda's dad now. He's dead, anyway – he couldn't hurt her.'

'Why else would she not say anything?' Swilley wondered. 'If not fear? Loyalty?'

'Loyalty to who? Amanda's dad against Amanda?' said Gascoyne. 'How would she even have known him?'

'Not Amanda's dad,' said Atherton. 'Her own. Say they were playing downstairs and got a bit boisterous. Her father comes rampaging down to complain about the noise – they were disturbing his genius, how could he concentrate with that unholy racket going on etcetera. And Amanda, who's used to rowing with her dad, answers him back, and he loses his temper and lamps her.'

They thought about that. 'Except that there were no fractures,' said Slider.

'Well, he caused her some kind of fatal damage in the heat of the moment,' Atherton said, 'without breaking bones. Strangled her, maybe. Now little Melissa, who's lost her mother and loves her daddy, has to make a choice – to the dead friend or the live father. I think in those circumstances, most kids would side with the father. Especially when he's right there, pleading with her.'

'You may have something there, Jim,' said Swilley.

'And you have to take into account the sudden dash away,' Atherton went on, warming to his theory. 'The holiday followed by complete removal from the scene, to Tetbury, never to return. That's very suggestive.'

'But still,' Gascoyne said, 'why wouldn't she tell the truth now? Her father's dead. It doesn't matter any more.'

'Because she's loyal to his memory. Doesn't want it tarnished,' said Atherton. 'Kept the secret all these years. Gave up her life to it, almost. Promised Daddy not to tell, and she's not going to break her promise now. She said to us, "I loved him," and she sounded genuine when she said it.'

'I suppose that's possible,' said Gascoyne, 'but—'

'But how did David Vickery manage to bury Amanda's body in her own garden?' said Slider. 'And even more to the point, why would he?'

'To throw suspicion on Ronnie Knight,' Atherton offered.

'Nasty,' said Swilley.

'But still,' Slider insisted, 'how? I know people are generally unobservant, but a man with a body to dispose of couldn't rely on that. *Would*n't rely on that. With the whole world to choose from, I can't believe an even slightly rational man would pick that particular place to bury his victim. No, it's got to be Ronnie Knight. He's the only one who could do it, who had even a chance, let alone a reason to bury her there. But then, what does Melissa know about it? And why won't she tell us?'

'Well, that dame is completely out to lunch,' Atherton said, 'so I don't think we ought to get hung up on her lack of frankness.'

'That's all very well,' said Swilley, 'but it puts us back where we were, not knowing how it was done or why. And we're running out of people to ask. Finding Melissa Vickery was our last hope, practically. Now we've found her, and we're no better off.'

'Go home,' said Slider. 'Nothing more to do here. Perhaps things will seem clearer in the morning.'

When Connolly opened the street door of her building, Julienne was there, hunched on the stairs, all spindly limbs, knees together and ankles splayed, arms wrapped round herself. There was a small rucksack and a carrier bag on the stairs beside her.

Connolly's heart sank. 'How did you get in?' she demanded.

'I made out I was buzzing someone till a bloke come along and he let me in,' said Julienne, unrepentant.

'Well, he shouldn't have. What are you doing here?'

Julienne gave her a doubtful, hopeful, pleading look, scrambling to her feet. 'I come to see you.'

'I know that, but *why*?' She noted the two bags and an unwelcome thought filtered in. 'Motherogod, don't tell me you've run away!'

'I can't stand it there,' Julienne whined. 'I hate it. They're all rotten to me. I wanna come and live with you.'

'I told you before—'

'I know, but think about it,' the child said beguilingly. 'I know you like me. We're mates. It could be great.'

'We are *not* mates. I'm old enough to be your mother.'

'All right then, be me mother,' Julienne said boldly. 'Whatevs. I don't care. Just s'long as I can stay here. Go on, it'll be fun.'

Connolly sighed. 'You'd better come upstairs while I ring the home. I don't suppose you told them where you were going.'

'Don't be daft!'

'You'll get me into trouble, so you will.' She had been leading the way upstairs, but turned abruptly to face the child, almost knocking her backwards. 'Do *not* take this as an invitation to stay. Do *not* assume, because I ask you in, that I want you there.'

'Jeez, all right! Keep your pants on!' Julienne, flapping a placating hand.

'Why the hell you'd do such an eejity thing I don't know,' Connolly muttered. They reached her flat door and she turned again. 'I don't live alone, you know. I share the flat. So while you're in there, don't touch anything. And if there's anyone else there, don't say anything.'

She let them in. Julienne stepped through with an air of wonder and willingness to be pleased. 'Cor,' she breathed. 'It's brill! Fantastic gaff!' She was only standing in the minute entrance hall, but from there she could see into the kitchen and down the passage into the sitting room. 'It must be great sharing with mates,' she went on. 'I bet you, like, have great parties and everything. No mum and dad, you can stay up all night if you want, and play music—'

'And eat ice cream straight outta the tub, I get it,' Connolly interrupted. 'A minute ago you wanted me to be your mother.'

'Only 'cos I knew you'd be cool.'

'I am not cool. I am far from cool. At the moment, I am red hot lava of *extreme* annoyance with you.'

Julienne only grinned. 'Yeah, I can see that. You like me, you know you do. You think I'm radical, like you.'

'Oh, for God's sake! Go in the kitchen, get yourself a glass of milk.'

'Milk? Got any lager?' Julienne said cheekily, but meeting Connolly's glare, did as she was told while Connolly looked for the number of the home. With glass in hand, she watched Connolly with an air of elation seeping away. 'You really sending me back?' she asked in a small voice.

Connolly looked at her, and felt a pang. 'I have to. You can't do stuff like this, Jule. I told you. There's laws and regulations and – Hello? I want to speak to the superintendent, please. Thank you. You've got to go back, put a shape on yourself, go to school, grow up.'

'I can do them things living with you,' Julienne objected.

'Even if I wanted you, they'd never let me look after you. Hello? Yes, this is Detective Constable Connolly. About Julienne Adams.'

Julienne's crest fell. She knew the game was up. She wandered disconsolately out of the kitchen, and down the passage to the sitting room. She was standing there looking about her like a 1957 visitor to the Ideal Home Exhibition, when Connolly joined her.

'I'm taking you back. And I hope you realize you are disrupting my plans for the evening in a way that is *not* acceptable.'

Julienne ignored that. She said, 'You got a great gaff. I like your couch. I like your carpet. I like them vase things over there. I like the colour you done the walls.'

'Are you listening to me?'

'I like that picture,' Julienne went on. 'It's a portrait, int it? Is it someone real? She looks nice.'

Connolly sighed. 'That's my partner.'

Julienne turned, eyes wide. 'You mean you're a lezzer?' she breathed in awe.

'That's not a nice word,' Connolly said. 'We don't use pejorative terms like that.'

'What's peejora-whatsit mean?'

'Disapproving.'

'Oh!' Julienne was enlightened. 'But I never meant disapproving,' she said excitedly. 'I think it's great! *Super* cool! Cor, I wish I was one!'

'You do not. And never mind me. I only told you so you'd know why they'd never let me foster you, even if I actually wanted to, which I don't. Mind me now, I *don't*.'

'Don't be daft,' Julienne said. '*Course* they would. You get priority these days if you're a – if you're gay. They *can't* turn

you down. There's this girl at the home, she says your best bet
of getting out is to say you're gay and you want to go to a gay
couple.'

Connolly sighed again. 'If she's so clever, how come she's
still there? She doesn't know what she's talking about. And it's
time I took you home.'

'It's not home,' said Julienne flatly. She looked at Connolly
without any wiles now. 'Please. It'd be great. And I wouldn't be
any trouble.'

'You're trouble now.'

'Only so's you'll notice me. I can be good if I want. I'd be
good if you took me.'

'Well, I'm not going to. No matter what stunts you pull. So
get it into your head.' She managed to glare at the child, though
it was an effort. 'Now I'm taking you back. And if you do
anything like this again, I won't come and visit you. Understand?'

'You'll come and visit me?' Julienne brightened.

'Only if you buckle down, obey the rules – go to school! Don't
get into trouble. And don't run away.'

'Will you come and see me on Saturday?'

'Mary and Joseph, did you listen to a word I said?'

'Keep your hair on. Course I did. What's her name, your
partner?'

'None o' your business,' Connolly said, bustling her charge
towards the door.

'Is she nice? She looks sort of posh in that picture. Maybe
pictures just make you look posh. That sort, the painted sort.'
Julienne prattled her way down the stairs. 'How come you had
her picture done, anyway? Was it like a birthday present or
something? If the two of you adopt me, I'll have two mums,
won't I? Would I call you both mum? How'd you know which
one I meant?'

Connolly made a point of not responding to any of it, and
thought in exasperation that now she'd got something on her
hands that would be hell to get off.

TWENTY
Matchless

P orson was not a happy bunny. Somewhere he had picked up a cold, and it had ripened by Thursday morning into its full chesty glory. Slider didn't need the flapped hand and terse warning to position himself well out of spray range.

'You don't seem to be getting on with this Laburnum business.' Porson tried to bark, but it came out as a croak, and set him coughing fruitily into his handkerchief. 'You should see what I'm bringing up,' he said as he wiped his lips. 'I swear the last lot had hands.'

'Get well soon, sir,' Slider murmured, with sincerity.

Porson gave him a sour look. 'Glad you've kept that famous sense of humour. I was worried you might be feeling low. I thought this case would be an easy job for you – get a result, boost your self-extreme, do you a bit of bon with our masters. But you don't seem to have got anywhere.'

'It's tricky when it was so long ago,' Slider said. 'Many of the principle players have died.'

'Excuses are all very well, but it's you I'm thinking of. A failure in something like this can leave a nasty taste in the eye. Let alone having to justify the budget expenditure on a bag of blasted old bones.' He blew his nose.

Not lovely old bones any more, Slider observed.

'Dammit, man, you get handed a sitting catch and you fumble it,' Porson went on. He emerged suddenly from the handkerchief and fixed Slider with a disconcerting glare. 'And what's this I hear about visiting Shannon Bailey?'

Damn and blast, the old man really did know everything, Slider thought, half admiringly, half in irritation. 'It was one officer only. And very discreet.' He couldn't help himself. 'How did you hear about it?'

'Walls have ears,' Porson said inscrutably. 'You know you

shouldn't have done it, don't you? I'm not going to have to tell you how wrong, dangerous and bloody stupid it was, am I?'

'No, sir.'

'Good. What did you find out?'

Slider hesitated, trying to untangle the facts from his own prejudices. 'She withdrew her testimony because she's unsure now what, if anything, she really saw.'

'She withdrew voluntarily?'

'Yes, sir.'

'She wasn't frightened into it?'

'No, sir. She'd been drinking and taking drugs, and her memories of the evening are unclear.'

Porson gave a grim nod. 'Right. Exactly. Just what everybody's been saying all along. So are you happy now?'

Slider didn't answer, unsure what the truth about that might be.

Porson began pacing. 'Let's put it another way. I know you aren't happy about the hit-and-run girl, and *I* don't like the fact that we've never found the driver, but these things happen in war. Are you prepared to accept that you don't have a case, that you never had a case.'

'Yes, sir,' Slider said.

'I blame myself for letting you run with it,' Porson said restlessly. He honked into his handkerchief. Slider could hear his chest rattling from here. The old man didn't look well. There was a shiny, sucked-boiled-sweet look to his eyes. 'I should have known better. Truth to tell, I fancied having a pop at the heads on the parapet myself, God help me.' He gave a mirthless grin, drew breath to speak and set himself coughing.

'I'll go and leave you in peace,' Slider said, turning away.

Porson flapped at him to stay. 'So,' he wheezed, when he could, 'we're all clear now on the Adams thing, are we? I'm not going to have any more temper tantrums? No more toys thrown out of the plane? You're all done with it?'

'Yes, sir.'

'Right.'

As Slider reached the door, Porson called after him, 'End of the week for this Laburnum business. Can't spend any more time on it. There are some big initiatives coming up next week and we'll need all hands.'

Initiatives, Slider thought as he trudged away. We used to fight crime, now we progress initiatives. Welcome to the twenty-first century.

It had got so that he could smell trouble. He felt the electric charge coming out of the CID room halfway along the passage. As he turned in at the door, all eyes turned on him. It was Gascoyne who spoke.

'Sir, the DNA test result on the remains has come back. It *was* in the non-urgent queue. I think they must have—'

'What's the problem?' Slider goosed him.

Gascoyne looked unhappy. 'It's not a match. No matches at all to Mrs Knight's sample. The remains couldn't have been Amanda's.'

'So where does that leave us?' Swilley looked round the assembled troops. They'd all got consolatory teas and coffees and sought their own or the edge of someone else's more convenient desk.

'All bets are off,' said McLaren. 'It's a whole new ball game.'

'Yes, thank you, we'll manage without the *Bumper Book of Clichés* today,' said Slider.

'I feel bad about your man, Ronnie Knight,' Connolly said, swinging short arcs on her swivel chair. 'Suspecting him all this time. It's cat!'

'Still prob'ly was him,' McLaren grumped. 'Who else could've done the burying?'

'Let's not forget, Amanda's still missing,' said Lessop. He tugged unhappily at his chin-plaits. 'Does that mean we have to drop her?' he asked Slider.

'I'm afraid so,' Slider answered. That poor girl would remain forever a misper, practically an un-person, her meagre file crumbling gently to dust in the basement. He threw them a counter-irritant. 'We can't spend any more time on her. We only have to the end of the week to sort out the bones. Ideas?'

'Well, we're back to square one, aren't we?' said Swilley. 'We don't even have a date to work on.'

'Local searches,' said Slider. 'Other missing persons. Other sex- and abduction-cases, possible links with. Other local perpetrators, similarities with MO.' They looked profoundly unexcited by this turn of events. 'Come on,' he said sharply. 'Let's not lose sight of the fact that someone died, and was probably murdered. A crime was committed. That is our proper concern, what the generous public pays our wages for, to catch criminals.'

'What if they turn out to be Roman bones or something like that?' Fathom said gloomily.

'Idiot!' Swilley said roughly. 'Doc Cameron said they're about twenty years old. I know it's an estimate, but he's not going to be a couple of thousand years out, is he?'

'What if it's the other side of twenty?' LaSalle said. 'We've been looking at the Knights because of Amanda, but what about the people who came after them?'

'The Barnards?' said Swilley.

'Oh! Guv!' Fathom said, jumping as though he'd been prodded with a sharpened pencil.

'We didn't look at them properly because of Amanda being a misper,' LaSalle went on. 'There was no point when it was obvious it was her.'

'Guv?'

'But now it's all thrown open again—'

'Guv, about the Barnards,' Fathom said, managing to get over the top of LaSalle.

Slider turned to him. 'Yes, you were looking for them, weren't you?'

'I found 'em,' Fathom said. 'I forgot to say. They're coming in this morning.'

The estate agent had got it all wrong. They had not sold the house in Laburnum Avenue because they were going to Australia. It was their *son* who was going to *New Zealand*, and they had sold their house to realize some cash for him and their daughter-in-law to put down on a house when they got there. The agent had thought there'd been a reference to Adelaide, but that was the name of the daughter-in-law, not the Barnard's destination. He hadn't properly been listening. He hadn't really been interested.

Meanwhile the Barnards were looking for something smaller for themselves and, having retired early and prosperously, and having no particular place in mind where they wanted to settle, they were renting in order to try out different places, until they found their spiritual home.

Laborious work and much dedicated cross-checking on Fathom's part – he might be slow, but he was *thorough* – had finally located them in North Norfolk. He had telephoned them and checked that they were, indeed, the Barnards who had once lived at 15 Laburnum Avenue, and when he told them about the skeleton and said there were some questions they wanted to ask them, they had volunteered at once to drive up to London and be interviewed.

'Well, that's not a good start,' Hart said. 'If they've volunteered to come in, they must be innocent. If they was guilty, they'd be having it away in the opposite direction.'

'Could be a double bluff,' said Connolly. 'If they've got away with it all these years, they'll be super-confident. If it was me, I'd want to come just to find out what the Pols really know.'

'If they was a Fred and Rose West couple, there'd've been more bodies,' Hart objected.

'Maybe that was the only one they buried on the premises,' Fathom said eagerly. 'The others could be anywhere – out on the moors or something.'

'The Shepherd's Bush moors?' Hart said witheringly.

'They got a motor,' Fathom pointed out. 'And twenty-five years ago there was no ANPR cameras.'

Slider was getting a headache. 'I'm going to my room, to go over what we've got that hasn't just fallen apart. Let me know when the Barnards arrive.'

He left them to it. There was something bothering him, had been bothering him since yesterday. Something he should have remembered, or should have known. Or had noticed without realizing it. At his desk he settled down to look at the story in the order they had discovered it, page by page, interview by interview.

Atherton came into his room. 'They're here.'

Slider, startled out of deep thought, jumped like an actor hearing the phone ring. 'Don't you believe in knocking?'

'No, only in constructive criticism. Downstairs just called up. There's a couple asking to see you. By the name of Barnard.'

'Ah. The moment of truth, perhaps?'

'Or *a* moment of truth. Or possibly more lies. D'you want me to come?'

Slider stood up. 'I wouldn't be so cruel as to deny you.'

Mr and Mrs Barnard were a respectable-looking couple in their fifties who were out of place waiting in the front shop with the sad cases. He was wearing a sports coat and flannel trousers and actually a tie – it was a long time since one of those had come in the front door without being attached to someone in uniform – and she was in a jersey dress and wool jacket with one of those enormous scarves that BBC female correspondents wear, looped about her neck and shoulders. They didn't look like serial killers. They didn't look like people who had come all this way to tell lies. They looked, in fact, eager, intelligent and very slightly nervous – quite a good combination, Slider thought.

'Are you the person dealing with the Laburnum Avenue thing?' the man asked as Slider opened the pass door and caught his eye.

'Yes – come on through.'

Atherton was waiting at the door of the interview room, held it for them, followed them in.

'Fancy it being our old house,' Mr Barnard was saying.

'Please sit down,' Slider said.

'It gave us quite a shock when that policeman rang up,' said Mrs Barnard, sitting. 'We hadn't seen anything in the papers about it, had we, Eric?'

'Not a thing, and I think we'd have noticed because you do, don't you, if you see your own name or the name of your street? You just naturally pick up on it.'

'I suppose being in Norfolk we're a bit cut off. It's so remote up there.'

'That's why we're trying it out, because it's so peaceful and quiet.'

'I think it might be a bit *too* quiet, though,' Mrs Barnard said with a nervous laugh. 'When your nearest neighbour's out of sight and out of earshot . . . I mean, you hear such awful stories about rural robberies, where gangs just come in broad daylight with lorries and take everything, because there's no one around to see them. And the police don't seem to be able to do *anything.*'

'Di,' Mr Barnard said warningly. 'They *are* police.'

'Oh, no offence,' she said quickly. 'I'm sure it's different here. Well, I know it is – we lived in Shepherd's Bush for most of our lives.'

'It was good of you to come all this way to talk to us,' Slider said, in the hope of stemming the flood.

'Oh, but we *had* to,' Mrs Barnard said.

'As good citizens,' said Mr Barnard. 'And to make sure we're not suspected of anything.'

'Because we didn't have anything to do with it, you know.'

'We had no idea there was a body buried in our garden,' said Mr Barnard. 'No idea at all.'

'Such a horrible thought,' said Mrs Barnard with a shudder. 'If we had known . . . Well, *I* couldn't have stayed.'

'We don't know who it is or anything,' said Mr Barnard, keeping to the important point. 'It must have happened before we lived there.'

'Or after.'

'Not after, Di,' he corrected gently. 'We've not been gone that long. It was a skeleton. That doesn't happen in one year.'

'Oh, yes. I forgot. But you do believe us, don't you?' she asked Slider anxiously. 'It's such an awful thing to be connected with, even though we're not, except that it was in our garden. All those years. With our children playing there. Horrible!'

'Let's just start at the beginning,' Slider said soothingly.

They had bought the house in Laburnum Avenue from the Knights, but had never met them. Their dealings had been all with the agents. 'Were you told anything about them?' Slider asked. They shook their heads. 'Why they were selling? Where they were going? Anything at all?' he prompted.

'No,' said Mrs Barnard. 'The agent didn't say and we didn't ask. I don't suppose he knew there was anything funny about them.'

'What about the neighbours? Did they tell you anything about the previous owners?'

They looked at each other and shrugged. 'We never really got to know the neighbours, not the first ones. Only to say hello to if you happened to be going in or out at the same time,' Mrs Barnard said.

Mr Barnard looked embarrassed. 'You know how it is in London. And we were very busy in those days, juggling careers, bringing up children.'

'The people afterwards, in number 17, the Slaters, we got quite friendly with them,' she went on. 'They moved in about ten years after us, and their children were the same age as ours.'

'So this . . . body?' Mr Barnard said hesitantly. 'It's something to do with those people, is it? The ones we bought from?'

'Because if it is, it's horrible,' she said with energy. 'To sell a house knowing *that*'s in the garden. And not say anything.'

'We don't know, Di. It could be people before *them*.' He looked at Slider, hoping for enlightenment, but Slider only looked back blankly.

Atherton recognized the symptoms of deep thought, and took over, easing the Barnards through some more routine questions about themselves, their family, Laburnum Avenue and the environs, while whatever it was brewed in his guv'nor's mind.

Slider came back a little while later when there was a pause. 'Tell me about the garden,' he said. 'You must have done things to it, over the years.'

'Well, not a lot,' Mrs Barnard said apologetically.

'You're wondering why we didn't come across the body ourselves,' Mr Barnard said shrewdly. 'But we didn't do a lot of digging.'

'I'm glad we didn't,' Mrs Barnard said, wincing, 'as it turns out.'

'We're not really gardeners, you see,' said Mr Barnard. 'Mowing the lawn once a week was as much as *I* wanted to do.'

'Once we had a lawn to mow,' she added, looking at him. 'Once we got rid of that hedge.'

'Oh, Lord, yes, I was forgetting. That hedge!'

'Hedge?' Slider asked.

'A great, big laurel hedge,' she said disapprovingly. 'Right across the bottom. Eight foot high.'

'Six, Di,' he corrected.

'Taking up half the garden,' she went on complaining.

'She's exaggerating,' Mr Barnard said hastily, with a little negating wave of his hands, as though Exaggerating to a Police

Officer might be an arrestable offence. 'But you know what laurels are like. They creep.'

'Creep?' Atherton asked. He was not a gardener. But Slider knew what he meant.

'They grow outwards, so you get a shell of leaves on the outside, and it's all bare on the inside, and every year it pushes out a bit more, so you get an empty space behind it,' Mr Barnard tried to explain, with much use of his hands. 'That hedge was really old, must have been there fifty years, I should say, so it was taking up about four feet of garden. It was practically pushing the shed down, as a matter of fact. The leaves were scratching against the boards.'

'It was an ugly thing, anyway,' Mrs Barnard said. 'I've never been keen on laurels. My grandmother had them all round her house. Made it so gloomy.'

'And you decided to cut it down?' Slider asked.

'Well, yes. The garden wasn't that big, and we felt we couldn't afford to waste so much of it,' Mr Barnard said. 'We moved in in the February, and we had it down in the September or October. No point in waiting for winter for something like that, because it's evergreen.'

'And what was it like, behind it, when you took it down?' Slider asked.

'Well, there was just a single trunk in the centre, all the growth came from there.' He looked to see if he had answered to Slider's satisfaction, and seeing more was wanted, went on: 'The hedge was just like a thin wall, making a sort of cave. Bare earth. And the fence was in very poor condition.'

'Yes, we had to repair it,' she jumped in. 'Though by rights it wasn't our fence, it belonged to the people behind, and they ought to have paid for it.'

'But they'd not long moved in, and they weren't keen on the garden, they didn't care about the fence. They said right away, if we wanted it done, we'd have to do it.'

'Despite the fact it was falling down,' she added.

'Falling down?' Slider asked.

'Well, a lot of it was sagging, and two of the boards had fallen right out – rotted away,' Mr Barnard said, 'So there was actually a big gap. If they'd had a dog – the people over the back – it'd have been in and out of our garden all the time.'

'Which we weren't keen on, with two small children,' Mrs Barnard put in.

'*Something* had been going in and out that way,' he said. 'I don't know if the people before them had a dog. Or maybe it was a fox. Or just cats. There was a gap under the laurel at that end, and a flattened place in the garden over the back—'

'Which was a wilderness of weeds, by the way,' she added disapprovingly. 'Terribly overgrown.'

'But once we replaced the missing boards, we never saw any foxes,' he concluded, 'so that put paid to that.'

'And the extra space you'd created,' Slider said, 'what did you do with it?'

'Turfed it. It made more room for the children to play.'

'And the water butt in the corner,' she reminded him. 'There was a terrible drought round about that time, and everyone was going on about conserving water. Funny when you think of it now, with all these floods. But back then, the garden gurus were always going on about planting drought-resistant plants, and collecting rainwater.'

'Yes, and the council was offering rainwater butts at a special price, so we took one and set it up to catch the rain off the shed roof.'

'Actually,' she said, 'the council's offer was back in the spring, but it was such a bargain we took one anyway, though we didn't have anywhere to put it then.'

'But when we had the hedge down, it all came together. There were even a couple of slabs there—'

'Slabs?'

'You know, like paving stones, but concrete. Someone had left them behind.'

'They were in that area, behind the hedge?'

'That's right. So we put the butt there, and I got some plastic guttering—'

'He doesn't want to know all about that,' she interrupted, with her own anxious look. Wittering On to a Police Office, another arrestable offence.

'So you didn't at any time do any digging in that corner?' Atherton asked, seeing Slider had lapsed again into silence, and knowing where he was going now.

'No,' said Mr Barnard. He looked from one to the other. A light bulb went on. 'Don't tell me – is that where . . .? Oh my goodness!'

Slider distracted them. 'So, the people in the house behind,' he asked, 'do you remember their name?'

They exchanged a glance. 'I don't think we ever knew it,' she said.

'But you say they hadn't been there long?'

'No, only about eighteen months more than us.'

'We only had a few conversations with them, mainly over the hedge,' he said, making it clear there was no abiding friendship.

Mrs Barnard took the ball back. 'I think she was a foreigner of some sort – Iranian or something like that. But she spoke good English. He was Scottish – he had a Scottish accent, anyway. I think he was in oil or something. And they had two teenage children, boys. But they didn't like gardening, and you did wonder why they'd bought the house, because that big garden would take a lot of looking after. And it was terribly overgrown. You'd think that alone would have put them off. There were plenty of modern houses with less garden they could have bought.'

She sniffed. Obviously their refusal to pay for the fence still rankled.

'Did you know that, about laurel hedges?' Atherton asked as they climbed the stairs back to his room.

'Yes, of course. Anyone who's ever *had* a laurel hedge . . .' They pushed through the swing doors. 'A laurel hedge is not for Christmas, it's for life. It's not something you want in a wee suburban garden. You end up with a big dry space behind it that can't be used for anything.'

'So you're thinking . . .?'

'We've always wondered how the body could have been buried without anyone's seeing.'

'But how does it help us? I don't really think the Barnards killed anyone, do you? And if Ronnie Knight killed some un-related teenage girl, why would he crawl behind the hedge to bury her? Even if he was a serial killer and murdered Amanda as well, there are so many places to dispose of a body, it never made sense that'd he'd bring her back to the garden.

Wherever he dumped Amanda, he'd dump Miss X as well. But it was a good place, behind the hedge. Unlikely ever to be found back there, as the event proves.'

'You ought to make a beeping noise when you reverse like that,' Slider admonished. They had reached his door.

Atherton went on: 'Maybe the body pre-dates the Knights. There's a depressing thought. Just tracing the people who lived there . . . And, I forgot, we've only got until the end of the week.' He followed Slider into his room. 'What are you going to do now?'

Slider reached for his coat on the back of the door. 'I'm going to see Kellington,' he said.

TWENTY-ONE
Pedes Fictilis

Kellington's daughter looked reproachful. 'He's not well,' she said. 'I don't want you upsetting him.'

'He asked me to come,' Slider said. 'He asked me to let him know what progress we made.'

'In that old case? I don't want him bothering about that. It was over years ago. He'd forgotten all about it till you came, now I can see it's on his mind.'

'Better to get it off his mind then, isn't it?' Slider said. *Or off his chest.* He didn't say that, though. 'Ask him if he'll see me.'

'He'll say yes,' she said, sticking her lip out. Slider stood his ground, trying to look both determined and unthreatening, until she crumpled. 'Oh, all right,' she said. 'I suppose you won't go away till you've seen him. You people have got no thought for others.'

A curious accusation, Slider considered as he followed her through. It was thinking about others that had brought him here.

Kellington appeared to be asleep, but when she roused him and he opened his eyes, he didn't seem surprised to see Slider there. 'Oh, it's you,' he said dully. 'I thought you'd be back. Sit down.'

Slider sat. Kellington looked much worse than at the last visit. There had been a sort of vigour then under his frailness – or, if not exactly vigour, a tautness, like a steel frame under crumbling concrete. Now the supporting structure seemed to be failing. The bridge was coming down, and coming down soon. Slider felt guilty and sorry – and determined. It would be better for Kellington, too, he thought. That thorn had been festering in his flesh for a long time. Better to get it out, even if it was painful.

'So,' said Kellington, 'you worked it all out?'

'Not all. Some.'

'It was Ronnie Knight, wasn't it? Who else could have done it? It was Knight killed her. Had to be.' It was a valiant last defence, but Slider could see the horrible doubts in Kellington's eyes, and it braced him, even while it engaged his pity. It is hard to have your idol exposed, even if you had long suspected the size twelves housed feet of clay.

Slider began. 'When I was here last time, and you said, "God damn him, he did it," you weren't talking about Ronnie Knight, were you?' Kellington stared, warily. 'You were talking about Vickery.'

Kellington took in a sharp breath, which started him coughing. He made Porson sound in the peak of health by comparison. This cough had its roots dug in somewhere important down inside. It was pulling at his actual life. The daughter appeared at his elbow with a glass of water and a pill, and he drank, washed down the pill, blew his nose and wiped his eyes. Slider waited implacably through all of this. It was not a performance, he could see that. But he would have his answers.

'Talk to me about Vickery,' he said, when equilibrium was restored. 'Your superintendent. He was your hero, wasn't he?'

Kellington looked sour. 'Don't talk bollocks. He was a good copper, and my boss, that's all. We worked together on a lot of cases. He was . . . effective.' The word was odd on his lips. It sounded like something he'd read somewhere.

'You admired him,' Slider urged.

'Why shouldn't I?' Kellington said roughly. 'Like I said, he was a good copper.'

'And brilliant. Came from a brilliant family. His brother, for instance – David.'

Kellington drew in a breath at the name, but it wasn't a gasp of alarm this time, merely a sigh of resignation. 'So you know about him,' he said flatly.

'I know about him. The talented younger brother. The high achiever. When did you realize his house backed on to the Knights' house?'

'Straight away. Soon as I went out in the garden, on the Sunday.'

'How did you know where he lived?'

'I'd gone there one time to pick up the boss. He was having

dinner there with his brother. Something'd come up, and I went
to fetch him.' He brooded. 'He was always going on about his
brother, Vickery was. David this and David that. Seemed to think
he was in a different class from him. As far as brains went,
Vickery could think rings round anyone, any time, my opinion.
But still he thought he was nothing next to David. You could,'
he added with delicate distaste, 'get tired of hearing about him.'

And jealous? Slider wondered. He thought of teenage girls
who had a crush on a pop star or a film star, and how bitter they
felt when he got married, how they hated the wife, wanted her
to be ugly and mean, made her so in their minds when she wasn't.
Kellington had had a crush on Vickery – of a different sort, of
course, based as much on real knowledge as fantasy; a grown-up
crush – but perhaps as powerful.

'So David lived in the rear-abutting house. But what made
you think he was involved?'

'I didn't. Why should I? Far as we knew, the Knight girl had
gone missing, done a runner or been snatched. David living there
– that was just a coincidence. How could it be anything else?'

'Then at what stage *did* you start thinking he was involved?'
Kellington was silent. 'All right, at what stage did your Mr
Vickery start taking an interest in the case?'

Kellington looked out of the window, sign of discomfort, but
he had capitulated now. He was admitting the inadmissible. 'I
rung him the Sunday after I'd got back from the house. He liked
to be kept updated. I mentioned that it was the house down the
back of his brother's, just as a matter of interest. He didn't say
anything at first. Then he says, "Are you sure?" Which is not
like him. I mean, I wouldn't say that if I wasn't, would I? So I
says, "Is there a problem?", and he says no, of course not. But
the Monday, when the kid hadn't turned up, and we were going
to search the house and garden, he says he's coming with us, to
have a look. Sounded quite casual about it.'

'But?'

'Eh?'

'You sounded as if you were going to say, "but".'

Kellington hesitated. 'He seemed a bit bothered. Like he wanted
me to think he wasn't interested, but he was really. And . . .'

'Yes?'

'I said something about his brother – just mentioned him, not meaning anything – and he said, Mr Vickery said, quick as a flash, "He's gone away on holiday".' Kellington brooded a moment. 'It struck me as a queer thing to say. I mean, what was that about? Why mention it at all?'

'Why indeed,' Slider said. If Vickery was pre-empting any suspicion, it must have been because there was suspicion to be had. Even Kellington, the good dog, the loyal hound, was copper enough to have sniffed that particular kipper and found it ripe.

'Go on. What did you do on the Monday?'

'We went down there. In separate cars. Ready to do the full search. I sent my boys out to look at the van and the shed. I interviewed the parents again. And Mr Vickery . . .'

Slider saw he was coming to the really bad bit. He had already guessed what it was.

'Go on.'

'He said he wanted to look at the girl's bedroom. Well, that's SOP. I thought he'd have wanted to hear what the Knights had to say, but he went up alone. When I was done, I went up there as well. He – he sort of jumped when I came to the door.'

'What was he doing? Was he reading something?'

Kellington raised mournful eyes. He was a bad dog. 'You know, then?'

'Tell me.'

'It was a diary, one of those five-year things with a lock on it. Red leather. I recognized it – they were all the rage round about then with young girls, to write their secrets in. Daft! Anyone could break the lock with one finger, but I suppose the point was they'd know if anyone did. Like their mum or dad.'

'What did Vickery do?'

'He sort of dropped his hand down the side of his leg, hiding it from me. He said, "All done?" I said yes. I asked if he'd found anything, and he said no. I said I was going out to have a look at the garden. He said he'd come and help me. And he sort of waited for me to go first.'

Slider nodded kindly. 'And he followed you?'

'Yes.'

'Straight away?'

'More or less.'

'And what did he do in the garden?'

'He watched for a bit. Then he said there was nothing to see, you could see the whole garden from where he stood, and he called the boys off. He said the girl had obviously run away, and we were wasting our time here. We'd do better talking to the neighbours.'

'What else did you do?'

'I told you all this before. We knocked on every door up and down the street. Asked in local shops, showed her picture at the tube station and the bus depot. Her mum said she went to the lib'ry a lot so we asked there. Then Mr Vickery says to drop it.'

'He told you to drop the case?'

Kellington looked briefly annoyed. 'Things were different then. There wasn't all this fuss. Girls run away all the time, there's nothing you can do. Vickery was right about that. He said, there's no reason to think anything bad's happened to her. No sense in killing ourselves over it. We'd got better things to do. So we filed it.'

'And the diary?'

'I never saw it again. Why?'

'It was missing from amongst her things. Her parents packed up the contents of her room when they moved. They kept them in a box, undisturbed. I've looked through that box, and the diary's not there.'

'Doesn't mean anything. Maybe they got rid of it.'

'Did you see the Knight file before it went to Missing Persons?'

'Course I did. Had it in my hands many times.'

'And was it thick?'

'Just normal. You know what it's like.'

'Yes, I do. Who took it down there?'

'How would I know?' Kellington said roughly. 'All that time ago? How would I remember?'

Slider studied him. 'But you do remember. Because you've wondered. Since I told you we'd found the body, you've been wondering a lot. Who took the file?'

There was no further place to go. Kellington looked down at his big bony hands as they lay in his lap. 'I took it into Mr Vickery's room and said, "Have we finished with this, then?" And he said yes. He said to put it on his desk, he'd got to go to

Records for something else and he'd take it down then. Save me a journey.'

'That was nice of him. And when did you next see it?'

'I never saw it again. Why would I? I've never looked at the case since. It was a misper and that was the end of it.'

'Yes, quite.' Slider relapsed into thought.

'Look,' Kellington roused him, 'what exactly are you suspecting? I thought you said you'd worked it out.'

'I know many things now. Why she was buried in the garden. Why she was never seen outside in the street. Now I know why her diary was missing. Why the file was so thin.'

'You don't know what happened to the file. Stuff could have been lost any time. Good God, man, it's been twenty-five years! And the diary – who's to say it wasn't the father got rid of it? What do you think was in it anyway?'

Slider didn't answer that. 'Vickery left the Job soon afterwards, didn't he?'

'End of September. He was burnt out. You could see it – they often go that way, your brilliant ones. Just suddenly had enough. Then he upped sticks and emigrated to Australia. Suppose he wanted a change of scene.'

'Is that where he is now?'

Kellington looked bleak. 'I heard he snuffed it not long after. Car crash. Up in the mountains. Car went through a safety barrier and down a ravine. It was in their papers, and some copper over there sent it to a copper mate over here who's a friend of a friend of mine who knew I knew him and sent it to me.' A pause, then he looked up. 'You don't think . . .?'

'That he couldn't live with himself any more?'

He was annoyed. 'I wasn't going to say that. Car crash was an accident. I was going to say, you can't think he was involved in the murder.'

'No, I don't think *he* was.'

'*Or* his brother, if that's where you're going. I don't see it. This Amanda Knight girl, what was she to either of them?'

'It wasn't Amanda Knight,' said Slider.

'Eh?'

'The bones. The DNA test came back. It wasn't Amanda.'

*   *   *

'So Vickery told them to cool off on the search?' said Atherton. 'He must have known, then.'

'Known what?'

'That there was funny business going on.'

'Is that what I think?'

'Look, it's obvious. Vickery must have spoken to his brother to know he's gone on holiday. And he wouldn't have mentioned it at all if it wasn't meant to be a sort of alibi. And then he left the Job more or less straight away. He must have given in his notice by the end of August to leave at the end of September. That's only two weeks afterwards. So he must have known something.'

'I think he did know something,' Slider agreed.

'And he doctored the file so that if the case ever got revived, there'd be nothing in there to implicate—'

'Yes?'

'Well, the brother, I suppose. I mean, it could hardly be our Mr Vickery. Or could it? Or both of them together? No, look, I assume you're thinking that the body, which is not Amanda, is a victim of David Vickery's and that Edgar Vickery for some reason suspected. Maybe David had done weird stuff before, and Vickery knew about it, or at least suspected it, and decided to protect his little brother. But this time it was too much for his conscience and he had a breakdown and quit.' He frowned. 'But that still doesn't make a whole lot of sense. Why would that stop them searching for Amanda? What's Amanda got to do with it at all? What does the diary have to do with it?'

'Melissa Vickery is the key,' said Slider.

'Well, I guessed *that*,' Atherton said. 'But give me a clue, will you?'

'I'll give you several. Amanda Knight had a crush on David Essex. She was mad about animals. David Vickery ran away with his daughter and never came back. Melissa Vickery never married.'

Atherton shook his head. 'Not there yet.'

Slider went on. 'And though the two little girls were superficially quite alike, there was one major difference.'

'Do tell,' said Atherton with taut patience.

'Melissa Vickery had brown eyes.'

*   *   *

Because of the firearms at the farmhouse, Porson insisted they get the local police involved. 'You don't want to be interviewing her at the house. And you don't want some kind of nutty siege situation developing. We need to get her out of there and interview her in some neutral place.'

'There are the firearms violations,' Slider said. 'Assuming she has a licence at all – which the locals will know – the guns are supposed to be kept in a locked cabinet, not hanging handily over the fireplace. They can ask her politely to come in to discuss certain irregularities, and we can talk to her at the station. As long as they make it sound routine, that ought to work.'

'All right,' said Porson. 'I'll have a word with their super. But what if she doesn't come in voluntarily?'

'I think she will,' Slider said. 'Her whole life has been dedicated to pretending everything's normal. But if she doesn't – well, she has to leave the house sometimes, to shop and so on. I'd recommend stopping her in the town or outside the supermarket or wherever. Just tell them not to alarm her.'

Porson regarded him for a moment. 'D'you think she'll cough?'

Slider thought. 'I think underneath she's longing to. It's a hell of a story never to have told anyone.'

Cirencester police station was, like so many of them nowadays, a yellow-brick barracks of no charm whatsoever.

'All serene?' Slider asked the custody sergeant, a good-looking young man with blue eyes and a firm jaw – a poster-boy for the Job if ever there was one.

'I wouldn't say that, exactly,' he said. The gentle Gloucestershire burr only added to his charm. 'She's not a happy bunny. We asked her to come in and discuss the renewal of her licence. When she got here we said there were irregularities, and someone was coming to talk to her about it. She's in an interview room now, waiting for you.'

'You didn't tell her—?'

'Anything about you? No, sir. Or what you want to talk about.' He grinned. 'I'm not sure we actually know. No, all she knows is we've discovered firearms irregularities. She's had a cup of tea, and the last thing she was complaining about was being delayed because she's got animals to feed.'

'Right. Thanks.'

'Do you need backup? Is she likely to be violent?'

Slider considered. 'I don't think so. I think she knows the game is up.'

'Well, there'll be one of our uniform lads waiting outside if you need him.'

'Thank you.'

TWENTY-TWO
Oh Spite! Oh Hell!

They had a peep at her before they went in. She was looking bored, wearing dungarees and the wellingtons, her hair dragged back unbecomingly behind. Under the dungarees was a man's red and green plaid shirt. He remembered the cord trousers. Did she keep all David's clothes to wear herself? Slider wondered. It was a rather horrid evidence of obsession, if so.

Despite her apparent sang-froid, she jumped when Slider came into the room, lurched to her feet, and if this had been a western saloon she'd have been reaching for her shootin' iron.

He got in quickly before she could speak. 'Sit down, please,' he said, so firmly that she obeyed automatically.

'Well, well,' she said sourly, 'if it isn't Butch and Sundance.' Odd that she was thinking the same thing, Slider mused. 'The old man and the talent. I suppose it was you that shopped me to the local plod?'

'I did tell them about your unsecured shotguns, yes,' said Slider.

'Didn't like me making you look small,' she sneered, 'so you got them to do your dirty work for you.'

'I wanted to have another little chat with you, and I thought it would be more comfortable here,' said Slider, sitting down. Atherton, prudently, took a lounging position behind him, near the door. She was not a big woman, but they knew she was full of passions, and strong from strangling chickens.

'Comfortable for who?'

'Oh, for all of us. We may be here a little while.'

'*You* may be. What if I decide I don't want a chat with you? What if I decide to leave?'

'Then I'm afraid we will have to arrest you. But it needn't come to that. Why don't we just talk, and see how we get on? I have some questions for you.'

She rolled her eyes. 'Oh, go on then. What do you want to know?'

'To begin with, why didn't you tell me that Amanda used to come through the hedge at the bottom of the garden to visit you?'

Her eyes opened wide. Whatever she had expected, it wasn't that. 'Why on earth should I? What does it matter?'

'She went through the hedge, like Alice down the rabbit hole, into a magical place, a world of possibilities,' said Slider. She looked at him quizzically. 'That's how she came and went without being seen,' he went on, 'without going out onto the street. And it made it extra exciting – like a secret passage that only she knew about. Added to the thrill of it all.'

'What are you *talking* about?' she said witheringly, but he saw she was alert.

'She came through every day during those summer holidays, didn't she?' he went on. 'Her parents were both at work, she had nothing to do, no friends but you. And most importantly, she was in love with David Vickery.'

She was still for a moment, then said robustly, 'Don't talk such rubbish.'

'I suppose it began with an ordinary teenage crush. He did look a bit like David Essex, didn't he? Even had the same first name. And it's a mistake to underestimate the power of a teenage girl's first love. It's all-consuming, it can burn down cities, and sometimes it lasts a lifetime – especially if, unusually, it crosses over from fantasy into reality. All those girls who screamed and fainted for the Beatles, never got to meet them in the flesh, never got to have sex with them, live with them. How did the reality match up, in the end? Was it worth it?'

'What are you asking me for?' she demanded, but her eyes were fixed on his.

'She was lonely, an only child, and very bright, and her parents couldn't keep up with her mentally. She was isolated at home – isolated at school, too, where all the other girls came from a different sort of home. She longed for someone who understood her, she was ready, *desperate*, to give her heart to someone. She wanted to love – and being the age she was, that emotional yearning got mixed up with burgeoning hormones. It's a potent mixture. David Vickery ticked all the boxes: handsome, extremely intelligent – and available.'

A little fire was burning deep down in those eyes now. 'What are you talking about – ticking boxes? Available? You make it sound like—'

'Yes?' No answer. 'I make it sound trivial?' He saw agreement in her face. 'I assure you, I don't think it's trivial. Far from it. I understand. I *get* it, I really do.'

'You don't know anything!' she exclaimed, standing up. 'And I don't have to sit here and listen to you talking rubbish. I'm leaving.'

He stood too. 'I did warn you earlier, that if you try to leave, I shall have to arrest you.'

'Arrest me for what? Not having my guns locked up?'

'Oh, there are any number of things I could arrest you for, some of which I hope we're going to discuss. But just for a start, and most easy to prove, is financial fraud.'

She looked at him searchingly, warily. 'Fraud? What are you talking about.'

'You know very well. You've been receiving money, royalties from patents owned by the late David Vickery.'

'He left them to me!' she said angrily.

'He left them to Melissa Vickery,' said Slider, holding her gaze. 'And you are not Melissa Vickery.'

She was silent, her mouth open, her mind evidently frantically computing behind the puzzled eyes.

'If we arrest you,' said Slider, 'we will fingerprint you and take a DNA sample. That's normal procedure. And we will compare your DNA with that of Mrs Margaret Knight – a sample of which we have already sequenced – and prove that you are, in fact, her daughter Amanda.'

She sat, slowly, looking dazed.

He felt, most unwillingly, sorry for her. He said, 'I've told you that I *get* you, Amanda. It's true, I do. And I would like to hear your story from *you*. This is your chance to tell it all, everything, from the beginning. No need to hold anything back now. I think you've been wanting someone to tell it to for a long time. Well, here I am. We've got as long as you like. No one will disturb us. Tell me.'

'Dear God,' she said faintly, hoarsely. She shook her head, but it was bewilderment rather than denial. 'Where do I start?'

'Start with how you first met them – David and Melissa,' said Slider. 'Start there.'

It was David she had met first, not Melissa. The earlier story about the gloves had been a lie.

She had been walking back from school one day, dawdling, bored, not wanting to go home to the empty house with its limited resources.

'When was that?' Slider asked.

'May. Some time in May.'

She had gone to the newsagent-tobacconists on the corner of Colville Avenue to see if the latest issue of *Jackie* was out. David was ahead of her at the counter and turning too quickly when he had finished, almost knocked her over. He caught hold of her to steady her, their eyes met, and she was in love.

'The way he'd grabbed me, his hands were sort of touching the side of my breasts. He started to say sorry, but he could see I didn't mind.' He had lingered outside the shop, and when she came out, he apologized again. 'He asked where I was going, and I said, home, but I didn't want to because there was no one in, my parents were at work. So then he said he had a daughter about my age, and would I like to go home and have tea with them.'

Nothing, Slider understood, could have stopped her. All those teenage girls who went into stars' dressing rooms at pop concerts were not more eager to embrace their fate than Amanda Knight that day.

She'd never seen Melissa before. 'She went to a different school. I didn't particularly like her when I met her. She was a drip. Nothing to say for herself. Never looked up, never spoke above a whisper. You practically forgot she was there. I didn't care. David and I did all the talking, which suited me just fine.'

It was a warm summer day, and they had tea out in the garden.

'I mentioned we lived in the next road, and David and I got up and walked down the garden to see if we could work out which was my house. It was just an excuse to get away from Melissa. While we were standing there looking, I could feel him sort of pressing against me from behind – like, accidentally-on-purpose.'

Finding that the Knights' house was just through the fence at the bottom was a bonus. 'I saw a bit of his fence was missing, and I said, "I bet I could get through there. It'd be a short cut".'

David encouraged her to try, knelt down by the hole and looked through after she'd gone in. 'It's like a cave in there,' he'd said. She'd discovered that she could wriggle under the laurel hedge at that end. '"Look at that," I said. "I don't need to go out into the road at all." And he said, "It can be our secret passage. Now you can come and visit whenever you like."'

'What did you think he meant by that?' Slider asked.

'Well, it could have meant, come and visit Melissa. But I was hoping it was more than that,' she said.

'What about Melissa's mother?'

'Oh, I knew she was dead. That came out when we were having tea. He told me Melissa needed a friend because her mother had died the year before. Then he said, "I think I need a friend, too. I work at home alone all day, and it can get pretty lonely."'

'So you think he was attracted to you from the beginning?' Slider asked, concealing his distaste.

'I know he was,' she said complacently. Her eyes were distant, and he could see she was reliving the early days of the romance, when her pop-star hero had taken flesh and dwelt right next door.

'And when did the relationship take on a physical aspect?' Slider asked.

'A couple of weeks later,' she said. 'I went through the hedge like usual after school—'

'Through the hedge?'

'I'd started going home first,' she said impatiently. 'To change. I didn't want to see David in my school uniform. Anyway, I went through, I walked into the house, and when I called out, "Anybody home?" he called for me to go upstairs. He worked at the top of the house. He met me halfway down, on the middle floor. He said Melissa had gone on an outing with a school club, and wouldn't be back until about seven. He said he hoped I wasn't disappointed. I said far from it. We were standing very close together. I was praying he'd kiss me. And he did,' she concluded simply.

They went to his bedroom and consummated her love. 'It was magical. The most wonderful moment of my life,' she said.

They had only managed to do it twice more before the summer holidays. But then, with so much more time on her hands, she had virtually lived at the Vickerys' house. 'At first, we could only do it when Melissa was out, but he managed to make sure she was out quite a lot. But after a while, we were so hot for each other, we took to going to the bedroom whenever we wanted, and just locking the door. Sometimes we didn't make it to the bedroom. We did it all over the house,' she said proudly.

'Your birthday,' Slider said, 'was in June, wasn't it? You asked your parents for a diary that locked.'

She looked surprised. 'You're not on about that diary again?' And then, unexpectedly, she blushed. 'You haven't found it? Oh God, you haven't read it, have you?'

'No, it disappeared. I assumed asking for one that locked meant you had something to write down that you didn't want your parents to read.' She looked away. 'You wrote down all about your affair with David, didn't you?'

She nodded. 'Every blessed word. Every kiss. What was I thinking? But they would never have peeked, my parents. They were stupid, my dad was an ass and a bully, but he was honest. He'd never have read it, even if I forgot to lock it.'

'Tell me about Melissa,' Slider said next.

'What about her?'

'Well, she must have started to suspect something. Eventually.'

For the first time she looked uncomfortable. 'Oh, Melissa. She really was a pain in the neck. I suppose she must have suspected. Even she couldn't be that stupid. I didn't care. I never really thought about her at all. She was such a *nothing*. It wouldn't have mattered, anyway, if she hadn't got jealous.'

'Jealous?'

'I mean, she still had him to herself all night. Actually, I'm not sure she liked that side of it, really. But since her mum died she'd been sort of looking after him, doing the cooking and washing and cleaning, sort of being like a wife to him, and I think she felt he ought to have appreciated her more.'

Slider felt cold all down his insides, as though he swallowed an ice cube. 'When you say she didn't like "that side of it",' he said as casually as he could, 'do you mean . . .?'

She shrugged indifferently. 'It started with just sharing the bed, because they were both lonely and upset. But one thing led to another. David was a very *physical* man. You'd think she'd be glad, really, that I took that over from her.'

'Weren't you afraid she might tell someone? Wasn't he afraid she might?'

'She'd never have said anything,' she said harshly. 'She worshipped him. And she was too much of a wimp. Like I said, she was wet. A complete drip.'

Slider thought of Edgar Vickery. Was that what he had suspected – or known? Or had there been something else in the past? 'I wonder,' he said, 'whether there were others before you.'

He thought that might cause an explosion, but she only shrugged. 'I don't know about that. There were others after me. He had a taste for schoolgirls. I had to keep an eye on him. But I never let it go too far. As soon as I saw the signs, I jumped on him. And it faded away as he got older.' She sounded almost disconsolate. 'The fire burned down, if you like. He'd look, but he never had the energy to touch.'

'Tell me about that last day,' Slider said. He felt Atherton tense behind him. This was the testing part. So far, she had talked freely, but she hadn't incriminated herself. He had to keep her talking without alarm, to get her to tell the rest, to run out the thread without knotting it.

'What last day?' she said absently, busy with her thoughts.

'Saturday the 18th of August, 1990. The day Amanda went through the hedge, and never came back. What happened that day?'

She thought about it, and her mouth turned down. 'It was all Melissa's fault, stupid idiot. There was no need for her to make a fuss.'

'What happened?' He pressed her gently.

'David was working on something up in his room. Melissa and I were sitting on a rug in the garden. It was really hot that day. I said, "I bet David could do with a cup of tea". We went in, and Melissa made tea, and I took it up in his special mug. Well, he was just ready for a break. Working always made him randy, especially if it was going well. So we started . . . you know. We were getting into it when Melissa came in and shouted at us. I was on his desk with my legs round him, and when she shouted it made me jump and I knocked the mug over. Luckily most of the tea went on the floor, but she started screaming about his papers on the desk and how important they were. What if the tea had gone all over his work and ruined it? I told her to calm down but she didn't. She started going on about what was I doing in there anyway? She said *she* was never even allowed into his room, but I seemed to think I could go anywhere I liked and do anything I liked.' She shook her head. 'She was raving. She was mad and scared and jealous and crazy. She said she was going to tell everyone and we'd be locked up. She wouldn't *stop*. She just – wouldn't – *stop*! Stupid girl!'

'So David stopped her,' Slider suggested, the merest breath of a question.

She was grave now, all the poke gone out of her. 'He didn't mean to – you know – be so rough, but he was angry. Well, a man doesn't like being interrupted at a moment like that. And she wouldn't stop screaming. He grabbed her by the neck, just to shut her up, really, but she fell over and he fell with her. They were both on the ground. She grabbed the coffee mug from the floor and started hitting him on the head with it, so I grabbed her arms, but she wouldn't stop struggling, so I knelt on them. When she stopped screaming he let her go and got up. He said, "Come on, Mel, get up now", but she didn't move.' She sounded sad, almost quite regretful. 'I think we overdid it,' she concluded.

You think? Slider said inwardly, in broad irony. What he said was: 'So then you had to decide what to do with the body.'

The sadness went, the grit came back. 'It was mostly me. David went to pieces. He wanted to go to the police and say it was an accident. I said, with those bruises? And what about me? God knows what would have happened to me. I said no way I'm going to prison. He said you won't, it was my fault, and I said at the very least they wouldn't let me see him again, and I wasn't having that. I told him to calm down, we could get out of this all right if we kept our heads.'

'And you came up with a plan. Which was, for you to become Melissa,' said Slider.

She shrugged. 'We were the same height, same age, same colour hair. I could fit into her clothes. But it had to be somewhere we weren't known. And we had to leave right away, because as soon as I went missing, they'd start looking for me. So I just didn't go home.'

'Then there was the problem of the body,' Slider suggested.

'Yeah. That was a hard one,' said Amanda. 'He wanted to take her out in the car after dark, but you only had to watch the news to know they *always* get seen by somebody when they do that. I said we had to bury her in the garden. But he said we couldn't leave any sign of newly dug earth. Then we both thought of the space behind the hedge – between his fence and our hedge. Nobody knew about it, and nobody would be able to see anything from the outside.' She shrugged. 'So that's what we did. In the middle of the night. We took turns holding the torch and digging, because there wasn't much room in there and it was difficult. But we got it done.'

'You put some paving slabs on top of the grave.'

'Oh, yes, I'd forgotten. David was scared cats or foxes would dig it up. He had some slabs left over from when the patio was laid, so we put a couple on top. And the next morning, he told the people next door we were going on holiday – he always gave them the keys when they went away, so it had to look natural – and we never came back. Well, David did, to collect stuff before the house was sold, but I didn't. I couldn't risk anyone *there* seeing me.'

'Did he telephone his brother during that evening?'

She had been thinking, and looked up, surprised. 'His brother? Oh, I know. No, the brother phoned him. They were supposed to get together or something on the Sunday, but David told him he was going on holiday.'

'Did he tell him anything else?'

'I don't know. I didn't hear all the conversation. He was on a long time.' She frowned. 'But he'd hardly have told him he'd killed Melissa, would he? I mean, you don't.'

No, Slider thought, perhaps you don't. But he'd told him something – enough, at any rate, for Edgar Vickery to put two and two together the following day and make a considerable sum, large enough to make him compromise his conscience, sully the law he served, and destroy his career. Enough, probably, to ruin his mental health and bring him to an early grave.

'Did David keep in touch with his brother after you left?' Slider asked.

'I'm sure not,' she said indifferently. 'That was the whole point – we had to make a clean break, go where we weren't known, and start a new life together. And we did.'

'You went to school in Tetbury,' he said.

'David said I had to, or the authorities would be after me. We had to pretend I was Melissa until school-leaving age. I went as little as possible, I can tell you. And as soon as I was sixteen, I left school and we moved out of town. To the farm.' She stopped, sinking back into thought. She roused herself a moment later, to say: 'And that's the end of the story.'

Slider and Atherton were both reeling from the casual recounting of so Gothic a horror story. Atherton recovered first. 'Did you never think, in all that time, of how your parents must be suffering?'

She looked up at him in surprise. 'No. Why should I?' she said. And then, perhaps thinking that did not reflect too well on her, she said, 'They wouldn't care. They didn't even like me very much. They'd think I'd just run away, and after a bit they'd forget me.'

'Your father was suspected of having murdered you,' Atherton said.

To their shock, she burst out laughing. 'No! That's rich! My dad, murder me? He'd never have had the nerve. He used to shout a lot, but that's all he did. He was scared of me, if you want the truth. He was scared of anything he didn't understand, and boy, he didn't understand the first thing about me! That's why he shouted so much. Shouting was all he could do, faced with anything above his level of intelligence,' she concluded contemptuously.

Slider heard Atherton take a breath, and stopped him with a movement of his hand. He wanted to keep her on side, keep her wanting to tell. 'So you had twenty years, more or less, living with David as his wife. Was it worth it?'

'What do you think?' she said; but then the animation faded. 'I knew it had to end one day. He was a lot older than me, after all. I didn't know it would be that soon, though. It's a bastard thing, that cancer.'

'It must have been awful for you,' Slider said gently, 'watching him suffer.'

'It was,' she said, her eyes inward. 'Seeing him go downhill. He wasn't my David any more. Well, he'd been going downhill for years. The fire went out of him, he didn't work any more, he just slumped about the place. I got fed up with him. Then he got ill. At the end he was just bones covered in skin.' She stared at nothing. 'He didn't smell too good, either,' she added out of the blue.

'So one day . . .' Slider prompted.

'You don't let them suffer,' she said slowly. 'I've always loved animals. I wanted to be a vet when I was a kid. And that was the first rule. You don't let them suffer. You put them out of their misery. I told him there was a loose panel on the hen house that needed fixing. I followed him out with the twelve-bore. He was kneeling down, trying to hammer a nail in. I got up close, called his name, and when he looked up, I shot him in the head. That way it would look like suicide.' She drew a sigh. 'I wanted to bury him on our land, where we'd been happy, but the regs were so complicated, in the end I had to let it go, and he's buried in the cemetery. They make simple things so difficult these days.'

'Yes,' said Slider. 'I suppose they do.'

Everything she had done had seemed simple to her, he thought. It was a function of obsession.

TWENTY-THREE
A World More Full of Weeping

They went up to the canteen to get a cup of tea while they waited for the duty solicitor to come in, so they could take her statement.

'She's mad, of course,' said Atherton. 'Mad as a ferret in a blender. How do you think this is going to go? We haven't got much except the confession. I'm surprised, really, she did.'

'What else would she do?' Slider said. 'He's dead. He was her whole life. There's nothing left for her but to talk about it, and no one but us to tell.'

'What a story,' Atherton said. 'If that's what love does to you . . .'

'Not love, passion. Love ages, puts on weight and gets comfortable, but passion goes on burning. The topless towers . . .'

'Topless Towers sounds like some kind of adult theme park.'

'I was referring to Ilium,' Slider said with dignity.

'I know. But that was Helen's face, not her passion.'

'Comes out the same,' said Slider.

Taking the statement took all night. They drove back to London as a pink dawn was breaking, and Slider went home for a shower and breakfast before going back in to start the ball rolling their end.

Despite his cold, Porson was in early, after their telephone conversation the evening before. 'You look whacked,' he said as Slider came through his door. He stood still, unusually, arms folded across his chest and chin lowered while he listened to Slider's report. 'So, no problem with the statement?' he said afterwards.

'No. She told it all the same the second time. Even added some detail. She seemed happy to have the extra audience. Cocky, almost.'

'Yes,' said Porson, broodingly. 'As well she might. I don't like it, don't like it at all.' Now he began walking. 'If she's as intelligent as you say, barmy or not, she'll know what the score is. She'll think she can get away with it.'

'Really?'

'It's a mess. I can't see the CPS running with it. They don't like going in when all we've got is a confession. No hard evidence.'

'The DNA?' Slider suggested.

'Doesn't tie anything down.' He paused to mop his eyes and nose. 'It's a hell of a complicated story. A jury might not get it. Or if they did, they might not convict. After all, it was him that killed his daughter, according to her.'

'She held her down,' said Slider. 'It's common purpose. And she's not a sympathetic character.'

Porson shrugged. 'A good brief can make anyone look sympathetic.'

'She's showed no remorse. She made her plan and carried it out. The people who got in her way didn't figure with her at all. She even killed *him* in the end.'

'Well, what's goose for the gander is good for other,' Porson said. 'And that raises the question of her sanity, doesn't it?' He stopped in the middle of his walk and faced Slider. 'I'm just trying to prepare you for disappointment, that's all.'

'Thank you, sir. You're very kind.'

Porson gave him a raised eyebrow. 'Oh, irony! You could cut yourself with that. Also, there's this Kellington-Vickery aspic as well. You've got to think about that. Another reason the CPS might give it the bum's shoulder. It wouldn't reflect well on the Job.'

'Vickery's dead. And Kellington won't last much longer, from the look of him,' said Slider. 'And it was all a long time ago.'

'There you are, then,' said Porson. 'Where's the public interest in prosecuting something that happened twenty-five years ago? But look on the bright side,' he added, walking again. 'You got it done – *and* before the end of the week.'

'On time and on budget,' said Slider. More irony.

Porson ignored that. 'You did good. This'll go in your record, whether they prosecute or not. I wouldn't be surprised if there wasn't a commendation for you in it.'

Take two attaboys out of petty cash, Slider thought. 'Yes, sir,' he said.

'Right,' said Porson, dusting his hands. 'When's she arriving?'

'She'll be on her way here after the statutory rest. So she'll be here this afternoon some time.'

'Good. That gives you time to set up a psychiatric assessment. That's the first thing. My guess is that she'll be found unfit and referred for treatment. So she'll get locked up, one way or another. And this way it's indefinite. So don't brood about it.'

'No, sir,' said Slider.

He was almost out when Porson said, 'Oh, by the way, I've got some news that may interest you. Shut the door.' When Slider had complied, he said, 'It's about Assistant Commissioner Millichip. I've just heard this morning he's been required to resign.'

'Sir?' Slider brightened. Required to resign, for the higher ranks, was the equivalent of being sacked.

'Yes, I thought that'd cheer you up.' Porson nodded.

'Is it over Operation Neptune?'

'No, it's not. I told you, Neptune's been filed. It's a Fraud Squad thing. The North Kensington Regeneration Trust. He was well involved, and as I understand it, there are going to be prosecutions. Quite a few of them. Now this is sub-judice, so don't talk about it, but I thought you deserved to know, seeing as you set so much store by it. Millichip's gone, Marler's been deselected, the parties have been stopped, all's well with the world, eh?'

'Yes, sir,' Slider said.

'All right, off you go,' said Porson. 'Go and bask in glory while you can. It doesn't last long.'

Slider didn't need to be told that.

The troops listened in silence as he and Atherton unreeled the story from Amanda's point of view, tacking it down here and there with a deft stitch to the evidence from their own end. At the end there was a thoughtful silence as they digested it all.

Then Swilley said, 'What gripes me is that he got away with it, David Vickery. He seduces a schoolgirl, kills his own daughter, and goes on to lead a normal life.'

'Until he got a twelve-bore in the face,' Connolly reminded her.

'I wonder,' Atherton said, 'whether that actually happened. It might have been fantasy on Amanda's part – what she feels in retrospect she ought to have done. It came out rather too pat in the confession. More likely he did it himself.'

'Why would she confess to murder and put herself in danger of prosecution if she didn't do it?' Gascoyne asked.

'Because she knows she's safe. We've got no evidence,' Lessop said. 'Can't go just with a confession.'

'She wouldn't know that,' LaSalle said. 'The public think a confession is everything.'

'I think David Vickery suffered his own punishment,' Slider said to Swilley, to comfort her. He'd used the same thought himself. 'He went into exile, and I'd like to believe he was haunted by what he did every day of his life.'

'It's not the same,' she sniffed.

'No, it's not,' said Hart. 'Boss, what *are* we going to get her for, Amanda?'

'I don't know,' said Slider. 'It depends on the psychiatric assessment, to begin with. And then on the CPS.'

'They won't touch it,' McLaren said with gloomy conviction. 'Too messy. Too long ago. And she's an obvious nut job.'

'So we busted our humps for nothing!' Fathom complained.

'It wasn't for nothing,' Slider said. 'We did excellent work. We solved a very difficult and obscure case. Two cases, in fact, a misper and a homicide. We should be proud of ourselves. I'm proud of all of you.' They looked back at him.

Connolly said, 'Talking of bodies . . .' Everyone looked at her. Slider's heart sank. She was going to bring up the point he had been trying not to think about. 'The bones,' she said. 'We're saying now they're Melissa? But how do we prove it? There's no rellies to get DNA from. And what happens to them?'

'Yes, and what do we tell Mrs Knight?' Swilley asked.

'And her sister,' Connolly added.

'I suppose we couldn't let 'em have the bones and say nothing,' Hart said wistfully. 'Let the Pearl and the Emerald give them a decent burial. Two birds with one stone.'

'That's really very witty,' said Atherton. 'Two birds with one headstone. I wish I'd said it.'

'Oh, have manners!' Connolly snapped. 'We're talking about human feelings here.'

'No, we're talking about processes of the law,' Atherton objected.

'Well, I bagsie you be the one to tell Mrs Knight that her daughter's been alive all along, but that she's a cold-hearted murdering bitch who let her mammy suffer all these years because she didn't give a tinker's about her,' Connolly retorted hotly.

'And that she'll never see her again because she'll be banged up in a psycho unit,' McLaren added. 'Nice one.'

'What *will* happen to the bones, sir?' Gascoyne asked, restoring sanity. 'If there's no relatives?'

'That'll be for the coroner to decide,' said Slider.

'Buried on the parish,' Swilley said.

'Don't get sentimental,' said Atherton.

'It will be done respectfully,' Slider said. 'And anyone who wants can go.'

There were no immediate takers. Talk was free, but free time was precious. But Slider thought that he would probably go. And glancing at Atherton, he thought that he probably would too, despite his slick words.

His missing night's sleep was beginning to catch up with him, so he went up to the canteen, as much for the exercise as for a cup of tea strong enough to trot a mouse across. When he got back, he found Joanna was there, with George, who was sitting on the edge of Swilley's desk, swinging his stout little legs and holding court. He loved company.

Joanna stepped aside to talk to him.

'What's that about?' he asked, cocking an eye to his son. George was flirting outrageously with Swilley, who was visibly melting. The very sight made him feel less tired.

'I saw how knackered you were this morning,' Joanna said, 'so I thought you'd need cheering up.'

'It's working,' Slider said. 'Thanks.'

'And I've got some news. You know my *Whistle* depping ends tonight? Well, I had a phone call this morning from Frank Samuels.'

'The fixer? You haven't heard from him in a while.'

She nodded. 'He's only just caught up with the fact that I'm back in circulation. But he's always liked me, and he's offered me a whole lot of sessions, starting next week. For the new *Star Wars* movie.'

'Oh, that's wonderful,' he said. 'They pay really well, don't they?'

'Yes, and even more wonderfully, there'll be an album afterwards, which means more work, and residuals.' She grinned happily. 'And I love session work. No cracked singers or potty MDs. Just lots and lots of lovely dots, and hanging around with all my favourite professional musicians. Pig heaven!'

'I'm very glad for you,' he said, with sincerity.

She eyed him carefully. 'And you've solved this bones thing. So you're happy?'

'I'll tell you all about it later,' he said. 'At the moment there are some administrative details to clear up.'

'Well, I won't get in your way, then. Boy and I will go and have a bun somewhere. Shall I see you before I leave tonight?' He hesitated. 'Probably not,' she answered herself. 'All right, later then.' She was going, but turned back to say, 'Oh, and here's one to tell Atherton. The keyboardist told me last night. Lloyd Webber's writing a new musical about a pit collapse. Do you know what key it's in?'

'Tell me,' he said obediently.

'A Flat Minor,' she said, and fled from his groans.

He got a phone call from a Vicky Rayner from Berkshire police's Victim Support Group.

'It's about Mrs Knight, Mrs Margaret Knight,' she said. 'They tell me at Reading station it was you that first put us on to her.'

'I went to interview her about her daughter who went missing in 1990,' Slider said.

'That's what they said. Well, I wondered whether you had any more information about her daughter, at all? Or any other relatives?'

'Why do you ask?' Slider said warily.

'Only, I'm sorry to say she's died. She had a heart attack last night. A neighbour who had her key found her and called the ambulance, but she was pronounced dead on arrival at the hospital. The neighbour didn't know who to call, but she found my card

by the telephone, so she called me, and I called the station, and they thought you might know something more, seeing as you were interested in her.'

One problem solved, Slider thought, and another one unfolding. 'I'm afraid I can't tell you anything about her daughter,' he said circumspectly, 'but Mrs Knight did have a sister.'

'Oh,' Vicky Rayner said, brightening, 'well that would be a help. Can you give me her phone number?'

It was very tempting, the idea of having someone else break the bad news. But it was not the whole story, and he could not divulge that to this stranger. He knew, with a sinking of the heart, that he would have to do it himself, go and see Pat Bexley and tell her everything, because if he didn't, it would haunt him afterwards.

So he said, 'Don't worry about it, I'll let her know myself. She's in my area.'

'Oh, well, that's very good of you,' said the woman, with an air of crossing it off her list. 'There'll be the remains to claim and a funeral to arrange. I suppose her sister will want to do that?'

'I think it's likely,' Slider said.

He took Gascoyne with him. Not only had he had the previous contact with her, but Gascoyne had a shiningly honest face and the innate look of a favourite nephew. Slider didn't tell him that – at his age you wanted to look tough and cool and Daniel Craigish. Gascoyne was just pleased to be singled out for the job.

Fortunately, Pat Bexley was past the age when many things make you cry. She listened composedly as Slider broke the news of Maggie's death, and all she did when he had finished was to sigh. 'I'm not too surprised, really, I was shocked when I saw how she'd aged. I went to see her, you know?' she addressed Gascoyne. 'After I spoke to you? She rang me, and I could hear how shaky her voice sounded, so I said right away could I come and see her, and I went the next day. I'm really glad now that I did. It'd've been awful if I'd put it off and she'd died before I could get there.'

'I'm glad you were reconciled at the end,' Slider said.

'Well, I think we were both a bit ashamed, after all this time, letting something like that keep us apart, when there was only the two of us left. I mean, it all seemed a bit silly, when so much else had happened. So I said, "I'm sorry, Mags," and she said, "I'm sorry too," and we hugged and had a bit of a sniff and that was that.' She touched a handkerchief delicately to her eye. 'Oh dear, so I suppose there'll be a funeral to arrange. And nobody but me left to arrange it. Poor Maggie. It makes you wonder, doesn't it – I mean, who'll there be for me, when my time comes?'

'There'll be no difficulties with your sister,' Slider said, to get over the point. 'You'll just have to get in touch with the hospital – they'll be able to help you through the paperwork.'

He saw in her bright eye that she had – unsurprisingly – made the association.

'Speaking of which, when are poor Amanda's remains going to be released? Because it will have to be me, now, won't it, that arranges *her* funeral, now Maggie's gone? And I'm thinking, what would be really nice would be to have them buried together – don't you think? After being separated all that time, it would be a nice gesture if they could be together again in death.'

'Ah,' said Slider. 'As a matter of fact, I have some news for you on that front. We took a DNA sample from your sister when we visited her, and compared it with the DNA from the remains. And it turns out that it wasn't Amanda.'

'*What?*'

There was a certain amount of astonishment, exclamation and disbelief to work through. 'It *must* have been,' she kept saying. 'I mean, who else would be buried in their garden?' But eventually she got to: 'But – then – who on earth was it?'

'I'm afraid I can't tell you much. It's all sub-judice. It turns out to be another girl from the neighbourhood, a friend of Amanda's.'

'Oh my *lord*!' Her eyes opened wide. 'Another girl? You don't mean – Ronnie wasn't a serial killer, was he? No, I can't believe that. Not Ronnie!'

'Ronnie had nothing to do with it,' Slider was glad to be able to tell her.

'Oh dear, now I feel bad about suspecting him. Not that I ever

did, not *really*. It was just, well, you think, who else could have
done it? But what was this girl doing in Ron and Maggie's
garden?'

'Again, I'm afraid I can't tell you.'

'And what about Amanda? That means she's still missing,
does it?'

'No, she's not missing.' He saw painful hope chasing painful
doubt across her face. Not missing – did that mean more remains
had been found? When he saw she couldn't ask, he said, 'I'm
sorry to tell you that she's in custody. She's suspected of having
something to do with this other girl's death.'

She sat back in her chair, her mouth open. 'Well, that's floored
me,' she said at last. 'I don't know what to say. You mean,
Amanda's been alive all this time? And never got in touch with
any of us? Oh my good lord, poor Maggie! Dying without
knowing Amanda was still alive.'

Gascoyne said quietly, 'That might be just as well, in the
circumstances.'

She stared at him. 'You mean – you think *she* did it? Killed
this other girl?'

'I'm sorry, but we're really not at liberty to tell you anything
else at the moment,' Slider said. 'But I promise that as soon as
we are, I will tell you the whole story.'

She was silent a moment. 'Well, I suppose that's the best you
can do. You've got your job to do, so I won't ask you any more
questions and embarrass you. But tell me this – can I see her
– Amanda?'

'Again, not at present. I will let you know when you can.' He
rose to leave, and she got up too, though her mind was obviously
busy elsewhere.

'This other girl – the bones. I suppose her parents will be
collecting her, when the time comes? I'd like to offer them my
condolences.'

'I'm afraid they're dead. She doesn't have any relatives.'

'No relatives *at all*?'

'Apparently not.'

'Oh, that's *sad*,' she said with feeling. She followed them to
the door, and as she saw them out, she said quietly to Slider,
'What's she like now? Amanda?'

What on earth could he tell her? In the end he said, 'Not like you remember.'

By going-home time he had gone past sleepiness into the rather featureless zone of post-exhaustion, where colours were muted, reactions slowed and sounds, curiously, were magnified, hurting his ears. He was praying the phone wouldn't ring when he was anywhere near it. Atherton popped his head round the door. 'We're going for a drink to celebrate. Coming?'

'Celebrate?' Slider said.

'You can call it a wake if it helps. Boscombe Arms?'

'All right. I'll be about half an hour. Couple of things to wind up.'

'Right. First pint's on me – you look as though you need it. See you down there.'

He thought everyone had gone, but a little while later Connolly appeared at his door, looking faintly guilty.

'Boss?'

'What have you done?'

'Not what I've done, what I'm doing.' She held out an envelope. 'It's my resignation.'

He was taken aback. 'What? Why?' She started to summon words, and he said, 'Come in, sit down. I thought you were happy here. What's happened?'

She took Atherton's perch, on the windowsill above the radiator, which had never worked in Slider's tenure of the room. 'I've had enough,' she said.

'Is there something I can do?' he asked.

'No, boss. It's not you.' She looked down at her hands and fiddled with a hangnail. 'I've enjoyed working for you, I really have. It's been a slice. I'm just burnt out. Me brains are mince. I've got to get out and do something else.'

'It's a terrible pity to give up your career. You're a good copper. You could go far.'

'I don't want to go far,' she said, looking up with a ghost of her old grin. 'I've seen what *that* looks like! No, I've done being a gard, seen it all, got the T-shirt. Now I want a change.'

'A change to what?' Slider asked, still hoping he could find a chink and talk her round.

'I keep thinking about those girls,' she said. 'I've never forgotten when I went to interview some of them at that home. I keep wanting to do something for them.'

'Social work?' Slider was surprised. 'You don't want to be a social worker. It's the dog's job after this.'

'I know. They have terrible case loads and no time to put anything right. But I want to make a difference in someone's life. You remember Julienne Adams?'

'How could I forget?'

'She wants me to foster her.'

Slider met her eyes, and realized this was something serious. He remembered Julienne's mother's funeral, and how the child had clung to Connolly. There had been a connection there.

'Are you considering it?' he asked quietly.

'It needs a bit of thinking about,' Connolly admitted. 'I might get married,' she said, and he couldn't tell if this was part of what had gone before or a new tack.

'Who's the lucky man?' he asked cautiously.

'It's no one you know.'

'No, I remember you said you'd never date anyone in the Job.'

'You see,' she said, restlessly sliding to her feet, 'if I did try and do something for Julienne, I'd have to get a job with regular hours. I'd have to be around for her.'

'Any ideas?' Slider asked.

'Private security – consultancy, I mean, not walking about with a dog. I can earn a hell of a lot more doing that, and choose me own hours. I'll be on the pig's back.'

'So all this – leaving – is for Julienne's sake?'

'Not all,' she said. 'It's for me, too. I can't keep looking at the woeful end of life and keep me sanity. I've got to get out while I can.'

'Well, it's your decision, but I shall be very sorry to lose you,' Slider said. 'I won't tell you to think carefully before you do anything because I know you will.'

She nodded. 'There's one more thing. When I tell you, you might be glad I'm going.'

'Go on,' he said warily.

'It was me told Shannon Bailey to go to the press.' He could only stare. 'I know we're not supposed to, but I was mad as fire about the whole thing. You'd been suspended, and I knew they were going to drop the whole thing. So I thought, if the press get hold of it, they'll have to do something.'

Slider managed to say, 'You were right there.'

'There was this girl I knew from back home, in Dublin. We went to different schools together. She went into journalism. She was brilliant. She was on the *Irish Times*, then she went to New York for a couple of years, and she'd just come back. We'd got together for a drink, and I talked to her about Kaylee Adams and the girls, and she said if I put her in touch with Shannon she'd run with it and make it happen. So I did.'

'Oh, *Connolly!*'

She went on: 'I'm sorry now I did, and not only because it came to nothing in the end, and not only because I let *you* down, boss. But because I know now what it did to Shannon. It put her through stuff she never needed to go through. I just made her life harder. But it's all over now, and I want to make it up to someone. Julienne's just at the age when she could go either way.'

'Do you have any idea what you'd be taking on?' Slider heard himself say in a faint voice.

She grinned. 'Oh, I think I do. I've nephews and nieces and a million cousins, and they're all hyperactive. Ten minutes with any of 'em and you're setting your hair on fire!' The grin disappeared. 'But the other thing, boss – I'm really sorry. Can you forgive me?'

It was all history now, and curiously irrelevant in his world of fatigue. He was glad to know definitively that it had not been Atherton, and slightly ashamed that he had suspected him. His life would be easier now that he could relax in Atherton's and Emily's company. Beyond that, he felt nothing.

'Tell me you're not leaving the Job so as to avoid being disciplined for leaking,' he said with mock severity.

She clapped a hand to her head. 'Found me out! I should never try and fool a grand detective like yourself, sir.'

'Enough of your cheek.' He waved her away. 'Get on down the pub.'

'Are you coming, boss?'

'Wouldn't miss it,' he said.